THE ELEMENTS OF THE STORM

THE ELEMENTS OF KAMDARIA

KAY L. MOODY

MARTEN

The Elements of the Storm
The Elements of Kamdaria, #3
By Kay L. Moody

Published by Marten Press
3731 W 10400 S Ste 102, #205
South Jordan, UT 84009

www.MartenPress.com

Cover by Angel Leya
Edited by Deborah Spencer

ISBN: 978-1-954335-07-3

ALSO BY KAY L. MOODY

The Fae of Bitter Thorn

Heir of Bitter Thorn
Court of Bitter Thorn
Castle of Bitter Thorn
Crown of Bitter Thorn
Queen of Bitter Thorn

The Elements of Kamdaria

The Elements of the Crown
The Elements of the Gate
The Elements of the Storm

Truth Seer Trilogy

Truth Seer
Healer
Truth Changer

**Visit kaylmoody.com/kamdaria to read the prequel
novella, *Winds of Flame*, for free**

Balance is the Greatest Enemy to Chaos

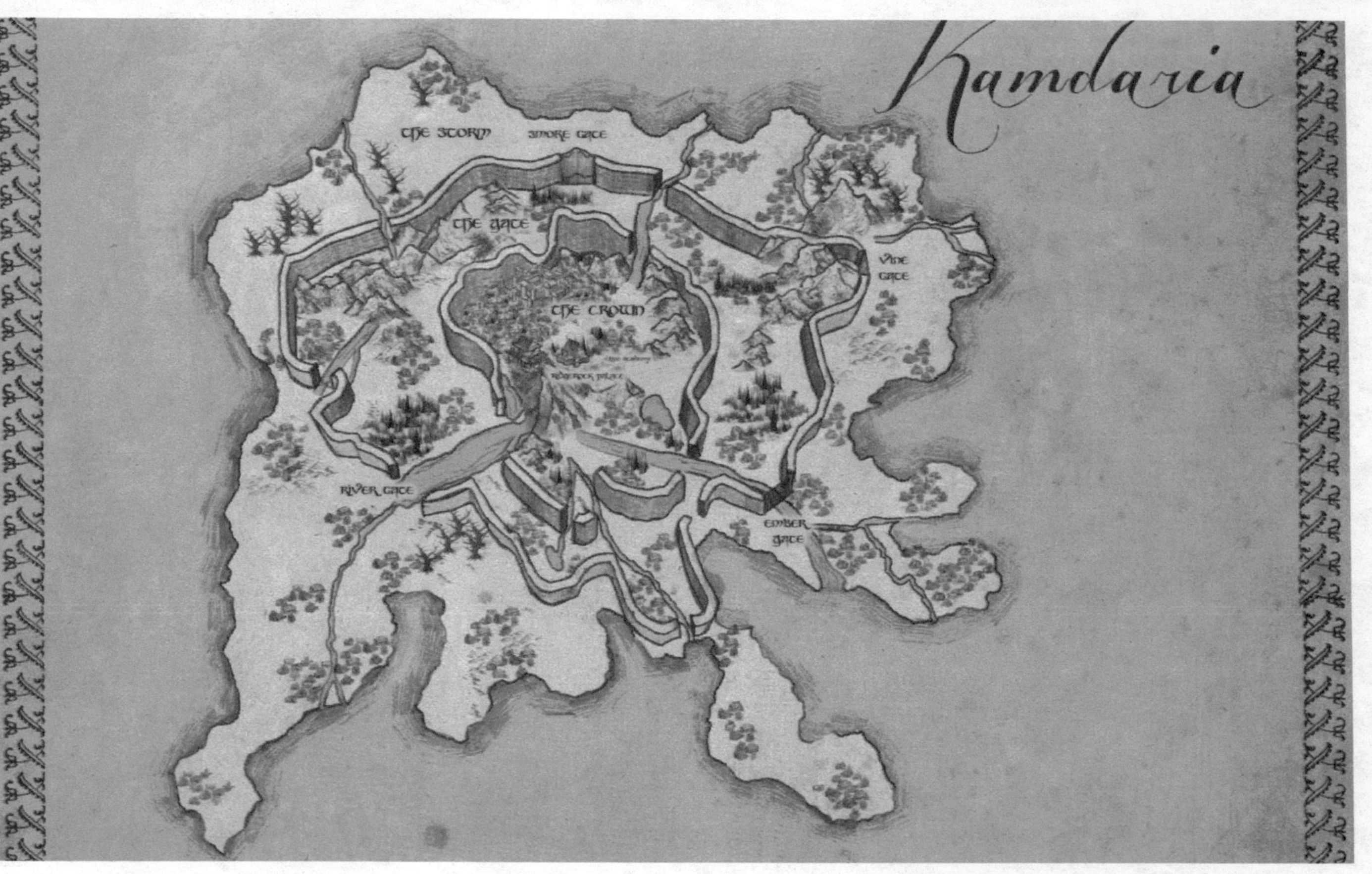

Kamdaria
THE STORM
SMOKE GATE
THE GATE
VINE GATE
THE CROWN
RIVER GATE
EMBER GATE

WATER

STORM

Chapter One

NOTHING COULD PREPARE A PERSON a person for the Storm.

Ice cold air accosted Talise from every angle. Shaping fire into her veins helped, but her friends couldn't shape fire into *their* veins.

For the tenth time that morning, she wished they hadn't all insisted on coming with her to the Storm. Rio, Fyra, and Tempest were soldiers, so they had a little training on how to handle difficult situations. Wendy was technically a soldier too but with far less training. She *was* an incredible shaper with an unbreakable spirit, which would help.

Even her brother, Cyrus, was a soldier. Although, since he had just spent summer and fall being cooped up in Kessoku's dungeon, he couldn't possibly be at full strength.

At least their only non-soldier companion no longer traveled with them. Claye. But he had also betrayed them and Talise's entire army to Kessoku, and apparently, had been a member of Kessoku for many years. His absence brought relief.

Annoyingly, it also hurt.

Steady footsteps at Talise's side moved with the precision of a soldier but with the grace of someone who had been raised in Kamdaria's inner circle of the Crown. His was the only internal temperature she *didn't* have to worry about. As the only living Master Shaper in Kamdaria besides her, Aaden knew how to shape fire in his veins just like she did.

Thoughts of him caused a stumble in her step. Like always.

Before that moment, she had done an excellent job of ignoring the quiet clink coming from her tunic pocket. Now the sound pierced her.

Each footstep made the green Forces tablet in her pocket tap against the flame-carved dagger right next to it. The Forces tablet came from Claye when he had declared his love to her. The dagger came from Aaden when he helped her escape a Kessoku dungeon during the summer. Both were mementos from young men she wanted to forget.

And remember.

Clenching her fists, Talise glared at the ground. Could she tune out the clinking from her pocket through sheer willpower? Not yet, but that wouldn't stop her from trying. And trying again.

She had no time to be worried about romance or kisses or frustrating young men. Much more important issues plagued her small group. With every footstep, she and her friends moved closer to their first city in the Storm. The. *Storm.* The outer circle of Kamdaria had far more danger and desperation than most people knew.

After a quick glance over her companions, she noted how they attempted to rub heat into their arms. Maybe they had agreed to help her, but none of them knew how difficult being here would really be.

The first edges of the city came into view, which caused a yank through Talise's gut. A thought entered her mind that had been lingering all day. *The others will regret their decision to help me.*

Her stomach sank again.

Once they saw how bad things really were, they would certainly want to return to the middle ring of Kamdaria and bask in all the safety the Gate could provide.

How could Talise ask them to stay in a place with such horrifying conditions? She couldn't. She knew that before they had even stepped through the hidden hole in the wall that led into the Storm. Already, she had spent the last few days looking for a way to let them go. If they could leave gracefully, things would be easier for everyone. Anyway, it would be easy to convince them once they saw how bad it truly was.

Anxiety spilled over in her gut. Without her friends, it might be impossible to accomplish everything she needed to do.

Talise had to rescue her soldiers and steal back the amulet from Kessoku. Again. Not to mention, end Kessoku for good. None of those goals seemed remotely possible, but compared to her final goal, they almost looked easy.

Even after retrieving the amulet and ending Kessoku, somehow, she still had to fix the problems in Kamdaria the emperor had caused. Just thinking about it made her belly ache.

Now was definitely *not* the time to worry about young men.

Her shoulders rocked with a shudder, which immediately sent Aaden's head turning toward her. Despite traveling with few supplies, he had managed to keep his goatee neatly trimmed. The look in his eyes questioned her before his mouth did. "Are you okay?"

She waved him off without making eye contact. It hurt how eagerly he jumped to her aid these days. He was here now, but where was he in the summer and fall when she had really needed him? Her attention immediately turned back to the land.

Since it was the outer ring of Kamdaria, the Storm was bigger than the Gate and much bigger than the Crown.

Cities dotted the unforgiving landscape. They were scattered everywhere. Some were situated near the wall that separated them from the Gate. Some were situated along the harsh ocean that surrounded the entire empire.

In some areas, the land stretched into the ocean like long fingers. Those areas often had two or three cities on them with only an hour of walking to travel between.

Mountains were rare in the Storm. Small, desolate mounds that could barely be called hills were much more common. Instead of forests, sparse clumps of dead trees peppered the cracked earth.

Rio still had the map of Kamdaria, which they had acquired months ago. Even after studying it for hours, Talise could not pinpoint where in the Storm she had lived as a child. The map only showed the location of cities and a few mountains and trees. So far, they hadn't encountered any areas that seemed familiar to her. Though, maybe that was just because they hadn't entered a city yet.

If they had wanted to visit a city sooner, they could have done it their first day in the Storm. Instead, they had chosen to travel the uninhabited wilderness of the Storm while they gathered their bearings. They'd been camping for about a week. Now, their water supply had finally dwindled enough that they decided to brave a city to use their well.

Dead trees lined a beaten path that led into the city. Tiny gasps sounded through the group as the houses came into view. Scorch marks and mud splotches darkened the clay walls of almost every home. A few homes even had splatters of a dark substance that looked eerily close to blood. Mold and grime trailed through the branches of the thatched roofs. Gaping holes appeared through several walls. Thin wooden doors hung crooked in their doorways. In some houses, only a wrinkled sheet of cotton functioned as a door.

In most of Kamdaria, plants and little gardens grew around all four walls of a house. In this city, houses were surrounded by dried up brush and stench-filled mold. They vegetation hung withered, clearly devoid of life for many years now.

An icy breeze sliced through the bare tree branches all around. It brought the stink of the city closer to everyone's nostrils. Only Cyrus was brave enough to plug his nose.

"I'm pretty sure your cell smelled at least twice as bad as this, so I'm not sure why you're plugging your nose." Aaden paired his words with a smirk before he glanced over his shoulder.

Cyrus let out a dramatic sigh in response. "I got used to things smelling nice for a change. It does smell better than you do after you practice sword fighting though, so at least that's nice."

It was strange to see Aaden chuckle in response. He had always been so serious and reserved. With Wendy's brother there, he never had trouble joking around.

Talise hated it.

It hurt to see him happy. And then she hated herself for hating him.

"*Shh.*" She shot them both with a glare before stepping closer to the city. "No sudden movements. If anyone in this town feels threatened, they *will* attack us."

Letting out a low whistle, Cyrus tipped an eyebrow up at her. "So, these people really are savages, huh?"

He probably didn't expect her to whirl around and grab his shirt collar. He definitely didn't expect her to use such a piercing tone.

"They are just trying to survive. The only way to do that in the Storm is to attack first." After releasing his collar, she took a gentle turn to face forward again. Her eyes roamed over the dilapidated houses, searching for a well. She finally spotted one behind a decaying tree.

Three children, about thirteen years old, played near the well. Unsupervised. And they weren't *playing* exactly. They threw rocks at a nearby house and snickered when the owner shouted at them. The tunics the children wore were either too short and too tight or much too big. Despite the blue tinging their lips, none of the children wore shoes.

Using a hand to urge the others back, Talise took careful steps toward the well. When she lowered the bucket inside, one of the children dropped herself onto the stone outer edge of the well.

"You won't get any water from there." The child's voice sounded croaky, as if recently plagued by an illness.

Using her gentlest tone, Talise asked, "Is the water frozen at the bottom?"

The temperature had dipped now that winter had arrived, but not *that* much. Still, there was no other apparent explanation for the child's statement.

A boy wearing a chunky tunic tied with string around his waist leaned on the well with one elbow. "Nah, it's 'cause the water is gone. The only water nearby is the river that comes through the Ember Gate, but that's a two-day walk away."

From behind them, someone had moved forward. Tempest's soldierly stomps and brash voice revealed herself. "The air isn't as dry here. I bet I could shape some water out of the air."

Sucking in a tight breath, Talise jerked around. "No."

But it was too late.

"Grab that bucket, will you, Wen?" Tempest used her chin to point toward the well. She had already pulled a sizeable amount of water from the air.

"Tempest." Nobody seemed to notice how Talise's voice trembled through the word. Their scratchy, thirsty throats did all the thinking for them. Clearly, they saw nothing but good in the water-shaper's actions.

Until a rock hit Tempest square in the face.

One of the children grabbed the bucket and caught the falling water, but it was an adult who tackled Tempest. The girl with the blue lips and croaky voice stomped on Talise's foot. A shower of rocks were flung toward their group. Attackers even chucked dirt into their eyes.

The rocks had no shaping behind them. People in the Storm were incapable of shaping. Technically, they *were* capable of shaping, just like every other Kamdarian. Malnourishment from living in the Storm stole the ability from them, usually only a few months after arriving in the dreadful place. Now they could only fight with rocks and sticks.

Unfortunately, they knew fighting well.

After throwing a wall of dust between her friends and their attackers, Talise jerked her head toward the edge of the city where they had come. They had to get away before things got worse.

When a flurry of rocks passed through the wall of dust, Aaden used earth shaping to drop the rocks onto the road. Running was their best defense, and they used it.

Even after camping for a week, they still had much more strength than the Storm citizens. It didn't take long to outrun their attackers and get to a safe distance away. Each member of Talise's group sucked in long breaths, eyeing the city with even gloomier eyes than before.

That ache in Talise's belly had returned. Now was as good a time as any to say what needed to be said.

Standing tall, she attempted to settle her features into a face that would command attention. "Who wants to go back to the Gate? You may leave now. And if you want to get into the Crown, Aaden can give you the password you need to do it."

The silence that followed could have filled an entire well on its own.

Talise pinched the bridge of her nose. "I *told* you this would be more dangerous than you realized."

Rubbing the spot on her forehead that had been hit, Tempest sneered at the city. "They attacked us for no reason."

A scoff puffed from Talise's mouth a little harder than she intended. "No reason? There was definitely a reason."

Cyrus threw her a sideways glance. "Because they're savages?"

Her deepest glare yet caused him to shrink in place. When she spoke again, it was through her teeth. "It's because they're thirsty and starving. They have to walk two days just to get water." Her head fell into her hand as she let out a sigh. "I know people from the Storm seem scary and dangerous, but it's just because they're desperate."

The others nodded, apologized even. They all insisted they wanted to stay, but that could change at any moment. For now, Talise decided they should head to the river coming from the Ember Gate. At least then they could get some water.

As they marched, she remembered a dream she'd had right after she'd been rescued from Kessoku's dungeon. It had been the height of summer then, but the memory of the dream stayed crisp, even now.

One part of herself had tugged her one direction, reminding her she was a Master Shaper. Another part of herself had tugged her in the other direction, urging her to be a princess. It had all seemed so frightening back then. But then Marmie's voice cut through the dream, leaving an imprint on Talise's heart. Her words were still clear as crystal in Talise's mind.

You must help them, love.

The thought of Marmie immediately turned Talise's thoughts to Marmie's gravestone. It was somewhere in the Storm, and now Talise was too. The gravestone sat somewhere bearing the dishonor of not a single mark. Talise hadn't been able to mark the gravestone because the competition for Master Shaper had been the same day. But maybe she could mark it now. Since no one in the Storm kept records of their graveyards, finding the grave could take years. Still, being in the Storm would provide a chance that had never existed before.

A glow blossomed in Talise's chest at the thought. She was even more determined to do what Marmie had asked in the dream. Help them. *Them* probably meant everyone in Kamdaria. But Talise couldn't do that now. For the first time since leaving the academy, she finally had a chance to help the people who needed it the most.

The Gate, the Crown, even the amulet, they would all have to wait.

Now, Talise would save the Storm. If she couldn't save all of it, she'd at least save the desperate city they had just entered.

CHAPTER TWO

IT DID NOT TAKE TWO days to get to the river. Even with a low water supply, icy wind, and aching limbs, Talise and her friends made it to the river far before nightfall.

The others rejoiced, but Talise only squirmed at the thought. How could such a short walk take people from the city two whole days? Malnourishment stole away their ability to shape, but it also ate away at their muscles. They were *so* weak. So helpless. Even something as essential as water took them two days to retrieve.

While her friends marched toward the river with grateful eyes, Talise kept glancing over her shoulder toward the path that led to the city.

Maybe the city just needed another well. If she used her water shaping ability, she could sense water under the surface of the ground. Then it would just take a little earth shaping to dig a new well with lots of fresh water. She cocked her head to the side. Maybe it would take a *lot* of earth shaping.

It could take at least a week to dig deep enough into the ground. With her friends' help, it might take less. Since they were just hiding, they didn't exactly have anything better to do. Her soldiers had to be rescued from Kessoku, but hopefully they would be safe for a little while. It probably wouldn't be smart to attack for at least a few weeks.

The crystalline river ahead flowed in a winding path. The bushes lining the river's edge wilted with the sick scent of decay. Winter could spread frost and ice over the branches, but it couldn't smother the smell.

At least the water was clear. Cyrus cupped some into his palms, ready to pour the ice cold liquid into his mouth.

Touching him on the shoulder, Wendy stopped her brother. "We should make sure it's clean first."

Cyrus raised an eyebrow and glanced back at the river. "It looks clean to me."

He hadn't been traveling with them, so he didn't know their procedures. Rio pulled one of the canvas packs off his shoulder and dug through it, probably for the water pouches inside. "Don't worry," the soldier said to Cryus. "We can clean the water if needed. We just like to check before we drink it. You never know what kind of things can hide in water."

Shrugging off her own pack, Tempest found the pot they used for cooking and pulled it out. After running a finger over the thick braid that fell past her waist, she tossed it over her shoulder. Her feet stomped into a solid stance and then she shaped a portion of water out of the river.

The water hovered an arm's length away from Tempest as she worked. It looked even more crystalline with the sunlight streaming through it. Closing her eyes, the water shaper held the water in place with one hand and used her other hand to pull any impurities out.

Usually Talise helped clean the water, but right now, another thought consumed her. She needed Aaden. Turning on her heel, she spun to find him. It took only one step before she nearly toppled into him.

Taking a step backward, she forced her heart to stop pounding in her chest. Why did he always stand so close to her?

His eyes were expectant when he stared back. Hungry for any sort of attention.

It took too much effort to pull her gaze away. Suddenly, brushing the dust off her tunic was *much* more important. She continued to avoid his eye, even when she spoke. "We should teach the others how to shape fire in their veins. They're freezing out here, even in the winter gear you packed."

Without looking at him, it was difficult to gauge his reaction. Then again, he liked to keep his face as still as stone, so maybe looking wouldn't have helped anyway. His voice did seem a little lower than normal though. Whatever that meant. "Shaping fire inside the body is not an easy technique."

"I know." She glanced at him just long enough to see his eyes flick toward Tempest. Since Talise and Aaden had taught the water shaper back when they both still lived at the palace, they knew firsthand that Tempest's fire shaping skills were less than ideal.

Even without looking, Talise could feel when his gaze landed back on her again. He didn't move, but he seemed to edge forward somehow. "And even *we* can't shape fire into our veins while we're sleeping. That's when the cold will be most dangerous."

She let out a little huff before finally looking at him. But she didn't look at his eyes, not exactly anyway. Instead, her gaze fell on the thick, white scar that went across one eye, from his forehead to his chin. When memories of him obtaining that scar surfaced in her mind, she dutifully shoved them away.

It only did so much. Even without thinking about it specifically, the memory was strong enough to warm her insides. Months ago, the palace had been attacked by Kessoku. The attackers had all died except one man. After the battle, she and Aaden had roamed the palace grounds looking for survivors. Instead, they had found the last living Kessoku, who then tried to kill her with a sword.

Aaden protected her without hesitation.

And got a scar in return.

"Princess." Rio's voice cut through the memories, bringing Talise back to the present moment again.

She jerked her head away from Aaden and nodded toward the soldier at her side.

Rio gestured toward the path they had taken to get there. "Fyra and I are going to find a spot to make camp. We figured it would be smart to stay near the water, but we probably won't stay *too* near."

The smile that broke onto her face probably looked as forced as it felt, but she didn't have the energy to try harder. "Thank you, Rio. That's a great idea."

As soon as he turned away, Talise glanced toward Aaden. Her lips pursed before she opened her mouth to speak. "Maybe shaping fire inside the veins *is* too hard for everyone else, but we have to do something. The nights will only get colder. Maybe we need to figure out how to keep our fires burning longer throughout the night or something."

Aaden pinched the facial hair on his chin as he nodded.

Sucking in a breath, Talise whirled around and moved closer to the river. It's not like she needed his help anyway. His shaping skills had always been incredible, so they probably could have come up with a solution faster if they worked together. But she'd still think of something just fine on her own.

After moving closer to the river, she saw Tempest gag before dropping a small portion of water into the cooking pot at her feet. Her long braid shook as a shiver went through her.

It only took an eyebrow raise for the water shaper to know what Talise wanted to ask.

"This water is disgusting. It's much filthier than it looks."

"Do you need my help?" Talise asked.

With a wave of one hand, Tempest turned away. "No, no. It's going to take me a little longer than usual, but I can do it no problem."

A bright smile filled Wendy's nearby face. She smirked at the water shaper's back before turning a knowing eye toward Talise. "Tempest likes doing things herself."

The chuckle that left Talise's lips was both sincere and pleased. Her best friend's presence always made the world feel lighter. They hadn't spent much time together with all the recent events, which made those short moments they did get all the more special.

Wendy bit into her bottom lip as she brushed her black hair over one shoulder. "Could you *try* teaching me how to shape fire inside my veins? I know air is my primary, so I probably won't be able to do it." She dug one toe into dirt. "But I'd love to try."

Tilting her mouth up into a true smile, Talise nodded. "Of course I'll teach you." She used one hand to beckon. "You too, Cyrus. Come stand next to your sister."

Cyrus stopped halfway through filling an empty water pouch with the water Tempest had just finished cleaning. The cooking pot holding the clean water was nearly empty when he finished it. "I'll be right there." He jumped to his feet and then downed the water in a single swig.

Once Wendy and Cyrus stood in position, Talise talked them through each of the steps. First, they had to feel the fire in their hearts. They had to feed it without allowing it to grow too large. For people whose primary element *wasn't* fire, it took a lot of practice.

Since Wendy and Cyrus were both air shapers, they kept feeding the fire with air from their lungs. Coughing fits abounded through their many attempts.

Talise soon realized this lesson wouldn't amount to anything. Air-shaping techniques were too ingrained in Wendy and her brother for them to learn the art of shaping fire inside the veins. But Talise wasn't about admit it. She chose to keep teaching anyway.

By the time Tempest had filled the cooking pot halfway full with clean water, she dared to chuckle at the failed efforts.

"You try it then, water-shaper." Cyrus glared at the back of Tempest's head. "I bet you struggle to make a simple fireball."

Wendy's eyes narrowed as she folded her arms over her chest. The tightness in her jaw seemed to cause a squirm all through Cyrus's limbs.

He gulped and whipped the hair out of his face. "I mean…" He spared a small glance at his sister, who looked even more serious than before. "I'm sure you'll get it in no time once you attempt."

Both of his eyebrows raised when he looked at his sister again, as if asking whether he had fixed things.

Wendy gave a subtle nod before closing her eyes and trying the difficult technique again. When Cyrus did the same, he managed to work for several seconds before coughing.

"Talise."

Aaden appeared from nowhere, standing close enough to Talise that she could feel heat from his arm. Using his chin, he pointed toward a small group of strangers who approached the river.

Between the four of them, they carried a wooden box with thin sides. Two long poles had been attached at the bottom in long parallel rows, making the box easier to carry.

Talise took a step away from Aaden before a hard swallow went through her throat. "It's fine. They're just getting water."

He nodded in response, but that didn't stop his gaze from becoming even more focused than before.

When one of the women in the group cupped water from the river into her hands, Talise jumped forward.

"Don't drink that."

All four of the strangers jerked their heads toward her before reaching for the daggers in their belts. Hollow eyes stared back at her. Their frail limbs only added to their frightening appearance.

With a gulp, Talise stepped forward again. She clasped her hands behind her back. Hopefully that would make her seem less threatening. "I just mean the water isn't clean. You need to boil it before you drink it, otherwise it will make you sick."

Their grips on their weapons tightened with each word she spoke.

Fear flooded her veins, which she tried to hide with a smile. "Or I could clean the water for you if you need to drink some right away."

The woman who had gotten the water drew her dagger first. A man with faded eyes pulled his next.

Talise let out a sigh. Less than a day had passed, and they were already in their second fight.

✳

CHAPTER THREE

THE AIR BUZZED WITH TENSE energy. Talise slowly lifted her hands, keeping the palms open. She dipped her head, hoping it would make her seem less threatening.

It didn't matter though.

While brandishing their rusty daggers, the strangers at the river eyed everyone *except* Talise. The moment one of them stepped toward her, Aaden lunged forward.

Using the sword he had brought in one of his packs, he smacked a dagger out of the attacker's hand. With a jab, Aaden's blade cut through the man's burlap tunic.

After a hard gasp, the man tumbled backward and fell onto the cold earth.

The other man in the group went to throw his own dagger, but the flat side of Aaden's blade slapped against the man's wrist. Soon, the rusty dagger dropped to the ground. When one of the women lifted her arm, Aaden shaped a blast of icy wind forward that knocked them all off their feet.

The last woman slapped a hand over her mouth as she landed with a thud. "They're shapers," she said through a whisper.

Her words brought shudders through her companions. In a single breath, they jumped to their feet and barreled away as fast as their legs could carry them.

It wasn't very fast.

Once they were out of sight, Talise gritted her teeth. She slammed both hands onto her hips as she rounded on Aaden. "Why would you do that?"

The slightest tremor of guilt passed through his eyebrows before he slipped his sword into its sheath. "You said the only way to survive in the Storm is to attack first, so I did."

Would it be wrong to growl at him? Probably. She stuck to a loud huff instead. "We don't need to hurt the people who live here; we need to *help* them."

"But I didn't hurt them." His head hung as he said the words. "I was careful to only keep them away. If I had wanted to hurt them, I would have used my blade, not the side of it."

She had noticed that, but a part of her hoped it wasn't deliberate. It was so much easier to hate Aaden when he gave her reason for it. Unfortunately this time, he didn't.

Another puff flared out her nostrils as she stomped away from him. "We can camp by the river tonight. In the morning, I'm going back into the city. I have to figure out a way to help everyone there."

"How?" Wendy twirled a bit of hair over her finger as she spoke. It did nothing to disguise the desperation sinking into her features. "There are so many of them and only a few of us. We don't have the resources we used to have."

Touching a hand to her forehead, Talise let out a sigh. "We still have a lot more than they do. We have strength, food. We have shaping."

"We can't give them our food." The expression on Aaden's face had hardened. "We don't have very much to begin with."

She wanted to snarl at him, but Tempest's frown stopped her. The water shaper glanced into their cooking pot that was still only halfway full of clean water. "We can't give them water either. It takes too long to clean it, not to mention transport it." She gestured toward the wooden box that lay discarded nearby. "Even if we use this thing they left behind, we don't have enough time to bring water back and forth to the city day after day. And if we did, it still wouldn't be enough water for everyone who lives there."

Cyrus made a tiny tornado above his palm. "And it's not like we can give them our shaping."

Sliding a hand over her long braid, Tempest stared at the ground. "Maybe it would be better if we stay away from the cities while we're here." She wrapped her arms over her stomach. "We don't want to lose our shaping because we gave all our food away."

Heat trickled into Talise's face as her jaw clenched. She tightened her fists, ready to scream something she'd probably regret. The only thing that stopped her was the sound of Aaden's voice.

"We still have the money we got from selling the horses we stole from Kessoku. Maybe I can sneak back through the wall and go into that small city in the Gate where I went before. I could buy an animal for butchering. We have enough money to get something that would feed the whole city for a few days. And maybe I could get some chickens too. Then there would be eggs."

All at once, the lump in Talise's throat hardened for an entirely new reason. She tipped her head up, eager not to glance toward Aaden. Or let him see how his words had softened her. Instead, she tried to don an emotionless mask like *he* always wore. "Yes, I think that will work. In the meantime, I'm going to dig another well for the city we just left."

Her words sent a shock through the rest of them, but she didn't stay around long enough to see their reactions. She just marched off to find Rio and Fyra so she could help them set up camp.

— ◆ —

DUSKY CLOUDS FILLED the sky when Talise and her friends entered the city the next morning. Perhaps she moved a little too confidently down the path, her friends too. At the sight of them, several citizens ran from the streets and back into their dilapidated homes.

Apparently, they had a reputation now. A child peeked through an open window and gasped at the sight of them. He ducked into his home, a chorus of whispers emerging from it a moment later.

A few brave souls lingered around the well, but Talise ignored them. At her side, Aaden reached for his sword. She ignored that too.

Closing her eyes, Talise stretched out her senses, feeling for any water that sat far below the land's surface. At first, she could only sense earth and *dry* earth at that. Even the gentle sway of air ruffling through her hair touched her shaping senses more than the non-existent water in the ground below.

No wonder the well didn't work.

But giving up never came easily to her. She found enough dirt inside Kessoku's base by the Vine Gate to convince the soldiers the ceiling was caving in. She could find water in the Storm too. She just had to keep looking.

Her fingers raised out in front of her, her one stretching forward. Squeezing her eyelids tighter, she felt for the liquid that could save the city. Bursts of energy pulsed through her eyes. It

30

had been years since she learned that water shaping came from the eyes, but she had never felt it more than in that moment.

Each of her breaths had to move at a glacial pace or it would destroy the concentration she had built. With her fingers reaching out, a cool droplet seemed to land on one thumb.

There.

One corner of her mouth pricked upward as she tilted her hand and reached into that same spot with her shaping. Now droplets seemed to prickle all over her hand. The sensation was only in her mind, but it told her what she needed to know.

Water *did* sit under the surface of the land. After reaching deeper with her water shaping senses, she could feel the droplets form into a puddle. And then she found an underground pocket of water. Now it would just take some digging to get the city a working well.

With her opposite hand, she reached directly above the water with her earth shaping senses. Once her senses found the surface, she punched a mound of dirt above it. Her eyes flew open the moment she finished, finding the little mound she had just formed.

It sat on the other side of the city. The houses were farther away from it than she would have liked, but at least it was closer than the river.

"Is that the spot?" Aaden tilted his head toward the mound.

She nodded once before marching toward it.

As they planned, she and Aaden used earth shaping to start digging a hole. She decidedly ignored how helpful it was to have another Master Shaper in their group. And anyway, even with his limited shaping skills, Claye would have been helpful for a task like this since it involved so much earth shaping.

Her nose wrinkled as she lifted a fresh pile of earth from the ground. Even with the green Forces tablet in her pocket, she had done a decent job of not thinking about the young man who had betrayed her to Kessoku. The one who ensured her enemy got both the true amulet *and* her entire army.

When she dropped the pile of earth next to the hole she dug, Wendy used her own earth shaping to pick it back up again. She couldn't carry as much as Talise had, but she managed a fair amount. Talise and Aaden continued to dig the hole with earth shaping while Wendy, Tempest, and Cyrus moved the excess dirt out of their way.

Rio and Fyra stood guard.

It didn't matter how many times Talise insisted it wasn't necessary to have anyone stand guard, she got outvoted on the matter. It didn't seem fair to be outvoted. She was a princess, after all.

Then again, she had seen how the emperor ruled, usually without taking advice from his advisors. She *didn't* want to end up like that, so she let herself get outvoted in the end.

After only a few minutes of working, one of the children who had been throwing rocks the day before got brave enough to come near. The girl looked to be about thirteen years old. She held one shoulder back as she moved toward them, almost like she wasn't quite sure if she should come or not.

Rubbing the side of her leg, the girl spoke in the same croaky voice she had the day before. "I'm Willow." Her eyes narrowed. "What are you doing?"

While heaving a mound of dirt upward, Talise couldn't speak. Aaden cast a small glance in the girl's direction, but he looked back to Talise almost as fast. Finally, she dropped the dirt onto the pile in front of Cyrus. She wiped the dirt from her hands while Aaden started digging out the next portion of earth.

"We're digging a well." Talise hoped her smile didn't look as worn out as the heaving in her chest indicated. "Pretty soon, you'll have water close by again."

Willow stared for almost a full minute without moving a single muscle.

When Aaden finished hauling out his dirt, Talise reached in with her earth shaping to dig another portion.

The girl finally spoke when the next mound of dirt emerged from the hole. "Why?" Her eyes narrowed at the earth, then at their group. "I know you don't live in our city because you didn't come here with palace soldiers. Plus, it's been more than a year since we got someone new in our city."

A frosty breeze cut through the air around them. Willow probably found it unwelcome, but to Talise's tired muscles, the cold felt marvelous. The sheen of sweat on her forehead grew every minute that she worked.

"Don't you want water?" Talise asked.

With a scoff, Willow rolled her eyes. "Obviously we want water. This year has been the worst ever. The river is low, the crops hardly grew. They never grow well, but this year was worse. And the emperor won't hire Storm laborers now, so nobody has work. Pretty soon, we'll have nothing left to eat except *fish*." A grimace overtook her face.

Talise knew the look well. She could recall her days in the Storm without any effort at all. The desperation. The hunger. Even now, fish always left her stomach feeling empty.

Tightness filled her throat when she opened her mouth again. "You're right. We don't live in your city, but we wanted to help you. This seemed like the best way."

The girl's eyes only narrowed further. "Why?"

When Talise glanced toward Aaden, he was already staring back at her. Even Aaden had suffered enough desperation to understand the girl's hesitancy. Still, it was difficult to explain such a simple thing to someone who had obviously never known kindness.

Remembering one of Marmie's favorite sayings, Talise tipped her mouth up in a smile. "I was taught that when you have more, you give more."

Willow folded her arms over her chest. "That's not the way we do things around here."

"I know." Talise let out a sigh along with her words. Aaden glanced toward her again, but he said nothing. What was there to say anyway?

When Talise and her friends returned to their camp that night, somber quietude filled the air. The evening meal got passed around with less vigor than usual. Even Cyrus refrained from his jokes.

They built a fire to help keep them warm through the night. Everyone made their beds around it.

When Talise dropped her head onto her pillow, an overwhelming heaviness pressed down on her. How could she save the Storm when there was so much to do?

Chapter Four

Ice cold air froze in Talise's throat when she sucked in a breath.

She sat up with a start, ignoring how her bed and hair were drenched in sweat.

Another nightmare.

An inky black sky hung up above. Glowing embers filled the pit where a roaring fire had been only hours earlier. It still gave off some warmth, but Talise shot a fireball to feed it anyway.

Wriggling out of her makeshift bed, she ran off toward a dead tree that stood nearby their camp. Her bare feet slapped against the frozen dirt. She rubbed her arms to stave off the chill, but soon, a flood of fire pulsed through her veins.

It felt almost the same as ice shaping. On the inside of her body, heat and fire raged. On the outside, frost bit into her skin trying to burrow down. Having a neutral temperature probably would have felt better, but she didn't mind the fight between fire and ice. It reminded her of how much she wanted to help Kamdaria… and how far she was from succeeding.

Touching a palm to the dead tree now at her side, Talise stepped around it to reach the fallen log she had noticed the day before. Her heart jumped when she found it already occupied.

Aaden rested his head in one hand, and his elbow rested on his knee. He glanced up at the sound of her footsteps, but nothing else about him moved. When he swallowed, the slightest flicker of pain stretched across his face. "Are you okay?"

Talise nodded quickly. For no reason at all, she dropped onto the log next to him. His method of holding his head with one hand seemed pretty good at the moment.

"What happened?" He stared at the ground, his lips barely moving with the words.

She waved a hand through the air in response. "It was nothing. I just had a nightmare about Forces tablets attacking me." She left out the fact that the tablets had all been green.

Now he lifted one eyebrow the tiniest amount. He even turned his face toward her slightly. "Forces tablets?"

A sigh left her lips as she dropped her head. "It's a long story. I'm fine. I just needed to breathe."

Silence stretched between them. Even his nod had been so miniscule she could have imagined it. Reaching for the hem of her tunic, she glanced toward him for one small second. "What about you?" Her eyes fell studiously to the ground. "Did you have a nightmare?"

The laugh that came out of him sounded almost like a scoff. "Yeah, I have a nightmare. You fell in love with someone else, and even though he betrayed you, you still don't want to be with me." He pressed his palms into his eyes after he glared at the ground. "Except my nightmare doesn't go away when I wake up."

Initially, yelling seemed like a good response. Or maybe complaining that he had left her with no hope for his return. How could he expect her to just welcome him back with open arms?

But the words died on her lips when she saw how he dug his fingers through his hair. That's when she noticed his puffy red eyes. He was in pain too.

Good.

He deserved it.

After a heavy swallow, she glanced back at the ground. "I can't give you my whole heart right now."

He reached out, not quite touching her hand but leaning toward her with every part of himself. "I don't care. I'll take as much as you can give."

"Even if half my heart still belongs to *him?*"

The words sent a flinch that rocked through Aaden's whole body. Clenching his teeth together, he went back to staring at the ground. Wetness glistened in his eyes, but she did her best to ignore it.

It might have been an exaggeration to say half her heart still belonged to Claye. His betrayal had cut deep. Still, *something* inside her still belonged to Claye based on all the dreams about Forces tablets she'd been having.

And anyway, that didn't change how much anger she had for Aaden. He could be as sad and as desperate as he wanted, but he still forced her to spend months alone. Did he really expect her to forgive him so easily? Just because he took care of Cyrus? And helped Talise and her friends escape Kessoku's base? And he gave information to the emperor that helped the palace soldiers take out Kessoku's smaller bases.

A sigh left her mouth before she could stop it. Aaden *did* have a few things going for him. But that didn't mean she would hand over her heart on a platter. Scratching a thumbnail over the hem of her tunic, she stared at the ground. "I'm trying to do the right thing. I don't want to be with you unless I can truly be committed."

His body tensed at the words. Even from the side of her eye, she could see how a grimace passed over his features before he buried his face in his hands. It took a long while before he emerged again. "Just tell me, because I have to know the truth, is there *any* part of your heart that belongs to me?"

"Of course there is." As it always did around him, the truth spilled right out of her whether she liked it or not. Her lip trembled as she looked away. "There always was."

Warmth from his hand finally turned her toward him again. As before, he reached out. He didn't quite touch her, but his skin was close enough to feel the heat coming from it.

When she finally glanced his way, he held eye contact before giving a nod.

"I understand," he said.

She let out a scoff in response. "You understand, but you don't like it."

He quirked an eyebrow up. "Do you?"

"No." There went the truth spilling from her mouth again. She *didn't* like it. Because now Aaden was here, and his presence warmed her like it always had. But a fracture had split between them. Even if it healed, it would never be the same.

The knowledge of what could have been mocked them both. It laughed at their desires and speared them with regret. Now their future was as uncertain as Kamdaria itself.

"Once we finish the well, I'll travel into that town in the Gate and buy the animals we talked about." Aaden's voice had hardened in the same way his face had. All the vulnerability was wiped away in a single breath. Now he spoke of nothing but business.

When she nodded at his words, he stood from the log. Before he could disappear, she said, "When you go to the Gate, I need you to do me a favor."

His face stayed as blank as ever, but a small twitch went through his fingers. "Anything."

She stood up to join him, ready now to return back to camp. "Will you ask around and find out anything you can about Kessoku and the emperor? And I know it's unlikely, but will you try to find out about my soldiers?"

He nodded as they both headed toward camp.

Once again, her fingers found the bottom of her hem as she walked. "I know we have to hide here for a while, but I don't want to forget there's a war going on. We still have so much to do."

CHAPTER FIVE

IT TOOK FIVE DAYS TO finish the well. No one from the city would use it though. Trust issues were probably to blame. Hopefully things would change once the citizens saw how Talise and her friends drank the water without even cleaning it first. The well water tasted better than the river water anyway.

The morning after they finished it, Talise sent Aaden back to the Gate to buy animals. She also told him to buy seeds for vegetables and rice. He argued that none of it would grow in such cold weather, but she just waved him on.

After that, she sent most of her friends into the city to build a stone wall around the well as protection. Rio even promised to build a roof over it too.

Everyone except Wendy disappeared into the city. After they all left, Wendy folded up the last of her bedding and stuffed it into a canvas pack. "Aaden is right, you know. Citizens of the Storm might need food, but seeds aren't going to help. Not until winter passes."

Talise allowed the lightest smile to creep onto her face as she pulled a worn leather journal from her own canvas pack. Words from Kamdar, the first emperor of Kamdaria, were preserved inside.

A glimmer sparkled in Wendy's eyes at the sight of it.

Releasing the buckle that kept the journal closed, Talise turned the pages with more reverence than she had ever shown the book before. "Remember when we were by the Ember Gate, and I was trying to find a way to bend metal?"

After tying off the pack holding their supplies, Wendy plopped to the ground. "Yes."

The earlier smile crept back onto Talise's face. "I remember reading about how Kamdar created a solid, transparent material by heating sand. He called it glass."

The glimmer in Wendy's eye faltered. "How is that going to help us?"

Turning pages brought purpose to Talise's fingertips. "Kamdar built a house with the glass and something about it helped trap heat inside. If we can build a glass house, we might be able to grow vegetables even when it's cold outside. Maybe we could create a ventilation system too, so we can build fires inside to help with the heat."

Fervent nods bounced her best friend's head up and down. Wendy dug through a canvas pack until she had retrieved one of the red journals. The red ones had been written by the guardians of Kamdar's amulet. Her fingers flipped through the pages before she spoke again. "I remember reading how one of the guardians used earth shaping to sense nutrients in the soil. If we can put the right nutrients into the soil, it should make it even easier to grow things."

As they had spent many days before, Talise and Wendy buried their noses in the books. Back at the academy, they had done it for school assignments. At the palace, they had done it to gain respect from the palace soldiers. Now they did it again with possibly the most important mission yet. They sought to save the weakest and most downtrodden of all Kamdaria citizens.

That evening, Talise traveled to the ocean that bordered one side of the city. Gritty sand filled the beach near the ocean waves. Her first attempts at making glass resulted in little more than scorched circles on the shore. After hours of practice, she managed to create a transparent pane only slightly bigger than her hand.

The next day brought even bigger and better panes. Now she had enough panes to build a glass house that could supposedly stay warm inside, even in the winter. Her heart pattered as she lifted a pile of panes to take into the city.

Upon entering it, people scattered at the sight of Talise. The citizens dove into their houses not even daring to look back. Ignoring it, she and her friends set to work on building the glass house. They chose a spot just outside of city in full view of the sun.

Talise's eyes closed each time she melded two glass panes together. A surge of fire sent out from her fingertips brought enough heat to melt the edges. Quick blasts of shaped air helped cool the glass until the melted pieces became one.

Everyone in her group helped to hold up the walls and arrange the panes so the house could be as structurally sound as possible. As possible for something made of glass anyway.

By the time they finished, a timid crowd had gathered at the edge of town. At one time, Talise would have been nervous to approach the citizens. But after her time in the Gate, it almost came as second nature.

She had gotten the people living by Kessoku's main base by the Ember Gate to help her once. Certainly, it wouldn't be hard to get help from people who needed it so much more. Even the speech came easily once she began.

"This special house will trap heat from the sun, which will make it possible to grow food in the winter."

Despite their hollow eyes and frail limbs, a spark of hope lit inside the eyes of many citizens. She smiled to herself, hoping it wasn't too obvious. Yes, giving speeches really was getting easier. Standing taller, she opened her arms toward them. "In order to finish the house, I need your help."

She didn't really.

Even with Aaden on his trip to the Gate, her other friends were all she needed to get the glass house finished. But people in the Storm were used to feeling worthless. They were used to knowing that nothing they did could ever improve their lives. Most of them stopped trying within a year of being sent to the Storm.

After having lived in the Storm herself, Talise understood the psychological damage many of these people shared. They didn't just need food and water and proper shelter. They also needed to know they could get those things for themselves.

Raising her chin, she let a pleading look cover her face. "The earth here does not have the nutrients it needs to properly grow food. I can use earth shaping to get the proper nutrients from deep in the earth, but I need your help preparing it for the glass house. And I need you to bring any pots or containers you can spare."

A flinch went through the crowd, but she had expected that. "You can have your pots and containers when we are finished. I only need you to use them while we are working."

They definitely weren't convinced. But it didn't matter because they *were* curious. Curious enough that a handful of people turned around to retrieve pots from their homes. It wasn't much, but she didn't need much. She only needed a few. The others would come around slowly as long as she kept at it.

With a nod, Talise dropped her arms and moved toward the glass house. Her friends waited for her right outside it. Cyrus used air shaping to blow some dirt into a small mound. He raised an eyebrow at her while he worked. "So, this is your thing, huh? You go around saving people whether they want help or not?"

Wearing a wide smile, Wendy nudged her brother. "Just wait until you see how she gets the nutrients from the ground."

She spoke loud enough that the citizens hanging at the edge of town could hear. As she had probably hoped, a few more citizens disappeared to find pots. But now the time had come for the real work.

Fear wriggled into Talise's gut, caring little for how important this plan was. Seeming to sense the fear, Wendy touched a hand to Talise's forearm. Her big eyes sparkled with the look of innocence that always lingered there. "You can do this. Just remember, you don't need to bring up all the soil, only the nutrients."

Offering encouragement was a lot easier than what Talise was about to do, but she appreciated it all the same. Not one of her friends held the slightest doubt in their eyes. Well, maybe Cyrus did a little bit, but not the others. They had all seen Talise do incredible shaping.

But that was mostly for show.

Now she had to do something extremely difficult, and it wouldn't even look very impressive.

Grounding her feet, she stretched out her hands and closed her eyes. She used the exact stance as when she had searched for ground water, but this time, her earth shaping senses were the ones to reach out.

The nutrients she needed—according to the journal entry written by a guardian of the amulet—were much farther beneath the surface than she expected. Tilting her hand down, she pressed her senses to their limit, reaching for the elusive richness that would promote food growth.

When she found it, her hands formed fists. That helped her grab a clod of dirt far beneath the surface, but the clod had more than she needed. And anyway, pulling that much dirt up such a great distance would tire her out quickly.

With the clod in her grip, she loosened her fist and pinched her fingers together, as if plucking out the pieces of soil that she needed. Sifting through the clod took longer than she would have liked. Hopefully it would get faster the longer she worked.

After pinching through it for a while, the clod was no bigger than her thumbnail. Even more important, the clump only contained nutrients. She flicked her fingers upward, which caused the clump to shoot through the soil above it.

Only a moment later, the tiny piece of earth broke through the surface and flew into the air.

Pursing her lips, Wendy pointed to the nearest citizen. "Quick, get your pot and catch that bit of dirt."

A man with white hair hobbled forward to catch the dirt before it fell to the ground.

Wendy gave a hurried nod. "Now, put several handfuls of dirt into your pot. Then get a little water from the well and mix it all together. Once it's thoroughly mixed, bring it into the glass house and place it in one of the wooden troughs Rio and Fyra are building."

With glowing eyes, the man began scooping dirt into the pot.

The look probably continued to grow, but Talise turned her attention back to the dirt. She dug deep with her senses again. As she had hoped, finding the right nutrients went a little faster the second time.

When a second tiny clump broke through the surface above, two different citizens stood ready to catch it.

Talise turned so they wouldn't see how she grinned.

By the end of the day, two dozen people had come to help. Mud splotches covered their faces and hands, but something even more important lingered in their eyes. For the first time in who knew how long, they had done something that might improve their situation.

Many thanks were sent to the citizens as they all headed back to their homes. That day was only the first of several that it would take to fill the glass house with enough nutrient-rich soil. Hopefully tomorrow they would get help from even more citizens.

After saying goodbye, Talise and her friends headed back to their camp. Talise hung back, and luckily her best friend seemed to understand why.

Wendy grabbed a piece of her hair, only to realize her fingers were covered in mud. Scowling at them, she dropped the hair and shook her head. "What is it?"

A lump seared through Talise's throat. She bit into her bottom lip as she stared at the ground. "Something is wrong with the soil."

Lowering one eyebrow, Wendy's eyes turned down as well. "Because it doesn't have enough nutrients, right? But you said it was like that when you lived here too."

"No." Talise lowered her voice even more. "It has always been hard to grow things in the Storm, but it's worse now. I can tell." She closed her eyes, reaching out with one hand and her senses one last time. "There are layers in the earth. The soil has been bad for a long time, which is why I had to dig so deep to get the nutrients we needed. But the top layer…"

Snapping her hand upward, Talise opened her eyes again. "It's much worse than the rest. Something happened recently, and it's still happening. Something that leeched nutrients from the ground."

Wendy already had a hand pressed to her mouth, but it didn't hide the heavy gulp that went through her. "What do you think it was?" she whispered.

Talise took in a deep breath. "I don't know, but I plan to find out."

CHAPTER SIX

THE NEXT DAY, EVEN MORE citizens came to the glass house eager to help.

"Will this pot work?" A child with dark brown eyes carried a pot so large, he had to rest it on one hip to help support it.

Talise nodded as she flicked a clump of nutrients up from the ground. "That pot is perfect. Here comes the dirt, get ready to catch it."

He wobbled under the weight of his pot but still managed to catch the clump.

Without a second thought, Talise pressed her senses deep into the earth again. It had gotten much easier with practice. Though she had just gotten help from the citizens in effort to make them feel useful, their help actually did make the work go faster.

Rio and Fyra had finished building the troughs that would hold the plants. Wendy and Tempest had devised a ventilation system that allowed two small fires to burn inside the glass house without getting the smoke anywhere near the plants. Then if the sun didn't heat the glass house enough, the fires could warm it up even more.

Cyrus worked with the people, encouraging them and laughing with them. He constantly thought of new contests to make the work more fun. Who could mix dirt with the nutrients and stay the cleanest? Who could mix dirt and get the dirtiest? Who could do it standing up? Who could do it the loudest?

His antics made the days go faster for everyone. Talise had never known Cyrus all that well, but she wondered if such things were just because of his personality. Or maybe after spending months in Kessoku's dungeons, he just understood desperation better than the others.

Everyone had sore muscles by the time they trudged back to camp that evening. The inner muscles on Talise's upper arm pulsed after so much shaping. At this point, the work was almost finished. They just needed seeds now.

A skitter went through her stomach when they arrived at camp. Four chickens sat inside a thin wire cage. Nearby, a large animal grazed from a pile of hay. Several bags had been draped over the animal's back. The person removing them brought another skitter through Talise, one she felt all the way down to her toes.

Aaden had returned.

It wasn't until that very moment that she realized a large part of her had expected him to disappear and never come back. Just like he had at the palace.

But as he lifted a pack, his eyes met hers, almost a confirmation that he was actually there. He actually had returned. The lightest smile prickled under her lips, which she did her best to smother.

"I made dinner," he said, pointing to a pot full of hearty soup already cooking over the fire.

Grabbing his head, Cyrus dropped to the ground in a heap. "No, Aaden. *Why* would you do that?" He peeked at the soup before dragging both hands down his face.

Aaden stepped toward the group shaking both hands in front of his face. "No, I didn't make it actually. I should have said, I *brought* some soup that someone *else* made, and now I'm warming it over the fire for everyone."

The grimace on Cyrus's face melted away in a single moment. He let out a long sigh of relief. "Thank Kamdaria for that." Smirking, he glanced toward the others. "Aaden is the *worst* cook in the entire empire, probably the worst that has ever lived."

Pulling out the woven mats they sat on for meals, Aaden raised one eyebrow. "Okay, but at least I never tried to make a fireball that somehow turned into a smoke-filled ball of water instead."

Cyrus took the mats and dropped them evenly around the fire. "That was *one* time."

They were both chuckling by the time everyone sat down. Fyra dug the bowls out from one of their packs, and Rio began scooping soup into each of the bowls. After Talise got her food, she glanced toward Aaden.

Already, his face had fallen. The scar across his eye caught the moonlight when he spoke. "I didn't find out anything about Kessoku." Now his eyes wandered to the ground. The corners of his mouth pulled down. "Or your soldiers. I'm sorry."

Thought she had known it was a long shot, her heart still sunk in her chest. Nodding, she looked down at the brown liquid floating through the noodles in her bowl. "Is there anything you did learn?"

He chewed slowly before answering. "I heard about shipments going into the Storm. They might be coming *from* the Storm, I'm not sure."

Rio dropped his bowl to his lap as he looked across the fire. "What's in the shipments?"

Aaden shrugged. "I don't know."

Tempest and Wendy shared a glance before Wendy asked, "What are the shipments for?"

"I don't know." Aaden's answer brought collective frowns all through their group.

Fyra had her bowl up to her lips before lowering it with both eyebrows raised. "What do the shipments look like?"

Aaden flicked his eyes toward Talise before he looked down again. "I don't know."

Letting a little huff escape from her mouth, Talise asked, "Is there anything you *do* know?"

Rocking the bowl in his lap, Aaden kept his eyes down. "The shipments supposedly come from the emperor."

With a dramatic flip of her head, Tempest's braid flew behind her back. "Great, so the only way to get helpful information is to go to the palace."

Though the soup was delicious, a pit in Talise's stomach made it far less appetizing.

"I can do that." Aaden continued to tilt his head downward, but he looked at Talise through the side of his eye. "The emperor did give me a password to get past the gateways and into the Crown. I've been dropping in for months to get information and any new instructions. I can ask him about the shipments."

Soup spilled from Tempest's bowl as she leaned forward. Her face may have been passive before, but a scowl overtook it now. "Great idea. You head to the palace just so you can reveal our location to the emperor." The scowl hardened as she leaned back onto her mat. "I don't think so."

A slight eyebrow raise disturbed the stillness on Aaden's face. "I would never tell him where you are." He turned his head, looking straight into Talise's eyes. "I think you know that."

Her stomach flipped and only carefully controlled breaths could calm it down again. It really wasn't fair how he could affect her so easily. Once the flipping stopped, the reality of his words settled in.

They could get information from the *palace*.

It had been so long since they had heard any news from the Crown. How could she pass up the opportunity? Giving him the slightest glance, she asked, "Could you find out about Kessoku too? See if the emperor is planning to attack their main base any time soon?"

The nod Aaden offered brought a sense of relief through her that she hadn't known in a long while.

She gulped and pressed her lips together before managing to get her next question out. "And can you ask if he knows anything about my soldiers that Kessoku has imprisoned?

With her soup bowl almost against her lips, Fyra gave a tentative glance across the fire. "You aren't worried he'll reveal our location?"

"I'm not worried about it." Wendy nodded once with a face as serious as she could manage.

Cyrus leaned back as he swirled the noodles around in his bowl. "I'm definitely not."

Fyra didn't look convinced. Neither did Rio. Tempest looked ready to tie Aaden to a tree to prevent him from getting to the emperor.

Thoughts danced around in Talise's head before she finally found one that might assuage everyone's fears. "We'll just move to another city as soon as Aaden returns. The glass house is already finished, and Wendy taught the citizens how to ventilate if they have to build fires. Tomorrow we can butcher and distribute the animal meat. We just have to plant the seeds Aaden brought, but after that, there isn't much more we can do to help this city anyway. We'll just go to another city when Aaden returns, and we'll make sure he doesn't know where it is."

Fyra nodded as she stared at her soup. "I guess it *would* be nice to have news from the palace." She glanced at Rio, raising her eyebrows high on her forehead.

At first, he didn't react. After another moment of her staring, he gulped, and a pink flush went through his cheeks. Now he looked toward Aaden. Before speaking, he gulped again. "Can you try to find someone for me? She's a soldier with an orange hem. Ember is her name." Rio's eyes dropped to his soup as one hand crept up his chest until it landed over his heart. "Just tell her I miss her."

Cold seeped around Talise, biting into her neck. She remembered Ember. The soldier had slept in Talise's bed when Talise escaped the palace to get back to the River Gate. Ember had done it to make the guards think Talise was still where she was supposed to be.

Rio had never once spoken about the soldier, but his eyes said plenty now. Guilt thrashed through Talise like a dagger. How much had her soldiers sacrificed when they chose to join her?

"And can you try to find my parents?" Fyra asked. "They help clean the palace. Just tell them I'm safe and that I love them."

A few other requests went across the fire until Aaden pulled out a parchment to keep track of them all.

At the end, Talise sent the last request but maybe the most important one. She allowed herself to look deep into Aaden's eyes and ignored how it made her stomach flop again. Setting her jaw, she said, "Be careful."

Tomorrow he'd be gone again. But this time, she had a little more hope for his return.

CHAPTER SEVEN

A SMILE CREPT ONTO TALISE'S face as she patted the soil around the little sprouts poking out of it. Even with the days growing colder and harsher, they had still managed to see some growth from the seeds they planted inside the glass house.

"Can we eat them yet?" Willow had come a long way since Talise had found her throwing rocks at a home. Now the girl spent her days inside the glass house, tending instead of destroying.

"Not yet." Talise paired her words with as much feeling as she could. "You have to wait until they are fully grown. If you pick them too fast, you won't get as much food as you could if you had waited."

Willow bent her head in a solemn nod as they both exited the greenhouse.

The sprouts brought hope, but they also brought worry. It meant Aaden had been gone a long time. Talise didn't expect him to be back already. He had to travel all the way to the palace and back, and he didn't have a horse this time. But his absence often made her remember her soldiers.

They were held captive in Kessoku's main base by the Ember Gate. It took Kessoku months before they killed their prisoners from the palace the first time. Even then, the prisoners were only killed because Kessoku's main base got attacked. Her soldiers were probably safe as long as the emperor didn't attack the base. Which he could do any day. And she'd never know.

Prickles tingled through her feet as she walked. The cold wind whipped through her hair. Every time she thought about her soldiers, something deep within her chest roiled and churned.

Why had it seemed like such a good idea to get information from the palace? It would take Aaden weeks to get there *and* weeks to get back. By the time he returned, the news he brought might be too late.

At least the glass house had done what it was supposed to. Glancing back at it, her stomach dropped out. A dozen people wielding daggers and heavy rods stormed toward her. Two of them had a chicken under their arms. When one member of the group ran inside the glass house, the others flashed their teeth and brandished their weapons at anyone who dared look at them.

Willow clapped a hand to her mouth. "It's the tyrants. They have a different name they call themselves, but that's what my father calls them. They're from the city across the river from us. They're always coming over here and stealing our things."

With hands curling into fists, Talise stomped toward the group. Even before she got close, the person who had entered the greenhouse now exited it. All the little sprouts she'd been admiring just moments before were peeking out from his hands.

Even when the group members swung their weapons around, Talise only continued moving closer. Soon, the members of the group turned and ran away from the city.

Talise barreled after them without a second thought. Despite the icy chill in the air, heat coursed through her veins with the force of a gushing river. Her fists clenched tighter with every step.

This group seemed much better at running than the people in the city she'd spent the last few weeks with. The *tyrants* never stopped charging toward the river, despite the squawking chickens they carried.

From behind Talise, several shouts rang through the air. She recognized Rio's voice first. He was telling her to wait for the rest of them. His words only pushed her to move faster.

Breathing got more difficult the longer she ran. To combat the problem, she just used air shaping to force steady breaths in and out of her mouth.

When the tyrants reached the river, they climbed onto a rickety rope bridge. One end of it had metal claw-like hooks that gripped a large rock. They passed over the bridge, each one looking over their shoulders at Talise as they went.

On the other side, one member of the group took the stakes out that held the bridge in place from their side of the river. With a swift shake, the bridge rippled up in a wave. When the wave reached the end of the bridge, the claw-like hooks came loose from the rock on Talise's side of the river. The woman across the river yanked the bridge toward herself and then rolled it up. She sent a sneer toward Talise before scurrying away.

The group continued to run farther away, but Talise watched carefully where they went. After gulping several steady breaths in through her nose, she flooded her veins with fire. Ice shot from her fingertips almost as fast.

Her friends continued to call after her, but they were still far behind. A weaker ice bridge would ensure none of them could follow her.

After sending just enough ice for a thin layer across the river, Talise stepped onto it. River water smashed through chunks of it just as she reached the other side. Not looking back, she stepped quietly up to the house the tyrants had entered.

A yellow cotton sheet hung in an open window. Cold air fluttered through it. With a little blast of air, she forced the sheet to whip hard enough that she could glance inside the house.

All twelve of the tyrants were gathered around a bed that had a coughing woman under its covers. Their hushed tones made it difficult to hear, but they offered the sprouts to the woman just as another cough shook through her.

The woman looked a little younger than Aaden's father. She wasn't old but few lived to such an age in the Storm.

Not needing to see anything else, Talise moved to the front of the house and barged in.

It only took a few puffs of air from her palms to knock away the daggers that had been thrown at her. Fear scampered across the faces of those carrying rods, but they still held them dutifully. She had to force herself not to roll her eyes. It would have taken almost no effort at all to knock them all off their feet. Taking in a deep breath, her fists curled tighter until her fingernails dug into her palms.

Tension rocked through her jaw as she spoke through clenched teeth. "Those sprouts are not enough to keep you healthy." She gestured vaguely out the door toward the rest of the city. "I need you to choose a spot where I can build a glass house for you. Then you can plant your own seeds and wait to eat the food until it's fully grown."

The weapons faltered as those holding them glanced at each other.

Now she pointed in the corner where the two stolen chickens had been placed. "Keep the chickens, but you have to promise to distribute the eggs evenly to everyone in the city."

When she stepped forward, nearly every single one of them flinched. That only lasted until they remembered the weapons in their hands. Now they swung the rods toward her.

A flick of her wrist sent the rods crashing against the dirt floor. With her other hand, she reached out to sense the water inside the cup in the bed-ridden woman's hand.

Talise pressed a hand to her forehead as she shook it. "That water isn't clean. Don't you know you have to boil the river water before you drink it?"

"We did."

Everyone scowled at the man who had spoken.

The words brought heaviness to Talise's gut. Even as she shaped the impurities out of the water, theories began forming in her mind. How could the river be so dirty that even boiling the water wasn't enough?

A crumble of impurities landed on the floor when she turned to face the others. "Then start boiling the water twice."

Their mouths hung open at the sight of her. When the woman on the bed let out a croaking cough, Talise reached into her tunic.

Her friends had made her promise not to share the food they had brought in their packs, but surely, they would forgive such a thing in these circumstances. Pulling out a fluffy bun, she pushed the food into the woman's hands.

If she knew anything about the healing arts, she would have used them for the woman. Still, food and clean water were probably the best medicine anyway. *If* it wasn't too late.

The woman eyed the bun with narrowed eyes when Talise held it out. Shaking her head, Talise pinched off a piece of the bun and stuck it into her mouth. While chewing she said, "It's safe, I promise."

As soon as the woman accepted the bun, Talise marched toward the door of the house. "I'll be back in a few days to start building you a glass house that will be warm enough to grow plants. Make sure you have a spot chosen for it by then."

Not a single voice accompanied her exit, but she could feel them blinking at her retreating form.

At the river, her ice bridge had been reduced to nothing more than a few chunks of ice clinging to the riverbank.

Rio had disappeared. Only Wendy stood on the other side of the river across from Talise. As always, her best friend wore an innocent smile.

After making another flimsy ice bridge, Talise crossed over it to join her best friend. She glanced around. "Where are the others?"

Wendy clasped her hands behind her back as she started walking. "Oh, I just told them to go back to camp before I drowned them."

A snort escaped Talise's mouth before she could stop it. "This is why we're best friends."

With a smirk, Wendy gestured across the river at the house with the tyrants. "I assume you chose the city we're going to help next."

Talise grinned. Her best friend knew her too well. As they continued making their way toward camp, the lingering heaviness in Talise's gut spread out through her limbs.

"What is it?" Wendy asked.

Talise brushed a bit of hair over her shoulder. It had grown so long now. The black strands fell several inches past her shoulders. "I do want to help. I want to go to every city in the Storm and give them everything they need and more."

Quiet steps crunched over the dry earth before Wendy spoke again. "But?"

Talise's head hung. "But the walls still separate Kamdaria into three rings. The soil is still leeched of nutrients here. If I don't figure out what's causing it, it's only going to get worse. Every solution I can provide is temporary." She let out a huff before digging her fingers into her hair. "And I'm still in exile. While the war is still going on, there's only so much I can do to help."

Warmth went into her forearm when Wendy gave it a quick squeeze. "We can't save everyone. Not yet. But the things you're doing *will* help. Don't underestimate your actions because they are temporary. Just do everything you can while you can."

It felt nice to have a smile creeping onto her face again. "Thank you."

Now Wendy's lips pursed together while a mischievous glint went through her eyes. "Oh, and Aaden's back."

The words brought a flood of emotions through Talise so fast, she had no possible chance of controlling them. Trying to catch her breath, she attempted to don the most neutral face she could manage. "He's back already?"

Despite her efforts to hide the emotion, Wendy seemed to see through all of it. Her eyes continued to sparkle with a knowing smile. "Yes, and he says he has lots of news."

CHAPTER EIGHT

EVEN AFTER RACING BACK TO camp, Talise's thumping heart still skipped at the sight of Aaden. He had returned.

Again.

"The shipments are definitely from Emperor Flarius." Aaden slipped his pack off his shoulder, somehow maintaining intense eye contact with Talise throughout. His hands dug into the pack, but still his eyes didn't pull away from hers. "The emperor started sending them a few weeks ago."

Under the guise of catching her breath, Talise dipped her head to one side. Glossy black strands fell across her face, hopefully hiding the heat rising in her cheeks. After a few moments, she was able to look up with an even expression. "How did you get back so fast?"

The slightest twitch jumped across Aaden's lips. When he gulped, his throat bulged. "I borrowed a horse."

From his side, Cyrus wiped mud from his boots. He let out a snicker as he glanced toward Aaden. "He means *stole*."

A vein at the edge of Aaden's jaw pulsed before he attempted a nonchalant shrug. "I brought it back. They didn't even know it was missing."

Wendy shared a look with her brother before she and Cyrus both let out chuckles.

The fracture in Aaden's perfect mask vanished as he waved off their reactions. "After everyone stopped hiring Storm laborers, the emperor decided to send shipments to the Storm instead. They have food, clothing, and a few other supplies. The shipments are supposed to help until Storm laborers can be hired again."

It sounded too good to be true. Since when did the emperor care about people from the Storm? Why would he choose to help them now after so many years of oppression?

Of course, those questions only served as distractions from the real one skirting around in Talise's head. But even as she tried to ignore it, the question came forward anyway. Could the shipments be related to the recent leeching of the soil?

She thrust the thought from her mind with a swift flick. That didn't make any sense. Why would the emperor hurt people from the Storm? For years, he benefitted from Storm laborers who were paid far less than laborers from the Gate. If anything, he probably wanted a way to reinstate that system. He wouldn't want people from the Storm to die.

Unfortunately, the others in the group looked as skeptical as Talise.

Rio and Fyra stared anxiously at the pack Aaden still dug through. Tempest just settled onto the ground with her back against a tree. Clasping her hands behind her neck, she asked, "How do we know these shipments are actually beneficial to the people here?"

"We don't." Aaden finally turned his eyes toward his pack and immediately pulled two letters out of it. After tossing one each to Rio and Fyra, he spoke again. "But I know how we can find out. I managed to get a schedule for the shipments. That's why I got back as fast as I could. Palace soldiers are delivering a shipment to a town across the river from here. We should be able to make it in time if we leave right now."

Talise only had to take a swig from a water pouch before she was ready to go. Aaden was already pulling a map from his tunic to show her where to travel before the others had even moved. No doubt, they would not be far behind. But that didn't mean Talise was going to wait for them.

Tapping a finger to the city Aaden had pointed out, she allowed a soft frown to cover her face. It wasn't the same city she had just come from, but rather the one closer to the ocean. It would have been nice to return to a city where she had made some allies, but hopefully they would still have time to see everything they needed to see.

At least it wouldn't be difficult to make an ice bridge over the river again. She'd just have to make it a little thicker this time so the others could cross with her.

"Kessoku sabotaged at least one of the shipments." Aaden's voice broke her from her thoughts. The way he stared at her brought a jolt through her gut. A crease appeared between his eyebrows before he spoke again. "They used the amulet."

Her feet pounded across the dead earth as her eyes widened. "What happened?"

He checked over his shoulder. Maybe he didn't want the others to hear, but maybe he just wanted to share the information as soon as possible. They could tell the others later anyway. "The ground rolled under foot in the whole city and then it snapped upward. Bursts of earth clods exploded all over the place." His face grew dimmer with every word.

Without meaning to, her voice lowered to a whisper. "Did anyone get hurt?"

Aaden nodded slowly. His eyes looked dimmer by the second. "Many people got hurt, but most of them were Kessoku."

Another jolt went through her that had an odd mixture of thrill and terror. It took great effort to even push the next words from her lips. "Did anybody die?"

He turned away. Not all the others had caught up, but Cyrus and Rio had. After a quick nod toward them, Aaden's face turned still and unmoved. "I don't know if anyone died, but the palace soldiers said many of the injuries could have been fatal if they weren't treated in time. I don't know for sure, but it sounds like the person leading the group could have been fatally wounded. They described the woman as tall with soulless eyes. They said the other Kessoku seemed to fear the amulet, but they feared the woman even more."

Even running at full speed, Talise couldn't ignore the sinking in her gut. "River?"

Aaden offered a tiny shrug. "We have no way of knowing for sure, but it does sound like her."

Just then, Cyrus clapped a hand on Aaden's shoulder. With a widening grin, Wendy's brother let out a laugh. "This is perfect. We don't even have to fight Kessoku. We can just let the idiots use their precious amulet until they all kill themselves."

Aaden gave a sideways glance. "Not all Kessoku are as bad as River."

A twitch went through Cyrus's eye before he shrugged. "That just means my idea is even more foolproof. The only people stupid enough to use the amulet are the ones who want blood as much as River does."

Talise eyed Aaden carefully. "You said the land rolled and clods of dirt exploded."

He nodded.

It would be impossible to hide her gulp, so she didn't even try. "You don't think that could have caused the soil to be leeched of nutrients, do you?"

Aaden let out a sigh. "I was wondering the same thing."

When they finally reached the flowing water of the river, Talise had to take a few deep breaths before she could shape an ice bridge. Aaden had led them down river quite a ways from the city she had just visited.

From behind her, the others finally caught up. It took so much energy to form a thick enough bridge, she almost didn't hear Cyrus's low whistle. "I can't believe she can shape ice. I thought that was impossible."

Talise turned toward the others just in time to see a smirk pass over Aaden's lips. "It used to be," he said before stepping across the ice bridge.

The city sat directly along the edge of the river. At the end of the city, the river flowed into the ocean. Coarse sand filled the freezing beaches.

They didn't have to wait long before the shipment arrived. A riverboat came from upriver. After dropping an anchor, two dozen palace soldiers climbed down the ramp, pushing a heavy wooden cart to the bottom. From inside the boat, a soldier with an orange hem shouted loud enough for everyone to hear.

"Emperor Flarius wishes good to all in his empire. He sends food and clothing with a promise to send even more. May you all remember how your great emperor loves you."

Talise had to stop herself from rolling her eyes. In fact, she didn't even manage it completely. Of course the emperor couldn't just give people the things they needed. He had to take all the credit and boast about himself too.

Still.

She lifted herself onto her tiptoes and glanced over the crowd to see inside the wooden cart. Stacks of wool blankets were folded neatly next to barrels of potatoes and rice. There were even a few boxes of smoked meats.

The citizens who stood on the streets had already started shoving and tripping each other to get to the cart first. Talise turned to her friends.

"We should probably get some of the things, so we can see them up close." She didn't add that she wanted to make sure nothing in the cart could cause soil to be leeched of its nutrients. But maybe she didn't need to say it because the others glanced around with knowing nods.

Wendy offered to go since she was probably the least recognizable of anyone in their group.

When the shoving in the crowd got worse, the soldier at the top of the riverboat only shouted again. "Form two lines at the bottom of the ramp. We have many carts on the boat, so everyone will get what they need."

That didn't stop any of the shoving, but the soldier just shook his head. With a flourish, he whipped a folded card from his pocket. The parchment had been covered in a protective wax.

Holding the card up high, the soldier spoke again. "You are required to show your ID card to get your items. Only one blanket and three food portions will be given for each ID card."

With feet faltering, Wendy stopped moving toward the riverboat. Instead, she flashed a sweet smile and fell back until she stood close enough to Talise to whisper. "I can't show them my ID card. Everyone in the Storm is supposed to have an X on their ID card, but my square is blank since I'm from the Gate."

Nodding, Talise held her best friend back. "Stay here. We'll just have to get our information through observation."

CHAPTER NINE

CITIZENS OF THE CITY LINED behind the palace cart. Perhaps this was not the first time the soldiers had brought a shipment because everyone tapped their toes lazily instead of trying to get a look inside the cart.

When Talise edged closer, Wendy and Rio closed in tighter on her sides. Since Aaden already stood close enough that his shoulder rested against her back, it wasn't the most comfortable position in the world. Knowing any request for space would be disregarded, Talise did her best to ignore them.

A solider from the riverboat glanced toward their group. The back of her neck prickled when his eyes met hers. Aaden managed to stop himself from grabbing her, but she could feel how his hand hovered a breath away from her lower back.

Maybe this would be a good moment to disappear behind a house. The soldier's eyes narrowed at her, and this time, Aaden did touch her. When the soldier opened his mouth, Aaden had already slipped his hand around her waist and pulled her closer. As unnecessary as it was, Talise still felt grateful to have someone watching out for her.

Because she realized—a little too late—the palace soldiers might recognize her. She didn't recognize any of them, which is why she hadn't thought to worry yet. But suddenly, her memory filled with the grand pronouncement when the emperor had presented her as Princess Talise Ruemon. Scores of soldiers had been present, including many she had never seen before.

Before the soldier could blink, Wendy was standing directly in front of Talise. Twirling the end of her braid in one hand, Tempest leaned on a house next to Wendy, further blocking Talise from view. The others moved ahead as well, even Cyrus. Everyone except Aaden, of course. He seemed intent on pulling Talise away from the riverboat.

"You there." The soldier's voice came out raspy as he shouted over the crowd.

Even with her view blocked, Talise already knew the soldier must have been pointing to her friends. Now Aaden tugged her behind the nearest house.

The soldier spoke again. "Pull out your ID cards and get in line for your goods."

"Scatter." Aaden only had to whisper the word before the others leapt into action. They all darted through the city in every direction. She didn't have time to check where they all went because Aaden had firmly grabbed her by the hand.

He pulled her behind one house where they only spent a few seconds before they were off again.

Was the shipment a ruse by the emperor after all? Had he sent goods into the Storm simply to find citizens who didn't have an X on their ID cards like they should have had? People like Talise and her friends. Which only begged the question, did the emperor suspect she might be hiding in the Storm?

She didn't want to believe it. But then again, he had never understood just how bad things were in the outer ring of the empire.

After being tugged behind yet another house, Aaden dropped her hand with a heavy gulp. "Did I pull you too hard? I get tense when I'm nervous and…"

He had a way of making her whole heart skip and flutter. But it wasn't just that he was handsome or sly. No, the moments that truly stole her breath away were when he was utterly and completely open. For someone who always hid emotions behind a mask, it made his trembling lip that much more powerful. His eyes shimmered as his lips turned down. She could have sworn Kamdaria itself stopped to hear his breath.

Glancing down at her hand, he asked, "I didn't hurt you, did I?"

Her hand could have been completely sliced off, and she probably wouldn't have noticed. Why couldn't he be cruel when she wanted to be angry at him? Instead he had to wear a trembling lip that sent her heart into hysterics. She had to twist away from him before she could even process his question.

By then, her hand was too sweaty to notice if it hurt or not. Truthfully, she had been squeezing his hand pretty hard too. It was difficult enough trying to survive among desperate, starving citizens and during the harshest season as well. It really wasn't fair if they had to survive palace soldiers too. Would the fear never subside?

Finally, her lips parted to answer the question. Before she could admit her hand was fine, a raspy voice sounded from only a few houses away. "I think I saw some of them run over here." The palace soldier let out a hacking cough. "They think they're so clever coming over from another city so they can get double the goods."

A female soldier responded. "Storm citizens don't have any smarts though. All we have to do is check the city on their ID cards, and we can quickly see they are trying to cheat the system."

Aaden had grabbed her hand again. She sent a cooling blast of ice through her fingertips just before he touched her. Hopefully that would keep him from noticing the sweat that had gathered in her palm.

The voices moved closer. It offered almost no relief at all to know the emperor *wasn't* using ID cards in an attempt to find her because now the soldiers had almost reached them.

When Aaden tugged her hand, she followed him without hesitation. They moved at a slower pace than before. This time, disguising their footsteps held higher priority than getting away. They moved past several houses, but the soldiers' voices sounded near. Too near.

With a jerk of the chin toward the houses, Aaden whispered, "Try to find one that's empty."

Only a moment later, they ducked past a flapping cotton sheet and settled into the corner of a single-room home. The soldiers passed by the house only a few seconds later. Both Talise and Aaden dropped their hands away from each other with a start. Aaden looked away. As if that could help.

He cleared his throat, which gave her the strong desire to smack him. Why couldn't he have joined Kessoku like she thought he had? Instead, he had to make things so much more complicated.

They sat in silence for a while. Just when it seemed safe to leave, a man with callused hands entered the home. He whistled a plucky tune as he dropped several items onto the only table in the room.

Pursing her lips, Talise glanced toward Aaden. Could they sneak out without the man noticing? Probably not. Aaden frowned as he glanced toward the door. He stepped forward only an inch, but the movement was enough to stop the man dead in his tracks.

The whistling stopped at once. Whirling around, the man turned to face the pair of them. His jaw dropped low. After another breath, he snatched a large rod from off the dusty floor.

Talise threw her hands up in surrender. "We don't want to hurt you."

A sneer overtook the man's face as he tightened his grip on the rod. "Oh right, you only want my food and blankets. Is that it?"

"We want to leave." Aaden had such a funny way of speaking to strangers. His words always came out stilted. He talked too fast or too slow but never just right. Then a twitch always appeared above one eye as he attempted to straighten his expression to one of indifference.

It probably would have been wise to spend more effort comforting the man, assuring him of their peaceful intentions. But a new thought resounded through Talise's mind with such strength that she could not ignore it. Lifting one hand toward the table, her shaping senses reached out.

Letting out a laugh, the man said, "You must be new to the Storm. You probably just lost your shaping, and you still think you can get it back."

The words drifted right through her as she continued to use her shaping to feel inside of the food the man had brought back from the emperor's shipment.

"What are you doing?" Aaden whispered under his breath.

Now her eyelids dropped closed, giving more concentration to the shaping. "I'm trying to sense anything that might have leeched nutrients from the soil."

"You think the emperor caused that?" Aaden couldn't hide the surprise in his voice.

Stretching her hand out, her fingers shivered with energy. "Of course I don't *want* it to be the emperor's fault."

Even with her eyes closed, she could hear how Aaden nodded his head. "But you want to make sure just in case."

Finding nothing in the food, Talise reached her senses toward the blanket from the shipment. Then to a cup of water sitting in the window. None of them yielded anything suspicious.

When she finally opened her eyes, she found the man staring back at her with his jaw dropped again. "You still have shaping?"

She offered a tiny smile in return. "I'm sorry we came into your house. We just wanted to hide from someone. Enjoy your food."

They started moving toward the door, and the man only shrugged. "I'm too old to worry about trespassers anyway." He dug a black fabric pouch from his pocket and set it down next to the food.

Aaden froze mid-step, pointing to the pouch. "What is that?"

The man let out a sigh. He fell into a chair and started removing his shoes. "It's just the food they bring for the fish. They dump it into the ocean and river after they distribute all the goods. But I always steal a little bag of it because I like feeding the fish."

A smile crept onto Talise's face at the thought. It only lasted a moment before her entire face fell like a hammer. Just to be thorough, she had reached out her shaping senses toward the fish food as well. Now guilt stabbed through her with gripping clarity.

When she turned to Aaden, no words were necessary. His hand had reached out too.

He turned to her slowly. When he spoke, the words came out strained. "That's what is leeching nutrients from the soil."

Chapter Ten

TALISE RAN A FINGER OVER the black hem of her Kessoku uniform. She never expected to wear it again so soon. Truthfully, it came as a surprise that an opportunity arose for her to wear it at all.

Luckily, the black tunic and helmet were all she needed to hide in plain sight from the palace soldiers. Even more fortunate, everyone in her group still had a uniform to wear. Now they just had to destroy the fish food that had been leeching nutrients from the soil.

The fact that the fish food came from the emperor was something Talise did her best to ignore. Her thoughts were much better suited to analyzing the poison inside the fish food. Her knowledge and ability to identify nutrients made it easy to pinpoint the poison. Her senses could recognize the structure of it and how it had been imbued.

But thinking of how the emperor himself was purposefully sending poisonous fish food to the Storm? What could she do with that? It brought back too many memories of how he had exiled her and imprisoned her inside the palace. Ignoring the emperor's involvement instead was much easier. Especially when she had work to do.

From behind a dead tree, Talise glanced at the palace cart rolling into a city. Using the schedule Aaden had retrieved, they had all gone to the city set to retrieve the next shipment.

"Are you sure about this?" Aaden's face stayed steady as he glanced toward Cyrus.

Throwing an arm over his sister's shoulder, Cyrus let out a chuckle. "Wendy and I could sell ice in the middle of winter. Her charm is impeccable, but combined…" He gave a wistful stare off in the distance. "We can get away with anything."

Aaden didn't look so sure. He nodded, but his jaw still tensed when he swallowed.

Wearing their scratchiest tunics, Wendy and Cyrus stepped out from behind the tree and began moving toward the palace cart.

The timing was tricky. They had to destroy the fish food, which was leeching nutrients from the ground. But they wanted to do it *after* the palace soldiers distributed the food and other supplies to the citizens.

Aaden moved closer to Talise, leaning on a withered tree. His voice lowered while the others looked on. Tempest watched Wendy and Cyrus intently, but Rio watched Aaden. A warning seemed to flare in his eyes. Fyra had her eyes to the ground as usual.

Leaning into the tree, Aaden tilted his head to catch Talise's eye. When she looked, he flicked his eyes backward at the siblings. "Are *you* sure about this?"

A smirk worked its way onto Talise's face. "I've seen Wendy get away with plenty. I'm actually very curious about how she'll work with her brother. She always claimed she and Cyrus were more devious together."

An audible gulp left Tempest's throat as they all stared at the pair heading toward the shipment. She bit into her bottom lip too. With such a frightening air about her all the time, it was slightly disconcerting to see Tempest nervous. Then again, Wendy and Cyrus did have the most dangerous part of the plan. They were the only ones who had to show their faces. The rest of them would have helmets to obscure their identities.

Wendy found a piece of her hair once they reached the shipments. She twirled it just as she gave a sweet smile to the three palace soldiers. Two of them nodded without much added interaction. They just kept coiling the ropes that had secured the supplies inside the cart.

A third soldier with broad shoulders and a square jaw returned Wendy's smile with a smirk. He cocked one elbow up on the cart and opened his mouth.

Before he could say anything, Cyrus stepped up to him. He slammed both hands against his sides. "Why haven't you brought supplies to our city yet? Everyone around us is getting these shipments, but we keep waiting."

In a flash, the smirk on the soldier's face turned to a glare. The palace soldier rounded on Cyrus. Just as his lips parted, Wendy touched a hand to her brother's forearm. Her voice came out sweeter than the cinnamon candy at Fire Festival. "I'm sure they plan to bring supplies to us too." She gestured toward the soldiers, giving special emphasis to the one in front of her. "Look how hard these soldiers are working."

The expression on the soldier's face had already softened. When Wendy flashed him another smile, it warmed even more.

Her finger twirled her piece of hair around it as she addressed the soldier. "You probably get exhausted after so much hard work."

Just like that, the soldier stood a little taller. "It's not too bad. The emperor pays us extra for the hardship of having to visit the Storm."

Cyrus let out snort as he puffed out his chest. "The *hardship* of visiting the Storm? We have to live here all the time, you know. I bet you spend all your extra money on ridiculous things like silk handkerchiefs or sugared pastries. Meanwhile, *we* can barely survive."

Guilt twinged across the soldier's face, but it quickly reverted to anger. Red burned into his cheeks as his fists curled.

Talise gulped. Maybe she'd had too much faith in her friend. Angering the soldier didn't seem like it would help them get what they wanted.

Wendy flicked her fingers on Cyrus's shoulder. "Ignore my brother," she said to the soldier. "You *earned* that money from the emperor. You should be allowed to spend it however you want."

The soldier's fists relaxed. Wendy tilted her head with her most brilliant smile yet and pointed inside the cart toward the poisonous fish food. "What is that?"

Such innocence laced her voice, the soldier seemed more than happy to comply. In fact, his anger toward Cyrus only seemed to boost his desire to do something nice for Wendy. And now Talise wondered if that had been their plan all along.

Everything continued to move fluidly in just the way they had hoped. The two other palace soldiers had moved closer to the ocean. They dug two shallow trenches in the sand for the cart wheels to rest while they dumped fish food into the ocean.

The last soldier—the one talking to Wendy and Cyrus—was supposed to stay back and protect the cart while they worked. Instead, Wendy's innocent eyes and persistent questions led the soldier several paces away from the cart.

Now the soldier explained how seeds grew, as if Wendy couldn't possibly know such a thing after growing up in the Storm. Despite his ignorance, at least he had moved away from the cart as they had planned. Not only was the timing of their mission critical, the position of the soldiers was critical too.

They wanted to attack as Kessoku would, but they didn't want to injure the soldiers. It would take careful work to make it look like a violent attack without actually being violent.

Rio lifted a fist in the air and glanced toward Talise. She nodded to him, indicating she was ready whenever he was. His back stiffened as he stared at the soldier and the siblings. With narrowing eyes, he seemed to be counting in his head. Letting out a breath, he dropped his fist and they all started running.

Hearing a loud whoop erupt from Rio's mouth came as a surprise. His stiff, soldierly behavior didn't usually allow for such mannerisms. But it wasn't as shocking as the wild shriek that left Fyra's mouth. Talise had never heard the quiet soldier even raise her voice.

At least the growl that came from Tempest seemed normal. Even through her Kessoku helmet, Talise could see how Tempest glared at the palace solider who spoke to Wendy.

As they planned, Rio and Fyra attacked first. They continued shouting as they pulled out their swords and headed to the sandy ocean shore. The two palace soldiers standing there barely had time to draw their own weapons before their blades clashed into each other.

Tempest whipped her long braid behind her back as she charged toward the arrogant palace soldier. Wendy let out a whimper before cowering behind another withered tree. Cyrus followed after her.

While the others distracted the palace soldiers, Talise and Aaden had the perfect opening to perform their part of the plan.

Flames licked out from their palms even before they reached the cart. Floods of fire shot toward the wooden cart, engulfing it in a matter of seconds.

Using a technique Wendy had suggested, Talise kept fire flowing from one palm but used the other to send a rush of air toward the cart. As expected, the added air fed the flames until they soared high into the sky.

Aaden used his own shaping to fuel the fire even more. Shouts continued around them, but Talise only cared that the flames had started eating through the wood of the cart. Now it began burning the poisoned fish food.

The colliding swords closed in from behind her, but it didn't steal her attention from the fire. She trusted her friends to fight off the palace soldiers. Wendy and Cyrus would join the fight if they had to, so Talise ignored the sounds.

Her hand reached out. Using her earth shaping senses, she found the fish food and the poison inside it. The round pellets of fish food contained particles of earth with almost opposite properties to the nutrients the soil needed. Because of those properties, it caused nutrients to be leeched away. With her earth shaping senses, she detected the poison, carefully waiting until it had been completely eaten by her flames.

Hot flames engulfed the fish food a moment later. She expected the poison to burn up until there was nothing left, much like nutrients or leaves would have when burned in a fire.

Everything around her seemed to slow as her attention focused on the flames eating through the fish food. The result made her breath hitch. Breathing became difficult.

No.

Impossible.

When the fire burned through the food, the poison didn't diminish at all. Instead, it released into the air with its deadly structure still in tact. Clouds of invisible poison floated above the cart now. Soon it would settle into the soil and *still* leech the nutrients out of it. Even worse, it might infect people. The poison could get into their lungs and do terrible damage.

In a flash, she shaped as many flames away as she could. "The fire." Her voice came out as little more than a gasp, but Aaden still heard. "We have to put it out." Using one hand, she ripped air away from the cart. Using the other, she pulled water from the air. But she needed more. And fast.

She turned to Aaden to explain, but his eyes went wide. A shout seemed to catch in his throat. Through his helmet visor, Talise could see the color drain from his face.

She had no time to react. By the time she recognized his fear, someone had already grabbed her around the waist. With a hard jerk, her body was yanked to the ground. Her jaw clenched as she reached for the dagger in her pocket.

While retrieving it, she didn't dare forget the revelation she had just discovered. "Tempest!" Her voice came out even louder than she expected. When a palace soldier pushed his knees onto Talise's chest, air left her mouth in a rush. Sucking in with a gulp, Talise shouted again. "Put out the fire. Put it out now!"

Just when the soldier on top of Talise aimed his sword toward her neck, she blocked it with the blade of her dagger.

He snarled as he moved his arm back to strike again. By the time he had reeled his arm back, Aaden was already there. The scar across his face pulsed with even greater tension than the rest of his face. The facial hair covering his chin rustled as Aaden grabbed the palace soldier by the shoulders and threw him onto the ground.

In the short moment it took Talise to get back to her feet, she quickly scanned the area. Rio and Fyra still fought against two palace soldiers. Tempest shaped water from the ocean and brought it toward the cart. Cyrus used an air tunnel to help move the water along faster. With any luck, the fire would be out soon.

Apparently, Wendy was still trying to maintain her cover. She grabbed the arm of the palace soldier fighting against Aaden. With pleading eyes, she said to the soldier, "You have to go back to the palace. I've seen these Kessoku fight. They'll kill you. You have no chance." She clapped a hand over her mouth right as Aaden swung his sword toward the palace soldier. "You have to run," she said in a breathless voice.

Another swift swing of Aaden's sword caused the palace soldier to duck. Talise held her dagger out, attempting to intimidate him.

But the palace soldier made a decision before he even noticed the dagger. Perhaps he was trying to take out the attacker he considered weaker. Or maybe he just wanted to escape Aaden's sword.

Whatever his reason, the palace soldier leapt forward, tackling Talise to the ground. But her dagger had still been pointed out in attack. A groan escaped the soldier's mouth right when she felt her blade meet his flesh.

Warm blood spilled over her hand. She jerked the dagger back as fast as she could, but it was too late. Her heart beat so fast she couldn't even feel individual beats anymore. Anguish fueled her as she jumped to her feet.

Was he still alive?

The soldier let out pained groan, which sent a flood of relief through her.

He writhed on the dirt for a beat before he slowly got to his feet. One fist pressed into his side where the dagger had cut him. Without a clear view, it wasn't obvious how serious the injury had been.

Aaden lifted his sword, a wild look in his eye.

The palace soldier stumbled back. "Let's get out of here," he shouted to his companions.

At the sight of the blood covering his side and hands, the other two palace soldiers ran away from Talise and her friends without question. Soon, only their backs were visible as they ran away.

A hand settled on her arm. Heat seared through it, but the fingers that squeezed her were gentle. "Are you okay?" Aaden's voice shook through the words, which caused an involuntary quiver inside Talise's stomach.

She nodded and glanced over her shoulder at the cart. Tempest's hands waved over her head as she moved a final splash of water to put out the fire.

The knot in Talise's gut released. "It wasn't much so we're probably safe, but..." She let out a sigh. "Burning the fish food released the poison into the air."

His thumb moved across her arm in a few tender strokes before he pulled his hand away. "I know. I could feel it too."

The grinding in her gut tensed her muscles. After shaping water from the air, she washed the blood from her hands. She tried to swallow, but too much tightness lined her throat. She looked straight into his eyes, which was a dangerous place to look, but she didn't care. It didn't even matter if he saw how her chin shook. "If we can't destroy the fish food, then how are we supposed to get rid of it?"

CHAPTER ELEVEN

BLACKENED WOOD AND HOT ASH littered the dirt in front of Talise.

After such intense flames had engulfed the cart, it didn't have much chance of survival. But now the remaining dry pellets of fish food sat in haphazard piles directly above the soil. Even as they stared, the poison was likely infecting the ground below.

"What if we move it?" Wendy asked. "Maybe we can't burn it, but if we bring it to a part of the Storm where nobody lives, at least it won't matter if the nutrients get leeched from that soil."

Talise nodded, but the others probably recognized the same thing she did. That solution wouldn't work forever. The poison had managed to leech from the soil in cities even when it had come from the ocean.

At least it wouldn't poison any fish if they dropped it in an uninhabited area. Without a word, Talise dropped to her knees and scooped the fish food into the bottom half of her tunic. Since the pellets were still dry, it was probably safe to carry. Hopefully. Carrying it inside a tunic didn't seem like the most efficient transportation method, but it would work.

With as much fish food in her tunic as she dared carry, Talise lifted her hem up as high as her belly. How lucky that they hadn't brought much with them on this little excursion, other than their weapons. Transporting the food would be easier with nothing else to carry along with it.

Rio pulled out his map of Kamdaria. The Storm areas didn't have the same detail as the rest of the empire, but the map still showed the basics. They had seen enough cities to know that at least the location of the cities on the map were accurate. So far.

"What about here?" Rio pointed to an area behind some hills and in front of the wall that separated the Gate from the Storm. They would have to pass through a small city to get there, but it was probably the safest place.

Aaden stroked a thumb across the hair on his chin while he looked at the map. "We won't arrive back at our camp until well past nightfall."

Donning a wide grin, Cyrus slapped Aaden on the back. "Don't tell me you're afraid of the dark."

A small chuckle escaped through Aaden's mouth, but his face remained as serious as ever. "I'm *afraid* that we haven't eaten anything since this morning, and we didn't bring any food with us. By the time we get back to camp, we'll be too tired to cook anything. But if we don't eat, we'll be weakened, which is dangerous in the Storm."

Gingerly lifting the helmet off her head, Fyra pointed to the city they would have to pass through. "What if we get food while we're there?"

Aaden narrowed his eyes at the map before glancing toward Talise. "I did bring a pouch of money, but it might not be enough to feed all of us."

"When has that ever been a problem?" The grin on Cyrus's face continued to grow as he wrapped an arm around his sister's shoulder. "What do you say, Wen? Should we trick a few more people out of their hard-earned assets?"

Tempest had been plucking specks of dirt from the tuft at the end of her braid. At the end of Cyrus's comment, she dropped her braid which sent it swinging behind her back. "People here aren't going to care about money when there's barely enough food to go around. And I don't like the idea of you tricking people out of food when they're so desperate to begin with."

A niggle of guilt swept through Talise's gut, but Cyrus seemed completely unfazed by the soldier's words.

He just tipped an eyebrow up at Tempest and threw her a knowing smirk. "Are you sure this is about tricking people out of food? Or maybe you just don't like it when Wendy pretends to ogle *other* people."

Wendy's cheeks flashed crimson as she sucked in a breath. Tempest looked ready to run a blade through Cyrus. Even Fyra took a step back. She stared at the ground like it might swallow her up and that would be the best thing that could happen to her in this moment.

The protective best friend instincts inside Talise moved her forward. She stepped between Cyrus and Tempest until their eye contact had been cut off. "We'll split up." She'd been practicing her authoritative voice, but it came out even better than she imagined. Cyrus even cowered a little.

Talise jerked her chin back as she looked over one shoulder. "Wendy, Tempest, and Fyra, you go back to camp and start cooking dinner so it's ready when we get there. Aaden, Cyrus, and I will bring the fish food to the uninhabitable area. Rio—"

"I'll stay with you, Princess." He glanced at Aaden through the side of his eye while the slightest wrinkle went through his nose. The expression disappeared so fast it might have been a figment of her imagination.

"Fine." She gave a quick nod and lowered the end of her tunic so Wendy could dump her fish food on top of Talise's.

Tempest dropped her fish food into Aaden's tunic without bothering to look Cyrus's way. Fyra gave hers to Rio. Soon, the two groups were off on their separate ways.

Aaden and Rio stood on either side of Talise, both glaring at the path ahead like an enemy could attack at any moment. She rolled her eyes, which did no good because neither of them could see it anyway.

Since Talise's last suitor had turned out to be a traitor, she could understand Rio's reluctance to trust Aaden with her life. And Aaden… well, he was just Aaden. Despite his stone-like expressions and his subtle reactions, he had more passion than anyone she knew. *Of course* he was going to protect her like his life depended on it. That's just how he was.

Cyrus's expression was more difficult to decipher. His eyes held intensity, but was it anger or something else?

Before he could open his mouth, Talise lifted her chin. "We need to come up with a different solution for the rest of the shipments. We can't keep bringing poisonous fish food out to uninhabitable areas and hope it won't hurt anyone. It *will* hurt people eventually. It will just take longer to get to them."

Cyrus gripped the hem of his tunic tighter as he held his pile of fish food. Tension rocked between his eyebrows. "We could throw the fish food into the air one by one and blast a fireball at each while it's up in the sky. Then the poison would be too high up to hurt anybody."

Talise tilted her head. Even if the poison was released high in the air, it would still float down and poison people and the ground eventually. Probably sooner than later, in fact. Could she point that out without offending Cyrus? He looked so sure of his idea.

Now it was Aaden who tilted his head. He leaned forward until he caught her eye. Tipping his head toward Cyrus, Aaden said, "He's not serious. It's supposed to be a joke."

After blinking twice, Talise nodded. On her other side, Rio let out a chuckle.

They were silent for a while after that. Eventually, Rio asked, "Could you build another glass house? Not for growing food, but to store the poisoned fish food?"

Talise bit into her bottom lip before she responded. "I thought about that. I would have to study the journals again, but I don't think that would work either. The composition of the glass isn't strong enough to keep the poison from leeching out."

"I had an idea." Aaden stared at the dry pellets inside his tunic as he walked. His jaw worked up and down for a few paces while he seemed to be concocting the right words. "We could ask Kessoku to store it in their base. The granite walls should be strong enough to hold the poison in."

This time, a chuckle came from Talise's own mouth. "Great idea. Why don't we ask them to play a game of Forces while we're at it?"

"I'm serious." Aaden's tone alone spoke to that, but his face was serious too. Even more serious than usual, which was saying something.

Rio stared past Talise straight at Aaden. Rio did nothing to hide the suspicion in his eyes. "You want us to work with the people who are trying to kill our princess?"

"I never said we should work *with* them." Aaden's face softened as his gaze turned to Talise. "Think about it. Remember how Kessoku used the amulet when they were trying to destroy a shipment? We know they want to stop the shipments just like we do. But they don't have the schedule I got from the palace, so they can't do it as easily as us. And they don't know that burning the fish food only releases the poison into the air. But if we sent them a message, they could have all that information and probably take out the shipments even more easily than us."

Talise kept her eyes on her tunic as she considered his points. "But the Kessoku would hurt the palace soldiers."

Aaden shrugged. "We hurt them too."

Memories of the warm blood gushing onto her hands filled Talise's mind. If she hadn't been holding fish food inside her tunic right then, she would have wrapped both hands over her stomach. "That wasn't on purpose."

When Aaden only responded with another shrug, Talise scowled at him.

She felt her lips twist into a knot before she shot an accusation his way. "You don't seem to feel any remorse over that palace soldier getting injured."

"He tried to kill you." Aaden's look pierced her the way only his could. A final shrug lifted his shoulder, though it was smaller than the others. "So, no, I don't feel bad that he got hurt. It was his own fault anyway. You didn't even do it on purpose."

She let out a huff. It didn't help to calm the increasing patter of her heart, but she still tried. "And what would happen when the palace soldiers are attacked by Kessoku? How much worse would the injuries be against a group that *is* trying to hurt them?"

One eyebrow twitched over Aaden's eye. "Not everyone in Kessoku wants violence. In fact, very few of them want to kill anyone," his eyes dropped to the side, "except you and the emperor." His head shot up again. "But they don't have to know the message comes from you. We could just say we're a group of people who are also against the emperor or against the walls or division or something."

Rio walked with his usual stiff movements, but his face looked more open than it had a few seconds ago. "Do you have a safe way to deliver the message? Can you make sure they get it and also make sure they don't know who it came from?"

Aaden nodded. "I could be back tomorrow evening."

Cyrus whipped his head back. "I think it's a great idea. We get other people to do our dirty work for us. What's not to love about that?"

The roiling in Talise's gut only increased the longer this conversation went on. "I don't know about this, Aaden."

His own head whipped toward her. Even though his expression remained mostly neutral, she could still see a flash in his eyes. Fear. Or it might have been desperation. With such subtlety it was hard to tell. He gulped. "Then what are we supposed to do in two weeks when there's a shipment on the other side of the Storm? We can't travel there that fast. And we still have no good place to store the poisonous fish food."

Her heart sank then because he was right. But working with Kessoku? The people who murdered her family members? She had certainly entertained the idea of working with them, more than a few times. But their insistence to kill her never wavered, not even when Claye tried to negotiate on her behalf. If they wanted her dead that badly, *how* could she work with them?

She gripped her tunic tighter, ignoring the ache that worked through her arms.

"I think it might be worth it." Rio's voice came out so soft, she almost didn't recognize it. He stared ahead, but the muscles around his eyes pulsed as if deep in thought. "I don't know if our group is big enough to keep taking out the shipments. If Aaden's plan works, we can focus on keeping you safe and even helping more of the cities in the Storm build glass houses for growing food."

Their steps all slowed as Rio turned to look Talise in the eye. He raised one eyebrow. "And if we help Kessoku, it might help us get your soldiers back from them at some point in the future. We'd have to admit we sent the message eventually, but we don't have to do it yet." His eyebrows lowered. "But we aren't going hide in the Storm forever. We can't get sidetracked by the issues here."

It helped to have someone who spoke the truth even when no one wanted to hear it. Deep down, she had already known they would have to go with Aaden's plan. They simply couldn't keep traveling to uninhabitable areas to drop off poison. But it was nice to know the ever-practical Rio agreed too.

Talise nodded and walked with a determined step. "Then let's discuss. What should we say in this message?"

CHAPTER TWELVE

ONCE AGAIN, BRAND NEW SPROUTS peeked through the rich soil beneath Talise's hand.

It had been a few weeks since sending the message to Kessoku, and even more weeks since the *tyrants* had stolen the fresh sprouts from the first glass house. But new ones were growing yet again.

Talise and her friends had traveled to three new cities to build glass houses for growing food. But a part of her held a special affinity for the first city they helped.

Talise turned to the young girl at her side. The child's eyes always lit up when looking at the plants. "Are we *ever* going to be able to eat them?"

The second growing of the sprouts was a lesson of patience indeed. But the longer it took for them to grow, the more Willow got attached to their care. Instead of picking fights outside, now the girl spent her days tending to the plants like a mother tending to a newborn baby.

Food and hope could do wonders for people who were supposed to be cruel and dangerous. Talise shook her head.

"They still aren't ready, but yes, you will be able to eat them soon."

The girl's body wilted, but it only took another moment for her to perk up again. "Can you teach me that earth shaping technique? I really think my earth shaping is starting to awaken."

A gentle smile moved across Talise's lips. Considering how skinny and frail the girl was, it didn't seem likely that her earth shaping would return any time soon. At this rate, it might take up to a year for anyone in the Storm to regain their shaping. But the techniques Talise taught would still be helpful for whenever the shaping eventually returned.

Tilting a head toward the door, Talise said, "It's easier if we do it outside. Earth shaping comes from the feet. When you are first beginning, it helps to have your feet against the soil. But you'll have to sit by a fire afterward, so the freezing air doesn't make you sick."

Willow bounded toward the door faster than a blink. Soon, she stood with feet shoulder width apart just like Talise had taught her. The girl bit into her lip as her hand hovered near her stomach with the palm down. She closed her eyes, seemingly unaware of the icy wind that whipped through her hair. "Start by feeling the earth against your feet," Willow said.

She quoted one of Kamdar's journals now. His early journals had excellent techniques for shaping beginners.

A scrunch went through Willow's eyes, as if trying to remember the next words. All at once, her face relaxed. "Let that feeling of earth flow up your legs and into your chest. Once there, let it bloom like a flower until it reaches your hands." One eyelid popped open for a brief moment as she glanced at the ground in front of her. Her eye snapped shut again. "With that feeling in your arm and hand, lift the soil upward until it becomes one with the feeling of earth inside you."

Watching the concentration on the girl's face always brought a smile to Talise's lips. Her early shaping days had been much stricter with intense instructors. Being palace trained did have its advantages, but it had never been fun.

The girl's face scrunched up for several seconds. Red filled her cheeks as she tried to lift earth from the soil.

She failed.

Both she and Talise had known it would happen, yet they both shared a disappointed sigh. Talise tried to smile. "You'll get it. You just need more food and a little more strength in your body."

When delighted shouts filled the air, they both turned their eyes toward the edge of the city. Wendy and Tempest were supposed to be gathering water from the well for their dinner that evening. It looked like it had turned into a water fight instead. Fyra worked in front of a house, helping the owner fit an actual door into the doorway to replace the cotton sheet that had been there earlier.

Only a moment later, Willow's father called her home for dinner. "I'll keep practicing," the girl said over her shoulder as she began jogging toward her home. "And I'll take good care of the plants."

Talise let herself smile after the girl. With all the chaos that had come with living in the Gate, she never expected to find such peace in a place like the Storm. But of course the feeling couldn't last.

Heavy footsteps sounded from a nearby path. She glanced up at the sky at the sound of it. The sun dipped low on the horizon, just about ready to duck behind it. Aaden, Rio, and Cyrus were right on time.

All three of them walked up to her only a few moments later.

"The message worked." Cyrus grinned as he stuffed his hands into his pockets.

Rio gave a stiff nod. "Palace soldiers brought the shipment to the city just like we expected. They passed out the food and supplies with no problem, but Kessoku showed up immediately afterward."

Somehow, Aaden had moved closer to her than any of the others. He stepped near enough that he had to duck his head to look her in the eye. "Kessoku came in fast with minimal injuries to the palace soldiers. They stole the cart that held the poisonous fish food, and now they are gone."

Cyrus waggled his eyes up and down and slapped a hand on Aaden's back. With a grin, Cyrus said, "You really should listen to Aaden more. He has the best ideas."

"There's something else." Rio stood as tall and as stiff as he usually did, but his words still managed to sound more uncomfortable than they ever had. As someone who always spoke the truth even when it was difficult to hear, it came as a surprise when he simply followed his words with a gulp. Then he looked at Aaden.

Cyrus dropped his arm to his side. A quick jaw clench sent a crack through his charming demeanor. He too looked toward Aaden.

With an even expression, Aaden took in a steady breath. He met her gaze, but his look immediately sent warnings pinging through her veins. "We talked to some citizens in the city we visited. They had very concerning stories. We dug around for more information, and…" He took in a deep breath before he continued. "We found a plant where the fish food is being made."

That sounded like good news, so why did the energy in the air feel tense enough for battle?

"And?" Talise prompted.

Both Cyrus and Rio looked down at the ground. Cyrus stuffed his hands back into his pockets.

Only Aaden seemed capable of meeting her eye. Still, his eye twitched, which sent pulses through his scar. "Workers are lured there with promises of higher pay. They get sick after only a few weeks. Most of them die within a month. Then, palace soldiers travel to a new city for fresh workers and start the process all over again."

Talise had both hands over her mouth before he even finished. Her gut churned, ready to spew whatever food remained inside.

With a flexing jaw, Aaden glanced away before he continued. "Sometimes they send shipments of only fish food. The shipments with supplies are only used as decoys to keep the Storm citizens from asking any questions about the shipments."

The churning in her gut increased, but that only made her more anxious to speak. Her hands dropped away from her mouth while words bubbled at the back of her throat.

"We can't destroy the plant." Apparently, he didn't intend to allow any argument.

Too bad for him, she wasn't going to let that stop her.

But he spoke again before she got the chance. He took a step closer and hardened his face even more. "The plant is too heavily guarded. The seven of us could never defeat all the guards, even with our shaping."

Her teeth clenched together, hands already forming fists.

From the side, Rio cleared his voice. He continued looking at the ground, but that didn't make his words any less sure. "The plant has palace shapers guarding it. And it's made of stone, which we'd never be able to penetrate with our weapons."

Now she folded her arms over her chest, glaring at all three of the young men in front of her. "But Aaden and I are both Master Shapers. We can get past palace shapers."

Cyrus cocked his eyebrows up. "Not that many of them you can't. Plus, there are small holes cut into the stone. Only earth moving at a high velocity has any chance of getting through those holes to do damage."

Giving a half nod, the journals already filled her mind. Did one of them mention anything about shaping at incredible speeds? She'd been studying the journals a lot lately, but she couldn't recall anything about that specifically. Still, knowing lives were on the line, might give her the proper motivation to find something.

"We know how to get past it." Aaden's voice came out darker than usual. When she glanced toward him, heavy intensity filled his eyes.

But when she gave him an expectant look, he didn't answer. Frustrated, she looked toward Rio.

The soldier looked down at the ground as he rubbed the back of his neck. "Remember how Kessoku used those earth cannons against us when we were by the Smoke Gate? And then Lucian used one on us in the base by the Vine Gate? Those can shoot dirt at a pretty high velocity."

Hairs stood on end all along Talise's arms. She tried to force her breaths to stay even. "So, you want to steal an earth cannon from Kessoku?"

"Come on." Cyrus raised an eyebrow at her. "You know we can't sneak onto Kessoku's base and steal an earth cannon. They'd catch us immediately. And besides, we still wouldn't have enough people to defeat the palace guards outside the plant."

Her stomach sank down and then it sank down further. Part of her had known this was where the conversation was headed, but she still refused to believe it. "What are we supposed to do then?"

They all stared back at her. Not one of them was brave enough to speak. In fact, Rio very distinctly took a step backward. Cyrus followed him a second later. They both glanced over their shoulders at the path that led to their camp. Only Aaden stood his ground.

That made it easier to glare at him. She felt her jaw clench through her words. "We are *not* going to Kessoku for help."

"Why not?" Aaden responded without a single fidget or flinch.

Rio squinted his eyes and suddenly looked very interested in the nearby city. "I, uh… I better go help Fyra. She looks like she needs help with," his eyes squinted more as he paused, "whatever it is that's she's doing."

Cyrus took several steps backward. "Oh, and I better head back to camp. They might need help with dinner."

Both Talise and Aaden continued to glare at each other with absolutely no acknowledgement of the two young men who had just scurried off. Venom pierced her words when she spoke again. "Kessoku is the enemy."

A single eyebrow raised on Aaden's forehead, and it only moved a hair's breath. But that didn't stop his entire expression from feeling like an accusation. "And what about the person who ordered these shipments? The one who is deliberately poisoning citizens. Is he the enemy?"

Stinging pain shot through Talise's throat when she tried to swallow. "That's different."

"Why?" Aaden used his most unforgiving voice to ask.

She huffed at him in response, as if that could count for anything.

He shook his head at her before glancing away. "What do you think is going to happen in this war? Even if we defeat Kessoku and go back to the palace, what then? Do you think you can just waltz into the throne room and say, 'Father, I noticed you were poisoning people in the Storm and paying them terrible wages too. You should stop doing that.' And then he'll respond with a cheerful, 'That is such a wonderful idea. Let's unify Kamdaria while we're at it.'" Now Aaden was the one to fold his arms over his chest. "Is that how you think it's going to go?"

Another huff escaped her before she turned away. She reached for the hem of her tunic, which only brought anger not comfort. Another swallow went through her stinging throat. "We can only deal with one problem at a time. Kessoku first, the other problems second."

A crease appeared between Aaden's eyebrows while pleading filled his eyes. "Kessoku is trying to accomplish many of the same things you are. Why not get help from them?"

She slammed a fist against her palm. "They are the enemy. Kessoku is the *enemy.*"

His mustache tilted down with his frown. "Maybe they are, but they aren't the only one. The emperor is your enemy too."

Breathing became too difficult. She stepped back, trying to ignore how her chin quivered. The emperor was her *father.* How could Aaden ignore something so significant? But then her eyes widened. Floods of anger pooled all through her. She leaned forward letting her nose wrinkle with each word. "You're doing this for *your* father, aren't you?"

Aaden looked taken aback. "No."

She stepped toward him, lifting her chin high. "Are you on *their* side or mine?"

Now he looked offended. "Always yours. I'm not saying we should join them. I'm not saying you should give up your right to the throne. But if they can help us, why wouldn't we turn to them?"

Her skin prickled in the icy air. Even her heels lifted of their own accord until she rocked forward onto the balls of her feet. She jabbed a finger toward him. "You're just trying to protect your father."

Despite her jabbing finger, Aaden didn't move. His face hardened into one that betrayed no emotion at all. Except she knew him too well to be fooled by his facial expressions. The curling fists at his sides showed his true feelings. "We can't take out that plant without help. I'm trying to do the best thing for Kamdaria. Just like you."

Shackles raised inside her. The little sanity she had left hung by a delicate thread. Taking in a deep breath, she glared like she had never glared before. Without meaning to, she addressed the part of the conversation she most wanted to forget. The words spewed from her mouth with absolutely no permission from her. "My father is not the enemy."

But even as she stomped away, the truth of those words lost certainty in her mind. Her feet faltered over the dirt path that led to camp. Maybe her enemy was even closer than she had ever imagined.

CHAPTER THIRTEEN

TEARS TRICKLED DOWN TALISE'S CHEEKS as she stumbled back into camp.

The cold air nearly froze the tears, causing her to send fire into her veins. When she got to camp, Tempest was stirring a bubbling pot that sat over the fire. Wendy sat at her side, arranging Tempest's waist-length hair into a braid. Cyrus sat across the fire from them with his feet propped up on one of the canvas packs.

His spine straightened at the sight of Talise. "Where's Aaden?"

Her teeth flashed as she spat words back at him. "I have no idea. Go find him yourself."

At the sound of her words, Wendy and Tempest froze in place before glancing toward each other. A question seemed to linger in Wendy's eyes. Tempest responded to it with a nod. She took her halfway braided hair and tied it off. "I got this."

Wendy offered a sweet smile before she stood.

When she glanced toward Talise, the tears had turned to rivers gushing from her eyes. Talise tried to take in a breath, but it was more of a shudder. Even the fire in her veins couldn't stave off the chill inside her.

With gentle prodding, Wendy guided her best friend to the nearby dead tree. Just on the other side of it sat the fallen log where Talise and Aaden had discussed their nightmares only weeks before. Due to a dip in the land, the earth even provided a bit of a sound barrier to allow private conversations.

They sat down on a fallen log.

"What happened?" Wendy's voice had just the right amount of sweetness to coax out anything.

Talise's lip trembled as she buried her face in her hands. "Aaden wants to get even more help from Kessoku. We'd have to work *with* them."

Even with her face buried, she could tell Wendy was considering her words carefully. At last her best friend continued. "And you think that's a bad idea?"

"I don't know." The tears continued to spill, but it took too much effort to shape fire in the veins. Letting the winter freeze her tears felt more appropriate anyway. Lifting her head, Talise took in a deep breath. "It would probably work, but I wish it were a bad idea because I hate Aaden. I hate that he left me, and I hate that he's with us again. It's so much harder to hate him when he's here, and I hate that too."

With shoulders heaving, Talise dropped her head back into her hands. Sobs shook through her while icy wind stabbed her skin. "How can I trust him after he left me? And how can I trust anyone after what Claye did? And why does love have to hurt so much?"

Wendy touched a hand to Talise's forearm, sending the first wave of heat into her now icy veins.

Then the sobs started all over again. "It doesn't even matter." Talise had to suck in a quivering breath between each of her syllables. "I shouldn't even care about my feelings for Aaden right now. We have more important things to worry about."

"Don't say that." Wendy's whisper came out only slightly louder than the wind whipping around them. "Your feelings do matter."

Talise let out a scoff as she wiped away a sheet of tears on one cheek. "But they aren't that important. The fate of the empire is at stake. Kamdaria is more important than my troubles with young men."

"No, it's not." Wendy's voice had never sounded so stern. Even more surprising, an actual glare had broken across her face. She folded her hands in her lap and looked into her friend's eyes with a deliberate stare. "Kamdaria *is* important but so is your heart. You got hurt by two different boys, and it happened to you in the midst of a civil war. You have every right to be angry and sad."

"But—"

"But nothing." Wendy's voice had taken on an even sharper edge. "Stop trying to close off your heart and pretend your feelings don't matter. If you keep doing that, you'll lose your humanity the same way the emperor did."

Talise's jaw went slack. The words cut into her. *Had* the emperor truly lost his humanity? She couldn't even answer the question inside her head because she already knew. *Of course* he had. He was poisoning his own people. And deep in her heart, Talise already knew why.

To control the population. To keep Storm citizens weak and dependent on the emperor. The leeching of the nutrients had been worse that year, but with her shaping, Talise had already figured out that it had been going on for many years. Everyone said malnourishment killed Storm citizens, but was it really malnourishment… or poison?

Physical pain accompanied the realizations. She held a hand over her chest, which tightened harder with every passing second. Things *had* to change.

Lowering her head, Talise wiped away another sheet of tears. The sobs had stopped. Now tears fell in slower streams. She looked at the ground as she spoke. "I *do* need to focus on Kamdaria right now."

A softened expression fell across Wendy's face when she nodded. "Of course you do. And you also need to let yourself cry and heal after being hurt by two very stupid boys."

When a chill shook through her shoulders, Talise tempered it with fire in her veins. Staring at the ground, she asked, "How am I supposed to let myself heal *and* save Kamdaria?"

With an unconcerned expression, Wendy shrugged. "I have no idea."

Talise couldn't help the tiny snort that escaped through her nose. "How helpful."

Wendy's face brightened with a smile as she raised her eyebrows. "You single-handedly broke through a dam that had been destroying lives for years. And you did it with a dagger and a *tree* that you literally ripped from the ground." Her eyes sparkled as her smile grew. "I'm sure you can figure it out."

It was impossible to not return the smile. Knowing her best friend believed in her always brought a glowing warmth inside Talise's chest. But it only lasted a moment before the cold snuffed it out. "I don't know if it's safe to trust Aaden."

Nodding thoughtfully, Wendy reached for a piece of her hair. "That's because Claye's betrayal made you forget how to trust yourself. But I think a part of you still knows how to do it. Deep down, is it fear or intuition that makes you question Aaden's intentions?"

The question seemed simple enough, but that didn't make it any easier to answer. "I don't know," Talise finally said.

"It's okay." Wendy reached out and gave a gentle squeeze to Talise's forearm. "You'll learn to trust again; you just need more time to heal. But you should know, *I* trust Aaden. Cyrus was telling Tempest and me about this plan to destroy the plant, and I think it's a good one."

Talise cocked one eyebrow up at her friend. "Is Cyrus still mad about you and Tempest?"

Wendy let out a soft chuckle. "He wasn't mad. He just likes forcing people to have conversations they've been avoiding." A blush filled her cheeks as she tucked a piece of hair behind one ear. "It worked out."

A shadow brought both of their eyes toward the dead tree near them. Aaden stood next to it with his head tilting down. Even his shoulders slumped forward.

Without a single word, Wendy jumped up and dashed out of sight. That left Talise sitting on a fallen log alone with the person who could twist her gut into a tangled mess like no other. When he glanced up, she nodded, knowing his question without him speaking it.

Whether her heart was ready or not, this conversation had to happen.

CHAPTER FOURTEEN

TALISE REACHED FOR THE HEM of her tunic.

Whatever cold had been in the air now seemed to vanish. Heat burned throughout her body, and she couldn't tell if she had any control over it or not.

Aaden stood with one shoulder pressed against the dead tree. Steady breaths made his chest rise and fall, but he didn't speak. He didn't move. Weariness filled his eyes.

At last, he let out a sigh. "I'm sorry."

"I'm sorry too." The tunic hem grounded her as she gripped it.

Aaden's face fell at the sound of her words, but was that a tease in his eyes?

He raised an eyebrow. "This is supposed to be *my* apology."

The ghost of a chuckle slipped through her lips. She gave a grand gesture toward him. "Go on then."

A flex went through his jaw, which made his facial hair bristle. "I'm sorry I was insensitive to the complicated relationship you have with your father."

"I'm sorry I yelled at you." Staring at her hands seemed like the best way to handle the situation. At least *they* couldn't give her a look that would make her stomach flop. After several seconds of silence, she let out a sigh and glanced at him. "I'm still mad at you for leaving me in the summer."

"I know." He didn't step closer, but his posture relaxed. He stared at her shoes instead of her eyes. "I'm starting to wonder if leaving was even the right thing to do."

Her eyebrows pinched together. "I think it was pretty clearly not."

It was almost scary how he could say so much with so few words. In this case, no words came out at all. He just looked at her. His face stayed even, his muscles still. But she could feel emotion coming off him in droves. Longing. Regret.

She glanced away. "Why didn't you come back sooner? You said you'd be back in two weeks." Now it was easy to look him in the eye. He deserved as much guilt as her stare could pierce him with. "I waited for you. I waited and waited. When Claye first tried to hold my hand, I yelled at him and told him I was still in love with you."

Love. The word slipped out without her permission. *Now* she had to avert her eyes. Her wringing hands provided the perfect distraction. "When I finally saw you again, you grabbed me by the wrist and tried to capture me for Kessoku."

His feet shuffled across the dirt, probably taking a few steps forward. "I wasn't really trying to capture you. I just had to make it look like that. But I helped you get away. I made *sure* you got away."

When she glanced up, he had indeed moved closer. "That doesn't explain why it took you so long to return to the palace."

One of his hands got stuffed into a pocket while his head hung. "The Kessoku didn't trust me. They would have killed me if I tried to leave any sooner. I thought my father's position would help more than it did. They never trusted me until that day when I pretended to try and capture you. By the time I returned to the palace, I realized you weren't coming back."

Of course he had a good reason. She should have expected it all along. Even still, the anger inside her didn't just vanish. She still needed time. Time to sort through the feelings. At least she knew the truth now. At least she could talk to him without being so angry.

Another sigh escaped her, this one even bigger than the last. "You were right about my father. He's poisoning people. He's making the division between the rings even worse. If we want to truly change Kamdaria, we have to fight against him. I've known it for a long time, but I didn't want to admit it." She dropped her head in one hand. "I knew I'd take the crown someday. I just never expected to take it *away* from my father."

Aaden stepped closer again. He leaned toward her without getting too close, but she could still feel how every part of him focused on her. Maybe it was a trick of the light, but the scar across his face seemed brighter than ever. He waited until she looked him in the eyes before he spoke again. "I believe in what you are trying to do. You are the leader Kamdaria needs." He swallowed, which sent his goatee bristling again. "No matter what happens between *us*, I will fight at your side until the very end."

Her heart couldn't possibly skip faster, but there it was, skipping like it had never known emotion before. She tried to smile. That failed. She tried to look down at her hands next, but Aaden held her gaze too completely to look away. Perhaps changing the subject was the only viable option.

Trailing a finger across her tunic hem, she sat up straighter. "Tell me more about this plan to destroy the plant. Why would

Kessoku even agree to help us? They have my army. They have the amulet."

A devious smirk quirked up one of Aaden's eyebrows. "But they don't know how to *use* the amulet. Not without getting hurt."

Talise felt her eyebrows raise high on her forehead. Her voice came out breathless. "The journals."

The smirk on Aaden's face grew as he gave a single nod. "Rio and I came up with a plan. We'll meet with them in the Gate but not at their base. We'll request that they only bring three people. If they bring more, we'll leave before they ever see us."

"Smart," she said, tapping her chin.

"Most important of all, they won't know our identities until the moment we arrive for the meeting."

Now a grin began forming on her face. "That is a brilliant idea."

The slightest smile hid beneath Aaden's lips.

Taking a deep breath, she rose from off the fallen log. "I guess it's time. Let's go make an alliance with the people who want to kill me."

CHAPTER FIFTEEN

FROM BEHIND A COPSE OF trees in the Gate, Talise had a perfect view of the fire pit she and her friends had just finished arranging.

Large flames burned in the center of the pit with plenty of extra logs nearby for fuel. Fallen logs and large boulders sat around the pit in a circle. Best of all, their spot behind the trees was perfect for spying. Rio and Fyra hid farther down the path, watching for the members of Kessoku who were supposed to arrive.

Now they just had to wait. It didn't take long before three people in black tunics wandered over to the fire pit. Talise's gut clenched when she saw Lucian Sato, Aaden's father, at the head of the group. Since he was the newest leader of Kessoku, it wasn't exactly a surprise. But it didn't fill her with joy to see him either.

Behind him strolled a woman Talise didn't recognize. Her eyes seemed to blaze with a simmering rage. A young man with soft black hair falling over his forehead entered the area last. Her stomach clenched even harder at the sight of him. Even in the freezing weather, her palms got sweaty.

Claye.

Why would Kessoku bring him? She wanted to huff at the sight but didn't dare. Aaden stood too close to her. He would hear the huff and interpret it in all the wrong ways. But the sight of Claye did make her think of the green Forces tablet he had given her. The one that was supposed to represent his love for her.

She had kept the tablet in her pocket for a few weeks after escaping Kessoku's base by the Ember Gate, but she had stopped that long ago. Now it probably sat at the bottom of one of their canvas packs. Considering how much the tablet meant to him, she probably should have kept better track of it. Then again, he probably shouldn't have betrayed her, so at least they were even.

After another few seconds, Rio and Fyra dashed toward her and her friends from behind a clump of nearby leafless bushes. Luckily, none of the Kessoku seemed to notice the movement.

Fyra pointed across the clearing with the fire pit and into another clump of bushes. "They have two men hiding over there. Lucian told them to attack if he stood up and snapped his fingers."

A twitch appeared at the side of Aaden's nose while his hand clenched into a fist.

Wendy's eyes darted across the clearing as she twirled a piece of her hair around one finger. "What do we do? Should we leave?"

Rio stood tall, still looking like a soldier even when he wore the common attire of someone who grew up in the Storm. "We think it might be better if we allow them to ambush us like they plan."

Smirking, Cyrus rolled back on his heels. "Gutsy. Is there a reason for that?"

The slightest smile broke onto Fyra's face. For someone who had been so quiet and reserved for months, it was always refreshing when a bit of her personality shone through. "It's a power move. We know where those two men are hiding. We know what weapons they have, swords, by the way. Rio and I can sneak up behind them. When they attack, we can all fight back and most likely win. They'll think they have the element of surprise but really *we'll* have it."

Rio nodded, his back looking even straighter than before. He looked Talise right in the eye. "It will allow us to prove you are a force to be reckoned with."

While leaning forward, Aaden's hand subtly shifted to reach for the hilt of his sword. "Did either of the men have a colored band around their cuffs?"

Fyra nodded. "Both of them did, a thin blue band."

Aaden's hand rested on his sword hilt. "Then their primary element is water."

"Perfect." Tempest's hair swung as she cracked her knuckles. "We can easily handle a few water shapers."

Rio's eyebrows went up. "They also had swords."

Cyrus gave a casual shrug. "No problem. All of us are skilled with swords, aren't we?"

Hopefully no one heard the enormous gulp Talise made. "Actually…uh. I can use a dagger but—"

"No." Aaden cut her off while shaking his head. "You should use shaping against them. Do something elaborate to show them how powerful you are. Use all four elements if you can manage it."

Her defenses had gone up when he interrupted her. She had been expecting him to suggest she sit on the sidelines and wait while the rest of them dealt with the problem. Instead, he trusted her to fight them. Hopefully no one would notice how her shoulders rolled back. "Then let's go."

Rio and Fyra snuck off first. Once they had been gone for a few minutes, the rest of them formed a line and began walking toward the fire pit.

Wendy went first. Tempest followed behind with Cyrus right behind her. Then Aaden and finally Talise.

At the sight of Wendy, Lucian scowled. But he didn't seem to recognize her from their adventure in the base by the Vine Gate. Instead, he said, "Why do you get to bring five people when we were only allowed to…"

The man's face fell when the fourth person in line came into his view. "Son," he said. And then he swallowed.

Still, it was nothing to the way his entire face convulsed once he caught sight of Talise. He jumped to his feet and snapped his fingers without any hesitation at all.

The two Kessoku water shapers leapt from their hiding spots behind the bushes. They used water from a nearby stream to form funnels of water that resembled tornadoes. Ice cold water flicked away at every angle as the water funnels moved closer to Talise's group.

It took no time at all for Talise to summon an element to combat them. With heat prickling through her arms, she shot flames from her palms until two large pillars of fire formed around the funnels of water. Water sizzled when it made contact with the fire pillars, evaporating into the air with pops and cracks. It would take several minutes to completely evaporate the water funnels with fire alone. They didn't have that kind of time, but hopefully the display was still impressive enough.

While Talise shaped the fire, the woman with frightening eyes ripped a dagger from her tunic pocket and prepared to throw it.

Wendy jammed both hands in front of herself, which sent a blast of air strong enough to knock the woman off her feet.

The hair on Claye's forehead rustled as he stood completely still in the midst of the fight.

Over by the bushes, Rio, Fyra, Tempest, and Cyrus all used swords to fight against the two water shapers.

In front of Talise, Lucian slowly drew a sword. Memories of him trying to kill her suddenly filled her mind. He wanted to starve her to death when she was imprisoned in Kessoku's dungeon during the summer. And when she tried to steal the amulet from the base by the Vine Gate, he used an earth cannon against her that should have killed her immediately.

Her limbs shook as she continued to shape fire around the funnels of water. While buzzing filled her veins, Aaden caught her eye.

He gave a quick nod, as if urging her to act. Yet again, he proved he really did believe in her.

With a deep breath, she shaped away the fire. Raising her hands, she lifted mounds of dirt under Lucian's feet just as he moved to step forward. The errant dirt mounds caused him to trip backward.

Once he caught his balance, she used fire shaping to heat the hilt of his sword.

With a gasp, the sword dropped from his grip. His palms burned bright red when he blew air onto them. By now, it had gotten harder to keep track of the fight. The woman with frightening eyes started shaping. Talise's view was blocked by both Aaden and Wendy as they fought against the woman.

Over in the bushes, Rio and Fyra took down the first water shaper. They retrieved a piece of rope they had brought and tied him up.

With a flick of the wrist, Talise brought a whirling tornado in front of herself. She punched her hand forward, which caused the tornado to blast into Lucian. This time, he fell onto his backside. Now Cyrus and Tempest had the other water shaper on the ground. They tied him up as well.

Talise's muscles pulsed as she pulled water out of the air. Once enough had been gathered, she shaped ice to form the water into ice daggers. Lucian flinched when she shot them directly at his face.

When they were mere inches away, she halted the ice daggers. Lucian flinched again at the sight of them hovering so near.

At almost the same moment, Aaden's sword knocked the weapon out of the hand of the woman he fought against. Wendy sent another blast of air toward the woman to knock her off her feet for the second time.

The moment she landed, Rio and Fyra came up from behind and tied the woman up. They even curled her hands into fists and tied those up to prevent her from shaping.

Maybe they had only won so quickly because they had the element of surprise and because they had already known about the ambush. Still, after losing so horribly when they tried to steal the amulet, it felt good to have such a solid victory against Lucian.

It seemed like the perfect time to ignore how Claye stood still doing *nothing* during the entire attack.

Lifting her chin, Talise smoothed the wrinkles from her tunic. "Now that we have *that* out of the way, shall we negotiate like we planned?"

The woman with frightening eyes tried to wriggle free of her rope. She stared straight at Talise and said, "I'll kill you."

With the most even expression she could manage, Talise let out a sigh. "Well, you certainly tried. Did you want me to award you a silver crescent moon on your ID card or something?"

The woman's face turned aghast, clearly trying to grapple with the suggestion.

Lucian looked to his son before he turned back to Talise. "You genuinely want to negotiate?"

Dropping herself onto the nearest boulder, Talise folded her hands into her lap. "Surprisingly enough, yes, I do."

Rolling his eyes, Claye whipped the soft curls off his forehead. He took a spot across from her on one of the fallen logs. He glared at Lucian before speaking. "I told you we would have to work with her eventually. You should have listened to me. You should have joined her when I suggested it."

The woman who was tied up let out a scoff. "You think she's here to give up the throne? Don't be naïve."

Claye shot her a look that curled his lip. "Don't talk to me like that, River. Talise has more power in Kamdaria than you realize. And it's not because she's the princess. It's not because of her incredible shaping skills either. It's because she cares about the people in this empire more than anyone I've ever met." He leaned closer to the woman, who must have been the terrifying River they had heard so much about. With eyes narrowing, Claye said, "The people can tell how much she cares. We need her. As long as you ignore that, we are going to keep losing."

Even with the rest of her friends taking seats around her, Talise's insides still writhed. How was it that after five years of friendship, she was only now seeing the true Claye? Apparently, he did believe in her. But he also only saw her as a tool to aid Kessoku. Luckily, Lucian spoke before Talise had too much time to think about the implication.

Aaden's father took a seat directly next to Claye. He looked Talise in the eye and asked, "What do you want?"

Her spine straightened. "I want my soldiers back."

A snort erupted from his mouth. "That's not going to happen."

Though everything inside her trembled, Talise resisted the urge to reach for her hem. Any sign of fiddling would most likely be construed as nervous tension. Maybe she was more nervous than she'd ever been in her life, but she wasn't about to show it. Instead, she tilted her head upward, doing her best to look down her nose at the man who had tried to kill her twice. "What would I have to offer for their return?"

"Your life." River spat the words from her spot on the ground. Rio stood directly behind the woman, and he didn't look eager to release her bonds. River's face twisted into a wicked smile. "That should be easy to give up since you love your people so much."

"No." Even sitting, Aaden gripped the hilt of his sword. He glared at River, not flinching at any of her snarls.

Talise ignored them and looked back to Lucian. "What if I offer you a chance to destroy the plant where all that poisonous fish food is being made? You wouldn't have to keep attacking all those shipments if you go after the source."

That had been Cyrus's idea. He said they shouldn't ask for Kessoku's help. He suggested they phrase it like they were doing Kessoku a favor by allowing them to help.

Lucian didn't look convinced. "Do you know where this mysterious plant is?"

Talise moved her hands to a more comfortable position before she answered. "Yes."

He raised an eyebrow. "Then why not destroy it yourselves?"

She glanced at her fingernails. "Oh, we plan to. Only the most skilled shapers can get past its defenses. But there are also many guards protecting it. And the stone walls have small holes that your earth cannons would be perfect against."

With a chuckle, Lucian leaned back casually. "You need our help."

Talise raised her eyebrows high on her forehead as she tilted her head to the side. "Hardly. We have people who would gladly help us. But I want my soldiers back, and I want Kamdar's amulet. I thought it would be a nice trade to allow you to help us."

Now Lucian leaned forward. He steepled his fingers and held them under his chin. "No."

With a shrug, Talise stood. "Then I guess we're done."

When her friends started standing too, Lucian raised a hand into the air. "Wait." He looked to the side as his eyes narrowed. "We can send people to help you destroy the plant, but we aren't going to release your soldiers to you." He leaned back again, somehow looking ridiculously comfortable on only a fallen log. "But we *could* be persuaded to take better care of your soldiers. We could promise to feed them well and keep them safe from harm."

It wasn't perfect, but that was probably as good as it was going to get, and she knew it. Before acting, she wanted to know what her friends thought. When she glanced at Rio, he gave the slightest nod. She looked to Wendy next, who also gave a short nod.

Glancing to her other side, Aaden didn't seem as eager to agree. His hand still gripped tight on his sword hilt. "What reassurance do we have that you'll keep your promise? We know how you treated your other prisoners."

"I'll tell you how they're really treated." Claye nearly lifted out of his seat as he leaned forward. All at once, his expression fell. With a huff, it hardened again. "I know you all hate me for what I did, but I just want unity for Kamdaria. Most of Talise's soldiers want the same thing. Many of them are my friends. I'll make sure they're treated well. And if they aren't," he shrugged, "I'll tell you."

Now that the truth was out, it was much easier to see Claye for who he really was. It strangely made it easier to trust him too. He wasn't a friend, but maybe he could be an ally.

When Talise glanced toward Aaden again, he responded with a short nod.

She looked back at Aaden's father. "I accept."

"Now wait just a minute," Lucian said as he reached for his chin. "We aren't going to help your soldiers just because we destroy one plant together. What can you offer us in return?"

Talise's heart pattered, though she tried to keep her face even. Now came the truly terrifying part of negotiations. The part where she laid out what she had to offer and hoped Kessoku would bite.

The tiniest gulp passed through her throat. "We offer knowledge and training."

Lucian's eyes narrowed. "We are well trained as it is."

His reaction did nothing to deter the steady expression on her face. In fact, it even allowed a tiny smile to twitch at the corners of her mouth. "Knowledge about the amulet."

Now Lucian sat up, his eyes widening.

The smile beneath her lips only continued to grow. "I have a vast collection of writings that explain how to use the amulet."

Despite how Lucian sat at the edge of his log, he tried to shrug off her words. "We don't need them."

Talise raised one eyebrow. "I know many of your soldiers were recently injured after using the amulet."

His mouth twisted into a knot before he let out a huff. With a resigned sigh, he asked, "Do you have the writings with you?"

"No."

He used both his hands to shrug. "Then how do I know you have a legitimate offering?"

Her heart pounded against her chest. Even knowing what she had to do, it took a moment to act. Finally, she glanced toward Claye and raised her eyebrows.

It took a few seconds, but then his eyebrows shot upward. "It *is* legitimate. She has those journals from Kamdar. I told you about them. The journals helped her learn how to bend metal in one day."

Lucian's face didn't move in response to Claye's words. But his mannerisms were so close to his son's, she didn't need his face to move. Just like Aaden, Lucian's fingers twitched. The leader of Kessoku clearly tried to hide it, but he was definitely intrigued. "So, you will deliver these journals to us after we help you destroy the plant?"

"No." Talise sat as still as she could. "I will teach everything in the journals to two people of your choosing. Those two people must travel to me, and I will train them." Now her back straightened. She gave the most determined glare she could possibly muster. "But only if *I* get to train with the amulet too."

Lucian said nothing. Still, the fact that he didn't immediately protest the idea proved he was considering it. He reached for his chin and stroked the goatee as he sat in silence.

At last, he narrowed his eyes. "The other Kessoku would never agree to it. You are our enemy."

"And you are ours. I don't expect that to change just because we start working together."

A crease formed between his eyebrows. "Then what happens afterward? What happens when the war is over? You want to control Kamdaria and so do we. We're not going to give you the power you want."

"Fine." Talise draped her hands in her lap, exhibiting the least amount of care that she could. "Eventually we'll turn on each other, but for now, our goals align. We might as well work together."

He raised a single eyebrow, but it didn't hide the admiration in his eyes. "You want to create an alliance with the express intention of turning on each other later?"

She shrugged. "We both know it's going to happen. Why should we pretend otherwise?"

The admiration in his eyes only grew as he let out a chuckle. "Fine, I accept. We'll help you take out the plant, and we will protect your soldiers. In exchange, you will train two of my best shapers on how to use the amulet." He tapped his chin. "Now to decide which two." His eyebrows rose, as if he suddenly had an idea. Though, Talise suspected he had already decided what he was about to say. "What about Claye?"

Aaden visibly flinched at her side. He even leaned forward when he spoke. "Claye's shaping is useless. He's just a gardener."

An amused expression filled Lucian's face as he glanced toward Claye. "You hid your skills even better than I realized."

Now it was Claye's turn to flinch. He squirmed in his seat and stared at the ground.

Lucian chuckled. "And who else? Ah, why not River?"

Aaden tensed again, which was followed by a scowl. They had been expecting that, but it was still riskier than they liked. But Kessoku had Talise's soldiers and the amulet. It wasn't as if Talise had much choice.

Now, they just had to work out the details to destroy that plant.

Chapter Sixteen

IN PERSON, THE PLANT DIDN'T look nearly as oppressive as Talise had imagined.

Solid walls of brown stone formed the oddly-shaped plant. Instead of a building, it looked more like a winding hallway that curved and bent over the dead landscape. Not a single window graced the brown stone.

Dozens of guards marched on either side of the hallway-like building. Every few feet, small peep holes had been cut into the stone, always at the guards' eye level.

Standing at the head of a company of Kessoku, they were still far enough away from the plant to speak without being heard. Aaden gestured behind him at the building before he addressed to the group.

"We spoke to the family of a man who worked in this plant and managed to escape. He only lived a week outside the plant before he succumbed to the effects of the poison. The stone is thick enough to keep the poison inside. The guards march on the outside of the building on either side. They look through the small holes to check on the people inside. Because the holes are so small, and because the guards wear helmets lined with leather and extra metal, they are not affected by the poison."

As he spoke, several Kessoku from the back of the group began moving their four earth cannons forward.

Aaden nodded at the movement. "When you shoot the air cannons at the plant, aim for those small air holes. That will incapacitate some of the palace guards on the outside. Hopefully, it also frightens the people inside enough that they will exit the plant."

It didn't take them long to get into position after that. Talise adjusted the helmet over her head before she glanced back the plant. A lump grew in her throat the longer she stood there.

She had worn a Kessoku uniform before, several times in fact.

But it was different now.

Before when she had worn the uniform, it had been a disguise. The helmet still hid her face, which would prevent any palace guards from telling the emperor of her involvement in this plan. But still, today she would fight *with* Kessoku. On their side.

She hadn't joined them, but she wasn't against them either. Even when the ice-cold air whipped into her skin, it didn't change how her gut burned at the thought.

Her father had sent her to the Storm at only five years old. He forced her to train at the elite academy for years just to hide her true identity. He subjected her to trials to earn the title of Master Shaper that she had already clearly earned. When she dared to defy his insistence that a dam that hurt people needed to stay, he locked her away in her room. And still. *Still*, it took until he sent poison to hundreds of innocent citizens before she finally realized he was her enemy.

Today she accepted what Kessoku had recognized long ago.

Her father had to be removed from the throne.

Destroying this plant was just the first step in a very long road to do it. Even if she expected to turn against Kessoku later, today she fought for the same thing they did. Today she fought against the emperor.

With the earth cannons in position, everyone turned to Lucian. Aaden's father stared at the plant, narrowing his eyes at the guards who marched along both sides of the stone fixtures.

As he stared, one of the palace guards marching around the plant stopped in place. He stared through a small hole in the stone and then started yelling. "I told you the pieces had to be dipped three times in the solution."

A muffled sound of protest sounded from inside the plant.

The palace guard scoffed in response. "I don't care if it burns. No, don't drop it on… oh, you should know there are consequences for defying orders."

Stomping away from the plant, the palace guard reached for a pile near one of the plant entrances. He donned several extra layers of leather, followed by a thin metal set of armor. He disappeared inside the plant only to emerge a few moments later jerking a man by the arm behind him.

Once he had carefully closed the door to the plant, the palace guard began pommeling the man's face with his fists. Cries erupted from the man's mouth followed by whimpers as he fell to the earth. It didn't slow the beating.

Sucking in a breath, Talise jerked her head toward Lucian. He stood with eyebrows tilted, as if fascinated by the display rather than horrified by it.

Knowing Lucian would be angry about it, Talise punched her fist forward. A mound of dirt formed at her feet only to roll over the earth until it slammed into the backs of the palace guard's feet.

His fists stopped flying as he whirled around, searching for the source of the dirt mound behind him. Before she could send another dirt mound toward him, Lucian scowled at her. And then he gave the signal to his soldiers.

Earth cannons blasted waves of dirt toward the stone plant. Showers of the icy dirt slammed into the building and against the guards. Several guards got hard enough blasts in their stomachs that they bent over in pain.

A second wave of blasts from the earth cannons went out before the Kessoku descended on the plant. Weapons flashed in the sunlight, elements shot from all around.

Talise's feet flew across the ground. Fireballs shot from her hands at anyone who dared come near her. When the fireballs weren't enough, walls of air blew guards off their feet. She was only halfway to the plant when people began spilling out of it. They screamed and covered their heads with their arms, but at least they moved.

The earth cannons had worked exactly as they had intended. Palace guards shouted at the citizens to get back into the plant. With the pandemonium all around, none of the citizens complied.

Everyone wearing a Kessoku uniform let the citizens run as far away as their legs could carry them. While the palace guards focused on trying to stop the citizens, it was much easier to take the palace guards down.

Three fireballs shot from Talise's palm just before she stuffed her nose deep into her elbow. When she entered the plant, she kept the other hand out, ready to shape any poison hanging in the air away from her body.

Aaden trailed in behind her using the exact same method. They didn't attempt to communicate once inside. They just scanned the stone hallway. Every citizen had gone now.

Small wooden cups and bowls covered large wooden tables. Piles of brown fish food sat in several corners. Shimmery silver liquid floated inside the wooden cups. In another part of the plant, large wooden barrels contained powder and liquid ingredients.

After they had traveled through the entire plant, Talise headed for the exit with Aaden directly behind her. They both used care to shape any lingering poison back into the plant before they closed the door.

Aaden grimaced as he looked back the brown stone. "Fire won't destroy the poison, but it will destroy everything else inside. It should make the building unusable."

"I agree," Talise said with a nod.

Tension rocked between his eyebrows. "But we still have to figure out a way to keep the poison inside the plant. If we burn everything inside, it will force the poison out of those small air holes at a much greater speed and volume than normal. I don't think we can set the inside on fire until we have a way to block those holes."

A skitter of anxiety worked through her, but she couldn't deny the excitement that moved along with it. Her eyebrows cocked up. "I know something that might work."

Before she could utter another word, high-pitched shrieks stole her breath. Walls of fire nearly crashed into her. In desperation, she shaped a tornado around her body, which sent the fire spiraling away.

Her feet stumbled as the ground rumbled beneath her feet. Blasting air from her hands, she knocked at least one palace guard of her feet. Another threw a dagger aimed right for Talise's heart.

Pulling water from the air, Talise encased the dagger with water before freezing it. The change from water to ice changed the velocity of the dagger enough that it shivered and dropped to the ground.

Talise had to duck a fireball before she could even catch her breath. With her body low, she managed to catch a glimpse of the chaos around her. The Kessoku wielded weapons with great ferocity. Palace guards were fleeing from every corner of the fight, but many remained.

Jumping to her feet, she sliced a whip of water at the nearest guard. The slap of the water whip caused a palace guard to drop the dagger he had been preparing to aim at Talise. Showers of fire rained down on her next.

After sucking in a deep breath, she pulled every bit of air away from her as she could. The fire drops vanished at the lack of oxygen. The woman who had shaped them also dropped to her knees while clutching at her neck.

A frown overtook Talise's face, but she still waited a few seconds before bringing the air back. She didn't want to hurt the palace guards, but since they *were* trying to kill her it was a bit difficult to avoid it.

Luckily, the woman on her knees seemed much too relieved to have air again to care about anything else. She jumped to her feet and bolted away from the fight.

All around Talise, palace guards continued to run away or get knocked out. A small group of Kessoku closed in on the last guard still fighting. It was the one wearing the extra layers of leather and the thin metal armor.

With his back against a stone wall, the guard yanked open a door to the plant. He pulled out a burlap bag and chucked it toward the Kessoku. A flame burst above his palm before he shot a fireball at the burlap.

Even before the bag caught fire, Talise knew the contents of it. She could sense the fish food and the poison inside it.

Unfortunately, this food had a much higher quantity of poison than any they had encountered in the cities.

Once the flame hit the bag, Talise was already screaming at everyone to back away.

In the chaos, the guard with the metal armor bolted toward a nearby path.

Poison crept into the air just as the man disappeared behind a thicket of dead trees.

Chapter Seventeen

SHIVERS RAN THROUGH TALISE'S ARMS as she reached out. Aaden had gone after the man in the metal armor, so she stopped worrying about him. Closing her eyes, she focused in on the poison seeping into the air.

If her shaping could sense the poison, that had to mean she could control it too. At least she hoped that's what it meant. In theory it sounded simple, but it didn't work as well in practice.

Her mouth twisted into a knot because the poison continued to drift away.

A hand touched gently to her forearm. Talise recognized her best friend's touch even before she started speaking.

"Would air help to contain it?" Wendy asked. "If you tell me where the poison is, maybe I can form a ball of air to keep it inside."

An eager nod bounced Talise's head. She gestured toward the poison, guiding Wendy's ball of air until it encased all the poison. When her ball wasn't thick enough to keep the poison inside, her brother joined and formed a second ball of wind around the first.

Together, they moved their wind balls over the earth until they reached a door of the plant. By then, Tempest had yanked open the door so Wendy and Cyrus could shape the poisoned wind inside it.

Tempest shut the door, closing the poisoned wind inside. Some of it escaped through the small holes, but the brown stone held most inside. Talise finally allowed herself to glance toward the guard who had attempted to get away.

He and Aaden used a series of fireballs and sword swings against each other. Neither one seemed to have the upper hand until Lucian snuck up from behind. Aaden's father used fire shaping to turn his blade red hot before he shoved it under the metal armor and into the side of the palace guard.

One last breath escaped the guard before he dropped to the frosted earth below.

The entire operation had only had one casualty that Talise knew of, but her heart still stiffened at the sight of the guard's dead body. Only days earlier she would have considered that man her ally and Aaden's father her enemy.

Seeing the dead guard caused an aching conflict inside her. Then again, the palace guard *had* beaten that citizen with absolutely no regret. Perhaps it was time to think of allies as people who did the right thing and not as people who fought on one side or another.

Talise's friends huddled around her as things settled down. To her surprise, even Claye wandered away from the Kessoku to check that she was well. She refused to give him the satisfaction of eye contact.

After brushing dirt off the sleeves of his tunic, Lucian rubbed a thumb over his goatee. "Now that we've removed the guards, how do we destroy the plant?"

Talise lifted the visor of her helmet before she answered. "Aaden will destroy the inside of the plant with fire." She glanced at him, which was easy since he stood closer to her than anyone. "Do you think you can shape enough fire to destroy everything inside by yourself?"

He stood a little taller before he nodded.

She turned back to Lucian. "While Aaden shapes fire inside, I will shape ice around the building to keep any poison from escaping through the air holes. There should be plenty of water in the nearby ocean for me to use."

For a beat, Lucian did nothing but stare back at her. Did he expect her to say something else? When she didn't, he tipped an eyebrow up high on his head. "You're going to shape *ice* around the entire plant?"

"Yes." It took everything in her to not roll her eyes. "And it has to be thick enough to keep the poison in."

Claye ripped off his helmet, which sent soft waves tumbling over his forehead. His dark eyes shimmered as he narrowed his eyes. "Are you serious?"

He glanced at Talise's friends but none of them returned the look. In fact, most of them pretended they hadn't even noticed he spoke at all.

Claye scoffed in response, shaking his head along with it. Now he looked straight at Talise. "That's a terrible idea. You got frostbite from freezing a tiny ice key. How are you supposed to shape ice around an entire building?"

Her fingers curled into fists. "That was different. I was too distracted to monitor my internal temperature when I made that key. I didn't have time to realize I'd gone too far until it was too late."

Kneading his temples, Claye's eyes hovered as if he was very eager to roll them back. "But Aaden is going to create a ton of fire inside the plant. How can you possibly make enough ice to combat that kind of heat?"

Talise shook her head. "That's not how ice shaping works. You don't use ice to cool the fire. You use fire to warm the ice. I can shape as much ice as I want as long as I temper it with enough fire inside my veins. It's all about balance."

Claye tightened his grip on his helmet as he glared. "This is a terrible idea." The helmet dropped to the ground as he threw his hands into the air. "Why doesn't anyone agree with me?"

The slightest shift in his feet brought Talise's eyes over to Aaden. He stood completely still, doing an excellent job of pretending Claye didn't exist. When Aaden looked at her, his gaze held more intensity than ever. "Do you really think you can do it? Safely?"

"Yes." She paired her response with an eager nod.

A smile twitched at the corners of his lips as he tilted his head toward the plant. "Then let's do it."

When a grin formed on her face, she almost felt it more inside her body than on her lips. Everything seemed easier when she had someone who believed in her.

Her arms reached out toward the nearby ocean. The water hurtled toward her with the force of a storm. A water storm.

As she pulled the water toward the plant, she flicked her eyes at Aaden. "Can you shape a fire inside the plant even if I surround it with a thick layer of water first?"

He narrowed his eyes at the base. "I think so. Surround the base first, and I'll try."

By the time he finished speaking, she had already pulled enough water from the ocean to surround the entire plant. Just to be safe, she brought in a little more. Moving that much water would have been impossible to do at once. But holding it in place took much less effort.

Once ready, she dug her feet into the earth and found a good stance.

After a nod in his direction, Aaden raised both hands and shot his palms forward.

It turned out he *could* shape fire inside the plant even through her layer of water.

Closing her eyes, Talise took in a calming breath. She'd shaped plenty of ice recently, but this was on a much larger scale. It required more concentration than ever before. She slowed her breath, paying close attention to the beating of her heart. The pulse of her veins sent a steady rhythm through her, which she matched with her breaths.

Only after knowing the internal state of her body did she move. Rolling her weight to the balls of her feet, she sent gentle rippling waves through the water that surrounded the plant. Freezing it all at once would disturb the careful steadiness inside her heart. Instead, she sensed the water directly against the stone.

Ice prickled at the ends of her fingertips. Her shaping sent it into the water around the plant. Frosty crystals stretched through, sticking to the stone as they simultaneously worked through the water.

The first hint of danger rocked through her. The ice in her fingertips worked in balance with the floods of fire inside her. But that wasn't the only fire. Inside the building, Aaden's flames licked at her ice crystals. They fought against each other, both trying to take over the other.

To combat it, she did the only thing she could think of. With a steady breath, Talise stepped to the side until her shoulder met with Aaden's. Whether through instinct or something else, Aaden seemed to understand exactly what she needed.

He lowered himself and stepped to the side until his arm sat directly against hers. Shoulder to shoulder, elbow to elbow, wrist to wrist. It didn't matter that his arm was longer than hers. It didn't even matter that his tunic and hers both had long sleeves. Even through the fabric, she could feel the fire running through his veins. Heat emanated from his arm, which then seeped into hers.

Now the fire inside the building wasn't some unknown entity that she could only guess about. The heat from Aaden's arm told her exactly how big the flames burned. More importantly, it told her exactly how much ice could balance it.

By the time she sent another wave of ice to freeze more of the water, everything inside her was in control. Her breaths came out steady, perfectly in sync with Aaden's. Every ice crystal formed in perfect time with the licking flames inside the plant.

The ice and fire no longer worked against each other but *with* each other. Toward the same end.

Even with such concentration, her mind drifted to many months earlier. She and Aaden had just snuck into the emperor's living quarters, hoping to convince the emperor to give them another chance to become Master Shapers.

Using their complementary talents, they had shaped trees of ice and fire and then traded branches so the elements could work together as one.

And here they stood, shaping ice and fire again. Working together toward a common goal. But this time, more than their own lives were on the line. This time, it was about all of Kamdaria.

As Aaden's fire continued to burn, Talise eventually froze every inch of ice that surrounded the plant. At almost the precise moment she finished, Aaden flicked his eyes toward her.

It didn't take a single word to know what was in his mind. After a deep breath from both of them, they dropped their hands to the side.

It was done.

Aaden stood up straight, but he didn't move a single step away from Talise. Even with his shaping finished, she could still feel heat from his arm sizzling into her skin. He glanced at the plant. "All the poison is floating in the air inside the plant, so everything inside it should be sufficiently destroyed."

Sending an extra blast of cold into her ice, now it was Talise's turn to glance at the others. "With the winter weather and how thick the ice is, it should stay frozen until spring. We can return at that time to determine if the poison is gone or not."

At the end of her words, Wendy folded her arms over her chest and gave a cloying smirk in Lucian's direction. Claye also had his arms folded over his chest, but he glared at Aaden.

The look in Lucian's eye kept dancing from fear to awe as he glanced from the plant to Talise and then to Aaden. After a swallow, he tilted his head. "It seems we do work well together after all. In one week, I will send Claye and River to the meeting spot we specified. Then you can all begin your training with the amulet."

CHAPTER EIGHTEEN

A ROARING FIRE FILLED THE large fire pit Talise and her friends
had just built the day before.

Once again, they were back in the first city they had ever
entered since coming to the Storm. Small children gathered
around the fire, their parents and aunts and uncles huddled
nearby. Many sat on blankets while others settled onto chopped
logs. When one of the children began humming a Kamdarian folk
song, a few of the adults joined in.

Talise's friends moved around the fire, offering blankets to
anyone who didn't have one yet. The shipments from the
emperor would not continue, but at least they had gotten some
supplies before they stopped.

It was such a change to see how Tempest and Rio, and even
Cyrus spoke to the people. When they had first arrived in the city,
Cyrus had called them *savages*. Now he sat laughing with a young
man who could make funny shadows with his hands.

Daylight vanished behind the horizon. Even as an icy chill
whipped around them, no one seemed to notice the cold. The

large fire and blankets provided warmth to a people who very recently had known no hope.

Once everyone had a blanket, Talise lowered herself onto a wide log. Even without a blanket, she barely had to shape fire in her veins. The roaring fire brought enough heat.

A man with soft gray eyes sat crisscross on the ground beside her. She recognized him at once. He was Willow's father. He offered a smile. "Willow said you wanted to ask me about something."

Talise nodded while quickly glancing over the gathered crowd. The little girl and her two friends were nowhere to be found. But perhaps they were just getting more blankets. At least Talise was pretty sure they weren't throwing rocks at a house like they had been when Talise and her friends first arrived in the city.

Turning back to the man, Talise lowered her voice. The question she planned to ask wasn't exactly a secret. But she didn't want her friends to worry she had lost focus on the war either. And anyway, she didn't want to have to explain to everyone in the city, so whispering seemed like the best solution. "Do you have a graveyard in this city?"

Both of the man's eyebrows jerked upward in surprise. "Yes. We still leave marks on graves, even in the Storm. Our graveyard is down a beaten path, but it's there. I can take you there tomorrow."

It took great concentration to keep herself from jumping out of her seat right then. Tomorrow was only one day away. She had waited this long, it couldn't possibly hurt to wait another day. But that didn't stop her from wanting to leave immediately. Taking in a calming breath, Talise nodded. "And do you keep graveyard records?"

Now the man's chin dropped to his chest. "No, we are forbidden from keeping records of any kind. Many of us do not even know how to read or write."

The excitement that had bloomed only moments ago now withered like a dry reed inside her chest. She tried to offer an understanding smile, but it probably came off looking more disappointed than she intended.

Of course she had known it was very unlikely that Marmie's grave would just happen to be here in this little city. If this area had been near where Talise had lived as a child, she would probably would have recognized it, just like she had recognized the city by the River Gate. But her heart still dropped in disappointment.

Without grave records, the only possible way to find Marmie's gravestone was to visit every single graveyard in the Storm individually and check each grave for her name. Shyna Mori. Her real name was actually Shyna Malksur, but no one in the Storm knew that when she died.

The man stared back at her, clearly confused. Giving off a tiny shrug, the man got to his feet. "We hope you will stay with us for another week at least before you travel again. Water Festival is coming, and I know the children have lots of plans that include you."

This time, an actual smile passed over Talise's lips.

As the man walked away, three people came down a path from the city and near the crowd gathered by the fire. Willow and her two friends wore wide grins. Each of them carried a wooden tray with food on top. Food from the glass house.

It had finally grown large enough to eat. One tray held crispy potato strips, another held fresh bean pods. The last had crunchy red radishes with a creamy sauce to dip them in. Even without many herbs and spices, the vegetables alone brought a magical energy to the group.

The children passed the food around with vigor while every person waited patiently for their turn. As they worked, Aaden dropped onto the log beside Talise.

For a moment, they just sat in silence. Nothing had officially changed between them, but she couldn't deny his presence brought her more comfort than it had when they first arrived in the Storm.

He stared at the fire, which made flames dance inside his dark eyes.

Her heart skittered, but this time, it had nothing to do with him. She twisted her fingers in her lap, anxious for something to do with them. "This war is coming to meet us."

He nodded, his eyes still on the fire. "It's more real than ever because now we have to defeat the emperor."

A clench went through her heart. "But how can we defeat him when Kessoku has my army?"

Aaden's head tilted toward the people around the fire. "Maybe you can build a new army."

The lump in her throat made it difficult to swallow. Her voice lowered again, making certain no one except Aaden could hear her words. "The people in this city have only just started to get regular meals. They are still weak. I could never ask them to fight when they don't even have the strength to shape."

From across the fire, Willow handed off the last of the vegetables on her tray. In a flourish, the girl stood on top of a log, waving her arms for all to see. "Princess Talise says we will all get our shaping back once we have enough to eat. Let's see if that day is today."

Talise let out a chuckle as she glanced to her side. Aaden returned the look with a knowing glance. The girl's hope inspired, but she would need to learn patience while she waited for her shaping to return.

Still, it was sweet to see how Willow closed her eyes and held out a hand over the earth. Her fingers shivered with the unquestioning trust of a child.

Silence fell over the crowd as they watched the girl. Nothing happened. Though expected, it still brought disappointment.

Just when whispers began flitting through the group, a clump of dirt flew upward until it smacked against Willow's palm. Her eyes flew open in a flash as she clasped the dirt and brought it closer to her face. "I did it." Her voice came out breathless. Sucking in a gasp, the girl held her hand out with the palm facing up.

The dirt lifted into the air above her hand, hovering for a few seconds before it dropped down again. A gleam filled both of the girl's eyes as she jumped off the log with an excited shriek. "I did it!"

Talise's jaw had dropped. Tingling spread through her arms, ending in a blossom that filled her chest. A sense of wonder probably filled her eyes as she turned to Aaden. His eyes seemed to say the same thing her mind was shouting.

Maybe building a new army wouldn't be so impossible after all.

PART TWO

AIR
STORM

CHAPTER NINETEEN

TIME WAS RUNNING OUT.

Claye stood between his parents trying to muster the devotion he had always held for Kessoku. It took more effort every day.

The fight had been going on too long. Nearly every soldier within Kessoku's ranks was losing resolve. They needed a quick and decisive end to the war, or the soldiers might be too defeated to ever fight again.

From atop a balcony inside Kessoku's main base, Claye could see how soldiers in the crowd before him stood with hunched shoulders. Their vigor had been lost over the summer and fall as the emperor slowly took out the last of their other bases. Now they only had the main base left.

They only had one chance to defeat the emperor. If they lost again, every member of Kessoku would lose hope in their cause.

"We're so glad you're here with us, Claye." His mother squeezed his hand before glancing out at the crowd again.

They dutifully stood behind their new leader, Lucian Sato, as he gave a speech meant to inspire.

So far, the man failed to accomplish his goal.

On Claye's other side, his father nudged him with his shoulder. His father's eyes brightened with a smile. "This is where you belong. With Kessoku."

Even through their vague whispers, Claye knew what message his parents really wanted to convey. They were glad he wasn't with Talise anymore. They were glad she no longer had influence over his thoughts and life.

His parents had not been happy with him when he showed up at their home by the Vine Gate with the princess by his side. Even once he convinced them how much Kessoku needed her to help them win the war, they only barely agreed to let her stay. Since his entire family had always been Kessoku, it had been difficult to hide their affiliation from Talise and her friends during their stay by the Vine Gate. His parents rejoiced when Talise escaped Kessoku's base, and their son was finally living amongst Kessoku once again.

Too bad for them, they didn't know about the secret meeting between Lucian and Talise that had taken place only a week before. His parents didn't know how Claye, and even River, would soon enter the Storm to train with the amulet. They didn't know he would start seeing Talise regularly. And they *definitely* didn't know how much Claye looked forward to it.

Learning how to properly use the amulet was supposed to help Kessoku win the war. But these days, Claye really only cared about seeing Talise again. About changing her mind. If she just understood how important Kessoku was to him—to his family— maybe she'd forgive him.

Lucian raised both arms high above his head as he addressed the crowd. "We are more powerful than we have ever been. It doesn't matter if the emperor took out our other bases. Now that we are all together as one, we are far too strong for him to defeat. Now it is our turn to defeat *him*."

Nods and short murmurs went out through the crowd. Some soldiers opened their mouths to shout in agreement, but their eyes would dull before the words came out. When other soldiers raised their own fists into the air, the attempts were only half-hearted.

They *really* had to win this war soon.

When Lucian dropped his hands to his sides, his spine straightened.

Even from behind, Claye recognized the mannerism as one Lucian's son would have made. Claye's nose scrunched at the thought.

His parents had been founding members of Kessoku over twenty years ago. As the son of such important members, Claye had often met Lucian over the years. For most of those years, the mysterious man was only ever referred to as *General*.

When Claye met Aaden at the elite academy, he had no idea the elusive general was Aaden's father. Now that Claye knew the connection, he couldn't stop seeing similar mannerisms from Lucian in everything he did. And every single time, it made Claye clench his fist.

Why did Aaden have to show up at the elite academy anyway? Everything would have been much easier if he had never become Master Shaper.

Lucian's voice deepened as it simultaneously got louder. That meant the speech was nearing its end. Lucian raised his hands into the air once more.

"Tomorrow we will celebrate Water Festival. We will laugh and relax and enjoy ourselves. But once it ends, we will do nothing but work. I vow to you that this war will end soon. By the time Earth Festival arrives in the spring, we *will* defeat the emperor. We will have unity for Kamdaria." He pumped both hands into the air. "We will win."

A cheer went through the crowd at the end of the words. It lacked the vigor that had existed in their ranks during the summer, but at least they attempted to be excited.

While the crowd continued to cheer, Lucian stepped off the wooden box he had been standing on and turned to face Claye and the others. While stroking his goatee with one hand, Lucian used the other to gesture toward the room from which the balcony came.

On the floor below, the soldiers dispersed throughout the base.

Claye filed into the room with the others around him. The group consisted of a dozen people, mostly made up of those who had been members of Kessoku for many years. Now that Claye had betrayed Talise, the others seemed to think he was worthy to join them. He was the youngest among them by far.

His age showed when he took a seat at the farthest end of the oval table. Velvet drapes hung over the windows. The others talked amongst themselves about battle strategies, economics, and about getting the soldiers excited about their cause again.

If Talise had been the one giving the speech, she probably could have motivated everyone within minutes.

While conversations continued, a man wearing a worn burlap tunic came in carrying a plate of crackers and some smoked meat.

The smell drifted into Claye's nose reminding him of when they visited Wendy's home by the Smoke Gate. He had already been betraying his friends at the time, but somehow, he felt more a part of that group than he did with Kessoku now.

The man in the burlap tunic pushed the tray toward Claye with an urgency about him. Claye chose a few crispy crackers but only one piece of smoked meat. He gave a short nod and said, "Thank you."

A jolt went through the tray when the man took a step back. He blinked at Claye while his jaw hung open. "What?" the man whispered, but it came out so quiet it almost wasn't audible.

It took more effort to swallow after such a reaction. Claye set his face and spoke more deliberately. "Thank you for bringing in the food."

The man stared back even more bewildered than before. After a few moments, he nodded and hurried over to the others. Claye's stomach sank when he noticed everyone else—even his own parents—took the food without a single glance toward the man in the burlap clothes.

Lucian even glared when the man let out a tiny cough.

The man immediately scurried out of the room after that.

A cracker crumbled in Claye's fist before he remembered it was still in his hand. He brushed the crumbs away while the thickening in his throat only worsened.

Slave.

The word sat at the front of Claye's mind where he tried to swipe it away. Several servants worked inside Kessoku's main base. The number of them had grown significantly over the past few years.

They all came from the Storm.

No one was allowed to call them *slaves* though. They were *servants*. And they were *lucky*. They had been saved from the torment of living in the Storm. Now they had jobs and a chance to earn money. It didn't matter if they were treated badly. Anything would be better than what they had to endure in the Storm.

All these years, Claye had turned a blind eye to them. He swallowed, but it didn't take away the tightness in his throat.

After his recent travels through the Gate, the ignoring had gotten more difficult.

Treatment of the *servants* almost reminded Claye of how the emperor treated anyone who lived outside the Crown.

Shaking his head, Claye glared at the ground. Kessoku was *different* from the emperor. They wanted unity. They wanted every citizen to have equal opportunity. Maybe they treated their servants poorly now, but it would be different once they took control of Kamdaria.

It had to be.

Without warning, everyone in the room began filing out of it. If Claye had been paying better attention, he probably would have realized the conversation had ended.

When he went to fall in step with his parents, someone caught him by the shoulder.

Lucian's face held nothing but a blank mask as he watched everyone leave. His grip on Claye's shoulder wasn't insistent, but it managed to hold Claye in place all the same. When his mouth pinched into a knot, the goatee around it moved in time. Again, it looked exactly like an expression his son would have made.

"Wait." Lucian uttered the word under his breath, keeping it too soft for anyone else to hear.

Claye glanced around the room and noticed one other person also hung back.

River.

Her tall stature always stood out in the base. The wildness in her eyes had been growing more intense by the day.

Once they were alone, River moved closer until the three of them stood in a tight circle.

Lucian sent a brief glance toward the woman before tilting his chin higher into the air. "You two will leave soon after Water

Festival. I'll give you the amulet, but you must be careful when you train with the princess."

Folding her arms over her chest, River flashed a frightening smirk. "You mean carefully murder her and steal her journals? Then we'll have everything we need to learn about the amulet, and we can get rid of her at the same time."

Claye could feel the exact moment when sweat broke out onto his neck. Years of practice allowed him to keep his face decidedly indifferent, but that didn't change how the muscles inside him constricted with horror. "That's not really the plan, is it?"

A heaving sigh left Lucian's mouth before he reached for his chin. "Unfortunately, no. The princess has more skill than I realized. As long as she actually trains you, I believe it will be beneficial to learn from her." He lifted one eyebrow. "For now."

River let out a huff that sounded as angry as her snarl looked. She spoke through clenched teeth while she glared at the ground. "But we're still going to kill her before we attack Ridgerock Palace in the spring, right?"

"Of course." Though Lucian's tone came out even, it didn't hide the glance he shot toward Claye.

It took everything inside of Claye to not react to the words. He had already spent so much effort trying to get Kessoku to work with Talise. He never expected them to work with her *and* still plan to kill her. But it didn't matter. As long as he could convince her to give up the throne, they would *have* to give up on killing her. He'd make sure they did.

With the slightest turn, Lucian managed to move his face out of Claye's eyesight. He moved toward River and lowered his voice a few notches. "While you're in the Storm…"

Even as Lucian trailed off, River stood straighter and gave a deliberate nod. "I know what to do."

Claye took a few steps forward, putting both of their faces back into his line of sight. "What? What is she supposed to do?"

Lucian and River exchanged a brief glance before Lucian shrugged. "She is going to train with the princess and learn how to properly use the amulet of course."

Claye rolled his eyes before speaking again. "I'm not stupid, you know. And I'm adult. I have my own ID card. I just spent months spying for you. I deserve to know whatever plans are in place."

Now River rolled her eyes. Lucian waved her off. "Go on. I have something important to speak to Claye about."

She didn't need another word. Her footsteps trailed out of the room before either of them could blink.

When Lucian turned again, the sinking in Claye's gut turned into a twist.

Lucian stroked his goatee as a scheming smile appeared. "You still have feelings for the princess, don't you?"

That twisting in Claye's gut only tightened. He chose not to answer the question. "Just tell me what you want."

After a short shrug, Lucian stared off into a corner of the room. "I think you should tell her how you feel."

Tension crawled through Claye's forehead as he brought his eyebrows together. "Why? So it will make her trust me, which will then make it easier for you to kill her?"

The slightest flash of surprise passed through Lucian's eyes. "Uh…" He stared for one second too long before giving an eager nod. "Yes, that's exactly the reason."

But it wasn't, and Claye could tell.

Now the twisting in his gut took on a new quality that made him ready to part with the smoked meat he had just eaten. At his sides, Claye made fists with both hands. "It's because of Aaden." Even he was surprised by how low his voice came out. "You think if I can get Talise to fall in love with me, then Aaden will come back home to you."

The stiffness in Lucian's jaw increased with every word. He let out a huff before donning a tight glare. "He's my son. He *should* be with me. First love is always strong, but he'll let her go if he has to."

Claye could only curl his fists tighter. He didn't *want* to be a puppet for Lucian, especially when his purpose had nothing to do with Kamdaria. It was Lucian's own fault for losing the respect of his son.

But now Claye had a dilemma because he *did* want to win Talise back. And he'd do everything in his power to do it.

CHAPTER TWENTY

OF ALL KAMDARIAN HOLIDAYS, WATER Festival had always been Talise's favorite. She tore a strip of fabric from the edge of a battered, old sheet. The stains and worn threads made it unusable, but the strips were perfect for a Water Festival promenade.

After ripping away the strip, she handed it to the young girl in front of her.

Willow grinned as she carefully placed the strip over her nose and then tied it behind her head. When handed a second strip, the girl wrapped it over her chin and also tied it behind her head. The grin on her face grew wider as she used a third strip to obscure her mouth.

"It will take ages for my father to recognize me when I have so much of my face covered." Dirt caked under Willow's fingernails. She had continued to spend most of her days inside the glass house that grew vegetables for their town. The dirt on her hands and under her fingernails had only increased now that she could shape earth.

Several people in the town had gotten their shaping abilities back, all because they finally had regular meals with all the nutrients they needed.

Talise ripped another strip from the worn sheet just as Aaden entered the little house. His muscles hung stiff. "I gathered the adults in the clearing by the town well. They are ready for the promenade as soon as the children are ready."

His eyes narrowed as he glanced through the rest of the room. All around, children used old threadbare sheets, sticks, and even mud to obscure their faces and outfits. Wendy, Cyrus, and Tempest all helped children as they created strange costumes.

At the sight of one child rubbing mud all over his arms, Aaden's eyes went wide. "Can't you use makeup to disguise yourself?"

Talise ripped one last strip of fabric from the sheet before she stood and looked him in the eye. "This is the Storm. They don't have makeup here or any of the elaborate costumes they have in the Crown. They have to use things they don't need anymore."

"Right." Pink colored Aaden's cheeks as he gave a short nod. He turned away. When he spoke again, his voice came out stilted. "Of course I knew that."

Soon, Willow declared her disguise perfect. Many of the other children said the same. Once all the children were ready, they formed a line outside on the street. Talise and her friends joined Rio and Fyra who stood near the town well with the other adults. Every adult who had a child stood at attention, peering toward the street with intensity.

A few moments later, the promenade began.

The children stomped down the street in their homemade costumes. They walked with strange motions and let out growls and moans to obscure their voices. The promenade game was simple enough to understand.

The adults had to identify their own children in disguise as quickly as they could. The child who was last to be identified won the game.

Children always loved dressing up and trying to trick their parents, but the message behind the promenade went deeper.

No matter how a person looked, family was always family.

Despite the careful disguises, it didn't take long for the adults to find their children. Willow's father pointed at her from all the way across a crowd. He barreled through the other adults just to wrap his arms around her and hug her tight.

The promenade usually took longer in the Crown. There, the children had access to finer costumes and ones that could more completely obscure faces and bodies. But even in the Crown, a parent never had too much trouble identifying his or her own children.

Aaden nudged Talise with his shoulder as he tipped his head toward the last child who hadn't been identified yet. The boy had wrapped sheets over each of his limbs. Sticks sat under the sheets, which made the boy's limbs look much thicker than they were in real life.

Once the boy's mother finally found him, she chuckled at the sight.

The corner of Aaden's mouth turned up in a grin. "I did that for a Water Festival when I was young, although I used pillows instead of sticks." He let out the softest laugh. "It took my father and mother forever to find me amongst the children."

"Did you win?" Something almost like a flip stretched through Talise's stomach. Why did it seem so strange, and yet, delightful to hear about Aaden's childhood? Maybe because the time he spoke of was clearly *before* his father gave secrets to Kessoku that led to the deaths of nearly all her family members.

It was before either of their lives had been ruined.

"No," Aaden replied, but his eyes stayed bright.

Costumes were shed around the town well as parents used the sheets to wipe the mud and dirt off their children's skin.

Watching the festivities brought a strange sorrow through Talise. As much as she had always loved Water Festival, a part of her hated it too.

Since family was everything in Kamdaria, it made sense that one of the holidays focused completely on children. Technically, children were supposed to make all the plans for Water Festival. Adults did help, but they also allowed their children the freedom to do things the way they wanted.

As such, the holiday turned out a little different every year. And it was always different depending on where in Kamdaria the festivities took place. But a few things remained constant in every part of the empire.

First, there was always a promenade. At the elite academy, children didn't always have family members to pick them out of a crowd, so the teachers would step in and do it instead.

Second, Water Festival always had games that required running. And the adults had to participate even if they didn't want to.

Third, it had *way* too many treats. Unlike the other holidays, no special desserts went specifically with Water Festival. Usually, the children just requested every single treat they could possibly think of. Since children were in charge of the planning, the adults had to allow the entire list of treats. Even in the Storm where treats were so rare, the adults always managed to find at least one dessert for everyone to enjoy.

After the costumes had been abandoned, children began directing everyone in the start of their games.

Willow raced up to Talise's side and waved her arms around in circles. "It's time, Princess Talise. You have to make the water tunnel like we practiced. Everyone who can jump through it without getting wet will get one point!"

Though thirteen years old, the girl still maintained the eagerness of even younger children. She raced back to her father. Her arms waved about once again as she explained the rules to everyone in the city. Soon, the adults begrudgingly walked over to Talise's water tunnel. They all hid their tiredness under thin veils of excitement.

But the children didn't care. They had enough delight for the games to make up for all the adults combined.

Talise pulled water from the air and spun it into a tunnel in front of herself. Soon, children and adults alike jumped through the swirling water. Even without cooling the water, the chill in the air still froze bits of the tunnel.

That made the running games a little easier to endure. At least the swift movements kept everyone warm in the dead of winter. As people jumped through the icy tunnel, Talise called out when someone made it through without getting a drop of water on them.

All around, other children began directing Talise's friends in new games. Aaden had to create tiny fireballs on the ground that people were supposed to smother with clods of dirt.

Wendy and Cyrus shaped thick walls of wind. Anyone who could run through the wall of wind in fewer than five seconds got a point.

Tempest dropped heavy rain down in one spot. People would use cups to gather the rain and then pour it into large bowls. If

154

they filled their bowls in a certain time limit, they would earn another point.

Even Rio and Fyra had games they were in charge of, but they stood too far from Talise for her to see.

Soon, the thinly veiled excitement on the adults' faces turned to actual excitement. They giggled and shouted with as much playfulness as their children.

Water Festival had a way of reminding people what really mattered most. Family.

Talise swallowed over a lump as she spun her tunnel of water even faster. Willow's father grinned as he hopped through the spinning water. He glanced back to see Willow skip through the tunnel with a wide smile.

Despite their desperate circumstances, every adult managed to have fun with the children. They set aside the anger and fear that went along with living in the Storm and just enjoyed their families.

Cold tingles went through Talise at the thought. She remembered celebrating Water Festival way back when she lived at the palace as a child. Back then, even her own father set aside the seriousness of being the emperor. His face always turned red during the running games. Even with six other children, Talise had always been able to make him laugh the hardest.

Her stomach sank, but she tried to hide it behind a tight smile. If she were home now, would he be able to laugh at all?

He wouldn't. She knew he wouldn't, and it hurt almost as much as it had to lose all of her other family members.

By the time everyone gathered to eat a nut and cinnamon pie, it was all Talise could do to keep a neutral expression on her face. As much as she loved Water Festival, it always reminded her of just how broken her own family was.

Wendy and Cyrus didn't understand. The two siblings laughed with the carefree attitude that only came from siblings who loved their families. Tempest seemed just as happy.

Rio and Fyra definitely looked like they missed being with their own families for Water Festival, but they were clearly still enjoying themselves.

From across the crowd, she locked eyes with Aaden. A wrench went through her stomach. Without a single word, she could read the thoughts in his mind. She could feel them inside herself. The wrench twisted, sinking until it weighed down on the little joy she had managed to find.

He understood. He felt it too. As wonderful as it was to have a holiday dedicated to family, it still hurt. Both of them.

Because Aaden's family was just as broken as hers.

The weight pressed in on her, lowering the corners of her mouth no matter how she tried to smile. She tried again. Even though it hurt, she didn't want to ruin the holiday for anyone else.

As the day progressed, the feeling only deepened. Memories of poison, dry pellets of fish food, and even imprisonment stuck in her mind. Her father had become her enemy. Her *father*.

After all these years, she could finally accept that his wrongful actions had caused Kessoku to attack the palace. His actions had caused the war. And things had to change.

She and her friends could forget their woes for a day to celebrate Water Festival, but this war was coming fast. And now was the time to prepare.

CHAPTER TWENTY-ONE

SIMPLE GRAVESTONES LINED ONE END of the graveyard. Talise walked past each with a growing pit in her stomach.

Even here in the Storm, every gravestone had at least three marks. Many had more. Her fingers trembled at her side as she tried to gulp down a lump. The simple marks honored the person's life. They acted as a symbol for the love their families held for them. The more marks a grave had, the more honored that person was considered to be.

It had taken Talise too long to finally enter the graveyard. She had accepted long ago that Marmie's grave would end up bare.

Her funeral had been the same day as the Master Shaper competition. Talise *had* to miss the funeral so she could compete before the emperor and become Master Shaper without revealing her true identity to Kamdaria.

But now Talise lived in the Storm. She actually had a chance to mark the grave. She just had to find it first. It would have been easier if the fear of disappointment hadn't been so paralyzing.

Another row of graves only speared her with disappointment. Regret. Guilt.

She fought back tears as she glanced over the names on several gravestones. She had missed Marmie's funeral just to keep her own identity hidden. And then her identity had been revealed a few months later anyway.

Despite knowing she had good reason, Talise still couldn't ignore the guilt of leaving Marmie's grave bare.

While tears pricked at the back of her throat, a young voice called from across the graveyard.

"What about this one?" Willow hopped up as she pointed to the grave in front of her.

Maybe it had been cowardly, but Talise was too afraid to ask for help from her friends. She couldn't bear to admit that she had let Marmie's grave go unmarked for so long.

Getting help from Willow felt different. The girl didn't even know the relationship between Talise and the person's grave they searched for.

By the time Talise made it across the graveyard, her muscles ached from squeezing her fists so tight. Heaviness trickled inside, sending her heart down to her toes. Her feet trudged over the icy soil, stomping nearer while she feared each step.

By the time Talise stepped in front of the gravestone, her heart crumpled into a tight ball.

Skye Maki.

Like many people in the Storm, Willow had never properly been taught how to read or write. Talise had written out the name Shyna Mori so the child would know what to look for on the graves. Willow *had* managed to find a grave with many of the correct letters.

But it still wasn't Marmie's grave. Hers would continue to be unmarked.

Talise shook her head, unable to form words that weren't filled with tears.

Willow shrugged and turned her attention to the ground below. Reaching one hand out, Willow scrunched up her face until her eyebrows nearly touched.

After keeping her hand hovering over the soil for several seconds, a cluster of pebbles rose from the earth until they hit the child's palm. She glanced up with a grin as she turned her hand over to examine the rocks.

Talise had to turn away from the graves before she could speak, glancing only at Willow as she finished. "You are getting much better. Your practice is really helping."

The smile on Willow's face only grew. "Are you *sure* this is going to help my city though?"

Once Talise had something to focus on, it was much easier to set aside the grief that threatened to shred her from the inside out. She stood a little taller and took on a teacher persona. It came naturally now that people in the city had started to regain their shaping.

"Do you remember when I shaped nutrients out from deep inside the earth?" Talise asked.

Willow nodded. "Yes, you used them to enhance the soil in the glass house where our food grows."

Now Talise nodded. "Once you learn to identify the different parts of the soil, you will be able to shape out nutrients too. Then you can always make sure the soil you use to grow food has the nutrients it needs."

The child screwed up her mouth as she glanced down at the ground. "And it's really going to help me even when I'm just separating rocks from earth?"

Talise couldn't help but smile. She remembered being young and thinking her early training had been too simple to be useful. "Yes, it really will help. You start with identifying rocks because they're the easiest. Once you get good at that, you'll start to identify the different parts of each rock and then the different parts of soil."

With a little shrug, Willow began shaping rocks from the soil again. Despite her hesitation, the girl did enjoy shaping.

Her distraction meant Talise could only go back to the graves. Her heart squeezed as she stepped through rows of graves again. Still, there was no sign of Marmie's grave.

When her chin began trembling, the desire to distract herself became a necessity. She had checked every grave. None of them bore Marmie's name.

Talise clenched her jaw as she jerked away. It hurt to see the graves, but the marks hurt even more. Turning to Willow did not take the pain away from Talise's heart. But it did help.

Her throat burned as she tried to swallow. "Plus, knowing how to shape rocks is helpful for all sorts of things. If you're ever in an attack, you can shape rocks to help defend yourself."

Another set of pebbles rose into Willow's palm as she nodded thoughtfully. "Like those people who stole our vegetables all those weeks ago. If people try to steal from us again, I can protect the glass house by throwing rocks at the attackers."

Now Talise's heart got tight for a whole different reason. She took careful steps forward until she placed a hand on the child's shoulder. "No."

Willow glanced up with a supremely confused expression. "Why not?"

Talise took a deep breath. She attempted to use the same comforting voice Marmie had always used. One that would teach without scolding. One that would empower change without attaching guilt to it. "If people are stealing food, that means they're hungry. You have to take care of yourself, but if you have the means to help other people, you should."

Now the child placed her hands on her hips while one eyebrow raised on her forehead. "Then why would I need to know how to shape rocks to defend myself? If I'm not going to fight people who try to steal from us, who else is there to fight?"

A sharp pain struck through the tips of Talise's fingers. The icy chill in the air had something to do with it, but so did the conversation. Would smiling help? It didn't matter anyway because Talise couldn't possibly smile at a moment like this.

The war brewed hotter every day. With all the atrocities citizens in the Storm had to endure, it made sense how unaware they were of the war. They were already so broken. So downtrodden. How could Talise possibly explain to them about the war?

How could she ask them to fight when they had already endured so much?

She could only mutter a vague response. "It's good to be prepared for anything. Just in case." The child deserved more of an explanation, so did the entire city, but not today. They still had time before things got *too* serious. They didn't need to know every detail about the war yet.

Shrugging, Willow skipped across the graveyard until she stopped in front of a short gravestone with crumbling rock. The name read *Violet Okada*.

A big smile grew on the child's face before she touched the stone. "This is my mother's grave."

The air tensed around them, but with a joyful sort of pain. Willow reached out for a small mark to the left of the engraved name. "She died giving birth to me, but my father made a mark for me on her grave. Once I got old enough, he helped me make it deeper with a chisel so it would be my own."

Though her voice carried sadness, it held pride as well. She touched the mark while taking in a deep breath. "Father says first generation Storm citizens never survive long. His family has been in the Storm for four generations, but my mother came here when she was eighteen. Father tried not to fall in love with her because he knew she would die, but he says he couldn't help it. He doesn't regret it though because at least now he has me."

Talise nodded, trying and failing to keep tears from her eyes. The grave boasted five marks.

Willow touched each of them in turn. "This is my father's mark. This one came from my father's sister and this one came from his brother. This one is from my mother's sister and this one is mine."

Her fingers lingered over the mark while her mouth twitched with a smile that also held a frown.

It didn't surprise Talise that none of the marks came from grandparents. People rarely lived that long in the Storm. When the child stepped away, Talise moved forward and brushed her own finger over the child's mark.

"You did a fine job making it deeper. Your mother deserves all the honor it conveys."

Willow stood taller at the sound of those words.

After stepping away from the gravestone, Talise's eyes wandered over to the one next to it. The stone crumbled at the sides with a lightly engraved name on the front. Only one mark adorned that gravestone.

From her side, Willow let out a snort. "I know what you're thinking, but trust me, he deserved it. That man was so mean. He and his sister came here when I was younger, and he was awful to everyone. Nobody liked him. Only his sister marked his grave, and honestly, I don't even know if he deserved the one mark."

Talise didn't care about the cruelty of the words. She probably should have been more sympathetic to the man who was probably only mean because his life had been ruined. But in that moment, she didn't care. All she could think about was how the one mark on the gravestone dishonored the man's life. And Willow only confirmed the same notion. One mark meant the life had been lesser.

Now her heart crushed in on itself because the pain of knowing Marmie's grave *still* stood bare was too much. Talise stepped back, eager to escape the graveyard. How could she travel to other graveyards to search for Marmie's grave if her heart would be shattered every time?

As she stumbled over the frosty ground, Willow sidled up to her. The child's head tilted to the side. "So, when a man commits a terrible crime, his children are punished for it and sent to the Storm, right?"

Talise nodded. For someone who had been born in the Storm, it made sense that Willow would have questions about how the system worked. She had never experienced it.

Now Willow scrunched up her face. "But my father just taught me that people can disinherit their children. If a man truly loved his children, wouldn't he just disinherit them after committing the crime? Then his children wouldn't have to be sent to the Storm because they wouldn't be his children anymore."

The horror that twisted over Talise's features probably did a lot to answer the question because Willow immediately wilted in shame. Talise tried to form a more pleasant expression on her face. "Family is everything in Kamdaria. There is no greater dishonor than being disinherited. And just because someone *can* disinherit their children doesn't mean they ever would."

Her own father came to mind. Talise imagined a future that was not completely implausible. In that future, she stormed the palace and fought against her father to steal the crown from him. Though Emperor Flarius could have stopped her by disinheriting her, he wouldn't. Even someone as corrupt as him would never do such a thing. As certain as Talise was that Marmie's grave wasn't in that graveyard, Talise knew her father would rather kill her than disinherit her.

Willow nodded thoughtfully. "I guess that makes sense." She glanced over her shoulder at the graves. "I'm sorry we didn't find the grave you were looking for."

Not wanting to give away the relationship she had with Marmie, Talise tried to shrug. "It's okay. I knew it was unlikely."

But how could she possibly keep looking for the grave when it hurt so much? Could she truly deal with that much disappointment? Over and over again?

Maybe once the war ended. Maybe once she had time to spend days and days on end just searching through graveyards. *Someday* she'd find Marmie's grave. Someday she'd mark it.

She just had to accept it wouldn't be soon.

As Talise and the child headed back toward the city, she could only think of how she would begin training with the amulet tomorrow. Even worse, the training would be with the two people in all of Kamdaria that she had no desire at all to see. River, whose lust for revenge was tangible… and Claye, who had betrayed her deeper than anyone.

Talise couldn't decide what would be worse: fearing for her life with the frightening River around or having to spend time with Claye.

✺

CHAPTER TWENTY-TWO

TALISE GAVE STRICT INSTRUCTIONS TO her friends to stay in the city when she went to train with River and Claye. They didn't like the idea, but they had been there when Talise made the arrangement with Lucian. They knew the negotiations required her to arrive alone. If she didn't, her access to the amulet would be ripped away.

Maybe she didn't have the amulet in her possession, but this training would still help her learn how to use it.

Of course, no amount of protest could convince Aaden to leave her side. He ignored every argument and every plea. When the others said River and Claye could refuse to train with Aaden there, he simply insisted they wouldn't care.

In the end, they all gave up and just decided it would be safer for Talise and Aaden to go together. Talise could only imagine how it would go with Aaden and Claye forced to be around each other.

When they reached the clearing they had chosen for amulet training, Aaden held a tight grip on his sword as he surveyed the area. He checked behind every dead tree and bit of brush. After turning two large rocks on their sides, he finally declared the area empty and safe.

Talise nodded and began using air to scoop clods of dirt from the ground before piling them up into a mound. Since she had come to train, it seemed smart to practice.

Aaden seemed to think it best to do practice swings with his sword. Only a few minutes later, River and Claye appeared riding magnificent horses with long, glossy manes.

River was scowling even before they reached the clearing. Claye's scowl didn't appear until he caught sight of Aaden. His face twisted in displeasure, which sent fits through Talise's stomach.

It had already begun.

Claye dismounted his horse and tied it to a tree while everything in his body language darkened. When he stomped across the clearing, his glare toward Aaden only grew.

Talise tried to take a deep breath before the fighting began, but Claye spoke before she had the chance to breathe.

Claye whipped the soft curls off his forehead. "You're not supposed to be here." Poison sizzled inside his words. Even the air itself felt wilted after Claye spoke.

Aaden stared back without a single wince or blink or anything. He held one arm at his side and gripped his sword hilt with the other. No amount of venom lined his words. Just a raw determination, a tone that no argument could touch. "I'm not leaving."

The words sent Claye's face into a tight knot. Heat speckled his cheeks as his jaw tightened. "That wasn't part of the deal. We are supposed to be alone with Talise."

He spoke with such strong diction that sputters shook out from his lips. He jerked his head toward River, expecting to gain an ally with his argument.

Instead, her glare looked no different than it always did. "Where are the journals?"

The fact that she didn't even bother addressing Aaden's presence meant the issue was already over with. No amount of complaining could change anything now because River clearly didn't care about Aaden's presence. And if River didn't care, then Claye couldn't possibly win.

Talise welcomed the chance to turn away from the others. She dug into the canvas pack that held the journals. Instead of pulling out all of them, she merely grabbed the very first of Kamdar's journals. It held the most basic information, which seemed like a good place to start.

Even though she had willingly chosen to work with Kessoku, it didn't seem prudent to share the biggest shaping secrets with her previous enemy just yet.

River snatched the leather-bound journal from Talise's hands the moment she caught sight of it. But when she cracked open the book, it was time for Talise to start asking questions.

"Where's the amulet?"

Her gut rocked as soon as she lifted her head to face the others. Claye was still glaring. His face had grown even more red. The veins in his neck and face pulsed with a palpable hatred. Despite her better judgement, Talise couldn't help glancing to the side.

In contrast, Aaden wore an even-tempered mask of calm. He stood with no anger and no other emotion in his features. Despite the lack of emotions, it was still clear that he was immovable in his decision to stay.

A sigh escaped Talise's lips. Maybe this whole plan would end up badly.

Before she could contemplate the idea further, River stopped flipping through the pages of the journal and jabbed one page with her pointer finger. "All we have to do is connect the amulet's power with our own raw desires. That's why the amulet hasn't worked for us yet." She let out a hateful chuckle before tossing the book to the ground. "Give me the amulet. I'm going to try something."

Her words managed to draw Claye's eyes away from his heated glares toward Aaden. His voice came out tentative. The way he leaned toward River showed that he was almost embarrassed to let Talise and Aaden hear his question. "But how do we connect the power with our desires? Just because we know what to do doesn't mean we know how to do it."

After lifting the book from the ground, Talise brushed the icy dirt away from its cover. "It's not that simple. Kamdar let the amulet overtake him when he used it. He was more corrupt than anyone knew."

All three of the others jerked their heads toward her with widened eyes. Only Aaden seemed to believe her. "Corrupt how?"

The pages of the journal crinkled as Talise flipped through them. "Kamdar was obsessed with power. He destroyed villages and forests just so he could control more people. The amulet has great power, but it took over his mind when he used it. He allowed it to happen because his moral compass was basically nonexistent."

With a snarl, River ripped the book from Talise's hand. "These are lies. Kamdar is revered. Everyone knows he sought to help the people of Kamdaria. He's the one who gave us shaping. Why would he do that if he was corrupt?"

Aaden threw Talise the smallest glance before he gripped his sword and went back to staring straight forward with a blank expression.

Claye seemed to have completely forgotten the conversation. He went right back to glaring at Aaden. This time, each breath that escaped his nose came out in forced puffs.

And River was back to reading the journal again.

A sigh played through Talise's lips. They didn't care about Kamdar's history. Even Talise hadn't believed it when Eben, the guardian of the amulet, had first explained it. Maybe it would be better to start with an actual exercise.

Talise held both hands out in front of her with the palms up. "The point is, you have to channel the power of the amulet, but you can't let it take over your mind."

For the first time, Claye's gaze left Aaden and landed on her. He stared at her hands and then glanced up into her eyes. A strange sensation went through her stomach at the sight of it. Life didn't make any sense sometimes. How could she be so angry at Claye and hurt by him, but still feel fluttery when he looked at her like that?

He ran a hand through his soft curls while a smirk filled his face. "So, I have to use the amulet but not let it use me?"

She could barely swallow when he stared at her with that expression. The urge to step closer to him came over her, but another part of her felt just as strong of an urge to step closer to Aaden. Instead, she looked down at the ground with a half-hearted nod. "Something like that."

With her eyes turned downward, she could still see when Claye reached into his pocket. River's eyes immediately snapped over to him. Greed oozed out of her as she leaned forward.

Claye pinched a metal pendant between his fingers. He held it angled away from River, but everyone could still see it clearly. At the top, the carving of a waterfall glinted in the cold light of the winter sun. The tornado and fire symbols looked exactly like they did on any Master Shaper symbol. At the bottom of the pendant sat an image Kamdarians had never associated with the element of earth. A mountain.

The amulet looked exactly as Talise remembered it.

Taking a deep breath, Claye pinched harder on the metal. He reached one hand out. Soon, one of the large boulders near them lifted into the air. A crazed look entered Claye's eyes right as the boulder shook. A moment later, it started to fall. If it continued on its same path, it would soon fall right on top of Talise and Aaden.

It only took one gasp before she reacted. With the boulder falling straight for her, she had to move fast. At nearly the same moment, she and Aaden lifted their hands and sent enormous blasts of wind at the boulder. The stone jiggled in the air, but a force seemed to be propelling it toward them no matter how much wind they used to divert its fall.

While shaping with all her might, Talise jerked her head. "Claye, stop! You're going to hurt us."

The moment her voice cut through the air, Claye blinked and shook his head. The crazed look in his eye pulsed as he released his pinch on the amulet. With a soft plunk, the amulet fell into his palm.

Now the boulder lacked the force behind it, but that didn't stop it from falling. It still took strong bursts of wind from her and Aaden to push the boulder away before it landed on top of them.

When a cloud of dust lifted around the fallen boulder, Claye let out an audible gulp. His feet shuffled as he reached an arm over his stomach. When he spoke, his voice wavered. "I'm sorry. I wasn't trying to hurt you. I could just feel so much power in my veins and…" He glanced up for a single breath before his eyes fell again. "I don't know what came over me."

After a deliberate step closer to Talise, Aaden narrowed his eyes at Claye. Aaden's gaze never wavered as he reached for his sword, gripping it with more purpose than before.

Even though Claye glared back, it didn't hold as much hate. Too much guilt painted his features to wear a true glare.

Talise's mind wandered back to Eben's garden back when Kessoku soldiers had stolen the amulet from her. She could see the memory with perfect clarity. A Kessoku woman had grabbed the amulet. When she used it, her eyes turned black and her smile wicked. She too had been overcome by the power of the amulet. It wasn't until a fellow Kessoku had punched the woman on the shoulder that she had been broken from the trance.

Biting into her bottom lip, Talise glanced toward Claye. "What did it feel like?"

For a moment, the shame in his eyes vanished, only to be replaced with awe. "It felt like I could control anything. Everything. I could sense every piece of earth around me for miles. I wanted to move all of it at once."

Aaden took a step forward. One shoulder edged in front of Talise the slightest bit, as if distancing her from Claye. Aaden's eyes narrowed. "Are you claiming that you *weren't* trying to kill me?"

The glare that had been so persistent before completely vanished from Claye's face now. His eyes drooped as he shook his head. "I wasn't trying to hurt you, I swear on Kamdaria. I just… I don't know what came over me."

Talise nodded. "That's the power of the amulet. You have to learn how to draw on its power without letting it control you."

River licked her lips as she greedily stared at the amulet. "You had a chance." Her eyes went ablaze. "Now it's my turn."

✺

CHAPTER TWENTY-THREE

TENSION TWISTED THROUGH THE AIR as River reached for the amulet. Terror seized in Talise's heart. Despite everything she had been through, the sight of River reaching for the amulet caused Talise to step back. At the same moment, Aaden edged himself in front of her.

As protective as ever.

Still, the way her heart pounded in her chest, she couldn't be annoyed by it. Maybe if she stood taller, she could trick herself into brushing the fear away. After a few deep breaths, she forced out a steady voice. "Maybe I should try it next."

The chuckle that left River's mouth had as much bite as it had humor. With a pointed look, the woman said a deliberate, "No."

Fear continued to work its way through Talise's veins, but a slice of anger managed to cut through it. "You saw what just happened with Claye."

River threw her head back with a short chuckle. "Yes, but I have self-control."

"No, you don't." Aaden stood with his same even expression. But again, he spoke in such a way that no argument could touch his words.

A grunt left River's lips as she drew her eyebrows together. "Why are you even here?"

Aaden maintained direct eye contact with River as he pulled his sword halfway out of its sheath. "You know why."

The woman rolled her eyes as she turned away from the rest of them. "It won't be like Claye. I've already used the amulet twice."

Claye dug a toe into the dirt as he spoke under his breath. "And you almost died both times."

She turned on him with a fury worse than any storm. "I might respect your parents, but that doesn't mean you deserve the same." Now she graced him with a smirk of her own. "What if there happened to be an *accident* with the amulet and you died? What could your parents even do?"

"Really?" Aaden casually drew the sword from its sheath and examined the blade. "I've seen your shaping skills. I know the amulet gives incredible power, but Princess Talise and I are both Master Shapers." He twisted the sword through the air in a subtle jab. "And you know how skilled I am with a sword." When his gaze fell on her again, the air crackled with energy. "I'll do whatever is necessary if you happen to *accidentally* lose control."

With a hiss, she turned away. But even the snarl on her face demonstrated a surprising truth. Though she might have hated Aaden, she clearly respected him more than Claye. Even more important, she feared him too.

She snatched the amulet from Claye's hand and took a careful stance on the frozen earth. "I'll start with something small." Now she gave the slightest glance toward Talise. "And I'll focus on keeping my mind in control like you said."

Her fingers tightened around the amulet as she shot her other arm out in front of her. After a breath, she brought her arm back and then punched her hand forward.

A gust of wind with the force of a tornado burst from her palm. The air shook through the branches of nearby tree. The trunk immediately began jerking from the force of the wind. After a few seconds, the trunk tipped to the side with roots rising out of the ground.

The wind continued for a few more seconds until the tree was halfway uprooted. River let out a slow, steady breath as she released her grip on the amulet and dropped it onto her opposite palm.

She tipped one eyebrow upward. "See? I do have control when I choose to." Both her eyebrows raised as a smile stretched across her face. "I bet you've never seen anyone uproot a tree with shaping before."

Letting out a snort, Claye ran a hand through his hair. "I've seen Talise uproot an entire tree, which she then proceeded to destroy an entire dam with." He gave a pointed stare in River's direction. "And she did it *without* an amulet."

A tight scowl broke across River's face.

But Talise's gaze turned back to the halfway uprooted tree. Turning slowly, she glanced toward the woman. "Your primary is air? Not water?"

The grunt that left River's mouth made all three of them jump. "My aunt served in Ridgerock Palace for many years, and do you know how much she got paid? Basically nothing. One night, the emperor threw a party. Even with all the guests, they had trays of leftover food. So, my aunt took some of it home to her family. Do you know what happened then?"

Nausea rocked through Talise. Could her heart sink lower? Apparently, it could.

River stomped closer, narrowing her eyes at Talise with every step. "Your father found out and immediately sent my aunt's children and grandchildren to the Storm. He cursed them to a broken life just because they ate food that no one else even wanted. My primary is water, but I make a point to shape air as well because that was my aunt's primary. I do it to honor her life." She flicked a hand toward Talise. "Your family, on the other hand, deserves no amount of honor at all."

For some reason, Talise's mind went straight to Marmie's unmarked grave. No greater dishonor was known in Kamdaria, except being disinherited. Talise tried to swallow over the lump in her throat. But Marmie would have been sympathetic to River's aunt. She deserved every honor and got none instead.

After another hard swallow, Talise snatched the amulet from River's hand. Tingles spread through her body as she glared at the woman before stepping backward. "It's my turn now."

All at once, the tingles changed to pulses which sent a strange warmth through her. When Talise opened her fist, the amulet sat with a faint lime green glow pulsing inside it. Warm power burst inside her chest. The power crackled for a few seconds before the faint glow vanished. Even after it disappeared, the air sizzled with the same energy as lightning.

It was all Talise could do to breathe.

The lime green glow, the burst of power, even the sizzling energy in the air. It had all happened before. When the two pieces of the amulet had joined together in Eben's garden, the amulet had done the same thing. All those months ago, Talise had felt power inside her chest when she first touched the amulet.

She remembered the stone cups and how Eben had encouraged her to find a way to balance taking care of herself and taking care of Kamdaria. Once she had finally realized she had to take care of herself and Kamdaria equally, the cups had popped and sparked with a green kind of magic. The two pieces of the amulet had joined together and created a power like she had never felt before.

But why was it happening again now?

"Are you okay?" Aaden's voice came out clipped. Worried.

Judging by the faces the others wore, no one else had notice the lime green glow or the energy in the air.

Claye stuffed his hands into his pockets. "Don't be nervous, Talise. I'm sure you'll do great."

He accompanied the words with a smile that was probably meant to be encouraging. It came off as patronizing instead.

Aaden stiffened at her side.

Yet again, it seemed appropriate to let out a sigh.

Talise decided ignoring them would be better.

Before she could close her hand around the amulet, River stepped forward. The woman's face glared at the amulet. When she glanced upward, fear danced in her eyes.

Had River noticed the glow? The energy? Her face hardened. She reached for the amulet, but Talise stepped away just in time.

With a scowl, River said, "I think that's enough training for one day. Return the amulet to us, and we'll be back again in a few days like we planned."

Talise took another step back. "But I didn't even get to use the amulet. I'm supposed to train with it too. That was the deal."

Though the woman looked ready to argue, Talise ignored it and tightened her hand around the amulet once more. The power in her chest hadn't disappeared, but it felt more like a part of her now.

She turned her hand and flipped it upward. At the same moment, the ground beneath all four of them lifted into the air. The earth moved like a platform, hovering several feet above the earth as it moved to the right.

A moment later, the hovering earth lowered down onto a new spot. Every movement came controlled. The power in Talise's chest pulsed as she carried the earth, but it stayed in her chest. A part of her, but not anything that could consume her.

When the earth dropped down again, River couldn't smother the fear in her eyes. She ripped the amulet away from Talise and stomped away toward her horse. She didn't even bother to glance back as she spoke. "We'll be back in a week. You'd better be ready to teach us more challenging techniques."

She had already untied her horse by the time Claye finally moved. He shot a quick glance toward River before turning fully toward Talise. "The emperor finally took out all our bases except the main base."

River snarled as she hoisted herself on top of her horse. "Don't tell her anything about us."

Claye didn't react. He just continued on as if River had never spoken. "Whatever the emperor has planned for us, it's coming soon. He's going to attack our main base next. We're planning to storm Ridgerock Palace before he has the chance. No matter what, Lucian promised this war would be over before Earth Festival in the spring."

By then, River had led her horse over to their group. She grabbed Claye by the back of the collar and dragged him over to his horse. "We're leaving now," she said with no small amount of bite.

As the two of them galloped away, Talise turned to Aaden while terror spread throughout her body. She hadn't been so naïve to think the war would fizzle out without a fight. But in the Storm, it didn't feel as urgent. In her weeks there, she had started to feel like it would be ages before anything important would happen.

But the truth was clear. The war was coming soon.

CHAPTER TWENTY-FOUR

FREEZING WIND SHOT THROUGH TALISE'S hair. The cold cut into her cheeks. She tried to swallow, to breathe, but how could she when horror had seized her so completely?

"We still have time." Aaden's voice came out firm, grounding her in spite of the wind. When he gazed into her eyes, it settled some of the fear. But another terror she had been avoiding came out even stronger than the other.

Could she ever look at him without feeling from every part of herself that they belonged together? Since the beginning, she had always been drawn to him. Her feelings still coiled with betrayal and anger, but maybe now she could set those aside and release the longing that filled her soul.

Only when she closed her eyes could she speak again. She let out a slow breath, which the air froze the moment it left her lips. "We don't have as much time as we need."

"Yes, we do."

He had reached for her. Even with her eyes closed, she could feel it. Maybe her shaping had sensed the ripple through the air, or maybe her skin could just feel the heat from his arm. But he had clearly reached for her. And then he dropped his hand back to his side before touching her.

Something about it felt like rejection.

Her eyes snapped open again. The weight in her chest tightened, but she tried to ignore it. Sometimes ignoring took too much effort. Icy wind trickled down her throat when she swallowed. "I need to get my army back from Kessoku."

Aaden let out a scoff. It almost hurt more than when he pulled his hand away. With an eyebrow tipping upward, he asked, "How do you plan to do that?"

Responding with a gaping mouth probably wasn't the most princess-like thing she could do, but she couldn't help it. The question had left her speechless. Did he think it would be impossible to get her army back? Did he think they should give up now?

As if guessing her thoughts had turned sour, his head dipped down. A gentle expression filled his normally rigid features. "You need to build a new army with people from the Storm. You know you need to, but you've been putting it off, and I don't understand why."

Something in his eyes shimmered as he spoke. She turned away just so she wouldn't have to face him. That same terror laced with longing filled her, but it didn't seem as frightening this time. "Everyone in the Storm has already been through so much. How can I ask them to risk their lives when they're the victims of the horrible system of marking ID cards? I don't want them to fight for me. I want to save them."

It only took a single step for Aaden to return his position in front of her. It seemed she could never escape him, even when she wanted to.

His head tilted. "But if they fight for you, they'll have a chance to destroy the system that has hurt them. You can stop the system of marking ID cards. Don't you think they deserve the chance to make things better for themselves?"

A growl threatened to erupt from the back of her throat, but she managed to only let out a huff instead. Why did he have to say such logical things all the time?

The growing tension inside sent her mind searching for another topic to discuss. Any at all.

A new thought came without hesitation. She caught hold of it, eager to let it turn their conversation. But bringing it up would take some finesse.

Hoping her movements didn't seem too suspicious, Talise began walking toward the path that would lead them back to camp with the others. Aaden followed immediately, still unaware of how the conversation was about to change.

Biting her bottom lip, she glanced toward him. She tried to don the most innocent face she could manage. "Aaden."

His shoulders tensed at once. So much for an attempt at innocence.

The veins in his hands pulsed as he tried to keep from balling his hands into fists. She had observed the same mannerism from him so many times, it was easy to sense his discomfort. Did he know what was coming?

With a light touch, she tucked a piece of hair behind her ear. "You mentioned the other day how your father and mother took forever to find you in your Water Festival costume one year."

Now his hands *did* form fists. Even his gulp was audible. He definitely knew what was coming. It was probably best to just get it over with.

Her words came out in a rush. "The whole time I've known you, you've never once mentioned your mother. Not until you talked about that costume the other day. I remember seeing her once when I was a child, but she's obviously not around anymore.

I always assumed she died when Kessoku attacked the palace and killed my family. Lots of people died in that attack.

Another audible gulp escaped from Aaden's mouth. His hands had relaxed, but he stomped forward with his eyes studiously looking ahead.

Talise sucked in a quick breath before she spoke again. "I only assumed she died because I thought your father gave up palace secrets on accident. But it wasn't an accident. He was Kessoku, and we never knew." Her throat ached more with each of the words. "But if he was Kessoku, he never would have let his wife die in an attack he knew was coming. He would have protected her."

Aaden's face offered no reaction. His steps had become even and measured, giving no indication to his emotion.

The nonreaction made it more difficult to continue, but it was too late to stop now. Talise froze in place. Her feet stood firm, waiting until his followed suit. A charge buzzed through her when her lips parted again. "Aaden, *where* is your mother?"

He let out a sigh when his own feet stopped. His body moved toward Talise, but he didn't look her in the eye. One hand casually disappeared inside his tunic pocket. When he pulled it out again, he held a folded card covered in wax between two fingers.

Even without seeing it clearly, Talise recognized it as Aaden's ID card. When he offered it, she took it without hesitation. The light wax coating rubbed against her fingers as she opened the card.

Though her fingers moved easily, she couldn't imagine how *this* was supposed to answer her question. But then her eyes landed on the family tree painted on the back of the card. A calligrapher had delicately painted Aaden's name over the tree trunk. On the left side, she recognized several names: Lucian

Sato, Blaise Sato, Seraphina, his grandmother. The names continued for four generations back. But on the right side.

It was blank.

Talise's breath stilled as she rubbed a finger over the spot where the name of Aaden's mother should have been. An empty box stared back instead. No grandparents sat above the blank space, no great-grandparents. Just empty boxes, as if Aaden's mother had never existed.

Only one thing could explain the half-empty family tree, and it was a far greater shame than having an ID card that bore a black X.

Forcing herself to look up, Talise desperately tried to control the emotion tugging through her throat. "She disinherited you?"

When Aaden nodded, it felt like a punch to the gut.

Talise's voice came out tighter than before. "After your father's trial when they condemned you to the Storm?"

Red colored his irises when he shook his head. "It happened a few years before that." The faintest puddle of tears gathered, but he quickly blinked them away.

Never before had she been so overcome with the urge to embrace him. Her lip trembled, but it was pointless to try and stop it. An ache squeezed through her chest, reaching out along every limb.

Maybe it didn't make any sense, but his hand seemed like the best place to look while she spoke. "I know it's supposed to be shameful, but your mother is the one who should be ashamed. You were only a child, and she left you. That's…"

At some point, her feet had moved her closer to him. Now his hand was nearly close enough to brush. She reached out for him.

"I'm so sorry." Her words came out barely above a whisper.

When they touched, their hands fell into a natural hold without any hesitation from either of them. She gave his hand the tiniest squeeze. He responded with the most tender touch.

"Thank you." He choked over the words, which only twisted her already fragile heart into something that hurt, but in the best possible way.

Looking him in the eye would surely break her completely. But she couldn't just stand there holding his hand. He needed more. *She* needed more.

Her head dropped against his chest, which made the icy air feel like a distant memory. Another moment, and she would have wrapped her arms around him.

He stepped away first.

It was probably for the best. They both knew where it would have headed, and they probably weren't quite ready for it. Still, when icy wind whipped in the space between them, Talise felt a sting in her heart.

To distract herself, she glanced down at the ID card in her hand. Her thumb ran over the blank boxes on the family tree before she turned it over.

On the inside of the card, Aaden's name, primary element, and residence had all been filled in by a calligrapher. Aaden Blaise Sato, Master Shaper, Ridgerock Palace. A large box filled the bottom half of the card. It said *Deeds* above the box. Inside, two distinct stamps could be seen. First, a large black *X*. Then, a shimmery, silver crescent moon had been stamped on top.

Aaden reached for the card right as her eyes fell on the crescent moon. He tapped the stamp before pulling the card back into his hand. "The emperor gave me that stamp as a reward for spying on Kessoku. He gave it to me last time I went to the palace."

She gave a hurried nod as he stuffed the ID card back into his pocket. She tucked another strand of hair behind her ear. "Oh yes, I actually knew… Tempest told us about how you were supposed to earn a crescent moon for being a spy."

With her eyes toward the ground, Talise rubbed a hand over her arm. "I didn't know you'd earned it already. Great… work." Her voice trailed off at the end. What was the appropriate way to congratulate someone for earning back the life that had been stolen away from him? Did one exist?

Apparently, Aaden felt even less clear about how the conversation should go. Rather than responding, he just continued walking forward once again.

For some reason, the silence made Talise's heart go tight all over again. Her thoughts returned to those blank spaces on the ID card. She shook her head. "You have the worst grandfather in the empire. You might not have the worst father in the empire, but he's at least tied with my father." She let out a sigh. "And apparently, you have the worst mother too."

Aaden's face screwed up in puzzlement. "My grandfather is not the worst."

Neither of Talise's other statements seemed to bother him, so why would he be against that statement in particular? Especially since she knew it to be true. Piercing him with a stare, she said, "He beat you."

"What?" The confusion on Aaden's face had only grown.

Now anger stretched through her, anger against his grandfather. If he had such horrible parents, did he even know how to be treated well? Would he justify his grandfather's actions because he didn't know any better?

Her stare hardened. They continued to walk, but her feet stomped a little harder on the frozen soil. "Back at the palace, the emperor kept being hard on me during our Master Shaper training, and you stood up to him. You told him to stop. You told him that you didn't care if he was the emperor."

A memory sparked in Aaden's eye. A puff escaped his mouth that almost sounded like a chuckle. He gave a single nod after that.

She raised an eyebrow before continuing. "The next day, you had bruises all over your face. You even had one over your scar, which was still fresh at the time. I thought my father did it to you, but you told me later that your grandfather did it."

Aaden shrugged. "That's not…" He shook his head. "My grandfather heard about how I stood up to the emperor, and he feared for my life. He just wanted to teach me that sometimes you have to listen to authority figures."

Her fingers tensed as she curled them into fists. "Are you trying to justify what he did to you?"

"No." Aaden brushed a hand through the air before he rubbed two fingers across his now-healed scar. "What he did was wrong. He admitted that himself. He apologized. He told me he wished he hadn't done it. If he had hit me again after that, his apology would have been meaningless. But he didn't. He realized he could have taught me the same lesson in a better way. He worked hard to help me learn from his mistake."

Talise grumbled as she folded her arms over her chest. "He still made a mistake."

Aaden stopped and turned to face her completely. "Mistakes aren't what make people good or bad. Everyone makes mistakes. What matters is what someone does after the mistake. Look at my father. He helped kill most of the imperial family. Instead of admitting how wrong it was, he tried to justify it and then left me, his only son, to go fight with an organization of people who want revenge. My grandfather definitely did something wrong, but it didn't end there. He tried to make it right."

Her heart fluttered inside her chest. Why did Aaden have to have such intensity? Such wisdom? She stomped forward once again. "You might be right." Admitting it immediately took the fight out of her. She let out a sigh. "You were right about the other thing too. People from the Storm do deserve a chance to fight against the system that hurt them."

The slightest smile broke through Aaden's even expression. He was proud of her; she could feel it. It only sent her heart fluttering even harder.

Pursing her lips, she took a deep breath. "Tomorrow morning, let's gather the citizens together, and I'll talk to them."

CHAPTER TWENTY-FIVE

SOMETIMES LIFE MADE A MOCKERY of plans.

The Storm had been aptly named. Living amongst desperation and anger felt like a constant storm inside. But the name hadn't come from that.

It came from the literal storms that plagued the outer ring of the Kamdaria. Some years, only one storm would hit. Some years, dozens of smaller storms would hit. In every case, they left the citizens even more hopeless than before.

Battering air slammed against homes, wriggled into cracks. It brought mud, heavy branches, and even disease through every city. The air storms had no respect for need or desperation. Whenever one hit, the citizens could do nothing but hide in their houses until it had passed. But the storm was just the beginning. Cleaning up afterward took even more work.

Days passed by with survival as the singular goal.

Talise had fully intended to speak to the citizens about fighting for her. The air storm had other plans. A few of her glass houses in cities throughout the Storm were shattered by errant, wind-blown branches. Repairing the glass houses took days.

Following the storm, a horrid sickness swept through the cities. Many citizens were bound to their beds. Even if they gathered the well ones, the crowd would have been miniscule.

Talise trudged down the frozen path between rows of houses. The cotton sheets they used as doors whipped fiercely in the unforgiving wind. Moans and grunts filled the air. Some of them were the last sounds those people would ever utter.

Each noise brought strains through her limbs.

Cyrus had taken ill. Her group had been safe from the illness at first. Likely, their frequent nourishment and strong bodies helped with that. But Cyrus had wasted away in Kessoku's dungeon for months during the summer and fall. Even with Aaden sneaking him food at every available opportunity back then, his weakness was clear now.

So, the call to fight had been forgotten. Talise couldn't imagine asking for help from people who could barely survive the winter. Many of them wouldn't even survive this sickness.

Pushing open a wooden door on crooked hinges, Talise stepped into a little clay home. The square house consisted of a large room with a fire pit in the middle. One corner had a simple screen that blocked off the area for cleansing and dressing.

A tattered mat sat low on the ground. Cyrus lay atop it, coughing into a crusty rag. Wendy was perched at the edge of the mat. Her hand shook as she dabbed her brother's forehead with a cloth.

Aaden stood across from the mat with his arms held stiffly at his side. Nothing about him seemed relaxed in the slightest.

Willow sat in the corner scratching at a piece of parchment. She probably didn't enjoy having her home taken over by Cyrus and all of Talise's friends, but the girl never once complained.

Reaching into her pocket, Talise pulled out a toasted bun infused with herbs that would supposedly speed Cyrus's healing.

She held it up for the others to see. "I got the bun, but it took twice as much money as we expected."

Aaden jumped at the sound of her voice. He quickly stepped to the side to make more room for her, but his jaw clenched tight. "You shouldn't have left without me. It's not safe for anyone to travel alone."

Wendy wiped away a few tears as she took the toasted bun from her best friend. A short nod was the only acknowledgement she could offer. Instead, she focused on tearing away a piece of the bread. Cyrus moaned and turned away when she tried to push the piece between his lips. After some gentle but persistent prodding, he finally allowed the bread inside his mouth.

A sigh of relief escaped Talise's lips at the sight. She glanced to her side and addressed Aaden's earlier statement. "I only went one city over, and I didn't have time to wait for you to finish building that fire."

His eyebrows pinched together.

"Besides." Talise tossed a bit of hair over one shoulder. "I got back safely, didn't I?"

When Aaden's eyebrows moved even closer together, it turned his scar bright white.

Before he could scold her, Talise addressed her best friend. "Where's Tempest? I know Rio and Fyra are still helping to gather more firewood for everyone, but I thought Tempest was in here with you."

At those words, Willow looked up from her parchment wearing a grin. "My father got mad at her for rearranging everything in our house." The grin on Willow's face made it clear that *she* didn't share her father's frustration. In fact, she seemed to find the whole thing rather amusing.

Even the pain on Wendy's face had softened. Her lips turned upward as she gave a gentle dab to her brother's forehead.

"Tempest can't hold still when she gets anxious. She's out making a soup for Cyrus, and she promised to purify the water at least three times. A nice woman who lives by the well told us Cyrus's sickness will improve if we can get him to eat."

Throughout the conversation, Talise's eyes had wandered back over to Aaden. The crease between his eyebrows had deepened again but not with a scold. Instead, fear controlled his features. He stared at the mat, apparently unable to stop worrying for Cyrus.

His concern only made Talise's insides flip. Her fingers found the hem of her tunic as she turned toward the doorway. "I'll go check on her."

By the time she left the house, Aaden had appeared at her side. He didn't say a word, but she still clearly understood that she wouldn't be allowed to sneak away again. Fortunately for both of them, she had no intention of trying any time soon.

They moved in the direction of their camp, but the meandering steps wouldn't get them there quickly. The time seemed much better spent contemplating the state they were in. Even after gaining the trust of citizens in the Storm, they still weren't safe. Even with food and blankets and money, which they only had thanks to Aaden, one of their group still might not survive the winter.

And people from the Storm? How much better were they from before Talise and her friends had arrived? They had vegetables now and fires to keep them warm. But it only took one air storm, and many of their lives were at stake.

But even worse was having Cyrus's life in danger. They had sacrificed so much to save him, and now he might die anyway.

When Talise glanced to her side, Aaden's face had twisted as he tried to keep his chin from trembling.

Talise bit her bottom lip as she reached for her tunic hem once again. "You wish you could have done more to help him while he was in Kessoku's dungeon, don't you?"

Aaden let out a long sigh as he rubbed one hand across his forehead. "Cyrus always acts like I'm the one who helped him." He frowned through a swallow. "Maybe I did, but he helped me too. He kept me sane while I hid among enemies. He was my *friend*. I've never had many of those."

Talise's heart squeezed in her chest. Another moment and tears would have filled her eyes. Instead, a distraction held her emotions at bay.

"That sounds like me." A gruff voice came from behind them.

Turning, Talise saw Willow's father, Ash, standing with a pack slung over one shoulder. He scratched the back of his leg with his other foot. "My parents died when I was young. I'm a fourth generation Storm citizen. We usually live longer, but it's never a surprise when people die here. With no parents, my siblings and I were separated and given to different families in our city. My neighbors cared for my physical needs after that, but I was as lonely as a person can be. I embraced it. I pushed people away and pretended I didn't care about them. Even my brother and sister."

The man pulled the pack off his shoulder as a twinkle appeared in his eye. "But then a lovely girl came along and ignored my brash exterior. She treated me like someone important. No matter how I resisted, it was all over from the moment I laid eyes on her."

A faint smile twitched at Talise's mouth. An involuntary glance turned her eyes toward Aaden.

He was staring at her. Intensely.

With a sharp swallow, he jerked his head away.

Ash reached into his pack. "I knew she would die early, all first generation Storm citizens do. But I have Willow now and…" His hand emerged from the pack holding a sparkly green pendant on a silver chain. "I guess all we can do is appreciate the time we do have."

Though his words were probably meant to inspire, it didn't change how grief weighed down his features. He didn't quite seem to believe that any of it had been worth it considering how much pain he had to bear.

Coughs erupted from the home nearest to them. A gurgling sound accompanied the hacking coughs followed by the distinct gasping for breath. The noises came to an abrupt halt a moment later. The silence that followed sent dread and sorrow into the stillness around them.

For almost a full minute, none of them moved.

At last, a woman with tear-stained cheeks emerged from the house. "Could you—" She hiccupped as she swiped away a tear. "Could you help us carry a body? My brother wants to move his wife near the fire. Just in case."

The last few words came out as a whisper, but they could all hear the hidden message inside. It was already too late. The woman's breathing had probably already stopped.

Still, Talise moved toward the house without question. Her heart thundered when she saw the woman who had just died. The woman had been strong. She would have made a good soldier. And now she was gone.

Working with Aaden, Talise moved the body closer to the fire inside the home. Her skin still gave off warmth, but she had no life left inside.

The tightness in Talise's chest only grew as the woman's husband wrapped her up in several blankets. It would be awhile before he accepted his loss.

A lump formed in Talise's throat, tightening through the soreness. It only grew the longer they stayed in the home. Willow's father stayed to offer comfort, but Talise had to leave.

When she stepped onto the path outside, she welcomed the icy sting that hit her lungs. Her breath frosted as she let out heavy pants. She had almost forgotten how much pain frequented the Storm.

Aaden came to her side, but his stride lacked the determination so characteristic of him.

She slowly turned toward him. "I cannot ask these people to fight for me. Not now."

He didn't seem to agree, but he also didn't argue.

Her hand slid down her cheek as she tried to suck in a full breath. Everything still seemed too shallow. "I have to wait at least until this sickness passes through. We have more important things to worry about right now."

Concern flickered in Aaden's eyes as he glanced toward the home where Cyrus lay. They had spent so much time helping the other family that it was probably useless to check on Tempest now. She had probably already finished making her soup.

Without a word, they both headed back toward Willow's home, hoping for something to lift their spirits.

They walked through the doorway a few minutes later. Immediately, Talise could tell a change had occurred. The energy in the air had gotten lighter.

Talise stepped farther into the room and quickly touched a hand to her lips. Cyrus no longer lay back, barely registering the things going on around him. Now, he sat up, though still propped up with several pillows.

When Wendy brought a spoonful of soup to his mouth, he drank it eagerly. The color in his cheeks that had been gone for days started to return.

Aaden let out a long breath while the faintest relief spread across his face.

That was it.

That was the face Talise wanted, but she wanted it for Storm citizens. She didn't want to make them fight. She wanted to save them. She wanted to see them happy, to see them allow themselves to believe things were really better.

Her heart pounded inside her chest as she swallowed. Tomorrow would be her second training with the amulet. Maybe she didn't need another army to win the war.

Maybe she just needed more training.

CHAPTER TWENTY-SIX

ON THE WAY TO THE next amulet training, Talise tried to temper her urgency with a strong dose of reality. The amulet had great power indeed, but soon, River and Claye would have the training necessary to access that power.

Still, Talise's heart skipped whenever she thought about touching the amulet again. It could give her abilities she had only ever dreamed of. If she'd been able to help the Storm with her regular shaping abilities, how much more could she do with the amulet? Even if others knew how to access that power, her training would still allow her to do more than ever.

Reaching for her tunic pocket, she pinched the folded parchment inside. Since the journals from Eben were their only bargaining chip with Kessoku, she decided to leave them back at camp for this training. Last time, River had been a little too eager to throw the journal to the ground. Instead, Talise had copied a few pages of instructions for exercises she wanted to try.

As she moved, Aaden tripped over his feet. He huffed at the ground as he tried to regain his inflexible walking posture. The eyebrow under his scar vibrated while he attempted to spread calm through his features.

Perhaps a smile would ease his nerves. Talise leaned toward him as they walked. "Cyrus ate three whole meals yesterday. I'm sure he'll be back to himself soon."

Fear stretched across Aaden's face before he gave a hurried nod. "That's what the villagers say as well." He reached for the hilt of his sword as they stepped into the clearing.

River and Claye had arrived early. They stood in the center of the clearing with no way to tell how long they'd been there. River had both arms folded over her chest as she tapped one toe. At the sight of them, Claye's face warped into a glare. His eyes followed Aaden.

Talise knew better than to let either of the young men have a chance to speak first. She pulled the pages from her tunic pocket and waved them in front of the others.

"I did more research. It seems mental fortitude is the key to not letting the amulet control you."

River snatched the pages away and scanned them quickly. Every few seconds, she brought them closer to her face. Her eyes narrowed with a sneer. "These are not pages from the actual journals?"

Shifting on one foot, Talise tried to hold her head high. "No. I copied them from the journals."

One of River's eyebrows shot upward. She stood to her full height, which was a feather taller than Claye. Not quite as tall as Aaden though. "How do we know you copied the words correctly?" River asked as she threw the pages to the ground. "Maybe you wrote the opposite of what the journals said, just so you could sabotage our training."

Talise shook her head but managed to stop herself from rolling her eyes. Mostly, anyway. "I'm doing the same exercises as you, so I wouldn't have any reason to sabotage our training. I'm still not sure exactly what *mental fortitude* means anyway, but I assume it just means we have to focus. Come on, let's all do something with water today."

After wrinkling his nose a little too directly in Aaden's direction, Claye reached into his pocket.

Luckily for River, Talise chose not to comment on how Claye was carrying the amulet. Again. Surely, it indicated how much the Kessoku trusted River. Or more accurately, how much they *didn't* trust her.

With the amulet in his left hand, Claye reached out. The clearing stood several paces from the ocean surrounding the outer ring of Kamdaria. A long ribbon of water slithered from the ocean and toward Claye.

His arms didn't even shake under the weight of the water. Normally, a person could only shape elements slightly heavier than what they could carry with their arms. The power of the amulet must have been at work because Claye carried the long ribbon of water without a single sign of tension in his muscles. The water he now shaped must have been at least twice as heavy as himself.

A tiny gasp escaped Talise's mouth as the ribbon of water transformed into a liquid house. Even made of water, the walls resembled clay, and the roof looked made of tiles. Soon, water bushes formed around the outside edges. Recognition hit Talise just as the final bush erupted. Claye's home.

He held the water sculpture steady for almost a full minute. Even River's eyes had widened by the time he finished. At last, he let the water fall into the soil.

"How did it feel?" Talise's question managed to stop River, whose hand had already started reaching for the amulet.

With a teasing smirk in Talise's direction, Claye ran a hand through his curly black hair. "Much better than last time." Now he stuffed one hand into his tunic pocket. "I did feel like something was missing though. I don't know how to explain it. I just felt like the amulet could do more, but I didn't know how to access it."

Talise nodded and reached for the parchment River had thrown onto the ground. Running a finger over the words, Talise soon found the passage she remembered writing the night before.

The amulet requires full mental commitment to work properly. You must give everything, or you will get nothing.

By the time she finished reading, two figures stood on either side of her. Claye wore an thoughtful stare that had clearly been exaggerated. He peered over her shoulder at the parchment, standing much closer to her than necessary.

And of course, Aaden stood on Talise's other side. His thumb stroked up and down his sword hilt as he stared at everything around them. Every time his eyes went over Claye, his fingers twitched.

Letting out an angry sigh, she pushed them both away. "Why don't you try next, River? You have to focus fully to get the amulet to work."

The corners of River's mouth moved into a frightening grin. Once the amulet met her fingers, the grin turned decidedly wild. First, she pulled the water from the ground that Claye had only just dropped. As it raised into the air, the water formed into a large funnel. It started spinning slowly, but soon, spun fast enough to whip water in every direction.

Splashes erupted from the funnel, landing on dirt, dead trees, and even on their clothing.

One large splash shot through the air until it hit Talise in the face. Rather than fall like it should have, the icy water clung to her skin. Cold liquid crawled into her mouth and slipped down her throat. Another portion of the water moved upward into her nasal cavity. With no warning at all, breathing became impossible. The freezing water blocked off every airway she had.

She couldn't shape the water away. While River used her own shaping to control the element, no one else could wrest control away.

Instead, Talise formed a ball of fire in both her palms and brought them toward her face. She also flooded her veins with fire. Having fire both outside and inside her body quickly evaporated the water away.

Still, her muscles shook as she fought to evaporate the last of the water. If she had just taken a deep breath first, it probably would have been easier. As it was, her arms went limp the moment her airways opened again. It took several gulping breaths before she could stand up straight.

The water funnel had disappeared. Aaden held his sword at River's throat, but she merely glanced at it casually. "Relax." Her hand lazily pointed toward Talise. "She's fine now."

His sword didn't waver as he gave a short glance over his shoulder. Once his gaze met Talise's, his shoulders dropped with relief. But then his jaw flexed hard as he turned toward River again. "You tried to kill her."

River had the audacity to laugh. "I knew she'd be able to resist my attempt to drown her." River cocked one eyebrow up. "But do you think the emperor's soldiers could? Would that method work to defeat them?"

Reaching for her mouth, a hard shiver rocked through Talise. Her body jerked at the horrifying prospect of being drowned while standing in the middle of a clearing.

The muscles in Aaden's arms shook as he pointed his sword at River's throat.

She let out a scoff. "That's why we're here, isn't it? To win this war. Or did you forget why we wanted the amulet?" Her eyes narrowed at Talise. "Did you forget we want your father dead?"

"Give the amulet to Talise." Aaden's voice didn't waver. Each word came out in punctuated bursts. He didn't drop his sword until after she tossed the amulet away.

Even with her heart beating wildly, Talise caught the silver pendant. The moment her fingers touched it, a warm glow flared in her chest.

She needed mental fortitude.

Whatever that meant.

Taking a deep breath, Talise reached out with one hand.

The power of the amulet strummed through her. The glow expanded out from her chest until it entered each of her limbs. Closing her eyes felt natural, but something stopped her. Would closed eyes make her give in to the amulet's power too much? The risk didn't seem worth the help it might give.

Instead, she reached out until she could sense water from the ocean lapping up the nearby shore. With a small flick of her wrist, she raised a large portion of water above the ocean. But she didn't want to bring it toward herself just yet.

The power inside her began to grow. It moved through her, coaxing. Begging. It wanted more from her. As Claye had explained, it felt as if the amulet had much more power than she used at the moment.

But maybe mental fortitude meant resisting the pull.

With outstretched fingers, she let her shaping senses move through the ocean water. Little by little, she identified the salt and other minerals inside the water. Her hand began moving in a sweeping motion. Each time it moved to the side, she pulled water away from the other minerals. After several sweeps, the minerals began falling away from the water and back into the ocean.

Normally, shaping salt out of ocean water took longer, so much longer that almost no one ever did it. With the amulet, Talise completed the process in a few minutes. Once the water had been purified, she couldn't help sending a little heat through it to warm away some of the iciness.

With one final sweep, she slid the water over the earth. Before letting the water fall, she spread it out as far as she could, warming and watering the earth as it went. Soon, water sank into the earth, moistening it as if a long rainfall had just occurred.

The moment she finished, River snapped her fingers at Claye. "Get the amulet back. That was enough of a lesson for today."

Claye bounded forward wearing a grin. "That was amazing," he whispered as he reached Talise. "She's only making us leave because she doesn't like how powerful you're getting." He offered a wink when Talise dropped the amulet into his hand.

"See you next week," he called over his shoulder as both he and River headed toward their horses.

A strange thing happened inside of Talise as she watched his retreating form. Even a few days ago, that wink might have done something to her.

It didn't now.

Instead, when Aaden stepped to her side, her stomach jolted in a delightful mess. His hand formed a fist as he glared across the clearing. "I can't believe she tried to kill you." Even muttering under his breath, the words came out crisp.

An entirely different kind of warmth spread through Talise now. She had managed to fight off River's drowning attempt on her own. A smile played on her lips. But it was nice to know Aaden would have stopped it if she'd been unable to.

She let the feeling warm her for only a moment before thinking back on the journals.

Claye had been right. They were missing something while using the amulet. The power was there, but they needed something more to tap into it.

A memory flitted through her until words burned across her mind.

Be careful who you choose to be. Power will only amplify that choice.

Eben, the guardian of the amulet, had taught Talise many things in her time with him. But those words were still the most poignant. Maybe those words were just what she needed now.

CHAPTER TWENTY-SEVEN

AMULET TRAINING TOOK OVER EVERYTHING.

Talise did little more than study the journals. When the time came to head for the clearing the next week, ideas filled her mind.

Once everyone arrived, she gave a deliberate step forward. "This time, we should try letting emotion fuel our actions."

She didn't want to explain in too much detail. The complexities of what Eben had taught would probably be lost on River anyway. Claye was smart when he wanted to be, but Talise didn't have the energy to explain.

At the heart of it, Talise assumed that who she chose to be had to do with her emotions. So, if power could amplify her choices, it made sense that emotion could tap into the power.

She just had to be careful to not let it overtake her.

At her suggestion, they decided to shape air that day. Claye didn't have much experience with shaping air, but they assumed the amulet would make him proficient enough.

River insisted on going first. She promptly shaped the air out of Talise's lungs.

Talise reached for her throat just as Aaden reached for his sword. But then River's face contorted. So did the rest of theirs. The world went black.

The next thing Talise knew, she lay flat on her back, blinking several times before her sight became clear again. The others lay on the ground next to her, also on their backs. But all of their eyes were closed. A few moments later, River, Claye, and even Aaden came to.

When they got to their feet, River reached for the amulet which now sat on the ground.

Aaden stepped on the silver pendant before River grabbed it. She huffed in response. "I wasn't trying to suck air from *all* our lungs."

"Just Talise's?" Aaden's voice came out scathing.

River ignored him. "I don't know what happened. The amulet took over."

At Talise's urging, Aaden lifted his boot from off the amulet so Claye could pick it up. He wrapped his hand over the silver pendant and closed his eyes.

Claye's shaping formed a tornado that spun with the grace of a dancer. It flitted over the ground, picking up only rocks of a certain size. All seemed well until the tornado began spinning at dangerous speeds. Claye's face contorted as the rocks began shooting all across the clearing. Just before chaos ensued, his eyes shot open.

He sucked in a short breath and threw the amulet from his hand. A shiver rocked him before he finally spoke. "I lost control." While tremors shook though his arm, his head dipped downward. "I'm sorry."

By now, it didn't seem like a good idea to let emotions fuel the shaping actions. Talise wanted to try it for herself to be sure.

With the cool metal in her hand, the same warm glow bloomed in her chest. Her thoughts turned to the cities she had helped in the Storm. Willow and her father filled Talise's mind. Water Festival. The sickness.

Emotions spread through her as she reached her senses into the air. Already, the power of the amulet seemed so much bigger than it had during her last attempt. She could sense all the air like she never had before.

A small pocket of cold air drifted above them near the wall that separated them from the Gate. Based on the wind patterns, she could tell the cold pocket moved toward the Storm. Taking a deep breath, she attempted to shape the wind patterns in a different direction. Perhaps she could get the cold pocket to move toward the Crown instead.

Thinking of the people she wanted to save, the wind patterns bent to Talise's will. But as soon as she seized hold of them, they rocked and rushed. The wind picked up around them until her hair whipped around at ferocious speeds.

Squeezing the amulet, Talise took in a deep breath and let it back out slowly. At her urging, the emotions that had fueled her immediately got replaced by emptiness. Her brain cleared in perfect time with the winds dying down in the clearing.

By the time she opened her eyes, River had already mounted her house, ready to go. Claye took the amulet without a word, and soon, they disappeared.

Aaden gave a subtle glance toward her.

She couldn't help frown. "I'll have to do more research. But first, let's check on Cyrus. Wendy said he walked all the way across the room without help this morning. I want to see if he can do it again."

A WEEK LATER, Cyrus had spent his first night sleeping outside. The sickness had weakened him greatly, but his strength grew every day.

The little clearing they used for amulet training looked the same as it always did as Talise and Aaden entered it. River and Claye stood waiting for them.

This time, they decided to practice shaping earth. Talise also suggested they try removing all emotion from inside before they used the amulet. Only logic would fuel their actions.

Claye turned his face to one of complete calm before he began shaping. Soon, a portion of earth as big as a hill rose from off the ground. He carried it through the air and over their heads. Then, he dropped it down on the opposite side of the clearing.

Though he expertly executed the incredible shaping, he gasped for breath once he had finished. The amulet dropped to the ground. He clutched his knees as heavy pants escaped him. It didn't take long for him to recover. Still… he hadn't needed any recovery after using the amulet the other times.

River stepped toward the amulet. A vein in Aaden's jaw pulsed as he glared at the woman. Though he didn't speak, his threat could be felt in the air.

With a shrug, River plucked the amulet off the ground. "I'll be careful."

Aaden didn't look convinced.

Unsurprisingly, he had every right not to be.

A sink hole formed in the clearing, directly beneath Talise. It swallowed her up immediately. Her heart leapt into her throat as she fell into the earth. Her hands flailed, trying to grasp onto the sides of her prison. But the earth kept sinking at her feet, making it impossible to hold anything.

Aaden's footsteps pounded across the earth above. Noise ensued, but from inside the hole Talise couldn't determine what was going on. When the sink hole stopped growing deeper, she took exactly one breath to ground herself.

Reaching out one hand, Talise shaped foot holes into the sides of the deep sink hole. They held their shape as she used them as a ladder to free herself.

As she climbed out of her prison, she could finally see what had caused the sink hole to stop growing.

Aaden had tackled River. His sword glinted in the sunlight as he took aim for the woman's heart.

"Don't." The word came out of Talise quieter than she intended.

Still, her voice froze Aaden in place as he whipped his head around. At the sight of her, the tension in his face released. The moment gave River just enough time to shove herself free.

But was River... panting? Her face didn't hold the same ferocity it usually did. Instead, exhaustion lined her features. She stepped toward the amulet, which was sitting on the ground.

Aaden let out a stiff scoff as he jumped between her and the amulet. His brandished sword forced to take a step back. He took one glance over his shoulder at Talise. Not a word left his lips, but Talise could see the question in his eyes. He wanted to stop River from ever hurting Talise again. Or anyone. His sword itched to be used.

With a jerk, Talise shook her head.

He frowned with a huff but lowered his sword ever so slightly. Once Talise retrieved the amulet from off the ground, he dropped the sword even more.

With a deep breath, she willed every emotion to leave her mind. Her focus had to stay on logic only.

The glowing that usually accompanied touching the amulet felt more like fire now. It burned within her, across every limb, inside every vein.

Reaching out, her senses found the last bit of earth inside the trees around them. She hadn't expected to find anything, but it turned out the trees were not completely dead after all. Deep in the roots, a bit of earth still remained.

With her eyes open, she let logic rule her actions. Her fingers stretched and prodded until she found nutrients deep within the earth. She pulled them upward toward the tree. Once the nutrients came close enough, the tree roots drank them in.

Talise's shaping didn't stop there.

After more tugging and more prodding, Talise shaped nutrients up through the tree trunk. With each tug, the trunk came alive. By the time she shaped the living earth out to the edge of a branch, a little green bud popped out.

Even as buds popped out along other branches, it still felt like something was missing. The power she had tapped last time when she used emotions was still there. Just unattainable.

With logic only, she had great power, but could she settle for less when she knew greater power existed?

When Talise dropped her arms, she finally noticed the stares around her. River's eyes had never been so wide. Claye shivered, almost with fear. Aaden grinned at the tree like someone who had just discovered sugar.

It hit her then. With no warning at all.

Just like in Eben's garden, the answer had been there all along. Something so simple that shouldn't have taken her so long to understand.

The cups in Eben's garden had been the perfect metaphor for how to use the amulet. Yet, she had ignored them completely.

Balance. Using the amulet required balance. With the cups, she had needed balance between caring for herself and caring for Kamdaria.

With the amulet, she needed balance between emotion and logic. Using one or the other would result in less control or less power. But using both together? That's what she had been missing.

After River and Claye left the clearing, Talise and Aaden began their walk back to camp. His fingers twitched around his sword hilt at even the slightest sounds.

He took a few measured steps before he finally spoke. "At the next training, when it's your turn, why can't you just steal the amulet and run away?"

She raised one eyebrow. "Kessoku has my soldiers."

A slight shrug tipped his shoulder upward. "I'm not sure how that's applicable."

Despite herself, Talise grinned. Mostly because she was certain Aaden *did* know how it applied. He just didn't want to admit it because he didn't want to see her in danger again.

Shaking her head, she smothered the grin. "Knowledge from the journals is the only leverage I have. I *could* steal the amulet, but then Kessoku would kill my soldiers without hesitation."

He had no response. With a huff, he continued stomping forward, probably trying to think of an argument. His silence revealed he had thought of none.

When she spoke again, the slightest tremble accompanied her words. "Thank you for keeping me safe from River."

His feet stumbled, as if he couldn't decide whether to stop or keep going. He gave her a single glance, which warmed her heart with no warning at all. But a moment later, he stared straight forward, a little too focused on the path ahead.

"Of course." A tremor of emotion pierced his words. He cleared his throat. When he spoke again, the words came out even and sharp. "I may have failed you miserably already, but I vowed I would do everything in my power to protect you."

The words brought back a flood of memories. The masquerade ball. The moment her friends realized her true identity. The fight with Kessoku afterward.

Aaden had first declared that vow only moments before their first kiss. Moments before three Kessoku kidnapped her and imprisoned her in a dungeon.

That evening had been the first time Aaden understood why she distrusted him. He finally realized how much his own father had hurt her personally. And she had finally accepted that Aaden couldn't be held responsible for his father's actions.

Despite her insistence that it wasn't necessary, Aaden had vowed to protect her. To right the wrongs of the past. How much had it hurt him to see her kidnapped before his eyes only moments after making that vow?

The muscles in his jaw flexed now as he gave a hard swallow. His voice came out low but as determined as ever. "I don't intend to fail you again."

CHAPTER TWENTY-EIGHT

WITH ANOTHER WEEK CAME ANOTHER training with the amulet. Talise had never felt so prepared. This time, she simply had to balance logic with emotion.

Aaden gripped his sword more vigorously than usual as they headed for the clearing. Talise glanced in his direction, unable to stop the smile that appeared every time he was near. "Why are you so on edge? Are you fidgety because of the sword practice you did with Cyrus? I thought you said his strength was back."

Sucking in a breath, Aaden shook out his shoulders. "It *is* back. I'm not worried about Cyrus." He turned toward her. Their eyes met for only a moment before he jerked his head forward again. "I'm worried about River using fire against you."

The same concern had been niggling in the back of Talise's mind for a few days as well. It might have seemed random that Talise chose to train with water first, then air, and then earth. However, the order had been extremely deliberate. As the most dangerous element, she wanted to train with fire as late as possible.

But the day had finally come. Now River would have the power of the amulet at her disposal while she shaped the most destructive element.

With fear filling her mind, she and Aaden arrived at the clearing. The moment River and Claye came into sight, Aaden drew his sword.

He marched forward and jabbed the blade toward the woman's chest. "I'll kill you if I have to, River. You know that don't you?"

A chuckle left the woman's mouth as she pushed the sword away with the back of her hand. "Why would you need to kill me?" Despite her offhand remark, tension split across her forehead.

Aaden moved the tip of his sword under her chin. "You better be careful."

Claye cleared his throat as he pulled the amulet from his pocket. He stepped closer to Talise with a not-so-subtle grin. "Do you have any new advice for us today?"

Talise's heart still raced at the presence of River, but she tried to make it less apparent when she spoke. "I think balance is the key. We have to let emotion fuel us, but we have to temper it with logic at the same time. I found this lovely quote in one of the journals. It sums everything up the best."

Balance is the greatest enemy to chaos.

She had penned the words on a small piece of parchment. To her surprise, Claye took the paper from her instead of just reading the words. His fingers lingered against hers as he took the page. She could tell it hadn't been an accident, but she chose to ignore it all the same.

As she dropped her hand to her side, she couldn't help glance toward Aaden. His face looked as expressive as a stone, but she *did* manage to notice when a slight clench went through his jaw.

Claye held the paper reverently. After a moment, he looked straight into Talise's eye. "I think you're right. This has to be what we were missing."

With that, he reached out. Sparks flew off his fingertips in a rush. Showers of fire fell from his hand with the force of a waterfall. The fire spread past the clearing and into the brush nearby. The fire grew, engulfing brush and dead trees with almost no effort at all.

Even more interesting, Claye's face didn't give any hint of strain. The fire seemed to grow without exertion. After a few moments, he dropped his hand and the fire vanished.

The moment he finished shaping, color drained from his face. He sucked in a long breath and stumbled on his feet. Only after he sat down on the ground could he breathe normally again.

Without thinking, Talise stepped toward him. "What happened?"

He clutched his chest. "While I was using it, everything felt perfect. I felt like I could finally tap into the power but have control while I used it." He stopped to breathe, which took more effort than it should have. "But once I stopped using the amulet," he gestured over himself, "I'm obviously not doing as well."

After stomping toward Claye, River snatched the amulet from his hand. She shook her head before wrapping her hand over the amulet. "You probably just don't have the strength to do it right."

Whipping her hair behind one shoulder, River raised one hand into the air.

Before she could do anything, Aaden had his sword aimed at her heart. "Remember what I said."

River scoffed. "Calm down. You two said you could heat yourselves from the inside using fire in the veins, right?"

Talise nodded, but Aaden only continued to glare.

With a shrug, River raised her hand back into the air. "That's all I'm going to do."

And she did.

Except River didn't do it to herself. Talise had never once thought to use fire shaping in such a way, but soon fire flooded her own veins. River shaped fire inside *Talise's* veins.

The heat came on so quickly, Talise barely had time to react. Her instincts kicked in, counteracting the intense heat. Since River controlled the fire, Talise could do nothing to shape it away. Instead, Talise sent a thin layer of frost across her skin. The burning inside immediately cooled down to a gentle warmth. Clenching her teeth, she glared at the woman. "I think you forgot how my ice shaping works."

A wrinkle twitched at the edge of River's nose.

Aaden stood stiff for a moment until he glanced at Talise's arm, which was covered in frost. His eyebrows flew up his forehead, and his sword slashed through the air.

His blade slapped against River's wrist, which caused her to drop the amulet. It also split her skin. A drizzle of blood oozed from the wound, though it didn't seem *too* serious.

She yelped and immediately grabbed her wrist. She touched it gingerly before hissing at Aaden. "Can't you be more careful?"

"You can't, so why should I?" Except he didn't look at River when he responded. He stared into Talise's eyes like she was the last thing he'd ever see.

Shaking out her arms, Talise let the frost melt along with the dying heat inside her body. Aaden's quick reaction had stopped River's fire shaping. Talise let out a slow breath before she spoke. "I'm fine."

He didn't look convinced. But by the time Talise reached out for the amulet, she had something new to grab her attention.

The color from River's face had drained. Unlike Claye, she still stood, but it seemed to be a matter of pride not strength. Her chest heaved every time she took in a breath. Her legs shook with the effort of standing. After a wobbly breath, she threw the amulet at Talise.

It flew through the air and Talise only barely caught it before it touched the ground.

The moment it touched her fingers, the familiar glow burned stronger inside her than it ever had. Even without calling on her shaping senses, power pulsed inside her. The amulet seemed not just able but *eager* to give her more strength. More power.

But Talise had trained hard enough to not be intoxicated by it. She took in a deep breath and found the perfect balance between emotion and logic. She drew on her desire to save the people of the Storm. She drew on the painful memories of people dying or losing their shaping.

Emotions stirred within her, but she let logic organize and direct them. Then she set out to do the impossible.

When she and her friends had first discovered the poisoned fish food from the emperor, they tried to destroy it with fire. But the fire had only caused the poison to be released into the air.

At the time, Talise could not create a fire hot enough to burn away the poison. Hopefully, the amulet could change that.

When she reached out, the amulet buzzed in her other hand. It was like the amulet could read her mind, like it knew what was coming. Fire burst from her palm, crawling outward until it burned only on a specific square of earth.

Though she had never attempted it before, she used the same hand that shaped fire to also shape poison up from the soil. In all her years of training, shaping two different elements took two different hands. Or at least, two different parts of the body.

Now, it took no effort at all to do both with one hand. Just as the poison began seeping up from the ground, she noticed the amulet was glowing green in her hand.

Ignoring it, she focused on the poison. She could feel how it drifted among the flames, unchanged by them. Squeezing the amulet, she pushed power into her fire. The orange and red flames immediately turned yellow then white and finally… blue.

It looked just like the fire flowers on the dress she wore to the masquerade ball all those months ago.

When her fire turned blue, it burned through the poison until nothing remained.

It worked.

She had hoped it would, but the success still took her off guard. Now came the real test. How would she feel once she finished shaping? Exhausted like River and Claye?

Using as much restraint as she could muster, Talise turned the flames back to orange and then slowly shrunk them down to nothing. At the end, she released her grip on the amulet and let it sit on her open palm.

The green glow it emanated had softened, but it was still faintly there. Waiting lasted too long. She kept holding her breath without meaning to and then had to breathe in twice as much. But nothing changed.

She waited more.

Still, nothing changed. Her breathing, her strength, all of it seemed normal. If anything, she felt even more charged after using the amulet. When she looked up, the others were staring at her.

Claye's head tilted to the side. "Why doesn't it drain you the way it does for us? And why was it glowing like that?"

Before anyone else could move, River snatched the amulet from Talise's hand. She yanked Claye by the arm and pulled him toward their horses.

The questions plagued Talise. Even as River and Claye disappeared she wondered why and how and what did it mean?

But along with her strength, her determination was more charged than ever. She whipped around to face Aaden, who stared at her without a word. A smile quirked onto her face. "We've been teaching the Storm citizens basic shaping to help them survive. They need that… but maybe I can teach them combat shaping that will help them defend themselves too." The smile grew. "It's all about balance."

CHAPTER TWENTY-NINE

STANDING IN FRONT OF A crowd got more natural each time it happened.

After living in the Storm, and then hiding her identity at the elite academy for years, Talise had never had any typical training for her role as princess. But months in the Gate and in the Storm had taught her more than any type of palace training could have.

She didn't just know how to speak to the people. She knew the people.

The eyes that stared back at her were less hollow than they had been when she first arrived. Sickness had swept through the city thanks to the recent air storm, but everyone had mostly recovered by now.

When she offered to teach them shaping that would better their lives, no one even thought to question the idea.

Now she stood in front of the crowd, calling on the training she had recently done with the amulet. Using it had made her feel more in tune with shaping. Hopefully, she'd be a better teacher because of it.

"Here's how you shape nutrients up from deep in the earth." Her fingers pointed downward, as if digging. "The actual movement you use isn't as important as your intention. It's like holding a hammer. Some people might use a slightly different grip than you use, but as long as you have the same end result, it still works."

In front of her, many heads nodded. Most of them stared at her intently, but a few stared at the earth beneath their feet.

Pinching her fingers together, Talise picked away the nutrients that she needed. "Once you identify the nutrients in the soil, use your shaping to pick them away. Only do small bits at a time and keep working until you have a little clump of the nutrients."

It took a few minutes, but soon Talise pulled the nutrient clump through the soil and up into the air. "Once you pull it above the surface, just mix it with a pot full of soil. It will be ready to grow any type of plant."

Dumbfounded expressions stared back at her. Maybe a smile would encourage them. "It will take some time before you can complete the process as quickly as I just did. But practice will help you get a little faster every time. And don't worry if you accidentally snatch a little extra soil along with your nutrients. It won't hurt to have it." She waved a hand out over the crowd. "You may begin."

Not one look of confidence covered the faces in front of her. Still, they lifted their hands and attempted to follow her instructions. They'd been learning how to identify the nutrients for the past few weeks. Now, she was eager for them to shape the nutrients out of the soil, so they could take care of themselves without her constant help. She weaved through the crowd as they attempted the new technique. She answered questions and corrected misconceptions as she went.

When a few hours had passed, several of the citizens managed to shape tiny crumbs of nutrients up from the soil. Hopefully, it wouldn't take long before they could do more.

Glancing over the city, Talise glanced at each of her friends, who taught other shaping techniques that would help Storm citizens. Purifying water, starting fires, even using walls of wind to protect against storms.

Once again, the oddity of teaching earth hit Talise. When they taught the citizens by the Ember Gate how to use shaping to defend themselves, Claye had taught earth, Tempest water, Wendy air, and Talise had taught fire.

Now Talise taught earth and Aaden taught fire. As before, Rio and Fyra focused on non-shaping techniques.

Spinning on her heel, Talise addressed the crowd again. "Great work, everyone. We will practice again tomorrow. Just for fun, let's try another technique that will hone your shaping skills. Why don't we try lifting and throwing rocks? It will help you get used to shaping earth."

No one seemed to notice how the technique would be perfect in combat. Though she had decided to ask citizens of the Storm to fight for her, that had been many weeks ago. When the air storm hit, the decision lost urgency. She still fully intended to ask the people to fight for her… just not yet. She'd wait to do it until it was necessary. By then, the citizens would already know several combat shaping techniques thanks to her frequent trainings with them.

Using earth shaping, she passed rocks to each person in her group. When her hand moved up and down, the rock in front of her did too. She raised it until it hovered high above her head and then she slammed it toward the ground with as much velocity as she could manage.

The faces in the crowd changed in an instant. Their eyes widened at how quickly the rock shot down. Would they recognize the technique as one that could be used in war? Maybe. Hopefully they only saw it as a means to protect themselves if necessary.

Though finding nutrients and minerals in soil was just as vital to their survival, the citizens shaped the rocks with much more vigor. Each time a rock slammed against the ground, another person seemed to be instilled with the idea that they could finally help themselves.

And that was just what she wanted.

They still didn't know much about the war or Kessoku. How much better would they take the news once they were armed with shaping techniques to defend themselves? War wouldn't seem so bad if they had the ability to fight.

Faces turned red as the citizens shaped and threw their rocks. Most of them had never shaped any elements until very recently. Their movements came jerky and unstable, but that didn't stop them. Since most of them had never shaped before, they weren't hindered by the illusion that they had to do things a certain way. Instead, they tried and tried with no embarrassment over their failed attempts.

After another hour or so, the citizens finally began dispersing to go eat their dinners.

Before Talise could join her other friends, Ash came forward with his daughter, Willow, at his side. He swept a piece of hair out of his face. "Willow told me you know how to throw a dagger."

Talise grinned at the girl, who was now standing tall. "That's right. I showed her the other day."

"She said you use shaping to help you aim." Ash tentatively pulled a dagger from his pocket. Rust speckled the blade, but the handle still looked strong and sturdy. "Could you show me how to do it?"

A lurch went through Talise's stomach. She preferred to teach subtler defensive techniques. Then again, she didn't want anything to happen to Willow or her father. They deserved to know how to protect themselves.

With a short nod, Talise grabbed her own dagger from inside her tunic pocket. The familiar flame carvings decorated the handle, looking as fierce and as beautiful as the day she had first touched the dagger.

Ash sucked in a gasp. He pointed to a mark on the side of the blade. "Was this made by Aritsan Graund? My wife had a knife made by him, but we had to sell it for food many years ago."

"Um." Talise rubbed a thumb over the mark while biting her lip. Could she admit that the dagger hadn't originally belonged to her?

"It's just like you described, Papa." Willow brought her face close to the dagger to examine the mark. "This must be a family heirloom. Didn't you say Mama told you how Artisan Graund's work is the best in Kamdaria. No one would willingly part with such a treasure."

A *treasure?* Talise's gut writhed at the words. Aaden had given her the dagger, but maybe he hadn't meant for it to be permanent. After a hard swallow, she shoved the thoughts away. "Let me demonstrate the technique. You'll have to practice once I show it to you, but it will get easier to more you practice."

By the time Talise finished with Willow and her father and returned to camp, guilt churned in her stomach. Rio and Cyrus huddled over a pot of food, both adding last minute items to it. Fyra gathered the bowls and spoons everyone needed. Wendy and Tempest worked together to purify water for them to drink.

Even though Aaden was busy preparing the sleeping mats for everyone, Talise caught his eye. She beckoned him to join her on a long log that they typically used for seating during meals. He gave a quick glance at the others around them before sitting by her side.

She pulled the dagger from her pocket. It hurt to do it, though she couldn't explain why. Maybe just because that dagger had been there through a lot of things. It had helped her when she needed help, and it had been there when Aaden wasn't.

But if it was truly as valuable as Willow and her father suggested, she didn't have much right to keep it anymore.

A sigh left her lips as she pushed the flame-carved hilt toward Aaden. "I probably should have given this back to you a long time ago."

He stared at it for several seconds before looking into her eyes. Despite the movement of his eyes, his hands remained clasped together in his lap, making no movement toward the dagger. His expression gave away nothing as he stared.

She shifted in her seat and moved the dagger even closer to him. "It's yours."

His eyes flicked to the flame carvings in the hilt before he met her eyes once again. "No, it's not."

She felt her eyebrows pinch together. "Yes, it is. You gave it to me when I escaped that Kessoku dungeon in the summer."

He gave a deliberate nod. "Exactly. I *gave* it to you. It's yours now."

Her finger brushed over the swirl design that Ash had pointed out. "But wasn't this made by Artisan Graund?"

Aaden reached for his chin, rubbing a hand over the facial hair. "Yes. Artisan Graund made it before I was born. The workmanship is impeccable though. It should last centuries."

A jolt ripped through her. *Before* he was born? If the dagger had been made before Aaden was even born, then it *must* have been a family heirloom.

She pushed the hilt closer to him as she turned her eyes away. "You have to take it back. I never should have kept it for so long. It's probably a family heirloom, and I've just been using it and carrying it every—"

"I'm not taking your dagger." Aaden had a way of speaking that made it impossible to argue. His hands remained clasped in his lap as steady as ever. He stared ahead with his usual expression that revealed absolutely nothing.

But then, a slight break in his mask opened up. His eyes flicked toward her while the faintest of smiles played on his lips. "I gave it to you on purpose. I want you to have it."

He stood and walked away before she could stop him. The guilt remained, but it was joined now by a hot current that sparked through her veins. How could she say *no* to that?

CHAPTER THIRTY

THE NEXT DAY, TALISE TOOK Wendy to gather more water for their group.

With each step, Talise's feet dragged across the frozen soil. Her heart pounded hard while every muscle in her face drooped.

A soft giggle escaped Wendy's mouth before she could clap a hand over it. When she lowered her hand a moment later, her face had been overtaken by a look of innocence. "Aaden will be back tomorrow evening. He's just traveling to the Gate to get us more food."

Talise snapped her head up with a start. "I know that." She tossed her hair over one shoulder and took more deliberate steps. "I was just wondering if he'd bring that awful smoked fish again, or if he'll actually have good smoked meat this time."

Wendy had to pull her lips between her teeth to keep her smile from growing. "Oh, I *know* that's all you were thinking about."

Heat burned through Talise's cheeks as she flashed a hard look in her best friend's direction.

A tiny chuckle escaped, but then Wendy pointed toward the river ahead. "Have we seen that group before?"

They had seen many groups in the Storm, usually ones that caused chaos and havoc everywhere they went. The crimes only stemmed from hunger and desperation in most cases though. Those groups were usually small and efficient. Each person had a job, and each person did it well.

So, when Talise glanced across the river, it took her by surprise to see a large group of two dozen citizens gathered. No one stood at the head of the group, at least not anyone she could see. No wagons or wares sat among the citizens. They didn't even seem to be trading weapons or food.

Something deep in her gut stirred, which brought fear slithering through her limbs. Trying to temper the feeling, she shrugged. "I haven't seen a group that large, but I'm sure it's fine."

Despite trying to convince herself she had no reason to worry, she had still found it necessary to point out that everything was fine. If that were true, she probably wouldn't have thought to point it out.

Wendy fluffed her hair and donned her sweetest smile. "Come on. We'll find out what's going on in no time."

The closer they stepped to the river, the more harrowing the feelings inside Talise got. It didn't make any sense to be afraid. Fearing a group of people like that was something the emperor would do. Wasn't that why he had poisoned the Storm? To decrease the numbers of citizens and thus make them less of a threat? To make them dependent on him.

Fearing people before meeting them did no good at all.

No matter how Talise tried to convince herself of those words, each step toward the group still felt like danger.

She tried to adopt the same demeanor Wendy conveyed. Even if the group *was* dangerous, they would probably be less dangerous if the two of them approached with their hands behind their backs and their eyelashes fluttering.

Eventually, they moved close enough to hear mutterings from the crowd. "We can't go on like this, but who says we have to?" "Maybe we can break through the wall, or maybe we can dig under it." "We have to get food from people in the Gate so we finally have enough to eat. Why should they have more food than us anyway?"

Tension continued to rock inside Talise as she and her best friend moved closer to the river. She couldn't blame the citizens for having such thoughts. But the ideas weren't perfectly sound either. People in the Gate suffered too. Maybe not as much as people in the Storm, but they didn't have plenty of extra food like the conversation implied.

When she and Wendy got to the water, the crowd had noticed them. Their whispers stopped and their stares hardened. But it didn't end there.

A woman pressed through the crowd until she stood at the front of it. She had soft eyes and a gentle smile that could probably make anyone trust her. She almost looked like…

"Aunt Avery." Despite Wendy's calm demeanor, a quiver shook through her voice. "What are you doing in the Storm?"

The woman's soft eyes dropped to the ground as her shoulders hunched forward. After only a moment, she gave her head a little shake and stood tall. "Everyone deserves a chance to improve their life, especially citizens from the Storm."

But the conversation implied more than just improving life. It implied fighting. Revenge. Who had taught the group that such things would solve their problems?

A moment later, the answer became clear. With eyes flashing with wildness, River stood up tall. Her jaw clenched.

The air stilled around Talise. Each breath and flutter of wind paused as the meaning of the words took hold. Buzzing ignited through Talise's arms while she tried to formulate a response. An argument. Anything.

Instead, her body took over and forced her to do what she had been dying to do since the moment she first saw the crowd.

She ran away.

Tears pricked at her eyes as she turned her back on the crowd. Her feet flew over the dirt while frigid clouds of dust puffed around her. Jerky movements caused her to scratch her cheeks when she was only trying to swipe tears away.

The pounding of her feet landed hard, but not nearly as hard as the pounding of her heart.

It wasn't until she moved past a clump of dead trees that she finally slowed to a walk. A few minutes later, Wendy caught up with panting breaths.

Wendy's features had fallen. Now *her* feet dragged across the soil. "I know we saw my aunt and uncle at the base by the Ember Gate after we escaped, but I forgot. I forgot they were working for Kessoku."

Talise gulped, which did absolutely nothing to improve the situation. "Kessoku is trying to build an army with people from the Storm." The words cracked as they came out. Even worse, River led the charge.

Wendy was breathing too hard to offer any response.

Squeezing her eyes shut, Talise punched several fireballs onto the ground ahead. The fireballs sizzled away once they met the frosty ground. She huffed at the sight. "I should have started already. I knew I should have built an army with people from the Storm, but I put it off. I thought I had all this time."

She dug both palms into her eyes, letting an explosion of stars fill the inside of her eyelids.

A gentle touch came to her forearm. "It's not too late." Wendy's voice came out as steady and sweet as ever. "Based on what we just heard, I don't think Kessoku has been here long. You'll just have to do what you can starting now."

Talise dropped her hands to her sides as an involuntary whimper let her lips. "But what *can* I do? What can I offer the people?"

One of Wendy's rare smirks graced her face. "You're the princess of Kamdaria."

Rubbing a hand across her forehead, Talise grimaced. "Kessoku has food. Why would starving people choose a princess over food?"

"Then give them hope." Wendy reached for a chunk of her hair and began twirling it around one finger. "Give them something to fight for that is better than revenge."

The words offered only a smidgeon of comfort. It might work, but it would have worked better if Talise hadn't waited.

Her thoughts turned to the amulet training that would take place in a few days. Maybe Aaden had been right. Maybe playing along and keeping leverage didn't matter anymore. Perhaps the time had come to steal the amulet and run away. What could River do if Talise had the amulet anyway?

Warmth sparked in her chest and spread throughout the rest of her. She had expected Kessoku to betray her at some point, but maybe she needed to betray them first.

Once she had the amulet, she would have a lot more to offer the people than just hope.

It was settled.

When training day arrived, she'd steal the amulet.

※

Chapter Thirty-One

Icy air bit into Talise's skin as she woke from her slumber.

Just like every morning, she sent a flood of fire through her veins to stave off the chill of sleeping outside. Her fingers groaned as she stretched the cold out of them.

Even lying near a large fire with plenty of fuel each night, the winter air managed to freeze everyone by morning.

Tilting her body upward the least possible amount, Talise opened one eye with the intention of shooting a fireball at the dying embers in the fire pit. Instead, she gasped and sat up straight.

A figure stood in the shadows on the other side of camp.

Her gasp came out loud enough to make everyone in the group stir. Aaden reached for his sword and jolted to an upright position. He always did that when a sound woke him. Tempest groaned at the sounds, but once she saw the standing figure, her face turned to stone.

Rio moved first. The soldier in him clearly made his movements automatic. But he probably had less emotional reason to be angry at the person standing in front of them. Rio lifted his own sword from the ground but kept the tip pointed downward. "What are you doing here, Claye?"

Claye bristled at the question. Even in the shadows, his reaction was easy to see. His features tightened, but then a casual calm took over. When he shrugged, it felt like a normal day at the elite academy. How had things gone so wrong?

Before he could open his mouth, Tempest jumped out of her bed and ran forward just to jab Claye in the chest. "I have a more important question. How did you find us?"

Now he rolled his eyes.

Everyone else began standing up. The glares directed at Claye only hardened by the second, except for Wendy's. She wore a calm smile that somehow, looked even more dangerous than a glare.

After another glance at everyone, Claye let out a scoff and ran his fingers through his hair. "I found your camp weeks ago. It was on one of my trips into the Storm, which by the way, I take quite regularly."

Aaden didn't say a word, but his jaw was clenched so tight it looked painful. He gripped his sword hard enough that his knuckles turned white. His movements had been slow enough to not draw attention, but Talise wasn't surprised when his shoulder bumped up against hers.

"Does River know where we are?" Talise's voice croaked as she spoke.

A pained expression worked through Claye's features. "Of course not. You really think I'd put you in danger like that?"

Her stomach churned at the question. He could act noble all he wanted, but he already *had* put her life in danger like that. Many times, in fact.

He tucked one foot behind his leg and looked to the ground.

"You didn't answer the question. *How* did you find us?" Wendy's dulcet tone had just enough sharpness to feel more like dagger stabs than words.

Claye let out a scoff and rolled his eyes again. "You really think it was that hard? Haven't you already figured out I'm pretty amazing at looking stupider and less intimidating than I really am? All I did was find a city in the Storm and then I went off about how, Oh the princess is so amazing. Can you believe she's actually here in the Storm? I heard she can do incredible things, but I haven't met her yet. I'm dying to meet her. Do you know where she is?" He shrugged. "It took me less than two days to find your camp. I never tried approaching you before because I thought you would all still be too mad at me."

Cyrus let out a snort as he moved closer to his sister. "At least you were right about one thing."

"Why *are* you here?" Fyra's face turned pink when the words came out. It was almost like she was more surprised than anyone that she had actually spoken. Even more surprising, the question hadn't been full of wrath or spite like everyone else's. Instead, she seemed genuinely curious.

The inquiry caused Claye to let out a sigh. "It's about the amulet."

Aaden inched even closer to Talise.

Claye rubbed a hand over his face. "It doesn't work anymore."

Despite the writhing anger inside her, the statement managed to quirk one of Talise's eyebrows upward. "You mean you get too tired after using it that you can't use it at all now?"

"No." Claye pinched the hair on one of his eyebrows. "I mean it doesn't work. When River and I try to use it, our shaping is exactly the same as it without the amulet."

Just as Tempest finished braiding her waist-length hair, she let out a huff. "Are you sure you have the *right* amulet? Maybe someone betrayed you by switching out the real one with a fake."

Claye scowled at her before turning back to the rest of them. "Yes, I'm sure. I helped make the fake, remember? I can tell the difference between them." He shook his head. "Something happened the last time we used it."

Aaden barely parted his lips, but his words came out heavy. "You mean when it started glowing green?"

Even though Claye nodded at the question, he glanced toward the opposite side of camp rather than making eye contact with Aaden. "We talked to some of the soldiers who were in that garden when Talise first got the amulet. They said it glowed green then as well." His hands dropped to his sides as he let out a sigh. He looked Talise in the eye. "We think you're bonded to the amulet somehow. When you finally figured out how to use it correctly, we think it recognized you as the person who retrieved it." He shrugged. "And now it will only work for you."

Talise tilted her chin in the air. "What does that mean? Did you come to give it to me since it will only work for me now?"

A chuckle left Claye's mouth, but nothing about it spoke of humor. "No. It means Kessoku is coming to kill you. You need to move camp immediately."

The words pierced her heart like nothing else had that morning. The strong desire to reach for Aaden's hand came over her. He stood close enough. It wouldn't take much effort to reach him. Holding onto him felt like the only thing that could ground her in a moment like this. But fear froze her limbs too completely to even reach for that small bit of comfort.

Stuffing both hands into his tunic pockets, Claye stared at the ground. "Once they find out I came to warn you, they'll want to kill me too." He gulped. "I was hoping I could stick with your group for a while."

"No." Aaden spoke, but his answer was mirrored on almost everyone's face.

Everyone except Fyra. Her eyebrows pinched together. "But they'll kill him if he gets caught. We're lucky he warned us, or they could have killed us all. We should help him."

She was right. Everyone *knew* she was right. But even without speaking to each other, it was clear they all hated the idea.

Claye stood a little taller. "You should probably start packing. The Kessoku don't know where you are, but they have a lot of spies in the Storm. It probably won't take them long to find you. And Talise?" He swallowed. "Can I please talk to you? Alone?"

She blinked twice before the question registered. All at once, she remembered the green Forces tablet that sat at the bottom of her pack. She had found it the day before after digging for a clean pair of socks.

"Yes." Near their camp, a large dead tree stood near a fallen log. It had provided the perfect place for conversations throughout their time in the Storm. Thanks to a natural dip in the earth, it also blocked sounds, making the conversations private. She waved her hand in that direction. "Go behind that tree by the fallen log. I just have to get something, but I'll be right there."

Her knees landed on the ground before anyone could protest. Maybe the others thought it careless, but this was something she had to do. Once she secured the green tablet in her palm, she dashed over behind the dead tree where Claye waited for her.

He had been sitting on the log, but he immediately stood at the sight of her. Color burst into his cheeks as a wide grin spread across his face.

She took a deep breath. Whatever he wanted out of this conversation didn't matter to her in the slightest. She'd say what she needed to say and then she'd leave.

When she held her hand out toward him, he reached out eagerly.

His face fell once he realized what she had dropped into his palm. He frowned at the green Forces tablet and pushed his hand toward her. "I still want you to keep this."

"I don't want it." The entire experience had only given her a few minutes to rehearse the words in her mind, but apparently, she didn't need any more than that. The words came out abrupt and short. They didn't allow for argument.

His lips tightened into a straight line before he spoke again. "My parents are Kessoku. They helped found Kessoku. I've been Kessoku practically since the day I was born. When they asked me to spy on you, I didn't have a choice. Family is everything in Kamdaria. I couldn't refuse my parents."

Her nose wrinkled. "Did you even *try* to convince them not to kill me?"

He reached for his forehead, rubbing it harder with each word. "Talise, I really do love you. I promise. But I also believe in our cause. I *wanted* to help Kessoku."

"Oh, I know how much you believe it, Claye."

"Are you still mad?"

Her eyes fell closed while a sigh of complete and utter disbelief fell from her lips. "*Mad* doesn't even begin to cover how I feel." She let out a hot breath, but it didn't compare to the heated rage inside her. "You lied to me constantly, about your shaping skills, about your beliefs. Even worse, you tried to kill me."

Both of his hands raised in surrender. "I did not. I—"

"You *said*—" Her jaw clenched tight. "When we were in Kessoku's base by the Ember Gate, you said you helped the Kessoku escape after the masquerade ball. Do you remember the masquerade ball? Do you remember what happened after the Kessoku were free?" She stomped forward. "They *kidnapped* me. If Aaden hadn't rescued me when he did, they would have killed me."

Claye gulped, trying to step backward as fast as he could. "That wasn't what—"

"You found out I was the princess earlier that night. That means, they only kidnapped me because you helped them escape *and* you told them who I was."

An attempt at a smile spread over Claye's features. "But you got away, didn't you?"

She let out a chuckle that made him cower. "And what about when the Kessoku found us by the River Gate? You made me believe Wendy was the traitor. You tried *so* hard to convince me to go hide in the elite academy. But why, Claye? Was there a band of Kessoku waiting to ambush me there? Is that why you were so upset when I decided to go to Tempest's house instead?"

A tree kept him from backing up anymore. His lack of response gave all the answer she needed.

Hard puffs escaped from her nose. "And what about by the Smoke Gate? I thought Aaden had followed me to the garden when I retrieved the amulet, but I realized the truth. You could have followed me any of the days before. Remember the day when you gave me candy and a pouch of water? You probably followed me that day so that you could lead Kessoku right to me when they came. I almost died the night Kessoku attacked the garden, and it would have been your fault."

Claye tugged at his collar. "I told you. It's only because I didn't know you back then."

"Funny." She tilted her head with a mocking smile. "I've known you as long as I've known Wendy. I kind of thought our five years of friendship would have been enough time to not want me dead."

He blinked at her, apparently at a loss for words.

Taking a steady breath, Talise stepped away from him. She shook out her arms and marched over the ground to calm the trembling that ran through her. After several deep breaths, she faced him again. "You can stay with us, but don't attempt to have a private conversation with me again."

His eyebrows lowered. His arms drooped at his sides. Even the color in his cheeks looked duller than before. "But I love you. What am I supposed to do?"

She let out a scoff and began heading back to camp. "Go pretend to be in love with someone else. You'll probably fall for her too."

Chapter Thirty-Two

TALISE STOMPED BACK TO CAMP, but she couldn't deny a perk lined her steps.

Something inside her chest felt lighter than it had in months.

Rio sat on a log on the other side of camp with his head buried in their map of Kamdaria. Fyra kept her head down, rolling up sleeping mats and putting away loose socks. Wendy brushed her hair with a little too much attention on the ground in front of her. Though they had all definitely heard Talise coming, they acted as if they didn't notice her.

Except for Tempest. The soldier leaned back against a log and stared. She twirled the end of her braid with an expectant gaze.

Talise glanced over the makeshift beds of their camp and the glowing coals in the firepit. Her eyes flitted out past camp, but that didn't provide any answers either.

"Where's Aaden?" The question came out perhaps a little too passionate.

Tempest gave an obvious smirk and glanced toward Wendy.

Wendy continued to brush her hair as if nothing significant had happened. "He and Cyrus are doing a perimeter check. Aaden wanted to make sure no other Kessoku are here."

"Good." Talise gave a stiff nod. Could everyone see her disappointment? "Rio?"

His head popped up from the map. "I already have a place in mind for us to go next. We'll have to cross the ocean twice, but with your ice shaping, it should be doable. Then we can hide in a city by the River Gate. But on the Storm side."

Sitting down, Talise found her boots and began shoving them on. "Excellent. Tempest?"

The soldier abandoned her position against the log and moved closer to the fire. "I'll make us a quick breakfast. Something we can eat while we're traveling."

Talise nodded as she tied off her boots. "Perfect. Wendy, you're coming with me into the city. I have to say goodbye before we go."

Wendy dropped her brush into a pack and began putting on her own boots. "I'll be ready in just a minute."

Talise stood and faced the last member of their group. Footsteps approached while she spoke. "Fyra, I want you to pack up the rest of camp with Claye."

Based on the footsteps, Claye had just appeared from behind the dead tree.

A highly audible groan left Tempest's lips as she dug through a nearby pack. "Really?" she muttered under her breath.

"Claye is staying." Talise whipped around to glare at him. "But all of us are going to keep a *very* close eye on you."

He responded with a signature smirk. "I'll win you back eventually."

Talise rolled her eyes and turned away. "Come on, Wendy. We need to hurry."

Despite her hope for it, they didn't run into Aaden on their way to the city. She still had plenty of time to talk to him. Pulling him aside after a meal or while traveling would be easy. But that didn't change how her heart longed to have the conversation immediately.

She wasn't sure how to tell him that yes, she had needed time, but she didn't anymore. That she loved how his strengths complemented her own. That his very presence had a way of making her better. Even when he argued with her, he only did it to help her see things she already knew but didn't want to admit, or occasionally to help her see a different perspective. But he never argued with the express intent to change her mind. She wanted to be with him not just now but always.

But since, they *hadn't* run into him, they just entered the city instead. Her gut did all sorts of flips as she walked. Though, the Kessoku were on their way to kill her, she knew the flips had nothing to do with it. Why did waiting have to be so hard?

They continued into the city, heading for Willow's home. Despite the early hour, a few people stood on the other side of town getting water from the well. The creaks and footsteps of early morning filled the houses. When they arrived at Willow's home, it was no different.

The young girl welcomed them inside before she plopped onto a rug to put on a pair of thick socks. "Papa went to get vegetables for everyone from our glass house. He said he might be awhile if the plants need extra tending."

Wendy managed to give a gracious nod before she glanced expectantly toward her friend.

Suddenly, the flips in Talise's stomach turned to clomps. Her chest constricted under the weight of the words she prepared to say. Swallowing, she looked at the window.

"I have some news."

Even from the side of her eye, Talise could see how quickly Willow's head snapped up. Her face had gone slack. "What is it?" A strain twisted through her words, giving away the bravery it took to speak them as well as the fear lingering inside. How had the girl known the news would be bad?

Talise's lip began trembling all at once. "We have to leave. We never should have stayed in one spot so long anyway, but we liked it so much and—"

"But why?" Willow's eyes shimmered as she looked up. "I know you're the princess and you want to help other cities too, and you have. But you mean that you aren't going to come back this time, don't you?"

The hem of Talise's tunic twisted between her fingers as she sought the right words. "We might come back if…"

When her words trailed off, Wendy gave her a little nudge. Talise looked at her best friend. Wendy returned to look with a solemn nod.

Maybe it was because they had been friends so long, but Talise knew exactly what Wendy wanted to communicate. Or maybe it was just that Talise already knew what she needed to say. They both knew. That group of people they saw by the river the other day had made it clear. It was time to recruit some Storm citizens.

A hard swallow wriggled down Talise's throat. "The truth is…"

This time, hesitation didn't stop her words. Instead, a loud commotion outside diverted all their attention.

Wendy inched closer to the door. "Maybe we should see what that noise is all about."

Once Talise nodded at the suggestion, Wendy ducked her head outside.

It didn't take long to understand what was happening. A small band of citizens waved rusted weapons around wildly. Two men and a woman flashed their teeth at anyone who dared glance their way.

While they waved their weapons about, a man crashed out of a nearby house holding a bag of grains. He joined their group and showed off his own blade. Another woman joined them after she jumped out of the doorway of a house down the street. She carried an armful of firewood under one arm and a bag of vegetables in the other.

Under other circumstances, Talise might have tried to talk first. But her emotions were already heightened and sparking, so she acted on instinct alone. A strong blast of wind burst from her palm. It shot against the bag of vegetables, which the woman involuntarily dropped.

Wendy shot her own blast of wind. It moved in the shape of a sideways funnel. The tip of the funnel bored against a man's hand until he lost his grip on the bag of grains.

When one of the rusty daggers flipped through the air toward them, Talise blasted it away with a shot of air.

Talise and Wendy moved down the street blasting air and frightening the small band until they began to run. Maybe an air storm had brought sickness through the city, but it was nothing like the air storm raining down on that group of citizens now.

They were just hungry. Talise knew that in her heart, but after working so hard to help Willow's city, she couldn't bear to see them hurt again. Not after what the sickness had done.

Talise's feet swept across the frosted ground. Air balls and funnels and whips of wind hit the small group. They ran faster with each step, but not fast enough to escape the shaping.

As they rounded a corner, they began shouting and growling. They threw daggers and rocks, anything they could get their hands on. Talise and Wendy deflected everything with ease.

When the glass house came into view, everyone in the group snarled, angrier than ever. Talise knew what they would do a moment too late. She could see in her mind's eye exactly how things would play out, but she didn't have the speed to stop it. Her gut clenched. Her fingers tensed, trying to shape the rocks away. To stop them.

She failed.

Two members of the group had plucked large rocks off the ground. They clutched the stones, as if waiting for the perfect opportunity to use them.

While Talise spent her energy attacking them, she had been too absorbed to notice when two of the citizens glanced at each other. By the time the rocks flew, they were nearly at their destination before Talise realized what they would hit.

That's when the glass shattered. Every wall in her carefully crafted glass house burst into thousands of pieces. The shards flipped and twisted through the air almost too swiftly to see. Even worse, most of the glass shot down inside the glass house.

Right where Ash stood.

His wretched cry sent a yank through Talise's gut. The man dropped to his knees as he cried out a second time. Blood was already beginning to drip down the backs of his hands when he brought them over his face.

More rocks flew. Then a dagger.

Even running at top speed Talise couldn't get there fast enough. A man yanked away the bag of food at Ash's feet. A woman pulled a rusty dagger from her tunic.

Talise shot a funnel of wind at the dagger. Wendy threw an air whip. Neither hit their mark soon enough to make any difference. The blade pierced through Ash's chest like butter. By the time the air funnel and whip hit the woman, the dagger had already gone deep enough that only the hilt remained visible.

The woman ran.

But how could Talise do anything about it when Willow's father had blood gushing from his heart?

No amount of breathing would ever calm the hysterics roiling through Talise. She reached for Ash, desperate to find some sign of life. Her mind went back to the man who carried his wife closer to a fire because he refused to believe she had died.

Talise knew there was no hope left. She *knew* he was already gone. But her hands checked for a breath anyway. She knelt at his side, bloodying her clothes, her hands, even her face. But what difference would a little blood make when nothing would change what had happened?

Wendy sobbed at her side. Talise only realized it when she saw her friend's face. The sound hadn't alerted her. Perhaps it was the shaking. Or maybe it was just the pain that hung in the air.

It was too late.

It was too late, and Talise didn't know what to do. How to go on.

But then a whimper sounded, and time stopped altogether.

"Papa?"

Even the group of citizens running away stopped in place. They glanced between Willow and the bloody man at Talise's side. They glanced at each other. And then they got a look in their eyes.

Their feet lifted, as if to run.

But they couldn't.

Fire burned across the frozen ground in a flash. It encircled each member of the group, warming the winter air at the same time. They stood rooted the ground, unable to move unless they wanted to burn some limb or another.

Heat seared through Talise, but it had nothing to do with the fire. Her boots crunched over shards of glass. She shaped fire around the group while crowds of people from the city closed in.

A reverent silence filled the air as the incoming crowd recognized what had occurred. Someone had gathered Willow into their arms. Quiet sobs were the only thing audible in the near silence.

Talise stood to her fullest height and gulped over a lump that filled her throat. Deep within her stomach, a heaviness brought weight and strength to her words. The fire helped to gain attention, but her voice alone forced everyone to listen.

"Kamdaria is at war."

If possible, the weight in the air deepened. She sucked in a breath, letting her chest rise and fall slowly. Her eyes moved from the group of attackers to Willow's dead father and then to the rest of the citizens. Involuntarily, she shook her head. "You fight each other when you shouldn't even be enemies. Your land has been poisoned, your food supply diminished. Stop hurting the people who are just as broken as you."

Everyone blinked back at her. They froze when she mentioned *poison,* but they shivered at the rest of her words.

Now for the truth she had too long avoided. In her effort to help the citizens, she had unwittingly become like the very person she needed to defeat. Secrets and lies had been her way of life for years. She had kept the truth from the people for too long. This was the reminder she needed.

Secrets did nothing but hurt. It was time for the truth to be revealed.

CHAPTER THIRTY-THREE

WITH FISTS CLENCHING, TALISE KEPT the fire burning around the small group of citizens who had attacked. Willow knelt at her father's side. Her quiet whimpers filled the air.

But nothing had silenced the people like Talise's words had. Everyone stared at her with gaping mouths. They knew the word *war*, but they didn't believe Kamdaria itself could be at war. Not now when their lives were so desperate.

Her spine straightened. "The emperor himself has been poisoning you for years. When the dam at the River Gate was destroyed earlier this year, small bouts of rebellion erupted. When that happened, the emperor sent even more poison than ever to the Storm in order to control you, in order to make you dependent on him."

Most citizens knew she was the princess, so to hear her speak against the emperor himself brought their eyebrows high on their foreheads.

She took in a deep breath. "I believe my father is treating Kamdaria wrong. It's not just the poison. He rewards those closest to him but only at the expense of others. The poverty in our empire is getting worse by the day, while the wealth of those in the Crown grows to disgusting levels."

Her feet rocked back and forth as the fire at her command let off sparks. "Trust me when I say that you should not be fighting each other." Rolling her shoulders back, Talise drew from a feeling deep within her gut to help her through the next words. "I am Princess of Kamdaria. It is my right and my duty to save my people from poverty and corruption."

Stirrings went through the crowd. They didn't speak to each other, but nods rippled among them. Determination lined every face. Her words had affected them in some small way at least.

All at once, she shaped away the fire holding the group of attackers prisoner. She let them free and glanced over the crowd with the solemnest face she could manage. "Of all Kamdarians, the citizens of the Storm have been hurt the most. You deserve a better life."

With a small swallow, her head hung. "I cannot make everything about your life perfect, no matter how I have tried." She stood up straighter and pierced the eyes of the attackers with her own. Luckily, they stood in place despite their prison of fire being gone.

A deep breath filled her lungs, which she paired with her straightest posture yet. "But I can give you a chance to fight for the life you deserve." She raised a fist into the air. "Fight with me and we will change Kamdaria together!"

No one cheered, but a wave of agreement went through the crowd. If she had been asking them to go into battle at that exact moment, the reaction might have been even worse. But hopefully they wouldn't need to fight for a while still.

After the speech, Talise gathered the attackers plus several citizens from the city. She asked them to begin gathering as many people together as they could so she could explain even more and actually organize them in some way.

It only took a few minutes. Talise couldn't bear to look at Willow during that time, but she already had a plan for the young girl. For now, the girl's neighbors would surely stay with her and help to bury her father.

Less than ten minutes had passed, but that didn't stop Wendy from touching Talise's arm with a stern nod. "We have to go. It could take Kessoku all day to find us, but they could also be here any minute. We'll build your army slowly. This was a good start, but right now, we need to run."

The words didn't *hurt* exactly. Wendy's words obviously held truth. But frustration filled Talise as she scolded herself for waiting so long.

They were desperate to improve their lives, and now they finally had a chance to do it. But with Kessoku on Talise's heels, now she would have to build the army through messengers and short, infrequent visits.

Giving a resigned nod, Talise began down the path that led to their camp. After a few steps, Aaden's voice drifted over from behind a patch of dead trees. Talise's stomach flipped at the sound of it. Once she heard his words, her stomach flipped again.

"We saw River and her team of Kessoku in the city right across the river. We already know the citizens have a bridge to help them cross. If we don't leave immediately, they'll find us."

Talise and Wendy rounded the corner, coming face to face with Aaden, Cyrus, and Rio. At the sight of them, Aaden's calm demeanor flashed with fear as his eyes landed on Talise's hands, then her clothes, and then her face.

His entire body went still when he finally looked her in the eye.

Glancing down at her hands, Talise quickly shook her head. "It's not my blood."

He stayed frozen, not reacting at all until a tiny wisp of a sigh escaped his lips. But along with it, his jaw flexed. He glanced away. It seemed to take him more effort than usual to keep his face straight. In a dark voice, he muttered under his breath. "I was only gone for a *few* minutes and—"

"This would have happened whether you were there or not." Her own jaw clenched as she pulled water from the air to clean some of the blood away.

His head whipped back to face her as he raised a single eyebrow. "You don't know that for sure."

He probably would have continued. His mouth hung open, as if ready to speak more. But something on her face must have stopped him because no sound left his mouth.

Talise pressed her lips together, hoping it would hide the trembling in her chin. "Willow's father is dead."

For a single moment, he didn't move. The earth was silent while the words sank in. Everything stood still. And then Aaden's face fell. He let out a dark sigh and rubbed a hand over his face. Pain twisted through his features, making his veins writhe.

No matter how she tried, Talise couldn't control the trembling in her chin now. "We have to take her with us."

Every single eye in the group widened at those words. Cyrus and Wendy exchanged a glance that clearly indicated they didn't agree with the idea. Rio frowned as he looked to the side. He looked ready to tell her *no*.

But he didn't have to because Aaden spoke before anyone else. "She can't come with us."

Talise swiped away a tear with the back of her hand, which probably drew another smudge of blood across her face, but she didn't care. "Her father just died."

Aaden stood firm. "And we might end up in a fight at any time today. You want to bring her into a fight? She's only a child."

With a mouth screwed into a knot, Talise snarled back at him. "Then where is she supposed to go?"

"Have you asked *her* where she wants to go? Doesn't she have an aunt and uncle in the city?" His face remained rigid, but the question came out gentle. "Don't you think she should stay here until she can at least put a mark on her father's grave?"

Ice air froze in Talise's throat before she turned away. With blood-covered hands, she couldn't reach for the hem of her tunic. But with nothing to fiddle with, her hands just closed and opened over and over again. Her voice cracked when she spoke again. "What about after the funeral? I don't know if her aunt and uncle are still alive. The glass house was destroyed. I won't be able to build a new one any time soon. Food is already scarce. I can't bear to leave her here with no family at all."

Especially since Willow's father had also been left without family as a child.

Taking a step forward, Rio bowed in her direction. "Forgive me, Princess, but we need to leave immediately. We can get back to camp for our things, but then we have to go."

The nod came automatically. Talise couldn't even feel her legs when they started moving. Trudging over the frosty ground only served as a reminder of just how cold the empire had gotten. Not just physically, but down deep inside the heart of it too.

Everyone around her moved with the same grim steps.

Could her heart sink any lower?

Silence stretched between them. To fill it, Talise did the only thing she could think of. After pulling a glob of water from the air, she finished cleaning the blood from off her hands. The water helped with most of the blood in her clothes, but a few of the stains would last forever. When she shaped the water over her face, she had to guess where the blood had been smudged because she couldn't see it.

A few minutes later, she prepared to let the water sink into the frozen soil at her feet.

Before she could drop it, Aaden raised one hand and pointed to a spot on her cheek. Rather than attempt to clean the spot herself, she flicked the water toward him.

It only took him a minute to finish cleaning the blood away. He warmed the water as he worked, which she hadn't thought to do. At last, the water fell. She looked at him then.

He locked eyes with her for a few steps. With a hard swallow, he glanced toward the ground. His voice came out husky but soft. "I'll come back in a week or two. After Willow's father has been buried." He glanced to the side for a moment before looking back to the ground again. "If she doesn't have any family in her city…" He swallowed again. "I know a place I can take her."

The urge to reach for his hand came even stronger than before. Like a coward, Talise merely stepped closer to him. She caught his eye but could only manage two words. "Thank you." Since she strongly believed the place Aaden spoke of was probably with his grandparents in the Crown, it did seem like Willow would be taken care of after all. But nothing would be the same for her with her father gone either.

Of course, even that small moment of peace had to be shattered almost as soon as it had come. Tempest burst through a clump of trees ahead with two packs on her back. Claye and Fyra followed after her wearing packs of their own.

"They're coming." Those were the only words Tempest needed to stay before the rest of them took off running.

※

Chapter Thirty-Four

Running had many different forms.

A jog around the garden could get a heart racing, but it didn't instill the body with fear. Running to get to something felt entirely different, especially if that something was going to be hurt or might disappear.

But nothing could compare to the absolute flood of emotions that paired with running for one's life. Talise's limbs shook as her feet pounded over the ground. Winter might have frozen the tree branches and puddles of water, but running brought intense heat inside her body.

Despite the heat and racing heart, ice still stabbed into too many places. The cold had nothing to do with it. Anxiety controlled the ice with every step. No matter how many steps they put between their group and River's, it wasn't enough.

And then came the trembling. With every other heightened emotion inside, why did trembling have to accompany it? The fear of tripping only made her limbs less steady, which in turn, made tripping more likely.

The vicious cycle continued with every step. Every pound of the heart.

River's voice called out to them. "Today is the day, Princess. Today you die."

Talise's friends formed a shield with their bodies to protect her as they ran. They blocked every possible opening that might let in a weapon or shaping. But both groups moved too fast for any kind of fight.

A carelessly thrown weapon flew by every once in a while, but it lacked the strength or the aim necessary to hit its target. Likewise, Wendy and Tempest shot whips and blasts backward at the attackers. But they had to expend so much effort on staying upright and keeping Talise surrounded that their attacks were deflected easily.

They ran for too long. Talise's chest heaved in pain. The burning in her legs brought tears to her eyes. The attackers began to fall back but not enough.

Wrenching emotion crashed through Talise's gut as she realized what they would have to do. It took several gulps of air before she could say a word. She glanced to Rio first. He protected her with the fierceness of a solider, but he would understand the importance of strategy too.

"We can't outrun them." Her words came out in a gasp.

Aaden tensed at her side, but she'd been expecting it. That's why she hadn't turned to him in the first place. She continued. "We need to stop and fight. It's our only chance."

Rio nodded and pointed ahead. "Once we round this bend. That hill will give us some coverage as we fight."

By the time Talise nodded, they were nearly there. After a few whispers, everyone had a plan.

They jumped down behind the hill. Talise shot out a wall of fire. It burned across the landscape until it reached the group of attackers. They let out screams before falling back.

As planned, Aaden followed the wall of fire with a rope of fire that tightened around the members of the small group. River pulled water from the air to put out his fire rope. It distracted the group just long enough for Claye to shape a diagonal slab of earth upward beneath the attackers' feet. The shaping had enough force to cause everyone in their group to stumble backward off their feet.

Only expert skill could have formed such a perfect diagonal slab of earth. It served as a reminder of how often Clayed had lied, even about simple things like how skilled his earth shaping really was.

Their planned shaping worked exactly as they had hoped. It gave Talise and her friends the upper hand. But the fight wasn't over yet. Now that they had been beaten down, the Kessoku were angrier than ever.

Fireballs blasted across the landscape. Earth rippled beneath their feet. Whips of water slapped across their arms, leaving hot, red welts in their wake.

Talise punched every weapon-like element she could think of back at them. Fire and water crashed into each other mid-air. Steam sizzled out, burning anyone who happened to be close enough.

Water, air, earth, and fire combined and fought and crashed as the fight continued. Talise and her friends had great skill, but River had obviously found the best shapers she could to accompany her.

With so much uninterrupted fighting, they didn't have time to create a better strategy. Instead, they could only survive with as much shaping as possible.

The elements continued to collide. The actions continued to tire them. With muscles already burning under the strain, the fear of death no longer seemed a strong enough reason to keep fighting.

Talise wasn't the only one. She could see it in the faces of the others around her. They were ready to give up.

"They're just as tired as we are." Aaden spoke as if he had read her mind. Then again, he did have a way of knowing what she was thinking most of the time.

Cyrus threw his head back just as he blasted a wall of wind forward. "What good does that do us? We're still not winning."

Rio inched closer with the ghost of a grin on his face. Did he understand Aaden's unspoken suggestion? "We don't have to beat them. We just have to make them think they can't possibly win against us. We just have to get them to retreat."

Rocks showered down on the Kessoku thanks to more of Claye's expert shaping. "You say that like it's an easy thing. But how are we supposed to convince them they have no chance when we're already doing the best we can?"

Suddenly, it became clear. When she looked into Aaden's eyes again, she could see what he already had. Sometimes, presentation mattered as much as shaping. They didn't need something stronger or more powerful than their attackers. They just needed something that *looked* impressive.

Jerking her head to the side, Talise looked over at the nearby ocean. "Tempest, I need you to shape as much water as you can over here. Wendy and Cyrus, do what you can to help her. I know water isn't your primary, but any little bit will help."

Now Talise just needed an object that would instill fear in anyone who saw it. The walls of Kamdaria came to her mind first, but maybe Kessoku hated the walls more than feared them. Perhaps a mountain would work better. After all, it had been a mountain that killed their last leader. A mountain shaped by the leader's own hand.

Talise couldn't shape an entire mountain of water on her own, not without the amulet. But if Tempest, Wendy, and Cyrus all helped, they could get something of a decent size. Then, Talise just had to freeze the outermost layer of it. If she did it right, it would look like the entire mountain was frozen instead of just a thin layer on the outside. Who wouldn't be intimidated by that?

By the time they formed the mountain of water, many of the Kessoku already had mouths gaping wide. Talise sat up straighter. "Now, we just need some whips." She glanced at Aaden and then at Claye. "Make them big ones."

The mountain of water blasted across the landscape toward their attackers. It was extremely fragile, but Talise had managed to fake things enough to make it look strong. Luckily, the fire and earth Aaden and Claye shaped jerked around like lethal whips.

After leaving only a few welts on the Kessoku, the soldiers seemed to have lost their determination. They eyed the mountain with an air of distrust. The distrust quickly turned to fear.

River snarled at the mountain before turning away from it. Talise watched as the woman pulled a dagger from her tunic and aimed it right for Talise's shaping hand, which was only barely visible from behind the hill where they hid.

Despite the danger, Talise didn't waver in her shaping. She kept her thin layer of ice frozen over the hovering mountain. When River's blade flew near, Rio easily slapped it away with his sword.

It only took one.

One Kessoku from the group stood, legs shaking. She backed away with slow steps. When the others in her group turned to look at her, she ran.

A man followed after her without any hesitation at all. Another woman followed next.

River hissed at the Kessoku who hadn't left yet, but that only served to make up their minds faster. Another moment later, River stood alone against the fragile mountain.

Her hands dropped to her sides, but her eyebrows pulsed. She glared at Talise, seething. She didn't have to say it. They both knew what thoughts were running through River's mind.

The next time they met, River wouldn't give up so easily.

Still, the woman was more than outnumbered, and she knew it.

When she turned on her heel and ran in the opposite direction, it only offered the smallest bit of comfort. Besides, their chests were still heaving and their muscles burning.

Everyone in Talise's group collapsed while they tended to each other's wounds. There wasn't much blood. Talise shaped thin layers of ice over anyone's muscles that had been strained too hard. The cold numbed the muscles enough to ease the aching.

No one spoke except to clean a wound or to knead a sore muscle.

They hadn't been there long. Even with the shattered glass house and Willow's dead father and Kessoku trying to kill them, Talise suddenly realized with perfect clarity… it still wasn't over.

She jumped to her feet and glared at the footsteps Kessoku had left behind. Her stomach twisted in knots as the truth became clear.

Whipping around to face her friends, she said what had to be said. "They just ran toward Willow's city. If they want revenge for this fight, they'll kill every person there."

Wendy brought a hand to her mouth as she reached for a strand of her hair. Her wide eyes could have broken even the strongest soldier.

Talise got to her feet. "We have follow and fight them again."

Chapter Thirty-Five

TALISE STEPPED FORWARD, FULLY EXPECTING one of her friends to stop her. Memories of a dagger plunging into Ash's chest were enough to keep her movements rigid and sharp. Her friends could disagree all they liked, but she was going back into that city whether they liked it or not.

But when she turned to face her friends, not a single word of protest met her. In fact, none of their faces even indicated protest. Except for Claye, but he didn't count because Talise really didn't care about his opinion.

"We still have Kessoku uniforms," Tempest said, tossing her braid to the side.

Aaden reached for his chin with narrowing eyes. "As long as we have more time to prepare, we can probably beat them."

Talise nodded, warmth growing in her chest when she realized the others would help. "Good. We'll sneak in and assess the situation. Then we can come up with a strategy."

It took much longer to get into the city than it had to run away from it. Not only did they march now instead of run, but their muscles were wearied too.

By the time they neared the city, scores of people moved in large groups across the paths. Talise and her friends ducked behind a house to determine why. They didn't have to wait long.

A large group of Storm citizens gathered near the well. River stood on its side, calling out to the crowd.

"The princess will be greatly pleased with the numbers you've already gathered for her army. Line up along that back path, and we will take you to her base in the Gate."

River waved the citizens on and then quickly waved over another group. Talise recognized some of the people among them, but many she had never seen before.

Her stomach dropped as she realized why. They were from another city. The Storm citizens had agreed to join an army for Talise. They had already gathered members from other cities. And now Kessoku was stealing them away before her very eyes.

They couldn't do anything now. Even if Talise jumped out and revealed herself, she could tell that many of the citizens were already long on their way to Kessoku's base in the Gate. The ones that would recognize her were probably the first to go.

Even if she asked these citizens to fight for her against River, the terrifying woman would surely do extensive damage, probably killing most of the Storm citizens that stood nearby. Talise couldn't possibly sacrifice them now. Not immediately after they had agreed to join her.

Instead, she stood in terror as the last of them wandered down the path. She had been so afraid to ask them to fight. And they agreed without a moment's hesitation.

Soon, River herself began leaving.

Not wanting to cause a scene in front of the remaining Storm citizens, Talise and her group quietly followed River until they reached an empty clearing.

"Stop." Talise's voice rang through the clearing.

River gave a lazy look backward before continuing to stomp forward once again. "If you need to rest, do it, but I'm not waiting for you. And if the princess comes and kills you for revenge, that's on you."

With a huff, Talise tore off the helmet covering her head. "And what if I've come to kill *you*?"

A jolt went through River before she whirled around. She ripped two daggers from her tunic and threw them one after the other. Talise ducked to miss the first, but a blast of wind blocked the second.

Talise wasn't sure which of her friends had shaped the air that saved her, but the block had been perfect. Tucking into a roll, Talise moved forward. When she got to her feet again, two fireballs burned above her palms.

They shot forward with the precision only a Master Shaper could boast. But River had a wild look in her eye. She dodged the fireballs and pulled out another dagger from inside her tunic.

The fight had moved so quickly, Talise wasn't sure how it had happened, but the woman stood close. Too close. One swift jab could have sunk the dagger into Talise's chest.

Just as River reeled her arm back, a sword sliced through her arm.

The same wild look existed in Aaden's eye as he swung his sword a second time. Though he aimed for River's neck, her dodge left him slicing through her shoulder instead.

She let out a cry as she ran backward. A whip of water shaped out from her palm, but it did no damage to anyone.

Aaden continued to go for the kill.

A string of cries left River's lips. Soon, a man emerged from a cluster of trees. He rode a black horse and had a white one at his side. A short whistle sent the white horse close enough to River that she could jump on.

Fire in all shapes blocked the woman's path to the horse. She jumped through all the flames, clearly ignoring the burns that blistered onto her skin.

Every member of Talise's group sent whatever weapons they could River's way, whether shaped or metal.

But the horse moved fast. Blood gushed from the two wounds Aaden had inflicted. River ignored them as her horse galloped out of their sight.

Reality began trickling in as they watched the woman disappear.

Talise had succeeded. She had gathered a second army, one full of citizens from the Storm.

And Kessoku had stolen it from her.

Just like her first army.

When River had almost disappeared, she shouted across the winter landscape in a shrill voice. "This is what happens when you face an enemy stronger than you."

Even from such a great distance, Talise could imagine the smirk on the woman's face.

Donning a smirk of her own, Talise shouted back. She used air shaping to send her voice further without having to speak too loudly. "You mean like how you've fought against my father all these years and done nothing but lose?"

A growl erupted from River's mouth before she spoke again. "You'll never come back from this. We just stole a *second* army away from you."

The words hit Talise with the force of a hammer. Pain writhed in her chest. The defeats she experienced sent twists into every pore. Losing her army. Losing the amulet. Losing Eben. Being exiled by her own father. Her shoulders hunched forward while tears burned in her eyes.

Claye's betrayal.

For months, she had faced defeat after defeat. Kessoku always found her. They stole from her. Tried to kill her. Pain had accompanied her every word during those months, her every move.

The memories carried back the pain, but with it came an unexpected clarity. Deep in her stomach, laughter bubbled. She let it out in a bitter chuckle. Her hands pushed forward, shaping the air around her laugh so that River would hear it too.

The woman's threat had been clear. Her words were meant to defeat Talise yet again. Instead, they did the exact opposite. Letting the laugh build, Talise chuckled again. "You think *this* is going to break me?" Her eyes fell shut for a brief moment while pain washed through her again. This time, a determined strength accompanied the pain. "Do you have any idea what I've *been* through?" She clenched her jaw tight. "*This* is nothing."

To her utter delight, River had no response at all. From across the great distance, they stared at her, but Talise's message had been clear. She would *not* be defeated.

After another moment of silence, Aaden raised his sword and began charging toward River with a frightening growl at the back of his throat.

Of course he had no chance to hurt her before she galloped off, but his action had forced her to move. The sight of him charging sent an all new sensation through Talise. It moved through her with the best possible kind of warmth.

There wasn't a moment to waste right now, but soon, she'd pull him aside. She'd tell him exactly how she felt about him.

Now, she faced the rest of the group, her lungs filling with air that felt charged.

"I'm about to take back everything they've stolen from me."

Chapter Thirty-Six

BY NIGHTFALL, TALISE AND HER friends arrived at Kessoku's base.

Aaden had acquired horses for them, though everyone was too afraid to ask where he had gotten them. Instead, they just took them and traveled as quickly as they could. He had also found a somewhat fancy dress for Talise, which she had requested but never dreamed he'd actually acquire.

Now, she wore the fire orange dress while riding toward Kessoku's base in the Ember Gate. Wendy sat behind her on the horse, arranging her hair and brushing out the tangles as they moved.

When they got to the base, they entered it through the same tunnel they had used to escape several weeks ago.

They moved as quietly as possible, but it wasn't too hard because everyone in the base had been gathered on the opposite side.

Soon, they entered a large room with an oval table and velvet drapes.

Just as Claye had explained, a balcony sat on the opposite side of the room. The balcony hung above the entrance hall of the base, making it the perfect place to give speeches to everyone.

And as they knew he would be, Lucian stood on the balcony. He addressed the crowd below which consisted of his own men as well as the Storm army they had just stolen from Talise.

Arrogant pride laced his voice as he spoke. "Welcome to our newest members. Our organization is known as Kessoku. For many years, we have fought for unity in Kamdaria. Now that the princess has joined our side, we are more prepared than ever to take the emperor down and return Kamdaria to its former glory."

The cheers that accompanied his words filled every space in the large room.

This was the moment.

Talise stepped forward without hesitation.

Behind her, the members of her group had hidden weapons ready to draw if necessary. But most likely, it wouldn't be.

River had made one fatal error in stealing away Talise's army. If the Storm citizens thought they were fighting for the princess, they would surely revolt if anyone tried to injure her.

Knowing she had finally gotten the upper hand, Talise marched onto the balcony next to Lucian. She offered him her most dulcet smile.

"Thank you, Lucian, for introducing our cause."

Shock rippled through his features. He took a step back and swallowed. He blinked hard but seemed surprised when Talise was still there.

She ignored him easily. In her fire orange dress and combed hair, she looked more like a princess than she had in months. And, unlike Lucian, she had done a lot to gain loyalty from the people in the Storm.

She held her chin high. "This war has gone on for too long. It is finally time to demonstrate to the emperor just how powerful we are. Some of you know that we now have the powerful amulet of Kamdar himself."

A hush went through the room.

Lucian fidgeted at Talise's side. As before, she ignored him. "With this amulet, we will do something the emperor cannot ignore. We will show him our fight for unity cannot be stopped." She raised a fist in the air. "We will…"

At this point, even the Kessoku in the crowd below were hanging on her words. They leaned forward, eager to hear what mystery she had planned.

To increase the eagerness, Talise waited another extra second before she continued. By the time she opened her mouth again, everyone seemed to be holding their breaths. The room sparked with energy even before the words left her lips.

"We will destroy the walls!"

Gasps went through the room, but the kind that were too excited to breathe. Murmurs rippled around with excited energy. Even the Kessoku joined along.

All of them asked the same question. "Can it really be done?"

The walls that separated Kamdaria into three rings were thick. They were strong. They had been there as long as anyone could remember. Kessoku had managed to dig a hole through one wall, but it was barely wide enough for one person to pass. And even then, it had taken many years.

Talise knew exactly how crazy it was to suggest she could destroy the walls. As she expected, the people *wanted* to believe, but they needed proof.

Cupping a hand over one ear, she turned toward the crowd. After a moment, she stood straight again. "I know it is hard to believe, especially since many of you are only hearing about the amulet for the first time. But I assure you, the power of the amulet is great."

Like fate itself had planned it, a small voice called out above the crowd. "Can you show us?"

Talise couldn't have stopped herself from grinning even if she tried. One eyebrow raised high on her forehead. "A demonstration? What a wonderful idea." Now she turned to the side. She held out one hand expectantly. "Lucian, the amulet please. The people need to see what it can do."

With an army that was hers in the crowd below, he couldn't possibly refuse.

And he knew it.

After all these months, she'd finally gotten back her army and the amulet in a single bound. Now she just had to do the impossible.

Take down the walls.

EARTH STORM

Chapter Thirty-Seven

SOLDIERS LINED THE GRANITE HALL. Talise's heart leapt into her throat every time she stepped forward. The sight of soldiers was normal enough, but these weren't just any soldiers.

They bowed as she passed. Each one held a fist to his or her heart before dropping to one knee. Even after their long imprisonment by Kessoku, her soldiers hadn't wavered in their devotion.

Her soldiers. She finally had them back again.

Their heads ducked in reverence at the sight of her, but it didn't stop her from seeing the gleam in their eyes. They believed in her.

After Kessoku stole her army of Storm citizens, she had promptly marched onto their base and took them back again. Those actions firmly cemented her place as a true member of Kessoku. But it had also gotten her original army back.

It had taken a few days of harsh words to force Kessoku to set her soldiers free. Ultimately, they didn't have much of a choice. The newly recruited Storm citizens were eager to fight but only because they fought on Talise's side. Her original army would only fight for her as well. Without her two armies, Kessoku's original ranks were too downtrodden and diminished to ever defeat the emperor.

They needed her, and they knew it.

Still, explaining to her original army how she had gotten them free had been one of the most terrifying moments of her life. She had to explain that she no longer fought on the emperor's side. She offered her soldiers a chance to return to the palace and to the emperor. Aaden promised he would use his influence to help them get into the Crown if they asked.

None of the soldiers accepted the offer. They chose to stay with her instead.

Apparently, they had all assumed she would turn against the emperor eventually. Many of them joined her *hoping* she would turn against him. The others accepted the change without any hesitation.

Another step forward brought another twist through Talise's insides. On her right, a male and female soldier stood next to each other. Similar scars plastered both of their arms and hands. Their skin was pocked and warped from past burns.

Talise recognized them, though she had never interacted with them much. They were brother and sister, which always reminded her of Wendy and Cyrus. Talise scanned the burn scars once more. The two soldiers had earned those burns during the battle with Kessoku by the Smoke Gate.

Now they stood in Kessoku's base, treating their previous enemies as allies instead. Even with Talise's subtle glances at their hands, the brother and sister ignored the scars. Instead, they focused only on their princess. The young woman's eyes glowed as she brought her mangled hand to her chest. Her brother did the same not a moment later.

They both fell to their knees, dropping their heads in low bows.

Tears stung in Talise's eyes. Both of them had deeply injured limbs. The scars would mark them forever. They even stood inside the base of those who had inflicted the injuries.

And yet…

They looked to Talise with complete devotion. They believed in their princess despite all they had gone through for her.

Writhing filled her gut. She appreciated their loyalty, but it terrified her too. Never had the responsibility of leading hit her with so much force. She tried to dig for some measure of confidence while walking amongst them. Her racing heart wouldn't allow it.

From behind her, the rest of her friends greeted the soldiers. Rio and Fyra knew most of them. They waved and quietly promised to catch up soon. Even Claye had many friends he greeted eagerly.

A tremor yanked through her at the thought of it. *Right*. Her soldiers still didn't know how Claye had betrayed them. They didn't know *he* was the reason they got captured by Kessoku in the first place.

Talise forced out a sigh, attempting to ease the crushing weight of her responsibility. That conversation would have to come another day. Her heart had been through as much as it could handle for now.

After reaching the end of the room, all the soldiers had bowed. At her beckoning, they began to rise again. She told them to move freely through the room and enjoy each other's company. They relished the simple freedom as only those who had recently been imprisoned could do.

The rest of her friends mingled with them. Conversations flitted around as everyone caught up with each other.

Soon, Aaden slipped into the room from one of the side doors. His brown eyes shined bright compared to his short black hair. The facial hair along his chin and under his nose had recently been trimmed.

When Talise's eyes landed on the white scar across his eye, her stomach moved in an all new way. Now it fluttered and flipped. His presence had a way of improving her mood these days. Maybe it had always been that way. It seemed more so recently, probably because she was desperate to be around him all the time.

It had been surprisingly difficult to find a moment alone with him. Not just difficult, but so far, impossible. Waiting wasn't easy when she had something so important to talk to him about. With the chaos of the past few days, she still hadn't confessed her feelings for him. But she would. Soon. She'd do it the first chance she got.

"They're ready for you." He stood tall, which only accentuated his broad shoulders and precise posture. If the perfect moment didn't come soon, she might just blurt out her confession without any preamble.

She reached to brush her hair over one shoulder before remembering she had cut it.

Once they had arrived at Kessoku's base from the Storm and actually had access to the proper tools, she immediately cut her hair short once again. Now it fell to just under her chin, the same length she had kept it for almost all her life.

To pay for the riverboat tickets to get Talise to her academy testing, Marmie had cut her own hair and sold it. In honor of that act, Talise had always kept her hair short. After Marmie's death, it had been especially important to keep the tradition.

But being in exile, Talise didn't have the chance to keep it short.

Aaden's eyes lingered on her hair as she whipped it out of her face. She could have sworn the lightest smile appeared on his lips at the sight of it, but maybe that was just her wishful thinking.

Together, they left the large room.

If they had been alone in the hallway, she probably would have told him right then how much she loved him. But of course, armed Kessoku soldiers roamed around with no respect for their privacy.

Instead of having the conversation she wanted to have, they merely talked about shaping.

Aaden casually rubbed one thumb across his sword hilt as he spoke. "My father and River found a large slab of granite in the forest just outside the base. They believe it will be the perfect width and strength to mimic the walls around Kamdaria."

Nodding, Talise thought very seriously about just reaching for Aaden's hand. Who needed conversations anyway?

With a tiny shake of her head, she brushed the thought away. "I still think granite is too strong to truly mimic the walls, but I guess it could work. If I can break apart the granite, then I should be able to break apart the walls as well."

"Do you still have the amulet with you?" His question came out stiff, but she could hear a subtle tremor of doubt between his words.

She lifted one corner of her mouth upward. "I keep it with me at all times. I even hide it inside my tunic while I'm sleeping, exactly like you suggested."

Now the corner of *his* mouth lifted upward. "Good."

Her stomach flopped. *Why* did there have to be so many random soldiers filling every single hallway in the stupid base?

Even when they left the granite walls of the base, soldiers still milled around. Across a short field, River's wild eyes turned hard as she noticed Talise crossing the clearing that separated them.

Aaden's steps became rigid at once. He gripped his sword hilt tighter, almost exactly the same as he clenched his jaw.

Now that Talise had truly joined Kessoku, River had to accept that killing Talise was out of the question. It came as no surprise when the woman vehemently fought the idea. Luckily, anytime Lucian or Aaden were around, River seemed capable of following orders. Though it didn't stop her from glaring.

Lucian beamed as Talise and Aaden moved closer. Like always, he ignored everyone except his son. He especially liked to ignore Talise, despite the importance of her position. Lucian moved to one side, allowing Aaden a place to stand immediately at his side.

After a short nod to his father, Aaden did stand next to him. He also stood next to the slab of granite that protruded from the earth.

At the sight of it, Talise's hands fell to her sides. The granite stretched out across the frozen earth at their feet. The width had to be as long as two men. It might have even been wider.

Ice clung to the divots and rough texture of the granite, making it sparkle even more than usual in the sunlight. All at once, an ache carved into her throat.

She had promised to take down the walls. She had *promised*.

The magnitude of that promise hit her with an unforgiving force. This granite looked strong enough to withstand any amount of shaping. Even with the amulet.

Just when her heart sank low, Aaden caught her eye. He raised both eyebrows expectantly. No, not just expectantly. With unwavering trust.

It gave her just enough courage to reach inside her tunic pocket for the amulet.

Warmth filled her chest the moment her fingers touched the silver pendant. Her fingers wrapped around it as she pulled it from her pocket. The warmth spread, reminding her of the great power she could now access.

Taking a deep breath, she cleared her mind. Once clear, she let an equal amount of emotions and logic fill her. Then, she raised one hand and reached toward the granite.

Her shaping senses moved outward. Every particle and mineral stood out in her mind with perfect clarity. Power surged within her, eager to tackle any sort of shaping.

But when she tried to crush the granite to dust, the amulet shook in her hand. Was it trying to protest? A shiver passed through her arm. She had to clench her jaw to stop the sensation. Maybe the granite *was* too strong to crush, which is exactly what she had assumed in the first place.

Squeezing the amulet, she made another attempt. Her fingers stretched, wriggled. Her senses squeezed into the granite, but the minerals were just too strong to penetrate.

Taking a deep breath, Talise expended one last burst of effort.

A loud crack sounded through the air. The horizontal crack managed to cut through the entire width of granite. But it didn't crush it like she'd been hoping.

Lucian raised a single eyebrow. Somehow, he looked both smug and annoyed at the same time. "A crack isn't going to help us take down the walls."

While the glow in her chest dimmed, Talise turned to the man. Her mouth twisted into a knot. She slammed a fist against the granite, hoping to loosen more of the hard material. The motion caused bits of granite to fly out from the crack. The crack *did* get bigger after hitting it. Her lips fell into a frown. But not enough.

Most of the granite debris landed on the soil beneath their feet, but a pile of it fell onto a nearby platform the Kessoku used for training exercises. The debris would need to be cleared away.

Almost as soon as it hit the platform, an aging woman wearing a worn burlap tunic rushed toward it with a broom in hand.

A memory sparked in Talise's mind. The burlap clothes reminded her of others she had seen in similar clothing. It took her a moment to place the memory. When she did, her head jerked toward Lucian.

The man already had one arm out, gesturing toward the platform. "Aaden, could you help clean up that mess?"

Aaden took one step forward before his body stiffened. He glanced back at his father.

Letting out a light chuckle, Lucian rubbed his goatee. "The princess will be safe. I promised you I wouldn't harm her. And anyway, you'll still be able to see her from the platform."

Aaden's eyes flicked to the side. "Only if River helps me too."

With a snide glare, River stomped toward the platform just ahead of Aaden.

Once they were both out of earshot, Luican raised an eyebrow and turned back to Talise.

Before he could utter a word, Talise folded her arms over her chest. Her jaw clenched as she spoke. "You keep servants here? How much do you pay them? Are they treated well?"

Lucian's mouth dropped as he touched a hand to his chest. "Servants? Of course we don't keep servants."

Taking a step forward, Talise narrowed her eyes. "I remember seeing people dressed in burlap clothes when I was imprisoned in your dungeon during the summer. Those people were certainly *treated* like servants."

"No." Lucian let out a laugh. "Sometimes we have our soldiers wear burlap clothes, but that's only if they have messy work to do."

She wanted to argue more, but his deliberate look at the crack in the granite clamped her mouth shut.

He scratched one eyebrow, which did a remarkable job of making her feel like a child. "Even if you went around and shaped hundreds of cracks in the walls, it would still take years of effort to break through them completely. You said you could *destroy* the walls, not crack them."

"I can." It came out defensive, but she couldn't help it.

Glancing toward the crack again, he tilted his head. "Really?"

Now she let out a huff. "Yes, really. This granite is denser than the stone the walls are made of. I need more practice with the amulet, but I can do it."

Lucian scoffed. "You'd better be diligent with your practice then because I'm only giving you one more chance. In a week, you're going to try again. But you'll do it in front of citizens from the Gate. If you fail, they'll have no reason to believe you can defeat the emperor." Now he stroked his goatee. "Let's just say your leadership is at stake."

Forming fists at her sides, she donned a cheerful smile. "Threaten me all you like, but I *will* destroy the walls. Just you wait."

⚜

Chapter Thirty-Eight

DISMOUNTING A GRAY AND WHITE horse, Talise eyed the city before her. The city nearest to Kessoku's base was large and bustling, but this city was quaint.

Little clusters of homes bunched together like chickens in a pen. The city had a market square, but it only featured a few booths. The citizens chatted and laughed with each other like old friends.

As Talise guided her horse down the path, her friends, Lucian, and a few other Kessoku soldiers stayed close behind. Many of the merchants behind market stalls greeted Aaden. He often considered their wares, though he didn't need any of them. Perhaps it was a sign of respect more than anything.

Just after he finished buying a definitely unnecessary pair of socks, Aaden glanced over at Talise. "This is the city I always visited while we were living in the Storm. I got our food and supplies from here, so the merchants know me well."

Could he see her cheeks burning? Hopefully it came off as a light flush. Maybe he'd think it came as a result of the winter chill in the air. "And the horses?" she asked. Aaden always seemed to have an endless supply of horses at his disposal while they lived in the Storm. He never kept any of them, but he had *borrowed* plenty. Though maybe he had stolen them from Kessoku.

The tiniest smile played on his lips. "Yes, and the horses."

Her stomach filled with flutters. That smile. She wanted to keep it forever. If only she could package it up and hold it in her heart, surely not a single bad thing could touch her ever again.

It came at the perfect moment too because they had reached a gathered crowd. Everyone was waiting for her. In a single breath, her shoulders hunched forward, as if a physical weight pressed down on them.

Today she wore a velvet dress in a deep forest green. Thick gold lace adorned the edges of her long sleeves. One of her soldiers had even made a little tiara out of the gold lace. It wasn't as elaborate as a true tiara, like the ones inside Ridgerock Palace. But the citizens seemed to enjoy seeing her look even more like a princess than ever before.

Even in her fancy clothes, Talise insisted on keeping a few items with her. The amulet sat safe inside a deep pocket of her dress. The flame-carved dagger from Aaden sat on her hip, attached to a delicately embossed belt.

She reached into her pocket for the amulet. With careful steps, she climbed the wooden platform that had been built directly in front of the wall that separated them from the Storm.

Lucian gave his son the same warm smile he had for him. His gaze turned cold when his eyes met Talise's. "I don't want you speaking to any of the citizens. Let me do the talking."

Perhaps she should have protested. She didn't. Terror gripped her too completely. Even after a week of practice, she still didn't know if she could actually destroy the wall.

She had to. She *knew* she had to. She got advice from Aaden and even Claye. She sought help from anyone and everyone she could think of. Claye's parents, Glen and Ivy, even gave her some earth shaping tips that would supposedly help.

Yet, in all her practice sessions, she had yet to actually crumble any portion of the wall. It wasn't completely because of inability. Both she and Lucian agreed that the first destruction of the wall should be public. Of course, it would have been safer to practice on a random spot of wall first, but where would be the drama in that?

No, the people needed to see her first attempt. And it absolutely could not fail.

Lucian raised both hands high above his head. "Welcome citizens."

At the sound of his voice, many heads turned. Near the back of the crowd, one woman's head whipped toward him with incredible speed. A thick gold chain necklace adorned her neck.

Her face twisted into a snarl. After a tense moment, a look of calm immediately settled over her features. When the calm took over, she promptly left the crowd and walked toward a cluster of nearby homes.

It probably wasn't a good sign that the mere sound of Lucian's voice had already made someone leave.

Talise sucked in a short breath. Yes, she definitely had to get this right. She had to destroy a significant portion of the wall, and it had to be impressive enough that everyone's mouths dropped in awe. Her finger stroked the amulet inside her palm. If she failed…

Just when her thoughts had turned their darkest, Aaden glanced toward her. His expression didn't change, but the look alone lifted her spirits for a few more moments.

"Separation has ruled our empire for too long." Lucian's voice gained volume as he neared the end of his speech.

Talise noted with no small amount of pride that the people looked especially encouraged after those words. She had suggested that particular phrase to Lucian, so to see it resonated with the citizens more than any other parts of his speech felt nice.

The encouragement in the crowd seemed to lift Lucian's spirits as well. His words became more than just loud, they became confident as well. His eyes turned passionate.

"No more will we let ourselves be divided. With the power of the amulet, we will destroy these walls!"

Cheers broke out, but they were tentative cheers. The people weren't ready to be too excited until they saw the actual destruction. Just as the soldiers had, the citizens didn't quite believe the walls could actually be destroyed.

Even their tentative belief would have been enough to lift Talise's spirits. Except she didn't fully believe it either. When Lucian finished speaking, she lifted the amulet into the air for all to see. Letting balance flow through her, the amulet glowed a bright, lime green.

All at once, the people were entranced.

As Talise knew they would be.

She turned her back on them to face the wall. As she moved, she noticed Aaden scanning the crowd. He did that sort of thing often, so it didn't surprise her. But something about his look struck her as odd. Was he looking for someone in particular?

Brushing the thought away, Talise raised her hands into the air.

Her fingers wrapped around the glowing amulet. For several moments, she let the power pulse through her. Warmth spread through her in a nearly identical way to how fire did when she shaped fire inside her veins.

Though she hadn't planned to do it ahead of time, she spent another few moments letting the warmth and power grow inside her. She had no explanation for why. It just felt right.

Was it the bond she had with the amulet?

Was it intuition?

Whatever the reason, she stood still and let the power of the amulet work within her. It almost felt like her body was a well, and she had to fill that well before she'd have enough power to destroy the wall.

The feeling started at her toes. Though power had been pulsing through her, the newest sensation was different. It sparked and sizzled like a current of energy. It began at her toes and moved upward with each of her breaths.

Noises and crowds moved around behind her, but in that moment, she could sense nothing but the power within.

Crackling energy continued to crawl up her legs and into her stomach. It felt wonderful, dangerous. Perhaps even intoxicating. When the sparks sizzled around her heart, the first flag of warning went off in her mind.

She ignored it.

Though it might be dangerous, she had to destroy that wall.

The sizzling continued until it reached the tip of her head. She could feel her skin burning and freezing at the same time. With a deep breath, she shot her hands forward.

Power burst from every pore in her skin. It no longer felt like *she* was shaping. It felt like the world itself was shaping the elements, but only at her command. Clay and minerals inside the wall beckoned her to command them. Begged for it. Suddenly, the thickness of the wall meant nothing. The sturdiness meant nothing.

She simply pushed her power forward and willed a portion of the wall to crumble into dust. A breath barely passed through her lips before the wall obeyed.

Grinding noises filled the air while the ominous wall crunched and crumbled. Dust puffed outward while large pieces fell to the frozen soil below. But even the larger pieces were nothing. They were only pebbles, no bigger than a thumbnail, left to litter the ground until a gust of wind blew them away.

Her heart jolted.

For a moment, it stopped. *Really* stopped.

The flow of blood inside her screamed to a halt. Her power continued to crumble and crush the wall in either direction. But when her heart stopped, the shaping stopped.

Deep down, she had known it would happen. She had known her body couldn't handle that much power at once. But she had also known she had no choice.

Luckily, once she stopped drawing on the power from the amulet, her heart started up again. It beat weaker than before, but if she smiled wide enough, hopefully no one would be able to tell.

Blood inched through her veins but not anywhere near the speed it needed to move to keep her alive. Still, the people needed a show. She could only hope the color in her face hadn't drained enough to worry them.

Whirling around, she punched one hand into the air. "For Kamdaria!" she shouted.

Cheers rang so loud around her that surely no one would hear how she gasped for breath.

Lucian's eyebrows lowered at once. With the people watching, he wouldn't throw her a true glare, but she could still see one behind his eyes. He had expressly told her not to speak to the citizens.

But when he glanced behind her, the glare vanished. The wall had crumbled almost as far as the eye could see. A sigh of awe escaped his mouth.

At her side, awe also filled Aaden's face. The smile he graced her with gave her just enough strength to climb down off the platform. In other circumstances, that smile could have made her fly.

She waved to the people as she began walking away. They flocked toward her. As they had planned, a team of guards blocked the citizens from reaching her. She gave nods and returned shouts. Luckily, no one seemed to notice how slowly her feet dragged across the street.

At last, she, Aaden, and Lucian moved behind a home. The citizens were finally out of sight.

Lucian turned around, ready to speak.

Before he got the chance, Talise gripped the arm that had been at her side the whole time. "Aaden." It came out breathless. Too breathless.

His eyes widened at the sound of her voice. He clearly hadn't realized anything was wrong until that very moment.

Words tickled her throat as she tried to explain. But nothing came out because the world began fading around her.

Her legs buckled. Aaden caught her into his arms, lifting her off the ground with ease.

Just as she tucked her head against his chest, the world went black.

Chapter Thirty-Nine

VOICES FLITTED AROUND TALISE, BUT they warbled without meaning.

Heaviness filled her eyelids, sticking them closed. It didn't matter. She didn't even want to open her eyes. Her body lay atop a soft surface that seemed perfect for losing herself in.

A deep part of herself knew the soft surface was only hay. Or maybe it was a blanket laid over thick grass. But those dark recesses of her mind were far too unreachable to bother thinking about anyway.

The surface felt soft beneath her, so what else mattered?

Even with her eyes closed, the world pulsed in and out of existence. Voices drifted around, as if coming from deep under water. But a moment later, the words would sharpen until their meaning *almost* became clear.

Despite the strange pulsing both outside and inside, laying still seemed the most wonderful thing in the world. No amount of pain trickled through her. The not-bed beneath her provided unimaginable comfort.

After a while, her brain tried to flicker. To wake. The effort only weakened her until falling back into the darkness sounded far more pleasant.

Time didn't exist.

Whatever state she was in, it could have lasted minutes. It could have lasted days. She felt like nothing, but the nothingness didn't hurt. So, why would she turn away from it?

Voices continued to wander around her. They'd been surrounding her for so long, she wasn't quite sure when she had noticed it, but there were three of them. Three distinct voices, all hovering over her.

One sounded quite anxious. Another sounded wise, deliberate. The third had the playful lilt of a child, but even that voice had a thread of fear running through it.

She liked the voices. The anxious one was her favorite, though she couldn't tell why. But then her mind sparked, and the voices grew even more distinct. Two females, one male. The wise voice belonged to an old woman. A young woman spoke with her, following directions like an apprentice.

The third voice came out deep and husky. He also followed directions, but his anxious questions came faster than the old woman had answers.

Aaden.

Just when the name entered her mind, her eyes fluttered open.

Somehow, she had known just where to look to see Aaden's face first. He bent over a collection of bandages and ointments, muttering something inaudible under his breath.

Her eyes flitted to the other side of the room. Hay, wooden stalls, and a trough full of water confirmed her earlier deduction. She *was* laying on hay. It must have been a horse stable. Across from Talise stood a pretty young woman of about fourteen years old. The young woman carried a large bowl, which made her tilt under its weight.

The old woman knelt at Talise's side. One wrinkled hand hovered over Talise's body. The woman's other hand held a rag, which she moved toward Talise's forehead.

As the rag came closer, the woman's eyebrows flew up toward her gray-streaked hair. "She's awake."

The words came out in a gasp.

Aaden jumped to Talise's side in less than a second, but he looked more anxious than ever. Both he and the old woman jerked their heads toward the other side of the stable.

The young woman was already setting down her bowl of water. In a few steps, she disappeared through a door. The moment she left the room, the old woman let out a sigh of relief.

Her expression was difficult to read, but soon it didn't matter because the woman placed the rag directly over top Talise's eyes. Before Talise could think to shake the rag off her face, a sweet smell entered her nose. Her eyes fluttered again, but this time, they closed.

The world was black again.

PAIN SHOT THROUGH every part of Talise when she woke again. Her body didn't pulse. No voices drifted around her. Strong pain ground through the things she had once called muscles. A whimper escaped her lips before she could stop it.

In the next moment, a warm hand brushed across her cheek.

Even before her eyes opened, she recognized the touch.

"I'm sorry about the pain." Aaden's voice grounded her, as it often did.

Finally, she allowed herself to lift one eyelid.

He stared back with a tender expression. His eyes dropped as he pulled a wool blanket up around her shoulders. Now he brushed a strand of hair off her forehead. "The pain will probably last for several days, but nobody knows for sure."

She gulped then, which sent knives through her throat. "It was real though, right? I really destroyed the wall?"

His eyes shined. A half smile tilted his mouth upward. Though it was only a half smile, it still diminished some of her pain. He nodded, reaching for another strand of hair. "Yes, it was real. You destroyed the wall all the way over to the mountains near the Vine Gate on one side. And on the other side, you destroyed it all the way over to a lake between the Ember Gate and the River Gate. One third of the wall is completely crumbled."

The words were nice, but she could only focus on how his fingers brushed across her forehead. Right as she leaned into his touch, a door slammed open.

Aaden jerked his hand away at once.

"She's awake?" Wendy stomped across the floor. Her eyebrows pinched closer together with each step. "You swore you would tell me as soon as she woke up. You *swore*—"

"She *just* woke up. Just barely." Aaden glanced toward the open door Wendy had burst through.

It took until that moment before Talise realized she wasn't in the stable anymore. She laid on a bed inside a room with granite walls. It was her room in Kessoku's main base, the place she'd been staying since she stole the amulet back from Kessoku.

When had she moved?

Wendy pushed Aaden out of the chair next to the bed. She grabbed Talise's hand and squeezed it as her face screwed up with concern. "What happened? We saw you destroy the wall, and we all cheered. It was amazing. Then you, Aaden, and Lucian disappeared into the crowd, and we thought you were going back to the base as planned." Her chin quivered. "But then Aaden showed up at the base even later than us, and you were completely unconscious—"

"Wendy." A warning flared in Aaden's voice. He strode across the room quickly and shut the door. Even after it had closed, he pressed a finger to his lips.

Wiping away a few tears, Wendy shook her head. "Oh, and of course we have to keep the whole thing quiet. Lucian doesn't want anyone to know you have a weakness. He doesn't want anyone to know something went wrong when you destroyed the wall."

Talise tried to sit up, which only sent shooting pain into her heart. A grunt escaped her. She pressed a hand over her heart as she tried to inch herself upward again.

"What *did* go wrong?" Aaden stood by the door. His voice came out quiet, but it didn't hide any of the urgency. "I had no idea anything was wrong, and suddenly you just…"

He held his hands out in front of himself, as if ready to catch something. With his hands in place, he stared down at them, apparently unable to explain any further.

Pressing a hand against her heart, Talise managed to sit up just a little bit more. "I think my heart stopped."

The two other faces in the room mirrored each other. First, an expression of shock filled their faces, followed quickly by an expression of anger. Aaden and Wendy both opened their mouths.

Talise lifted one hand in the air to silence them. "I know. I can't do that again. I think it would have been fine if I had stopped earlier, but I wanted to give the citizens something incredible to see."

An innocent smile broke across Wendy's face. She laid her hands neatly in her lap and tilted her head to the side. "If you kill yourself helping the people, I will never forgive you."

With a chuckle, Talise nodded. "I'll keep that in mind."

Aaden moved as if he was going to take a step forward, but then he rocked back onto his heels instead. "How does your heart feel now?" He swallowed. "And can you breathe okay?"

Talise closed her eyes while she pressed her hand against her heart once more. After a few careful breaths, she opened her eyes again. "I think I'm okay. But I had a strange dream or something. There was a stable, and—"

"What?" Aaden's eyes narrowed as he reached for the facial hair on his chin. "I did bring you into a stable when I got my horse to take us back to the base. But we weren't there for long."

Nodding, Talise sank back into the bed. "That must be what I'm remembering."

The drifting voices, the old woman with the rag. They all muddled in her mind. Maybe it had mostly been a dream.

"How are you feeling now?" Wendy pressed the back of her hand across Talise's forehead, probably checking for a fever. Her face soon relaxed, so she must not have found anything troublesome.

Talise pulled the blanket up to her chin. "I think I'll be fine. I might not be strong enough for a lot of physical activity tomorrow, but I'm sure I'll be able to walk around after I rest for a night."

"I'm leaving tomorrow." Aaden swallowed after he finished speaking, his face frustratingly blank.

Did her frown take over her entire face? Could she even speak without a whimper? "Where are you going?"

The slightest smile twitched at his lips. "I promised you I would go check on Willow."

Talise's heart soared as she remembered the girl she had befriended in the Storm. The joy only lasted for only a split second before her heart dropped again. The only reason Aaden had to check on the girl was because her father had just died. Talise dropped her chin to her chest. "I wanted to go with you."

He raised an eyebrow before throwing a pointed glance at the bed.

Her heart sank even deeper. "You're right." It was amazing how he could communicate so much without speaking a word. "I won't be well enough to travel."

Though he clearly agreed, the slightest disappointment flashed in his eyes. "It won't take me long. I can travel to Willow's city in less than a day. If she has any family left in that city, I can bring them all to a safe place in the Gate. I should be back in less than a week. And if she doesn't have any family left, I'll be back sooner."

Talise nodded, but a rush of thoughts filled her mind. He wasn't planning to take Willow to his grandparents in the Crown? It seemed like a terrible idea now that she thought about it. Tensions were too high between the Gate and Crown. Even Aaden wouldn't be able to travel there without trouble. But if he wasn't planning to take Willow to his grandparents, who else did he know well enough?

"Don't worry about Aaden. I'll keep you busy while he's gone." A grin split across Wendy's face. Her eyes brightened as she brought her fists up to her chin. "You'll never guess what we're going to start doing tomorrow."

Even Aaden had a gleam of excitement in his eyes.

Looking back to her best friend, Talise raised one eyebrow. "What?"

Wendy clapped her hands together. "We're going to reunite Storm citizens with their families in the Gate."

Chapter Forty

Talise's limbs ached. Even after two full days of rest, riding a horse felt as comfortable as running into a stone wall. Each time the horse's hoof hit the ground her spine jolted.

Her body *did* feel stronger now, but her heart still pattered weakly in her chest. Her arms and legs still creaked with pain. It took more effort than she liked to paste a smile on her face whenever she caught sight of a citizen.

It didn't help that Aaden's absence hit her harder than she expected. If she had just been able to speak to him privately before he left, everything would have been easier. But she hadn't.

The horse's gallops joggled her fragile body. If she had known how painful the ride would have been, she might have asked to stay at Kessoku's base to rest even longer.

Wendy rode a horse at Talise's side. Rio, Fyra, and Tempest had already traveled into the Storm a few days before. Cyrus and Claye rode their own horses just behind Talise.

At least the horses moved fast enough that not much conversation could occur. Every few breaths, Talise had to suck in extra hard. Even then, her chest screamed for more air. When she pressed a hand over her heart, pain crushed through her.

Wendy must have noticed. Her eyes sparkled as she offered a smile. "Let's slow down. They don't need us right away."

Even though the words brought comfort, they stung a little too. Talise was the princess. The people were *supposed* to need her. How much would her weakness ruin things?

Seeming to notice the dark look in her best friend's eye, Wendy leaned forward on her horse. "It's incredible how much Kessoku has done already."

Talise bit into her bottom lip. "Are people from the Storm really finding their families in the Gate?"

Several bouncy nods sent Wendy's dark hair flying. "Yes, it's amazing." A subtle grin filled her face with even more sweetness. "I always assumed the worst of Kessoku. Some of them *are* terrible. Like River." Wendy shuddered. Letting out a sigh, she continued. "But there are others who are so sweet. All the talk of unity and bringing people together, they really mean it. They really want Kamdaria to be a better place."

In other circumstances, the words probably would have made Talise smile. Unfortunately, her horse gave a particularly spirited step that sent her stomach into a writhing mess. With one hand on the reins, she used the other to clutch her stomach.

Wendy's eyes turned soft. "Are you okay?" Her voice lowered to a whisper. "Do you want to go back to the base?"

Talise wanted to nod. She ached to nod. Her body was already weary from only an hour of horse travel. She wanted to return to the base and sleep for the rest of the day.

But she didn't want to disappoint the people either.

Remembering Eben's cups, the need for balance filled her mind. She couldn't only take care of Kamdaria, she had to take care of herself too.

The thought only solidified her earlier decision. Today, the people needed her more than she needed rest. She had already abandoned them for a few days of rest. As long as she moved slowly and didn't work herself too hard, she'd be fine.

Lifting her chin, she gripped the reins tighter. "I can do this. The people need to see that I will always be there for them."

Wendy's mouth pinched into a knot, but finally, she nodded. Luckily, they arrived at their destination only a few minutes later.

Talise dismounted her horse with absolutely no grace at all. Claye rushed to her side to help, but Wendy immediately batted him away. "I can help her. You and Cyrus go find the others."

To everyone's surprise, Claye and Cyrus *did* leave to find the others. The simple action released at least some of the pressure inside Talise's chest. It also helped that Wendy waited several minutes before she expected them to walk again.

When they did finally move, Talise saw the setup Kessoku had built. Lucian stood on a platform, raising his arms above his head. He spoke loudly to a group of citizens.

The action reminded Talise of how much her father enjoyed sitting on his throne, staring down at citizens.

Unlike at the palace, the faces in the small crowd looked up to Lucian with eager faces.

Stepping forward felt like a chore. Breathing made her chest constrict. She offered smiles to the citizens all around, but she could only hope the smiles looked gracious and not forced.

Once atop the platform, Talise smoothed out the full skirt of her powder-blue dress. Today, her short hair had been topped with a silver-braided circlet made from ribbon. Everyone was getting quite creative on how to adorn her with crowns when none were available.

She stood tall and took in a deep breath. The moment the air hit her throat it gave her the urge to cough. Speaking over it was all she could do. The people had been waiting for her, and they were expecting a speech. "For years, the walls around Kamdaria have separated families." She gestured toward the crumbled wall to their sides. "Today, we are finally free from its separation. I am honored that I can take part in reuniting you with your families once again."

To finish, she held a fist to her chest before lifting it into the air.

Her words came out strong enough, but the original message was supposed to be much longer. She was supposed to explain in more detail. She was supposed to have the citizens form a line.

But now, she could only take careful breaths that covered her unsteadiness. The others in her group stared at her a second too long.

Luckily, Lucian seemed to understand she no longer had the strength to go on. He recovered much more quickly than the others. Without a word, he continued where she left off. His arms waved about as he directed the citizens.

A line formed in front of the platform. Families bunched together in tightly knit groups. Children bounced up and down as their parents tried to calm them. At the front of the line, a young mother held a baby against her chest with one arm and a toddler's hand with the other. She stood with an older couple who had gray streaks in their hair. Her husband didn't stand with them. Perhaps he was home with an illness, but Talise knew it was more likely that the husband had died.

Her heart ached at the sight.

Still, the young mother's face shone as she stepped up to the platform. "We wish to find my husband's parents. I know they will want to mark their son's grave."

Talise's heart sank low. Still, nothing about the woman's face looked downtrodden or upset. Rather, joy filled the woman's eyes at the prospect that her husband might have the honor of his parents' marks on his grave. An honor that would have been impossible only days ago.

Lucian gave a stiff nod. "I'll need the names of your husband's parents. If you know what city they live in, or even which gate they live closest to, that will help. But we can probably find them as long as you have the names."

Shivers ran through Talise's legs. Her knees wanted to buckle for no reason at all. Why hadn't she thought to stand somewhere that had something she could hold onto?

And why did Aaden have to be gone? He would have offered an arm to steady her if he'd been there. He would have brought comfort with his mere presence.

The woman spoke to Aaden's father for only a few moments. Soon, he pointed to a wooden crate with rows of crisp parchment inside. "That should be the crate you need. Head over there, and my people will help you."

With a glowing grin, the woman gripped her two children tight and headed toward the crate indicated. Behind her, the older couple with the gray-streaked hair looked more skeptical. Still, the sight of the crates gave them a flash of confidence.

Another family moved to the front of the line next, but Talise continued to watch the young mother. She got to the crate. A Kessoku soldier stood behind it. Their conversation was too far away to hear, but they only spoke for a few minutes before the soldier reached into the crate.

He rifled through a short stack of parchment until he had found the one he wanted. While staring at the paper, he read something out loud.

As he spoke, the young mother nodded. Her nods became more vigorous, and soon, tears streamed down her cheeks. Her grin turned even wider still.

The soldier in front of her matched the grin with one of his own. Grabbing a blank piece of parchment from a nearby pile, he copied information from the first parchment. Once he finished writing, the soldier handed the young mother the copied information and waved her down to a group of soldiers who stood among horses.

Now the young mother and her family moved even farther away, making the conversation even more impossible to decipher. But Talise didn't need words to know what had happened. The Kessoku were ready to take the young mother and her entire family into the Gate right away. Soon, she would be united with her husband's parents, whom she had most certainly never met before.

Hope sparked in the city all around. It was so tangible, it even helped Talise stand.

But even more than the hope, something else became apparent. Something she hadn't been expecting.

The Kessoku were organized. They had records and systems. Lucian directed citizens with the ease of someone who had years of experience doing so.

While her limbs ached with weakness, an almost frightening thought came to her mind. Would it really be so bad if Kessoku took charge?

Yes, Talise had gained loyalty from citizens in the Gate and in the Storm, but it had been *their* idea to reunite Storm citizens with their families in the Gate. Talise probably would have had the same idea if she hadn't been injured after destroying one third of the wall.

But even if she *did* have the idea herself, her little group of friends never would have been able to execute the plan as seamlessly as Kessoku did now. She would have had to take families one by one. It could have taken her weeks just to find out exactly where their families in the Gate lived.

But Kessoku had crates of records that helped people find their families right away. They had organized soldiers who helped find families within the records. They had horses standing by, ready to deliver citizens into the Gate.

Her heart leapt at the thought. Kessoku still had people like River among them. Some of them just wanted revenge, no matter what the cost. But some of them truly did want unity like Wendy had said. And they were clearly willing to do the work to bring it.

"Where did they get those records?" Talise's voice came out scratchier than she expected. The moment she finished speaking, she had to cough away some thickness in her throat.

She had directed the question to all three of her friends on the platform, Wendy, Cyrus, and Claye. But Claye was the one who opened his mouth.

"We keep our own records. That was actually one of the things that got Kessoku started in the first place. It's a long story, but my parents and a few others were working with some Storm laborers. They found out there are no records in the Storm, especially not grave records, which makes it impossible to mark a grave unless you are at the funeral when it happens. Understandably, my parents thought that was pretty messed up."

The words carved into Talise's chest. Thoughts of Marmie's unmarked grave sent prickles all over her skin. Biting her bottom lip, Talise squeezed one hand into a loose fist. "So, does Kessoku have grave records for the Storm then?"

Claye gave a flippant shrug as he glanced out at the crowd. "No. Not yet unfortunately."

Her face probably fell. Her limbs definitely felt heavier. Hope had sprung inside her only to be dashed to pieces again.

Raising one eyebrow, Claye looked back to her again. "But that was just the beginning. Once my parents and the others realized the Storm had no records at all, they started paying attention to what records existed in the Gate. They got very angry when they found out how insufficient the Gate records were too. So, they traveled to Ridgerock Palace and requested better records. Then they found out palace records were perfect, and that made them even angrier. Then they realized how much wealthier Crown citizens were and that made them even angrier. A lot of things happened before they formed a group and named themselves Kessoku, but you get the idea."

Talise could barely stand. Luckily, her weakened body caused it this time. How interesting that a simple thing such as badly kept records had been the catalyst that eventually caused the deaths of her family members.

"Claye." Wendy tapped her chin as she looked out at the crowd. She gestured toward the other side of the city where the rest of Talise's friends stood helping citizens. "I think Fyra is trying to move mounds of dirt out of a home."

The moment her best friend mentioned it, Talise also noticed how Fyra was using one foot to slide dirt out of a crooked doorway.

"Oh." Claye tilted his head as he watched the strange method. A small head shake sent black curls whipping off his forehead. "I bet a storm blew the dirt in. I should go help her with my earth shaping."

The faintest smile played beneath Wendy's lips when Claye jumped off the platform. She twirled a strand of hair over one finger as the smile grew. When Talise caught her eye, the look immediately vanished.

Dropping, the strand of hair, Wendy flashed an even sweeter smile. "It will be nice once Aaden returns. I'm anxious to know how Willow has been."

Though Talise agreed, she longed for a lot more than just hearing about Willow. Maybe once he returned, it would be easier to find a moment alone with him. The thought sent a flood of warmth through her.

Almost immediately, the sensation ended when an ache twisted in her chest. Her hands curled into fists, but she managed to stop herself from clutching her heart.

The brightness stayed in Wendy's eyes, but her mouth set into a firm line. "You need to rest."

Talise opened her mouth to protest, but it only took a single eye raise from her best friend to close her mouth again. Wendy was right. Talise had shown her face to the citizens. She had done as much as she could for Kamdaria today. Now she had to take care of herself.

When Wendy led them back to their horses, Talise didn't object. But on their way back to the base, her thoughts turned once again to Aaden.

While they had been living in the Storm, she and Aaden had plenty of spontaneous moments alone together. Why had it been so difficult to find one now?

Her heart hammered in her chest as she squeezed tighter on the reins.

No matter. If a moment alone wouldn't happen spontaneously, she'd just have to manufacture a moment instead. Her eyes slid over to her best friend riding a horse at her side.

And she knew exactly who to go to for help.

Chapter Forty-One

THE RIDE TO THE BASE felt like it took at least twice as long as it should have. It took even longer for Talise and Wendy to bring their horses to the stable. Once they reached the hallway with their rooms, Talise began dragging her best friend down the hall.

She pushed open her door with a burst and let out an involuntary sigh of relief once inside. Wendy stepped in after her, and Talise promptly slammed the door shut. She was out of breath by the time she flopped onto her bed.

On the end of the mattress, Wendy pulled her legs up to sit crisscross. She let out a chuckle as a bright smile stretched across her lips. "I've been waiting for this."

Just as she settled her back against the pillow, Talise jerked her head upward. "For what?"

The smirk on Wendy's face grew before she covered it with a sweet expression. An air of innocence spread out around her. "Oh, nothing. What were you so eager to talk to me about?"

Talise let out a groan and buried her face in her knees. Heat trickled up through her neck until it filled her cheeks as well. "Am I really that obvious?"

Wendy only chuckled in response.

Tucking the embarrassment away took almost no effort at all, especially since Wendy seemed not just willing to help but excited too.

Biting her bottom lip, Talise smoothed away some of the wrinkles from her powder-blue gown. "It's about…"

The slightest eye roll went over Wendy's face. "Aaden." She chuckled as she shook her head. "I know."

Talise's cheeks filled with heat once again. The embarrassment didn't last long this time either, mostly because she was desperate for help. "Aaden and I had lots of time alone together in the Storm. We'd travel to the river for water or to amulet trainings. Even if it didn't happen spontaneously, it was easy to pull him aside if I ever wanted to. But things have been different since we got to Kessoku's base."

Grinning cheek to cheek, Wendy rested her chin on two fists. "Go on."

Now a twist went through Talise's gut. Her head hung. "I almost wonder if he's avoiding me on purpose."

A loud snort erupted from Wendy's mouth. She didn't even bother to try to cover it up. Her hand disappeared into a pocket and came out holding two shiny, silver wires.

Talise glanced at them briefly before leaning into the pillow at her back. "I'm serious. I know there are lots of people on this base, but I've been alone with you and Tempest and even Rio and Claye. And anyway, I told Aaden I needed time. I pushed him away." Without any warning at all, her chin quivered. "What if he doesn't want to be with me anymore?"

Saying the words hurt, but not as much as seeing the moment her best friend realized they might be true. Wendy had been bending one of the wires, but her fingers froze. She stared straight into Talise's eyes, not saying a word.

Sitting up taller, Talise bit her bottom lip again. "If I have to force us to have a moment alone together, I want it to be special. I want him to understand how important he is to me."

Wendy's face turned serious, as serious as it ever did anyway. As always, her eyes still gleamed with sweet innocence. "What if we arranged a dinner for the two of you? Maybe something outside where no one would bother you. Tempest and I could set out little cups filled with bark that you set on fire. Then you could have soft firelight surrounding you."

Warmth sparked inside Talise, right in her stomach. With a tentative smile, she reached for the dagger hanging from the belt over her gown. "I love that idea. And I was thinking maybe I could get him a gift of some kind."

After giving a serious nod, Wendy turned her attention back to the silver wires in her hands. Her eyebrows pinched as she twisted and bent the wires over her fingers.

Talise raised an eyebrow. "What are those?"

Her best friend gave a shrug in reply. "Oh, they're just for a project Tempest and I are working on. She's teaching me something. But forget about that. What kind of gift were you thinking of?"

Leaning back further into the pillow, Talise looked off to the side. "I'm not sure, but maybe something useful. I'd love to find something he could use every day." She bit into her bottom lip again. "If it's something he uses every day, then maybe he'll think of me more. That doesn't sound *too* devious, does it?"

Wendy only chuckled as she continued to twist the wires. "It sounds perfect. I have some other ideas too."

Plans for the special evening came together quickly.

As they worked, Talise thought back on how well Lucian handled the people in the Storm. He did have some good qualities. Now that he had stopped actively trying to kill Talise, he had undeniable leadership skills. And maybe he'd try to kill her again at some point, but with her armies on his base, he didn't have much chance.

Even without thinking it directly, she knew the thought she was avoiding. She'd been thinking the same thing from her earliest days of living in the Storm. As always, she longed for a life where she wouldn't have to rule.

The Storm reeked of desperation and fear, but Marmie had always made it bearable. More than that, she made it wonderful.

When Talise went to the testing to get into a shaping academy at seven years old, she didn't want to leave Marmie. She didn't even want to leave the Storm. But mostly, she didn't want to return to the palace.

A part of her always longed for a quiet life away from the pressures of leadership. When Marmie died and Talise had to choose between the funeral and the Master Shaper competition, it had never been about the competition. Instead, her mind filled with a dilemma that had been in her heart since the moment she entered the Storm.

Talise didn't want the crown. She never had. She just wanted to run away to Marmie and hide for the rest of her life. Though she had since accepted her duty, a part of her still dreamed of a life as anything but a ruler.

The fact that Lucian had done so well with the citizens did nothing to erase those thoughts. Especially now, Talise dreamed of a life where her greatest worry was whether she'd find the perfect gift to present to her beloved.

If her body remained as weak as it was now, perhaps it was time to truly consider giving at least some of her power away.

CHAPTER FORTY-TWO

TALISE GRIPPED HER STOMACH AS she inched across a market square. Her feet dragged across the cobblestone. Her head hung.

Once at the nearest booth, she gripped it with both hands and let herself pant loudly.

She didn't wear a gown today. Frayed burlap clothes covered her body, giving off a light stench. Her hair twisted and matted against her head. The amulet sat deep in a pouch hanging from the belt hidden under her clothes. Her flame-carved dagger hung next to it.

"Please." The words came out in a gasp.

The man in the booth barely lifted his gaze, but others on the street turned at the sound of her voice.

"Princess?" A woman in a palace uniform stepped across the cobblestone toward the little booth.

A gasp erupted from Talise's lips at the sight of the soldier. She clutched her stomach and stumbled backward.

Now two other palace soldiers joined the first.

After a stumble that nearly brought her to her knees, Talise froze in place. Her eyes widened as she sucked in a breath. "I…"

She wrapped her arms over her stomach. "I want to go back to the palace. Please, can you take me home?"

The three soldiers glanced between each other while matching gleams appeared in all their eyes.

Finally, the woman bowed. "Of course, Your Highness. We can leave right away."

Talise stared at the hand that beckoned her. She took a tentative step forward. On her second step, she limped.

A palace soldier with rough hands raised both of his eyebrows. "What happened to you?"

Gulping, Talise clutched her stomach even harder than before. She glanced over one shoulder as a shiver went through her. When she spoke, her voice came out as a whisper. "Kessoku."

The word had barely left her lips when a low rumbling shook the ground.

Before her, color drained from the faces of the three soldiers. One of them reached for her but not fast enough.

A horse galloped down the cobblestone path followed by dozens of others. Every figure on the horses wore a Kessoku uniform. When the first horse got close enough, the figure on top yanked Talise off the ground.

She writhed in his arms, screaming for help.

At the sound of her screams, palace soldiers emerged from all over the market square. They formed ranks quickly, showing off their years of training. Weapons were drawn and shaping hands raised.

Talise continued to scream until the horse carrying her turned a corner, leaving the market square out of sight.

At once, her body relaxed as she leaned back into the rider. "Do you think they bought it?"

Aaden pulled her closer before he answered. She felt him glance over his shoulder. "I think so. You definitely looked helpless."

Smug satisfaction sent her spine a little straighter. It had been months since any soldiers from the palace had been seen in the Gate. When tensions got too high during the fall months, the emperor ordered all palace soldiers to stay in the Crown. No one could pass through the wall between the Gate and the Crown unless they had a special password.

So far, the only times palace soldiers left the Crown was when they attacked Kessoku's smaller bases. The last of those had been taken weeks ago.

This time had been different. Palace soldiers had traveled in a riverboat to the city by the River Gate. A small platoon arrived in the city but not with large enough numbers for combat.

Perhaps the emperor had heard about the destruction of the wall. Perhaps he sent soldiers to find out if the rumors were true.

Whatever the reason, the opportunity had been too great to pass up. If palace soldiers dared travel in a riverboat without the numbers to protect it, then how could Kessoku *not* steal the riverboat from them? Having a riverboat would make it much easier to help people travel between the Gate and Storm.

Plus, their plan had the added benefit of making it seem like Talise had been captured by Kessoku. Now, the emperor wouldn't know for sure that she was actually working with Kessoku. It only hurt a little bit that her role had been reduced to mere bait.

Her strength was returning every day, but she wasn't ready for a fight yet.

At least Aaden had returned. He arrived at the base late the night before. She'd only seen him for a few minutes that morning when Lucian and the rest of Kessoku's head soldiers solidified their plans for the attack. Hopefully she'd have time to ask him about Willow soon.

After riding to an area behind some hills, Talise and Aaden joined the group waiting for them there. Talise sucked in a deep breath before she attempted to dismount the horse. Even with the deep breath, her body still tilted. Her head went woozy as she attempted to remember which way was up and which was down.

A strong hand gripped her around one elbow. Another hand grabbed onto her hand. The heated skin sizzled against hers. Even while her head continued to sway, she recognized Aaden's grip.

In a single moment, she had been righted once again. He held her for another few seconds, just enough time for her to feel solid on the ground. But then, his hands fell right to his sides.

She very nearly let out a sigh. Why couldn't he have held on just a little bit longer?

"Did it work?" Claye looked too anxious to even complain about how close Talise stood to Aaden.

She gave a short nod. "I think so."

Cyrus moved up to his tiptoes before throwing a pointed smirk in their direction. "How scared did they look? I probably would have fainted on the spot if I saw that many soldiers charging me at once."

Aaden let out a chuckle before moving to tie up his horse. "I wasn't paying attention to their faces."

Wendy pulled a rag from her tunic pocket. "I have to say, we did an amazing job with these dirt streaks. You look like you haven't slept in days."

Talise smiled as her best friend began cleaning the dirt streaks off her arms and face.

After running a hand through his hair, Claye moved next to Talise in the spot Aaden had been before he went to tie up his horse. Claye's eyebrows moved together as he leaned toward her. "Are you okay?"

She took a step back before nodding. "I'm fine."

While cleaning away the dirt streaks, Wendy glanced over her shoulder at Fyra.

The soldier stood alone with one hand hovering over her tunic.

"Do you need help?" Wendy's eyes brightened with the question.

Fyra let out a defeated sigh. "I got mud in my tunic, and I'm afraid it will stain. I thought maybe I could shape the earth out." She let out another sigh that indicated how well her shaping had gone.

With an apologetic frown, Wendy continued to wipe away more dirt streaks. "Oh, sorry. I probably can't shape out that much mud either. Not when it's so deep in the fibers." She glanced toward the rest of their group with an expectant face.

Claye rolled his shoulders back before he sauntered over to Fyra. "I can shape out the mud no problem."

"Oh good. I'm so glad Claye can help." Wendy grinned wide, but something about it seemed… devious.

By the time Aaden finished with the horse, even he wore a slight smile. He now stood in the exact spot Claye had been only moments earlier.

With her stomach coiling, Talise turned back to the city. She could only see part of it from where her group stood, but it was just enough. The market square sat directly in front of the riverboat, which bobbed in the gentle river waves.

Kessoku continued to charge against the palace soldiers. By now, the palace soldiers had gotten more organized. Swords flashed as they swung through the air.

Even as the weapons flew, another objective became clear. While the palace soldiers fought, they simultaneously inched backward. In only a few minutes, they had nearly reached the riverboat.

From one side of the Kessoku ranks, several soldiers raised their hands high into the air. The action shaped a wall of earth upward. It blocked the palace soldiers from reaching the riverboat.

All at once, the fighting changed. The swords clashed with more fervor. The swings turned deadly.

Talise sucked in a breath at the sight of it. If only she could help. If only her body wasn't still weak from destroying part of the wall. She ached to join the fight. She ached to stop it.

Kessoku needed the riverboat. *She* needed the riverboat. Having it would make it easier to bring people from the Storm to their families in the Gate. Plus, such a decisive victory would prove to the emperor just how strong they were.

But if people died in the fight for that riverboat, would it be worth it?

Tangible fear yanked through the calm Talise tried to settle inside herself as she stared at the fighting soldiers. The distance between them was just far enough that she couldn't make out if the swords actually struck their marks.

One thing she could decipher though. The palace soldiers were winning.

Her hands formed fists as she tried to force herself to breathe properly. One of her friends probably would have tried to calm her down, except they were all doing the same thing. Every eye was turned toward the fight. Watching. Waiting.

Just when the palace soldiers raised their hands to shape some element, a new group of people joined the fray. The newcomers let out wild shouts as they ran past the palace soldiers and toward the river.

The sight of this new group immediately stole the attention of every palace soldier. Their bodies turned toward them. Their weapons sought new targets.

A loud wail pierced the air. Someone had definitely been injured. But who?

She didn't want to accept it, but Talise already knew it was someone from that new group. The truth hit her at the same time as another horrifying truth. Every member of that new group wore a burlap tunic. The worn tunics were the same as that woman had been wearing when she cleaned up the dust when Talise made a crack in the granite.

Lucian insisted the woman wasn't a servant. He insisted she only wore the burlap because she had a messy job to do. But fighting soldiers wasn't messy. Even if it was, it surely would have been better to wear a uniform during the fight instead of burlap.

A dark chill spread across Talise's shoulders. So why was there a group of people now who all wore burlap And why had they entered the fight in the most dangerous way possible? And why did one of them get injured first?

The chill didn't leave. It frosted inside Talise while she continued to watch the fight. Kessoku had gotten the upper hand again, thanks to the people in the burlap clothes.

The moment Talise realized it, her stomach clenched. *Kessoku* had the upper hand. Nothing would stop them from fighting with the ferocity of people who hated their enemy. She clenched her jaw to prepare for a scene of death.

But none came.

To her surprise, many of the palace soldiers escaped the fight. Even more importantly, the Kessoku let them. While the palace soldiers retreated on foot for the safety of the Crown, the Kessoku only seemed intent on stealing the riverboat.

None of the soldiers had any of the bloodthirstiness Talise expected of them.

The fight did have a few casualties. Some of the palace soldiers refused to retreat. They fought hard for the riverboat. And when they tried to killed members of Kessoku, those members defended themselves.

Eventually, not a single palace soldier remained. The riverboat was theirs.

For a moment, Talise allowed herself to appreciate the victory. Joining Kessoku had helped both of them more than she could have expected. She enjoyed their organization and their records, and they enjoyed the extra soldiers she brought to their ranks. Every step went better for both of them now that they were working together.

After enjoying the victory, she allowed her thoughts to turn again. They got the riverboat, and they did it without Talise.

Did they really need her at all?

Her friends began cheering and celebrating at her side. Though she smiled, her thoughts were too focused to cheer. She turned to Aaden, who was already staring at her. "How's Willow?"

Her offered a smile in return. A warm smile. "She's good. She misses you."

He stood so close, but the rowdy behavior of her other friends wouldn't allow her to react the way she wanted to. Still, she longed to stand closer. To reach for him.

It wasn't the right time.

That truth sank her heart, but it wouldn't last for long. Now that Aaden was back, she had a plan. The evening she and Wendy planned was ready.

And this time, Talise would make sure he heard what she needed to say.

CHAPTER FORTY-THREE

THE OUTSIDE AIR PRICKLED ACROSS Talise's skin. It danced over goosebumps and quivered through her skirt. Her trimmed short hair hung loose, lightly brushing against her cheeks and chin.

Wendy begged Talise to wear a heavy brocade dress with pink and orange swirling designs. The threads would have shimmered with a beautiful opalescence in the moonlight. But tonight wasn't about looking like a princess. Tonight was about looking like Talise.

Luckily, Tempest had convinced one of the female Kessoku soldiers to let Talise borrow a black dress. The long sleeves and narrow skirt had a simple design, but it was still elegant. Talise did allow her best friend to put a few decorative combs into her hair, but that was the height of her adornment.

Now she stood on a clump of frozen grass at the edge of a forest clearing. A thick wool blanket sat on the ground inside the clearing. Small cups of fire surrounded the blanket, giving off soft, romantic light. Tempest had prepared the meal. Thin noodles floated in a brown broth with perfectly roasted vegetable morsels among them.

Biting her bottom lip, Talise glanced into the clearing once more before taking a few steps to the side. As long as Aaden approached from the direction he was supposed to, he wouldn't be able to see the blanket or fire cups or anything until Talise led him inside.

Her stomach jolted when she heard Wendy's voice. Through a cluster of trees, she could just barely make out Wendy's walking form. Another figure walked beside her best friend.

"I think it's a good idea to train the three different armies together, but we'll have to make sure Talise has just as much time with them as your father does."

"I agree." Aaden's voice sounded even stiffer than usual. He continued walking, but Talise couldn't make out his face from behind the trees. "Remind me, why are we having this conversation in the forest? I need to get back to the base."

"I told you." The sweetness in Wendy's voice came out more sparkly than ever. "I have to find the perfect stick for a project Tempest and I are working on."

"And none of the other sticks we've passed will work?" Even without seeing his face, Talise could hear the eyebrow raise that went along with Aaden's question.

"I'm sure I'll find the right one soon."

Talise very nearly rolled her eyes. What an *amazing* job her best friend had done at coming up with an excuse to get Aaden into the forest. She must have spent *hours* coming up with that story.

"I should get back—" Aaden started.

But the moment he began speaking, Wendy raised her voice and spoke over him. "Do you know when we're supposed to travel again? Your father keeps being evasive when I ask."

Aaden let out a sigh. The two of them were getting closer now. "That's because he doesn't know either. We want to be sure…"

He stopped as soon as he saw Talise.

Instinctively, she tucked a piece of hair behind one ear. Her stomach had so many flutters inside, she couldn't possibly keep them straight. Everything from her toes to her head warmed at the sight of him. Tingles buzzed at her fingertips, which made it difficult to breathe, but she didn't care. Everything about the moment felt right. She wanted to hold onto it forever.

Taking a few steps forward, Wendy smiled. "Oh, Talise. I forgot you were still out here looking. I still haven't found the right stick, but—" Her mouth dropped with far too much exaggeration. She dropped to her knees and plucked an extremely ordinary stick from off the ground. "This one is *perfect*. I have to show Tempest right away."

Wendy scurried off into the forest, disappearing from view almost instantly.

Aaden hardly seemed to notice her retreating form. He gazed at Talise almost without blinking. A faint smile pricked at his lips.

Those almost-smiles of his had a way of making Talise forget how to stand. She leaned into the nearest tree and offered a smile of her own. "Hey."

The single word forced his almost-smile to grow into a real one. He looked at the ground and ran a hand over the perfectly combed strands on the side of his head. One second later, the smile vanished. Now he looked as even and emotionless as ever.

"I'm glad I ran into you. My father said you told him that you were ready to destroy another section of the wall, is that right?"

She could only nod because her heart was busy beating right out of her chest.

His eyebrows moved together. Only a sliver of concern broke through his even expression, but it was enough to turn her heart into a skittering mess. "Are you sure you want to try again? I know you said you would be careful and stop before it injured you, but you were weakened greatly last time. I don't want…" The slightest tremor moved through his words. He cleared his voice and swallowed. When he spoke again, the words came out as even as ever. "I don't want that to happen again."

With one hand, she tucked another small piece of hair behind her ear. Then she bit her bottom lip. He swallowed at the sight of it, which could have been unrelated, but then again, maybe not. The tingles in her fingertips had spread into her arms and shoulders. "I do think I'm ready. My strength has returned, and I've been training with the amulet every day. I know my limits now."

Somewhere along the way, Aaden had stopped listening to her words and started staring at her instead. She couldn't put a finger on what had changed, but she could see it in his eyes, his posture. Heat flushed into her cheeks, which only made his gaze more intense.

Time for the gift. She pulled a pair of small, metal scissors from her pocket. Delicate carvings ran over the silver handles. There were swirls representing air, vines representing earth, waves representing water, and sparks representing fire. It featured all four elements but with symbols different from the usual waterfall, tornado, tree, and flames.

The carvings made it perfect for a Master Shaper like Aaden. Plus, the blades of the scissors could come apart to be used as razors.

"I got these for you." When she reached out, he took the scissors without question. Heat pulsed between them when their hands brushed against each other. But he pulled away quickly.

His lips parted as he brought the scissors closer to his face. Words failed him.

She tucked her hands behind her back. "It's for your beard. The pieces come apart so you can use each blade like a razor too." She ran a finger over her lower cheek. "For the parts that you do shave."

He looked up. Blinked. Glanced down at the scissors. Blinked again. Still, no words left his lips.

In moments like this, she wished he would show even a *fragment* of emotion.

His thumb slid over the handle of the scissors for several painfully silent seconds. Finally, his eyes lifted to hers. "How did you buy this? Do you have any money?"

The questions hadn't been accusatory, but her stomach squirmed all the same. She *didn't* have money. She had spent the last of it in their early days in the Storm. Since then, she relied on the money Aaden got when he sold the horses they stole from Kessoku. But that money had lasted longer than it probably should have.

Her feet shuffled over the ground. Could she admit that the shopkeeper offered her the scissors for free? That she had used her status as princess to get something she wanted? Wendy had said there was nothing wrong with it. And Talise *did* intend to pay the shopkeeper back… someday.

"Um." Hoping it might distract him, Talise took a step forward.

He gulped.

With a little shrug, she gestured toward the scissors in his hands. "I just wanted you to have something nice for your…" Now she touched her chin with her thumb and forefinger.

Aaden's free hand immediately went up to his chin where he touched his goatee with his own thumb and forefinger. "It's a family tradition."

A light smile passed over her lips. "I assumed."

He ran a finger over the facial hair lining his jaw. "My great-great-great grandfather Igniteous Sato started the tradition. The parts we shave and the parts we grow are very specific. The idea is that we can spot a fellow Sato man anywhere just by seeing his face. It's supposed to keep our family connected no matter how big it grows."

Her smile grew bigger and so did the warmth in her chest. It seemed like a good moment to take another step toward him. "Aaden."

He blinked several times. "Willow has an aunt and two cousins who are still alive."

As much as Talise loved hearing about Willow, the timing of it made her jaw clench. Letting out a small sigh, she tried to smile. "How were they?"

Aaden stared at the scissors sitting on his palm. "They were not good. Obviously. No one in the Storm is, although it is better since we've been there."

"And now?" Talise tucked a bit of hair behind her ear, even though it hadn't moved much since the last time she tucked it.

The scissors still held Aaden's attention. "I brought them to the Gate. They're staying with a good family now. Willow wants you to visit her, but I told her that probably wouldn't happen until after the war."

"I'd like to visit her. Maybe I can find a moment one of these days. How far away is she?"

He looked into her eyes at last. His fingers curled over the scissors as he put them into his pocket, but he still didn't break eye contact. "I know you want to see her, but now is not the best time."

Talise nodded, knowing the truth even before he said it. But something else about the words struck her as well. Why were they even talking about Willow? Of course she wanted to hear all about the girl but not when there was a dinner and fire cups waiting.

Something in her face must have changed as she leaned forward. Though, he continued to hold her gaze, his expression shifted.

"You never trusted me." He blurted the words out. His eyes grew wide, blinking way too often.

Rooting herself to the ground, Talise tilted her head. "What?"

After a hard swallow, his face slowly reverted back to its usual stone-faced expression. "At the palace. During our Master Shaper trials and while we taught the soldiers, you always held back. I was kind to you, and I helped you, but you never trusted me."

The words struck her with the force of a punch. "I trust you now."

His eyebrows lowered. "You should have trusted me then."

It felt like a knife had sliced through her gut, through her mind. Through her heart. Pain shimmered in his eyes as he stared back. They only brought more agony.

Never before had a censure broken her so completely. It didn't hurt that he accused her. It hurt that he was so painfully right.

She *should* have trusted him. She judged him based on the mistakes of his father, never once bothering to learn the truth of his own character. By the time she finally did trust him, Kessoku kidnapped her and imprisoned her in a dungeon.

And when she was rescued, Aaden left. But after being treated the way she had treated him during all that time, why would he have stayed?

Maybe he hurt her when he left to spy on Kessoku, but she had hurt him too.

Hot tears filled her eyes. She jerked her head away just in time to hide them from Aaden's sight. So much for her perfect plans.

With a trembling chin, she managed to swallow away the ache in her throat. "I just need a minute."

Her feet flew over the frozen soil as she disappeared into the clearing. Bright flames twinkled in the small cups surrounding the area. Her stomach lurched as tears spilled over her cheeks.

Of course she would apologize. Once she stopped the tears, she'd turn around and apologize for the dismal way she had treated him at the palace.

But what would happen after that? Had she been right all along? Had he been avoiding her? Did he no longer love her the way he once had?

Fire burst from her palms as her stomach knotted. Her flames joined those in the cups until she whisked them all away with a wave of the hand. No more twinkling lights. No more warmth.

Could she ever make things right?

All at once, she wiped the tears away. Speculating would get her nowhere. However Aaden felt, she needed to hear it from his own mouth. And *he* needed to hear how she felt.

Hadn't he said that mistakes didn't necessarily make a person good or bad. It was what a person did after the mistake that mattered? Maybe she had hurt him by not trusting him, but it didn't have to end there.

She'd make it right.

But when she left the clearing and returned to the forest, Aaden was gone.

Icy air stabbed her skin, mocked her pain.

Never in her life had she felt so alone.

After running across the frozen soil, she threw herself onto the wool blanket. Just when despair took hold of her heart, a bright thought dawned in her mind. She had asked him for time, and he gave it to her. Maybe now *he* needed time.

She wouldn't give up on him. Not now. Not ever.

Rather than fling the food into the forest and crumple up the blanket, she took a deep breath instead. Afterward, she bent to neatly fold up the blanket. She lifted the food carefully in her hands. The now-empty fire cups, she ignored. They could stay in the clearing until another day. Now she returned to the palace with a heavy determination.

Maybe she could focus on the war for a while. With another section of wall to destroy, Kamdaria needed her more than ever.

And she wasn't about to let everyone down.

Chapter Forty-Four

T̲ALISE STOOD AMONG ANOTHER CROWD of Gate citizens. This time, she stood at the base of the mountains by the Vine Gate. She wore a rich, chenille gown in a bright red hue. A crown of paper flowers was pinned in her hair.

When she raised the amulet into the air and vowed to destroy the wall, the citizens cheered loud and long. Rumors of her power had spread throughout the Gate. People knew that part of the wall had already been destroyed. No one feared the Kessoku soldiers who accompanied her when she got to the wall. Rather, they welcomed them.

Gripping one hand tight around the amulet, Talise turned and reached toward the wall. As before, a spark started at her feet, crackling as it crawled up her legs. It filled her like a well. The power buzzed inside, just waiting to be released.

When it reached her stomach, her eyes fell closed. Her full attention stayed on the power. She felt it rise, but with her control, the rising moved slowly. By the time it reached her lower chest, her body tensed.

It still took great concentration, but she managed to stop the power from rising up to her heart. Last time, that had been the moment that told her she had gone too far.

But a strange thing happened when she stopped the power from filling her to the top. Even without knowing it before, she realized the power didn't come from the amulet. It came from *her*. The amulet acted as a conduit to pull power out from herself so that she might use it to its fullest extent.

Once she cut off the amulet from using her own power, it stretched out. Her shaping senses felt when tendrils of energy spread out of the amulet. They reached until they grasped onto another source of power.

The invisible tendrils curled around the nearest person to her left.

Lucian.

Once the tendrils reached him, power sparked at her feet once more. Where her own power had been warm and buzzing, this new power felt completely different. It was cold but had great strength. Instead of buzzing, it ground up her ankles like rocks rolling over each other at the bottom of a rushing river.

The power stopped at her ankles. It took a moment of feeling it to figure out how to stop it. As soon as she realized how, she did it at once.

But no matter how she tried, she could not return the power back to Lucian. It stayed inside of her ready to aid her in destroying the wall.

After a hard swallow, she glanced to her side. Did he know? Could he tell what she had stolen from him?

He was staring at the palms of his hands. The moment she turned toward him, he jerked his head her way. As always, his expression wasn't easy to decipher. But he had been staring at his hands. Intensely staring. Did he know?

She could only hope the effects of using his power wouldn't harm him permanently. Hopefully, it wouldn't harm him at all. Maybe stealing his power would simply drain him temporarily as it had done for her. And hopefully it wouldn't drain him as much since she had only taken a small amount of power from him.

Her arm shook as she reached it toward the wall. Could everyone see how her hand trembled? Would they guess how terror filled her?

Punching her hand forward, a portion of the wall crumbled at her command. Pebbles and dust blasted into the air before floating to the ground below.

The crowd behind her cheered, but she merely glanced to her side once again.

Lucian inconspicuously held a hand out in front of his stomach. With his back turned away from them, no one in the crowd could see his palm.

But Talise could.

A spark appeared over his hand, which then turned into a bright orange flame.

He smirked at the sight of it. The flame vanished a moment later when Lucian shaped it away.

"Talise." Aaden's voice came out quiet but as intense as ever. From her right side, he took a step closer to her. "Are you okay?"

She hadn't thought to consider herself. For those terrifying moments, all concern had been on Lucian and whether his shaping was still intact. But as his fire had just confirmed, he *did* still have shaping. And even if stealing his power had weakened him, it clearly hadn't weakened him much.

A short breath of relief escaped her before she could finally pay attention to her own body. Her limbs did feel weak but nothing like they had before. She felt as if she had just shaped for a long hour. But she didn't feel ready to collapse.

With a few quick nods, she replied. "I'm fine. I stopped before it could drain me like it did before."

That satisfied Aaden. But when they moved down off the platform, he stood even closer to her than he had before. Lucian remained on the platform, telling the crowd how they would achieve unity by destroying the walls.

The citizens responded to every word with great enthusiasm. Talise smiled as she left the crowd and headed for the horses on the edge of the city. It gave her great pleasure to note that the parts of the speech the crowd loved most were the parts she had helped Lucian write.

When Lucian got to the part about removing the emperor from his throne, the crowd lost almost all its enthusiasm. Now they merely listened instead of cheering along.

Her heart sank as she mounted a horse. That was one area in which Kessoku did not have an advantage. Though the people agreed that change was necessary, most of them still believed Emperor Flarius had a right to the throne.

They wanted change but perhaps not at the expense of putting Kessoku's leader in the emperor's place.

A cry rang out, heralding an attack. They'd expected one, but the timing still came as a surprise.

Before she could turn her horse to head down the path ahead, a shower of rocks fell down on her and her companions. They beat down on her head and shoulders. Swift whooshes of air above pushed the rocks down even harder.

Pain shot through her shoulders, stinging each muscle in bursts. She gasped. The horses stomped and jittered angrily. The shock of everything came too quickly to react.

By the time a second wave of rocks fell, she was ready.

Her fingers gripped the amulet. With a flick of one hand, the entire wave of rocks moved to one side before dropping to the earth.

She clenched a fist and shot it upward. Soon, a wall of wind shot above. It blew so strong that the other whooshes of air vanished inside it.

Even without filling a well of power inside herself, the amulet still magnified her shaping greater than it had ever been. She turned around, eager to face her attackers head on.

Another barrage came for them, but this time, they used fireballs as weapons. The glowing orbs shot toward them, burning bits of dust in the air as they flew. She recognized the skilled execution. The fireballs had been perfectly formed, but they were perfectly thrown as well.

Those techniques came from months of training, but it wasn't only training that had taught them. Those fireballs were products of Talise's very own teaching.

She and Aaden had spent hours teaching the palace soldiers how to use fireballs in combat. And now those fireballs were being used against her.

Around her, elements filled the air to combat the attack. Tempest pulled water from the air and drowned a few flames while her long braid flipped around her. Wendy shaped air away from the fireballs until they vanished. Claye smothered the balls with clods of dirt. Aaden's arms moved fast, using every element to smother and push the fireballs away.

Taking a deep breath, Talise squeezed the amulet again. Before she could shape anything new, Aaden touched her arm.

"Talise." He pulled his hand away immediately. "Let Kessoku fight them. We need to focus on our goal."

Though she was tempted to at least throw a wall of ice at the attackers, she knew Aaden was right. They had planned for an attack from palace soldiers. And they had planned for Talise to run away from it.

Already, ranks of Kessoku began forming around the palace soldiers. The horses began galloping away at top speed.

Technically, she wasn't running away. Unlike when they stole the riverboat, she had more than one simple job to do.

The wall separating the Gate from the Storm hadn't been completely destroyed yet. She wasn't sure how far her destruction went this time, but at least one third of the wall still remained. It was probably even more than that since she had used less power this time than she had the first time.

Now she had to do more than just run. She had to travel around the Gate to find the next portion of wall. After resting, she'd use the amulet to destroy as much of the wall as she could. And then she'd start the process all over again.

By the time she returned to Kessoku's base again, the entire wall separating the Gate and the Storm would be completely destroyed.

They knew the action would force the emperor's hand.

Whether ready or not, the end of the war was coming swiftly to meet them.

CHAPTER FORTY-FIVE

TALISE SAT AT A LONG oval table. Aaden and Wendy sat on either side of her. Rio and Claye sat at the table too. Members of Kessoku filled the rest of the table. Now that the wall separating the Gate and the Storm had been completely destroyed, they were making preparations for a final battle.

River sat across from Talise, sneering like usual.

The oddity of it struck Talise. She had lived in the palace for months. She had earned the title of Master Shaper. She was the emperor's daughter and heir to the throne. And yet, the only time she attended a council meeting with the emperor was when she burst in uninvited.

Now she sat at just such a meeting among people who had once been her fiercest enemies. And they actually cared about her opinion.

Lucian led the meeting, listening dutifully to everyone who spoke. He didn't make fun of a single suggestion. Nothing got ignored. Even when he didn't agree with others, he took the time to think about what they had said. He still came across as gruff, but perhaps that had more to do with his personality than anything.

Despite the shock of it, Talise admitted that he made a good leader.

A woman stood, addressing the rest of the table. "Skirmishes still happen daily, but they are dying down. The palace soldiers are not appearing in the numbers they were even two days ago."

She sat and gestured toward a man at her side. Now he stood. After giving a nod to her, he continued. "We believe the emperor is gathering his forces. The palace soldiers are all heading into the Crown. The gateways are still blocked. We believe the soldiers will soon be gone from the Gate completely."

Lucian stroked his goatee as he gave a slow nod. "You believe they are preparing for a more focused attack?"

The man and the woman who had spoken both nodded. The man sat back down in his seat.

At Lucian's side, a woman raised one finger. Talise recognized the woman as the one who had been at the River Gate when Talise destroyed the dam. Celina.

Her soft eyes squinted as she spoke, as if trying to get the words just right. "I believe we will have a better chance against the emperor's army if we attack first. They have more training and precision, but we have the numbers to beat him now. If we are prepared, attacking first will let us fight on our own terms. It will give us the upper hand."

"I agree." Lucian didn't even stroke his goatee before he spoke. The words came out too quickly. "But we need a way to attack hard and on all fronts."

River sat tall in her chair, folding her arms in front of her chest before speaking. "Why don't we have the princess destroy the entire wall separating the Gate and the Crown in one go? The emperor's soldiers won't know what do with themselves if all their protection is removed at once."

"That is a nice idea," Claye said as he raised an eyebrow. "But it's probably impossible."

Lucian cleared his throat, which immediately brought all eyes toward him. He gave a pointed glance toward Talise. "Do you think you could do it? Destroying the entire wall at once *would* give us a distinct strategic advantage."

Squirming filled Talise's gut while everyone stared at her. The wall around the Crown was much smaller than the one around the Gate had been. And after accidentally drawing power away from Lucian, she knew it technically *was* possible. But only if she stole power from others, which she had no intention of ever doing again.

Maybe the smaller wall would be possible to destroy on her own anyway. She gave a short shrug. "I don't know if I can do it. I'll try, but don't plan on it."

In a flash, something in Lucian's demeanor shifted. "We have a team we can send in first. They'll keep the rest of us safe."

Talise immediately thought back to the team of Kessoku who wore burlap when they stole the riverboat. Members of that team had been injured more than anyone else. Some had been killed. Scratchy, dryness filled her throat at the memory.

Lucian's appearance sharpened. A gleam sparked in his eye that looked every bit as wild as River. He stared at Talise with an intense gaze. "I know something you *can* do."

Her stomach jolted. Warning bells went off in her mind. She had the urge to leave the meeting, but no excuse came to her mind. Soon, it was too late. Lucian revealed her secret.

He sat up tall, the gleam in his eye growing colder by the second. "The princess can take shaping away from others."

Aaden jerked his head toward her.

Her face grew hot as she stumbled over words. "I don't know if I can do that. I mean, I can." He *knew* she could. "But I've never done it on purpose. I have no idea what the long-term effects would be. I don't know the limits."

Lucian ignored her. "Before she takes down the wall, the princess will drain the shaping away from every person she can inside the Crown." He looked to her again. "Drain them until they are weak. Until they have nothing left. If draining them too much ends up killing them, then all the better for us."

Her mouth hung open, but no words came out.

The energy in the room had shifted. No longer did strategy or listening ears rule. Now the tangible taste of revenge hung in the air all around.

At the head of the table, Lucian's smile tilted with a heavy smirk. "Once you've drained as many people as you can, then take down the wall."

She found her voice again, but it took a moment. The words tumbled out of her faster than she could think of them. "I could never hurt people like that. I'm not even sure—"

"And Aaden." Lucian spoke over her, cutting off her every objection. "I have a special job for you. You will take a small group inside the Crown the day before our attack. Get into the palace and gain the emperor's trust. Tell him anything about our plans until he trusts you. Then, as soon as he does, your group will attack. Kill everyone inside the palace, everyone that you can. Take no prisoners."

Horrific memories played through Talise's mind. Flashes of her childhood came back like hammers pounding into her skull. Kessoku had done the same thing back then. They attacked the palace when everyone's guards were down. The Kessoku killed without abandon. They targeted the imperial family, but they murdered anyone who stood in their way.

With Marmie's help, Talise had only barely escaped with her life.

And now Lucian wanted to do the same thing again.

But he wanted Aaden to lead the charge.

"I'm not doing that." Aaden's voice came out soft enough that everyone leaned forward to hear him. The words still pierced the air with the strength of a sword.

A twinge passed over Lucian's face. It wrinkled his nose and put tension through his eyebrows. His teeth only barely parted when he spoke again. "Son."

Aaden sat up taller in his chair. His fixed his gaze on his father, letting each word out deliberately. "I will face my enemies with honor. We will both know when the fight begins and ends."

The vein in Lucian's forehead pulsed. More than once, he opened his mouth, but Aaden continued. His voice still came out quiet, yet as piercing as ever.

"I refuse to sneak in and murder people who trust me."

All around the room, thick tension filled the air. If anyone didn't recognize the jab Aaden took at his father, they were in the minority. When the palace had been attacked in Talise's childhood, it was all thanks to Lucian, a renowned member of the palace army. He gave away secrets that allowed Kessoku to sneak in and murder people who trusted them.

The unspoken accusation lingered over the table. It forced the pulsing of Lucian's vein to throb. Red heat trickled into the man's face.

Aaden sat in silence, still pinning his father with an unwavering glare.

Every breath in the room came out slow, waiting.

Lucian opened his mouth.

Aaden interrupted him again. "And I can't go into the Crown anyway. I am going to stay with *Princess* Talise during the entire fight. I will not leave her side."

The heat in Luican's face moved from a light pink to a dark crimson. His teeth clenched so tightly together his jaw looked ready to crack. He closed one hand into a fist. "Her side?" He spat the words out, speckling the table with his spittle. "You are not fighting for *her*. You are fighting for Kessoku."

Despite the clear expectation for a response, Aaden sat as still as ever. His mouth stayed closed without a single twitch to convey it might open soon.

Squeezing his fist even tighter, Lucian slammed it against the wooden table. "I am your *father*. You will show your loyalty to Kessoku in whatever way *I* decide."

Again, Aaden stayed silent. His limbs looked incredibly relaxed compared to his father's. Apparently, no amount of coercion could move him.

That wild gleam in Lucian's eye returned. On instinct, Talise reached for the amulet. Maybe it was overkill to assume she'd need it, but maybe it wasn't. Darkness like she had never seen before writhed in Lucian's eyes. Whatever he said next would surely be horrible, and most likely irreversible.

Lucian's mouth slanted upward, too frightening to look like a true smile. "If you continue to defy me, I might have to disinherit you."

Everyone at the table gasped. Even Aaden.

Especially Aaden.

The word very well could have been considered a curse in Kamdaria. Not even the worst criminals threatened their children with disinheritance.

But Talise knew what almost no one else at the table did.

Aaden had been disinherited before. His mother left him at a very young age.

If Lucian disinherited his son, Aaden wouldn't have any family left at all. No parents. Not even his Grandfather Blaise and Grandmother Seraphina who still lived in the Crown with the emperor.

No greater shame could be brought upon anyone in Kamdaria.

The breaths in the room no longer came out slow. They didn't come out at all.

Not a single muscle moved while everyone waited to see if Aaden would bend to his father's will.

Aaden's face looked *almost* as serene as ever. Knowing him as well as she did, Talise could see how his eyebrows pinched just slightly too close together. She could see that his hands curled in a not quite natural curve. His jaw pulsed the tiniest amount. It indicated that instead of having a relaxed face like it appeared, Aaden was actually holding the expression tight in place.

He stood. Every eye in the room gazed at him without interruption. For the first time in that meeting, his jaw clenched a little too tight. He glared at his father. "My loyalty does not belong to you."

For a moment, he just stood there. The words plowed into the air, keeping everyone still as stone.

But then his hand twitched. It dropped into his tunic pocket with the grace of someone raised in the Crown. When his hand emerged, he held the scissors Talise had given him only a few nights before. During her epic fail of trying to tell him how she felt about him.

His hands moved with precision. They didn't fidget or tremble. He pulled the two blades apart and held one in front of his face.

And then the blade met his chin.

In one perfect swipe, the facial hair along his jaw fluttered to the table. One more swipe, and he shaved the other side. Pulling his bottom lip between his teeth, he brought the blade down his chin, shaving away the rest of his beard.

His father blinked. Swallowed. He shook his head and clenched his fists. But no matter how he fidgeted, it didn't change the actions of his son. His face turned crimson once again.

Pulses shook through Lucian's jaw, as if trying to think of something to say. His eyes shimmered with anger. After several long seconds, he finally sat back in his chair. His eyebrows pressed down over his forehead. "Your grandfather will be disappointed in you."

The blade quivered in Aaden's hand. His eyes widened. His hand dropped to his side. He didn't say a word, but the determination that had been apparent in his face only moments before vanished. He gulped.

Lucian folded his arms over his chest. "You were born a Sato. Sato blood will always run through your veins. You can shave your face, but you cannot change who you are."

One beat of silence went through the room. Aaden curled his fingers over his blade and then he rested both fists on the oval table in front of him. Staring at his father, he spoke in a crisp, decisive tone. "I am who I choose to be."

And then he left the room.

No one tried to stop him, not even Lucian. By now, most people were staring at their hands or trying to shrink away. There wasn't complete silence anymore because people were brushing their tunics or playing with their hair.

But if no one had anything else to say, Talise was happy to take advantage of the silence.

She rose from her chair in the most fluid movement she could manage. Donning a regal expression, she floated across the floor. Her feet only barely brushed the ground with each step. By the time, she reached the head of the table, Lucian seemed to know what was coming.

He leaned back in his chair. It had probably been an attempt to look casual. Instead, it gave the impression of him shrinking at the sight of Talise.

Gritting her teeth together, she leaned toward him. She had told him to rot in flames before, but those words wouldn't be sufficient this time. Her eyes narrowed as her lips parted. "If you ever threaten Aaden again…" She paused for a moment to let the words sink in. Then, she leaned in even closer. "I'll kill you."

He must have sensed the truth in her words because this time he did shrink deeper into his chair. She whirled around. Holding her chin high, she addressed the others. "This meeting is over now. We will meet here again later."

With a wave of her hand, everyone left the room.

CHAPTER FORTY-SIX

COLD FILLED THE AIR AS Talise trailed down a hallway. The granite walls lost their sparkle at this time in the evening. It had taken her a few hours to decide her next moves. Wendy had been there to talk things through. Even Tempest offered valuable insight.

Talise knew what needed to be done. Now, she just had to do it.

Her heart leapt every time she glanced into a new room from the hallway. Most of these doorways led to sitting rooms where soldiers could talk and rest with one another. She never found the face she *wanted* to see, but eventually she did find the person she was looking for.

Claye.

She would have gone to Aaden first. In fact, she *had* gone to him first. But despite spending far too long searching, she hadn't been able to find him anywhere after the meeting. She strongly suspected he wasn't even inside the base anymore, but where else could he have gone?

Claye lounged on a plushy chair, grinning at the Forces board in front of him. Fyra sat across from him, biting her thumbnail. When he reached forward and moved one of the tablets, a giggle burst from her lips.

"I bet you weren't expecting that, were you?" he drawled.

Fyra's giggle turned into a snort, which only deepened the smile on Claye's face. Just when their grins looked ready to split their faces, Claye sat up with a start.

"Talise." He swallowed and sat up even straighter still. "Hi."

A bright red shade filled Fyra's cheeks. She jumped to her feet and gave an awkward bow. "I should probably get back to training." Her voice came out in a quiet squeak. As soon as the words left her lips, she shuffled out of the room.

When Talise sat down across from Claye, he tugged at his collar. Her eyes narrowed at the Forces board for a moment before she glanced toward the doorway where Fyra had just disappeared.

Her gaze turned back to Claye. Now red splotches broke out across his face. Talise raised an eyebrow. "Have you two been spending a *lot* of time together?"

"No." He squirmed. "Maybe." Two fingers tugged at his collar once more. He offered a guilty frown when he looked into her eyes. "I would spend time with you if you…"

"No." Even as he trailed off, Talise responded with ease. She even managed a smile that held no amount of spite or jealousy. "I'm glad. I like Fyra." She let out quiet chuckle as her eyes found the Forces board once more. "But it seems like you know her a lot better than I do."

The smirk that filled his face looked as Claye-like as ever. For the first time since leaving the palace, things felt natural with him. Finally.

He leaned forward. Genuine concern glowed in his eyes, showing how much he did care for her, even if it wasn't in a romantic way. "You're not mad?"

"No." She gave a quick shake of her head before dropping her hands into her lap. "But I do need to ask you about something important. You're not busy right now, are you?"

Another signature smirk filled his face. "Not anymore. What do you need?"

Her chest filled with a breath before she let it out slowly. With one last glance at the empty doorway, she looked Claye in the eye. "I've seen a few people around here who wear burlap tunics."

His nose wrinkled at the words. He grimaced at the floor before responding. "They're called servants, but they're treated like slaves. I don't think they even get paid. They get a place to live and food to eat. Nothing else."

Closing her eyes, Talise rested her forehead in one hand. Pain bloomed in her heart. She did nothing to stop it. How could she? If people had been treated that badly, didn't they deserve to have at least one person to mourn their condition?

When she opened her eyes again, an equal amount of pain cut through Claye's eyes. Her hand dropped into her lap once again. "I had guessed as much. Is there anything else I should know about them?"

Tilting his mouth upward, a glimmer of hope burst through the anger filling Claye's face. "They're from the Storm. Kessoku made that hole in the wall and then lured people here to the base with the promise of a better life. But once they got here, they barely got more than food and shelter." He gulped and turned his eyes downward. "For years, I didn't even realize how wrong it was. I grew up seeing them, and I treated them the way everyone else did. But it *is* wrong. I think we should do something about it."

She sat forward, letting a small smile onto her mouth. "Good. Hopefully you aren't the only one who feels that way." Resting her elbows on the table, she continued. "Here's how you can help me. Tell me everyone you can think of who might agree with us."

With a chuckle, he sat back in his chair. "What do you have planned?"

She raised an eyebrow. "It's going to be unforgettable."

— ◆ —

AFTER RETRIEVING A basket of herbed rice balls, Talise entered her room in the base. Several people squished into the small room, filling every corner.

Tempest lay on the bed with her hands behind her neck. Wendy sat next to her, fiddling with a cluster of silver wires. Every so often, Tempest would offer a word or two of instruction. Wendy's twisting did make the wires prettier, but they didn't seem to form anything in particular.

Fyra sat against one wall with her knees up to her chest. Claye sat next to her looking infinitely more relaxed than she did. Rio leaned one shoulder against a wall while he studied a piece of parchment. Cyrus sat on top of a rug, shooting short bursts of air at the ceiling.

Talise set the basket onto the ground with a little too much force. "Aaden's not here yet?" She let out a huff. "I need someone else to help me look for him because I can't find him anywhere."

At the sound of her words, Cyrus stopped shaping. He glanced toward her without moving his head and without lowering his hand. "Aaden is…" His eyes danced around the room, looking toward the ceiling for half a moment. "Busy." He gave a forced smile along with the final word.

Her head jerked toward Cyrus. "You know where he is?"

340

His eyes widened as his hand finally dropped into his lap. "Uh…" He extended the syllable long enough to make it clear that no answer was coming.

She huffed again, narrowing her eyes along with it. "Is he safe?"

"Oh. Yes." Cyrus shook both hands, as if in surrender. "He's definitely safe."

A sinking feeling filled her gut. Could she hide the slight tremble in her chin? "Where is he?"

The corners of Cyrus's mouth lowered as he gave an apologetic shrug. "I don't know exactly."

Her mouth twisted into a knot, but it was nothing to the twist in her heart.

From the bed, Wendy's head popped up. "He probably just needed some time to be away after…" Her hand gestured at nothing in particular as she trailed off.

Talise nodded, but her feelings only ripped and shredded. It made sense that Aaden would need time away after that meeting, but still. Why hadn't he gone to *her?* She could have been there for him. Was it because he didn't trust her as much as she wanted him to?

Her throat thickened at the thought. If she didn't do something immediately, tears would follow.

Lifting the basket of rice balls, she began distributing them out to her friends. She gave a pointed glance at Cyrus as she worked. "Will Aaden be back tomorrow evening?"

With a rice ball in hand, Cyrus frowned once again. "He said he'd be back in two days."

Talise slumped onto the floor as she plucked the last rice ball from the basket. "Fine. Then we'll postpone the meeting until then. In the meantime, we have a lot of work to do. Claye?" She gestured toward him. "Why don't you explain?"

CHAPTER FORTY-SEVEN

TWO DAYS LATER, TALISE SAT at the oval table once again. People filed into the room, people she and her friends had carefully chosen. The chair at her side remained empty. Her fingers ached from how hard she clenched them in her lap.

At the head of the table, Lucian prepared to speak. Talise's heart nearly stopped.

But just as the meeting was set to begin, Aaden noiselessly entered the room and slipped into the chair at her side.

She could have filled a room with the sigh of relief that escaped her. Despite her effort to keep it silent, some of the sigh stayed audible.

Aaden gave her a single glance, which was enough to set her heart on fire. It sizzled and glowed in her chest while she tried to maintain eye contact.

He didn't smile or frown or give any sort of expression, but something in his eyes looked different. Peaceful. Did he know what she had said to his father? Had someone told him? His face was clean-shaven now. Even the short mustache under his nose had been shaved away. As much as she liked his facial hair, he still looked as handsome as ever without it.

Lucian stood from his chair, keeping his eyes as far from his son as he could get them. "Welcome everyone. We need to discuss—"

"Excuse me, Lucian." Talise rose to her feet gracefully. "I have something I would like to discuss first."

A twitch pulsed at the edge of Lucian's nose. His hands formed fists at his side.

She didn't wait for him to give an answer. Instead, she addressed the others in the room. "I asked two people to join us today, people who have been a part of Kessoku from the beginning." She gestured across the table toward Claye's parents. "Glen and Ivy, would you please remind us how Kessoku first got started?"

Lucian continued to stand at the head of the table, but no one paid him any attention. Claye's parents stood, smiling at each other before they began.

Ivy spoke first. She set her jaw with a smile, but it was laced with determination. "Kessoku has always sought unity for Kamdaria."

When she glanced toward her husband, he gave a nod and then continued. "We discovered that poor and unkept records in the Gate made it so we were unaware of how much less we had compared to people in the Crown. And we were cut off from people in the Storm, so we could only assume they had even less than us."

Ivy gave an eager nod. "We just wanted resources to be distributed evenly throughout all three rings. And we didn't want to be separated from our families in the Storm anymore."

"Thank you." Talise gestured that they should be seated once again. Now her gaze turned to the most frightening pair of eyes in the room. "And River?"

The woman's terrifying eyes widened at the mention of her name.

Talise gave her a pointed stare. "What do you fight for?"

River's mouth tilted into a snarl. Her hand curled in a fist, which she brought down on the table. "I fight for my aunt's children who were sent to the Storm. I want the emperor to suffer like they did."

A stiff nod seemed like the best response. "Thank you." Talise glanced over the entire table once again. At some point, Lucian had returned to his seat. She tried not to be too excited about it. "For years, two opposing goals have existed in the hearts of Kessoku. If we are to win this war, our goals must align. I will not allow dreams of revenge to infect my soldiers anymore."

With a sputtering cough, Lucian lifted his head high. "*Your* soldiers?"

Her head turned toward the man slowly. By the time she locked eyes with him, he squirmed in his seat. She held her spine as stiff and as straight as she could. "Today you must choose, unity or revenge."

That twitch in his nose returned. He flashed his teeth before speaking again. "*I* am the leader for Kessoku. You cannot tell me how to lead my own people. They answer to me."

She let silence fill the air for a few moments, just enough time to make him eager for her response. Rolling her shoulders back, she spoke again. "I am princess of Kamdaria, heir to the throne. It is my right and my duty to protect my people. You may rule Kessoku, but I rule the empire. Your army answers to me."

He jumped from his chair, reaching for the sword hanging from his hip. "I should have killed you when I had the chance."

Though the group at the table had many of the same people in attendance at the last meeting, they had all been carefully chosen. When Lucian reached for his weapon, the four people sitting nearest to him jumped to their feet. Celina, Ivy and Glen, and another man whose name Talise didn't know. Each of them grabbed their own weapons, drawing them without hesitation.

Talise glared back at Lucian. "You did *try* to kill me. We shouldn't forget that." Her eyes flicked to those standing guard at the edge of the room. "Soldiers, remove this man from my presence."

Lucian backed away from the table with slow steps. He kept shaking his head but nothing changed when he did.

Settling back into her chair, Talise glanced across the table into a pair of frightening eyes. "Anyone else who only wants revenge should also leave. If you don't leave willingly, we'll remove you forcefully."

River sprinted from the room before Lucian did, but he followed soon after her.

In another life, perhaps Talise could have let someone else be in charge. Perhaps she could have lived simply in a secluded part of the empire. But in this life, she had to accept what she'd been trying to avoid since all her siblings had been killed.

The fate of Kamdaria rested on her shoulders. And the empire needed her now more than ever.

Silence filled the room for several beats after the two of them had left. Aaden was the first to break it. "River has a team of shapers who will follow her. They're the strongest shapers we have. Our army will be weaker without them."

A knot twisted inside Talise's chest. It took great concentration to keep her eyebrows from rising high on her forehead. "Do you think we should have let her stay?"

"No." He shook his head, confirming the sincerity of that one word. "I just thought you should know."

"Oh." Her heart pounded, but no other response came to her.

Aaden glanced around the table before reaching into his tunic pocket. "I have a letter for you from Willow."

Her head tilted as she reached for the folded parchment. "Thank you."

At her other side, Wendy let out a little cough.

It took a firm shake of the head before Talise had been righted once again. She tucked the letter into her pocket and glanced toward the soldiers by the doorway. "Bring them in, please."

The two soldiers bowed before disappearing through the doorway. When they returned, at least three dozen people filed in after them. Each of the three dozen people wore threadbare burlap tunics. Unkempt hair topped their heads. Hollow eyes filled their faces.

Nausea might have churned inside Talise at the sight of them if she hadn't had a plan already. Standing again, she addressed the people before her. "From this day forward, you will all be paid for your service inside this base. If you wish, you can join the army and become soldiers. If you want to leave, you are welcome to do that too."

Nothing short of astonishment filled their faces. Many open mouths and widened eyes stared back at her, but it seemed like no one had any idea what to say. Then again, for people who had never known freedom, it made sense they had no idea what to do with it.

She offered them a smile, hoping her expression had softened with it. "These two soldiers will help you. Please, take your time deciding. We want you to do what you want to do. And as long as you stay on the base, you will be paid."

After a gesture toward the soldiers, the crowd of burlap-clad citizens left the room. She made a mental note to check on each of them that evening before going to bed.

Her eyes turned back to those at the table. "We will spend one more week to prepare, but then we must start the final battle against the emperor."

Celina raised a hand into the air before speaking. "I still think it would be most beneficial if you destroy the wall around the Crown all at once. We could place armies around the whole wall before it's destroyed. Then we'd be ready to attack any army, and they would have no warning."

Talise's throat filled with an ache that couldn't be swallowed away. "I will try my best, but I don't know if I can take down the whole wall at once."

Rio sat up straighter. "Before we take down the wall, we should gather the citizens of the Gate and explain our plan. That will give them a chance to get to safety if they need. It will also give them a chance to join us if they are willing to fight."

"Yes." Talise gave an eager nod. "I can travel to a few cities, and we can send messengers to relay our plan to any other cities."

A woman at the other end of the table raised one finger. "We still need to decide where the main assault will occur. Will it be wherever you destroy the wall? If so, where should that be?"

"I have an idea for that." Aaden leaned forward. That same peace emanated from his eyes, but a gleam of excitement joined it. "I know where we should destroy the wall, and I know exactly what cities we need to visit along the way."

CHAPTER FORTY-EIGHT

MESSENGERS LEFT THE VERY NEXT day. Soldiers began traveling through the Gate in preparation for the final battle.

Only two days were reserved for last-minute training. After that, an entire company of soldiers accompanied Talise on what might be her last tour through the Gate.

They started in the small city where Aaden had gotten their food and supplies when they lived in the Storm. It was the same city where she had been weakened by destroying the first portion of wall.

After a rousing speech, the people cheered and many vowed to help Talise in her fight. Whenever Lucian had talked about removing the crown from the emperor, the people could only give half-hearted agreement. But now that their princess fought for their protection, the people couldn't join her fast enough.

Because she had something Kessoku never had.

A right to the throne.

After the speech, she spoke with as many citizens as possible. Eventually, tents had been set up at the edge of the city for Talise and her army. The tents brought back memories of when she had traveled through the Gate before.

Just as she settled into her tent, a young voice came from just outside it. "Talise? Princess Talise?"

Jumping to her feet, Talise yanked open the tent flap.

With eyes sparkling, Willow stared back at her.

Talise pulled the girl into a tight hug before any thought could stop her. After several seconds, she released the girl and pulled her inside the tent. "I'm so glad you got my message. I worried you wouldn't get my response in time."

Willow giggled as she sat crisscross on the tent floor. "Yes, I got the message almost as soon as your army entered the city." She let out a sigh, but it didn't seem too heavy. "I've missed you."

Reaching for her heart, Talise took in a deep breath. "I've missed you too." She gulped, thinking of Willow's dead father. "How are you doing?"

Though the words were not specific, the girl seemed to intuitively know the real question being asked. Tears brimmed in her eyes. She hugged her knees to her chest while squeezing her eyes shut. "I don't think the pain will ever go away." Her chin trembled when she looked up again. All at once, the tears slowed. "But I have good days too."

Swallowing over a lump in her throat, Talise reached for the girl's hand. There weren't words that could express how she felt, but it didn't matter. Willow felt it too. The two of them knew grief more intimately than most others. Talise had lost almost all of her family. And then she lost Marmie. Willow had lost her mother as a baby. And then she lost her father. In that moment, a touch said more than words could. They shared a painful bond that would never leave. But it didn't have to end them either.

After another swallow, a true smile came across Willow's face. "I'm living with another family now. It's my aunt and my two little cousins, and in the other family, they have a mother and father, a grandmother, and they have a daughter only one year older than me. She and I get along really well." Her face bloomed with an even bigger grin. "It's like having a sister."

Thinking of Wendy, Talise returned the grin. "I'm so glad. And how is your shaping?"

Talise probably shouldn't have kept the girl up so late, but she didn't care. They both needed that talk. Almost everyone had gone to bed by the time they stepped out of the tent.

Talise grabbed a gray shawl and wrapped it around her shoulders. "I'll walk you back to your house."

Of course Willow agreed because it meant more time for talking. Besides, they had dozens of shaping techniques they still had to discuss. A few snores erupted from some of the tents near her.

A peaceful chill filled the air around them as they strolled over the cobblestone streets. It wasn't until they nearly arrived that Talise realized she'd have to walk back to the tents on her own. There would probably be a handful of people who would have protested the idea if they knew about it. But with so much of her life becoming public, Talise craved these short moments of solitude. Then again, she wouldn't have minded the presence of a certain someone.

Once they turned onto a new street, Willow gave Talise one last hug and darted toward a doorway. Something about the doorway seemed familiar as the girl disappeared through it, but she couldn't pinpoint what.

At least not until Aaden emerged from the doorway only a few minutes later. He held the door open just long enough for her to see a large stable filled with hay and rows of horses.

Memories pricked at the back of Talise's mind. She tucked herself around the side of a nearby house, so Aaden wouldn't see her right away.

Smells drifted from out of the stable. She remembered them. The same smells had hung in the air when she went in and out of consciousness after destroying the first portion of wall. Aaden said he brought her to a stable to retrieve their horses before he took her back to the base. But this wasn't the same stable their horses had been at.

This was a place she had never seen before.

Standing the shadows of the doorway, Aaden glanced up and down the street. He carefully closed the stable door before he darted across the cobblestone.

But the door opened again once he reached the other side.

"Aaden." A young woman emerged from the doorway holding out a cloak. "You almost forgot this."

He glanced up and down the street before darting back to her.

The entire world froze around Talise. That young woman had also been in the stable when Talise moved in and out of consciousness. When the old woman had realized Talise had woken, both she and Aaden had looked at the girl. When she had disappeared through a door a moment later, Aaden almost looked worried for her safety.

Even as it thundered in her chest, Talise's heart sank low.

Was this the reason Aaden had been avoiding her? Was this where he had disappeared after the meeting when he shaved his face?

From across the street, Talise could just barely make out Aaden's lowered voice.

"Promise me you'll be safe, Cascade. You stay here with your parents like you promised."

The young woman gave a hurried nod before she threw her arms around Aaden's neck. When he gave her a gentle embrace in return, Talise thought maybe her heart should just stop altogether.

After pulling away, the young woman—Cascade—squeezed Aaden's hands and then disappeared through the door once more.

She was young, too young. She only looked about fourteen, which was much too young for a nineteen-year-old like Aaden. But then again, maybe she just looked younger than she was. Either way, Talise hated her. That probably wasn't fair, but she couldn't help it.

And she didn't want to believe it.

Aaden fastened his cloak and crossed the street once more. It only took a few steps until he discovered Talise hiding around a corner.

His feet stopped in place. "What are you doing here?"

It would be a miracle if she could get through this conversation without tears. She swallowed. "I was just bringing Willow back."

"Alone?" His eyebrow raised.

With a shrug, she looked to the ground. "I wasn't going to be out long. Most people are asleep anyway."

He nodded, but his eyebrows moved down over his eyes. "Are you okay?"

"Yes." Her voice came out too soft.

He still heard though. After letting out a slow breath, he glanced over his shoulder at the stable.

Talise's heart pounded. "You brought me here after I destroyed the wall. While I was still unconscious."

A hard swallow moved through his throat. "Yes." When he began walking back to the tents, she fell into step beside him.

He spoke without looking at her. "They weren't supposed to be helping me. I promised them you'd never even know. But then you woke up." He shook his head. "I was just trying to protect them."

She nodded but kept her eyes toward the ground.

Aaden's voice came out rushed as he continued to explain. "When you remembered it, I probably would have told you everything, except Wendy was in the room. I trust her, but not as much as I trust you. And I promised them no one else would know."

By now she had glanced up to see his face.

He was staring at his hands. "Cascade, she's…" He gulped. "She's not supposed to see me. Her parents would have punished her if they found out."

Roiling filled Talise from her head to her toes, but she managed to keep her expression somewhat even. So, not only did Aaden have a new young woman in his life, he also had a secret, forbidden love. She didn't want to believe it, but who else would he trust enough to take care of Willow and her family?

Talise's lip trembled. In the dark, he probably couldn't tell. He was still staring at his hands anyway. Perhaps her heart was failing, but she couldn't get angry with him. After everything they'd been through, he deserved that at least. She swallowed over an aching lump in her throat. "She's beautiful."

Now Aaden's eyes flicked upward. The sweetest smile covered his lips. He only replied with one word. "Yeah."

Knives stabbed into Talise's gut. Maybe he deserved better, but jealousy took over. "But don't you think she's a little young for you?" At least the words didn't hold as much bite as she had in her heart.

Slowing his pace, Aaden turned to her with an expression of confusion so pure, it turned his eyes bright. "Young for me to what?"

They continued to stare at each other for several steps. The confusion on his face only grew. Suddenly, his expression twisted. He closed his eyes and shook his head and maybe even gagged a little. "No, it's not like that."

Was it wrong for Talise to float at the sound of those words?

Now a chuckle escaped Aaden's lips. He brought a hand to his forehead. "She's my sister."

The words brought a hope so fierce through Talise's entire body, it could have kept her alive for days. "Your sister?" Such words had never sounded so sweet. But now her own face twisted in confusion. "I thought you were an only child."

He gave a heavy nod. "I *am* an only child." He rubbed one hand across his forehead, flinching underneath it. "She's my mother's daughter. And technically she's *not* my sister since my mother isn't my mother anymore." He gave a short shrug. "But we do share blood. And we both see each other as siblings, no matter what the law says."

The clouds themselves couldn't have climbed as high as Talise's heart did now. "Aaden, that's wonderful. You have a *sister*. How did you find her?"

His mouth tipped upward, filling his face with a glow. "My father helped me when I first pretended to join Kessoku. I was actually looking for my mother, but she didn't want anything to do with me." The words brought a wrinkle through his forehead. Almost at once, it disappeared. "But my sister did want to see me. She's helped us more than you know. Her parents raise and sell horses, so anytime I needed one, it was easy to borrow one for a few days without anyone noticing."

Talise smiled as another memory shot through her. "And the orange dress you found for me when I finally stole the amulet back from Kessoku?"

The smallest chuckle came out. "Yes, that came from Cascade."

They had nearly reached the tents, which didn't seem fair at all. She didn't want this moment to ever end. Perhaps more questions would force him to stay. "What about the other woman who was there? An older woman. She held her hand over my body."

His shoulders went rigid. "That was Cascade's grandmother. She's a healer."

The way he was so quick to use Cascade to explain the relationship seemed suspicious. Talise raised an eyebrow. "Is she your grandmother too?"

They both knew the law claimed that Aaden's only grandmother was his Grandmother Seraphina, who lived in the Crown. But Talise didn't care what the law said. Aaden's mother had still given birth to him. She couldn't be rid of him completely. And that meant Aaden's mother's mother was still his grandmother.

He nodded. Slowly. "I don't think she recognized me. Cascade didn't tell her who I was, she just said I needed help. I hadn't seen her since I was very young." He shrugged. "But maybe I look too much like my father. Still, even if she recognized me, she *did* help." His eyes lowered to the ground. "Without her help, you might have died. Kessoku has healers, but they're not very good."

They had finally reached the tents. Aaden glanced at his tent twice before he turned to Talise again. He opened his mouth, but Talise wasn't about to let him get away so easily.

"You've been avoiding me." She crossed her arms over her chest for good measure.

His face fell as he let out a silent sigh. "I haven't been avoiding you."

She raised an eyebrow.

Now he scratched at his perfectly combed hair. "I've been communicating with someone, and it's kept me busy. I'll be able to…" He shook his head, as if brushing away the words. "Soon, I can—" The words stopped as abruptly as they had begun. His face scrunched up as he let out another sigh. This one was audible.

He reached out and dropped both of his hands onto her shoulders. Her shoulders warmed at his touch but nothing like her heart did. Was it skipping now?

He leaned a little closer. "I promise, I am as devoted to you as ever."

And then he left. Abruptly. He disappeared behind a grouping of tents while she was still busy catching her breath.

A delightful tingle stayed in her shoulders, trying to memorize the feel of his touch. She shook her head at the cold night around her.

How could he be so frustrating and so wonderful all at the same time? She let out a huff, but it was half chuckle too. While her skin still tingled, she brushed a finger across her lips.

Whatever happened, she was determined to tell Aaden once and for all that she loved him. And she'd do it before the final battle. If she had to announce it in the middle of a camp in front of everyone, she'd do it.

He couldn't evade her forever.

CHAPTER FORTY-NINE

ON THE WAY TO THE location for what they hoped would be the final battle, the last city they visited was in the Storm. Aaden had suggested it. It seemed fitting to give extra attention to a part of Kamdaria that had been neglected for so long.

Plus, the city was near the River Gate. Using the riverboat they had already stolen from the palace army, they could easily travel up the river to the wall between the Gate and the Crown. They had chosen that spot as the perfect place for the final battle.

It seemed fitting that their final night before the battle they stayed in the Storm.

The entire way to the city, Talise wrestled with what she would say in that final speech. What would her final words be to an empire with so much hurt? So many broken people?

It came as no surprise that Aaden stayed at the forefront of her mind during these thoughts. Even though he had been born in the Crown, Aaden's life had been far from charmed. His own mother disinherited him. His father made a grave mistake that branded Aaden's ID card with a black X. After months of devoted spy work for the emperor, he still never got the X removed. He just got a silver crescent moon unceremoniously stamped on top of it. And because of his mother, half the family tree on his ID card would always remain blank.

He represented so much of what was wrong with Kamdaria. Destroying the walls would help. Evenly distributing resources would help. But Talise wanted something more. Something that would show Aaden he no longer had to be ashamed of the mistakes of his parents.

By the time she stood in front of the citizens that evening, her decision had been made. She gave the same speech she had given in every other city so far. When she called people to join her, they cheered with the eagerness of people who could taste change.

She had rehearsed the next words in her head many times while traveling from city to city. Now they stuck in her throat. Everything about them was perfect except one thing. She didn't know if the people would agree.

But she needed them to. She needed it like she had never needed anything before. Her fingers longed for something to fiddle with, but she couldn't do such a thing during a speech. Instead, she just forced even breaths in and out of her mouth.

The people waited expectantly.

With one last breath, she finally said the words. "I have one final request to make."

Her friends' faces all twisted toward her with varying expressions of surprise. They had heard her speech several times before, so they noticed the deviation at once.

Talise tried to stand a little taller. "Tomorrow morning, we will approach the Crown. I will destroy the wall, and the final battle will begin." She gulped. "But I would like to make a gesture once we enter the Crown. We need a symbol of how devoted we are to changing Kamdaria."

All around her, heads nodded. They might not be so willing once they heard her idea.

Her fingers twitched when she spoke again. "I request that we throw our ID cards into a pile and burn them all to ash."

Now came the murmurs she knew would come. She fought to keep her lip from trembling. "I know citizens in the Gate and in the Crown have their family trees recorded in many places besides their ID cards. For citizens of the Storm, I know that your ID card is the only record you have of your family tree."

The murmurs faded away as she addressed what she assumed would be their greatest objection. The listening ears gave her courage. "Let us spend this evening making family tree records for any Storm citizens who would like to join us in burning our ID cards."

She bit into her bottom lip. It was only the slightest fidget, but she immediately regretted it. Hopefully the people wouldn't fault her too much because she had never been so frightened of a reaction.

"No one will be forced to burn their ID card. Anyone who wants to keep their ID card will be allowed to do so without threat of malice or disappointment." Her shoulders rolled back as she tipped her chin a little higher. "But we will be indebted to anyone who does choose to burn their ID card. The more people who join us, the greater we will symbolize just how far we are willing to go to bring about change."

A few eyes looked brighter, but it didn't give her confirmation of how they felt about the idea. She probably wouldn't know for sure until the next day when she threw her own ID card onto the ground. Perhaps hers would be the only one to burn.

She raised a fist into the air. "Tomorrow the final battle will begin, and we will finally bring unity to Kamdaria once more."

Cheers erupted. If the idea of burning their ID cards brought hesitation through the crowd, it hadn't dampened their excitement to make Kamdaria better.

Even as Talise stepped off the makeshift platform, the people continued to cheer. Hope sparked all around. Being among the citizens when they were so charged was amazing.

But tonight, Talise had something more important to do. Something she had put off for far too long.

She found Aaden at the edge of the crowd. His face looked even stiffer than usual. When she approached him, he didn't say a word. He didn't move. He just swallowed. With a half flick, he gestured toward a path that led out of the city.

A smile formed on her face as she nodded. Together, they left the cheers behind. Finally, she had found a moment to steal him away. And finally, he let her.

After a few silent steps, he glanced toward her. Red rimmed his watery eyes. "You did that for me?" He swallowed. "Deciding to burn the ID cards?"

It would be easy to claim that she had done it for everyone. Burning the ID cards would destroy the card marking and the separation of families in one fell swoop. And it *was* for everyone. But she still did it for him. Because his ID card bore so much shame.

"Yes." She tucked a strand of hair behind her ear.

Even seeing a shred of emotion seemed like a lot for Aaden. So, when his chin quivered, and his eyes grew even more watery, it gave her the urge to throw her arms around him even tighter than ever.

But she had some things to say first.

He brought his fist to his chest just as he finally controlled the quivering of his chin. His words came out raw and deep. "Thank you."

Her feet stopped then. She looked him straight in the eye, ready for the words to spill.

"I have to…," he started. *Of course* he stopped her before she could get the words out. It didn't matter, she'd blurt them out before the night was over no matter how he tried to stop it.

Gently nudging her shoulder, he urged her to continue down the path once again. "I need… just… we need to keep walking."

She almost smiled at his awkwardness. How lovely to know she had rendered him speechless.

He scratched his forehead. Then his hand slid down his face. When his fingers touched the part of his jaw that used to have facial hair, he cringed. He glanced toward her, as if checking to see if she had noticed the reaction. She had.

After looking into her eyes, he let out sigh. "My grandfather *will* be disappointed in me when he finds out I shaved."

She let out a soft laugh. "I'm sure he won't mind once he learns why you did it."

Aaden's eyebrows drew together. "It's been a family tradition for six generations, and I'm the one who broke it."

With a shrug, she gazed into his eyes a little more directly than she had before. "If you could forgive your grandfather after he hurt you, don't you think he can forgive you for this?"

With feet nearly stumbling on the path ahead, Aaden's eyebrows rose. He let out a slow breath. "Yes, I guess you're right."

He chose that moment to stop. Touching her arm with the softest touch, he turned her toward him.

If he was going to do something like that, nothing could stop her from taking full advantage of it. She stepped closer to him. He sucked in sharp breath.

But of course, she couldn't end there. She reached out for his now-clean-shaven jaw and brushed her thumb across it. "Besides, it will grow back if you want it back again."

He closed his eyes and leaned into her touch. When he breathed in, it was like nothing in the world existed except her.

This was the moment. Her lips parted.

But of course he interrupted her yet *again*. She kind of wanted to punch him.

"I'm sorry it took me so long to find." A twinge of pain stretched through his words.

Her eyes narrowed as she tried to decipher what he was talking about. "Find what?"

He looked down at the ground, reaching for the end of his tunic. "I've been searching ever since we were living at the palace." He glanced up for a single moment before turning his eyes down once again. "You probably don't remember, but I looked up your testing record from when you were seven and got into the elite academy."

The conversation continued to turn in the most unexpected direction yet. "Aaden, what are you talking about?"

His mouth lifted in a smile when he looked into her eyes. "You were so angry with me about it." He shrugged. "In retrospect, I'm pretty sure you were afraid that I'd discover you were the princess." A playful chuckle left his lips. "But I *never* would have guessed that."

Her mouth twisted into a knot. This was it. She was just going to blurt the words out. He'd interrupted *her* enough. Now she'd do the same.

But when he continued, confusion stole every word from her lips.

He leaned an inch closer to her. "I was just trying to find out her name." One of his eyebrows raised. "You actually told it to me later that day, which worked out well for me." He let out a sigh. "But there are no records in the Storm, and I had to rely on messengers. I'm sorry it took me so long to find."

At some point, her heart had started beating into a frenzy. She wanted very much to demand an explanation, but the words caught in her throat.

With gentle hands on her arms, he turned her around.

She blinked as everything came into view.

A graveyard.

He had led her to a graveyard.

In the Storm.

CHAPTER FIFTY

AT SOME POINT, TALISE HAD grabbed onto Aaden's arm. Her fingers gripped him like he was the only thing that could save her. And maybe he was.

Her feet stumbled over every step. If it hadn't been for his gentle tugging, she never would have been able to move. She had forgotten how to walk. Every nerve in her body, every vein, every pore, all rushed with too much emotion. Too much heat.

It felt like a dream. It felt like a wish.

But it definitely didn't feel real.

Every breath she took entered as a short gasp. Every breath out came in bursts.

She gripped harder on Aaden's arm. It probably hurt, but his presence was the one thing that grounded her. The one thing that proved this moment was real.

"It's right over here." He gestured just before they turned a corner. His steps fell sure and even. He had been here before. He must have come ahead of time to confirm the location, to make sure she wouldn't be disappointed.

And then she couldn't breathe.

All those times she had thought he was avoiding her, but really he was *communicating* with someone. It was about this. Even without asking, she *knew* it was about this.

About Marmie's grave.

Just as suddenly as he had brought her into the graveyard, he stopped. A modest gravestone rose above the cold soil beneath his feet. The gray rock had flecks of black and white. The flecks sparkled in the dimming evening light.

Talise's chin quivered at the sight of it. Reaching out, her fingers trailed across the sparkling stone.

Marmie had a voice of honey and sparkles. How fitting that her gravestone should sparkle too.

Talise's knees fell onto the soil just as her eyes fell closed too. Leaning forward, she rested her forehead against the stone. It gave off an icy chill that cooled the heat burning inside her.

Steady tears streamed down her cheeks, cooling her even more. For a moment, she didn't move. She just knelt with her head against the gravestone. Breathing. Remembering.

Though Marmie was technically Talise's aunt, she had still raised Talise like a mother would. And in the Storm, no less. She chopped off her long hair to pay for the riverboat tickets that would get them to Talise's testing. Marmie gave up her own food to ensure Talise never lost her shaping. Through ten years of academy training, Marmie wrote letters to Talise, constantly giving encouragement and offering praise.

She never should have lived as long as did. Even Willow's father said that first generation Storm citizens never lived long. But Marmie did. She had probably survived on the strength of her heart alone.

Clutching her hand into a fist, Talise's chin quivered once more. But then Marmie had to die only weeks before Talise could have saved her.

Once Talise became Master Shaper, she was supposed to send a ticket to bring Marmie to the Crown. Marmie was supposed to disguise herself as a palace servant. By then, enough years had passed since the empress's sister was supposed to have died. And after her years in the Storm, no one would have recognized her.

But malnourishment took her the same way it had taken many others from the Storm.

Breathing became a chore once again. The cold tears trailing down Talise's cheeks brought the release of years of pent up anger. Regret.

Why had her aunt, the one who gave Talise undying love, been forced to live in the Storm for so long? Why had her life been cast away and forgotten?

Sitting back on her heels, Talise finally braved a glance at the front of the gravestone.

Shyna Mori.

Her aunt didn't even have the honor of having her real name on her gravestone. Instead of her family name of Malksur, Marmie had been buried with the fake last name she used in the Storm.

A knot twisted through Talise's heart as she ran a finger over the smooth stone surrounding the name. As she had known it would be, the grave sat unmarked.

It conveyed shame to all who looked upon it.

At once, Talise sucked in a deep breath. She reached out with her mind until she could sense every bit of earth in the stone. Then, her forefinger bent. A scratch appeared in perfect time with how Talise moved her finger. The shaping was more precise than anything she had ever done before.

The mark started wide, but then narrowed the farther it moved down the stone.

After it was finished, she dropped her hand into her lap and let out a sigh.

Aaden knelt next to her, close enough that heat from his chest warmed her arm and back.

"It's an icicle." She reached out and touched a finger over the mark. "Because her death is the reason I learned ice shaping."

Marks didn't have to be shaped like anything. A simple line using a chisel and hammer still showed honor for the person who had died. But since Talise had expert shaping skills, it made sense to leave an intricate mark.

Without warning, another puddle of tears spilled out of her eyes. She dropped her hand into her lap again while trying to control herself. She didn't mind crying, but the sleeve of her gown wasn't the best thing to wipe away tears.

But then Aaden pulled a handkerchief from his tunic pocket.

Of course.

Of course he had thought of that too.

Her tears turned to sobs as she buried her face in his chest. The handkerchief caught most of the saltwater, but he didn't seem to mind when his tunic caught some too. He wrapped an arm around her, gently rubbing one hand up and down her arm.

The motion grounded her once again.

She felt better in his arms. Safer. More able to bear the pain inside.

Despite the length of time she spent crying, he never made any move to hurry her along. He waited with the patience so indicative of him.

By the time her tears slowed, aches stung through her throat. But something tight had been released inside her chest. Something that had been brewing for almost a year.

With one arm still around her shoulders, Aaden reached forward. He ran his own finger over her mark slowly, as if memorizing every intricacy.

Talise's head hung. "She deserves more than just one mark. My mother's grave has hundreds, which she also deserves." She sniffed. "I just wish Marmie could have more as well."

His head tilted to the side. "But you're a Master Shaper. You get to leave four marks on her grave, one for each element."

If joy could have split apart her chest, it would have in that moment. She was almost too happy to breathe.

Soon, three more marks adorned the grave. A circle of wind, a mountain, and a flame with the same design as the flames on the hilt of her dagger.

Finally. *Finally*, Marmie's grave had the honor it deserved.

Talise touched each mark one last time. And then Aaden did the same.

He helped her to her feet.

Where she had entered the graveyard with stumbling steps, she left it with floating ones. Her heart had never been so full.

Aaden led her just outside the graveyard in exactly the same place they had been standing before.

"I love you." Her lips sparked with fire when she finally got the words out.

A twinge of pain passed over Aaden's features. He took her hand and pressed her knuckles against his lips. His eyes fell closed as another twinge went through his face. "I lied to you."

He let the words out with the weight of a confession, like he couldn't accept her words until she knew the truth. "I told you I never lied to you, but I did once."

Why wouldn't he open his eyes?

He probably could have confessed to murder and she wouldn't have cared at that point. But since it seemed so important to him, it would probably be better to let him explain. "When?" she asked.

His eyes flicked open. A gleam of hope appeared in them, perhaps grateful she hadn't immediately run away. He gulped. "I made you believe I left the palace because I wanted to see my father." Now he released her hand from his and gulped again. "But that didn't have anything to do with my decision."

She felt her eyebrows come together, but it didn't help her understand. Was it because of the silver crescent moon the emperor promised? Did Aaden agree to spy on Kessoku because he couldn't bear the black *X* on his ID card?

Picking at one fingernail, Aaden stared at his hands. "Your father told me I couldn't marry you."

She blinked. "What?" The word came out sharp.

He cleared his throat, but it didn't steal his attention from his fingernail. "When you were still in Kessoku's dungeon, he told me he would never allow his daughter to marry someone who had a black *X* on his ID card. That even though I was a Master Shaper and could live in the palace, my ID card still bore a black *X*."

Aaden curled his fingers and kneaded his forehead with his knuckles. "But…," he let out a humorless laugh, "he said if I spied on Kessoku and did well, he would stamp over the *X* with a silver crescent moon." Aaden's eyes lifted, meeting hers tentatively. "He made it clear that was the only way I could be with you."

Her mouth hung open for several seconds of stunned silence. When she did speak, the words sputtered out. "Why didn't you tell me?"

The twinge in his face appeared for a third time. He dug both hands through his hair, ruffling the neatly combed strands. "You had only kissed me *one* time and then you got kidnapped right before my eyes. You had only *just* decided to trust me. I knew how I felt, but…" His fingers curled into fists, which he pressed against his forehead. "I couldn't figure out how to explain without it sounding like a marriage proposal. I didn't think you were ready for that yet."

More silence followed. Her mouth had dropped open the widest yet, but this time, no amount of thinking could help her decide what to say.

Aaden's hands fell. His hair stuck up in messy chunks. "I knew you'd be mad at me for leaving. I knew you might never forgive me." He let out a sigh, staring at the ground once again. "But I kept thinking, if I stayed, you'd be happy, and I'd have you then." Now he looked up, piercing her with an intense gaze. "But I knew that wasn't enough. I didn't just want you then. I wanted you forever."

He bit into his bottom lip, letting his gaze fall once again. "And since your father is the emperor, I decided to play by his rules. I never would have dreamed of a day we'd turn against him and burn our ID cards."

A memory flickered through her mind. During their trials for Master Shaper, the emperor had told Talise he knew exactly what he was doing. Is this what he meant? That he could see how Aaden felt about her and that he intended to use it to his full advantage?

Her nose wrinkled as nausea twisted through her gut.

Aaden's lips fell into a frown. "I know I messed up. I know I hurt you, but I've been trying to make it up to you. I've been—"

She cut him off by raising one hand. Fear danced in his eyes.

"Just kiss me, Aaden."

The fear vanished as complete and utter astonishment replaced it.

Her mouth curled upward. "And don't stop until I'm breathless."

Now his astonishment turned to a hunger so deep she could taste it. He reached around her waist, tucking her close. His other hand went into her hair, digging deep but in the gentlest possible way.

And his lips. They pressed against hers with a passion so fierce it would change her world forever.

Fire sparked between them. Inside them. It grew and pulsed, sending bliss with every touch. Just when she felt her heart would burst, he pulled her even closer still. And the feeling only grew.

After digging through her hair, his fingers trailed down. They slid down her neck with a feather light touch. At the bottom, his thumb brushed across her collarbone, sparking another fire inside.

It turned out, *breathless* didn't even begin to cover what he could do to her.

She never wanted to leave his arms. Never wanted this moment to end.

She didn't just want kisses *now*. She wanted them *forever*.

When he stopped to let her catch her breath, he whispered, "I love you," into her ear. And then his lips were the ones trailing down her neck.

Her heart melted all over again.

Whatever happened in the future, she knew one thing for sure.

She would fight for Aaden. Always. By his side until the very end.

✺

Chapter Fifty-One

An ominous air boarded the riverboat along with Talise's soldiers the next morning.

It would take some time to travel up the river through the Gate. They wouldn't reach the wall around the Crown until the afternoon.

Sitting in a small room by herself, Talise pulled the amulet from her pocket. Her thumb touched each element in turn. A waterfall, a tornado, a mountain, and a flame.

Could she destroy the entire wall at once by using its power?

Despite its smaller size compared to the other wall she had already destroyed, it didn't seem likely. The wall around the Crown was probably thicker. It had probably been made a little better. And anyway, even if she did manage to destroy the entire wall, how weakened would she be?

Their plan didn't allow for her to go unconscious again.

Having people who believed in her brought her so much hope. She had citizens, soldiers, and friends who stood with her. But they also believed she could destroy that wall in one go.

For once, their belief in her was probably a little too strong. Even though she kept explaining that she didn't know if she'd be able to destroy the entire wall, they kept making plans like she would.

Would it ruin everything if she failed?

This was why she had hidden herself away in the room. She just needed a bit more time to figure out how to take down the entire wall. Gently opening a suede pack, she pulled out a red journal from within it.

The pages of Kamdar's journals were practically imprinted on her mind now. She had read them all so many times. Still, she leafed through the pages, eager to find something that would help her through this dilemma.

Just as she skimmed her third page, a male soldier entered the room. "Your Highness." He gave a deep bow. "Is there anything we can do for you?"

A female soldier entered after him, carrying a cup of water. She placed it at Talise's feet.

Perhaps it had been too much to hope that no one had noticed her when she slipped into the small room. Apparently, her soldiers knew exactly where she was anyway.

The female soldier gestured toward the journal on Talise's lap. "Can we help you look for something? Maybe a pair of fresh eyes is all you need."

Talise shook her head, feeling the weight of her responsibility deep in her gut. "No, I can figure this out. I don't need help."

Standing stiffer, the male soldier said, "But we *want* to help you."

Talise tried to smile, but the weight in her chest only deepened. "I don't even know what to do."

"I do." Wendy's head popped in through the doorway. Her eyes shined as bright as ever.

When the male and female soldier looked Wendy's way, she shooed them out of the room.

But just when Talise expected her best friend to give some sort of explanation, other people began filing into the room behind Wendy. Cyrus and Rio came in and sat against one wall. Tempest swung her long braid around before standing at Wendy's side. Claye came in next and then Fyra. Finally, Aaden entered the room.

Talise's heart leapt at the sight of him. He sent the tiniest smile her direction, but it was enough to make her stomach flip.

When he shut the door behind him, the weight of what had just happened finally hit. Talise began to eye her friends suspiciously.

Aaden trailed across the room with casual ease. Once at Talise's side, he brushed a bit of hair out of her face. "It's a good plan. You have to at least consider it before you refuse."

She narrowed her eyes at him before turning to glance at each of her friends. Her eyes narrowed tighter each time she looked at someone new.

When everyone else sat down on the ground, Talise followed them. But that didn't make her relax. "What is this mysterious plan?"

All eyes turned to Aaden. He glanced toward Talise, taking in a small breath before he spoke. "My father said you could drain power out of other people."

Her chest constricted with a sharp burst. "I'm not going to steal power out of our enemies just to ensure our victory."

"We would never ask you to do that." As Wendy spoke, she pulled piece of silver wire from her pocket and began bending it around her fingers.

Tempest leaned further back against the wall behind her. "We basically just want to know how it works."

Claye leaned forward. "And also, how did Lucian know you could do it? None of the rest of us knew."

"Well." Swallowing didn't help Talise speak, but it did give her an extra moment to find the right words. "I accidentally stole some power out of him when I destroyed the second portion of wall around the Gate."

Several eyes blinked back at her but not with any measure of understanding.

She let out a sigh. "When I use the amulet while doing regular shaping, it gives me incredible strength. But when I destroyed the first portion of the wall, it did something different. I discovered I could use the amulet to fill a well of power inside me."

Rio tapped his chin in thought. "But that weakened you."

Talise nodded. "Yes. I can't fill the well too high with my own power, or it will take too much out of me. But when I got ready to destroy the second portion of wall, I stopped the power before it could fill me completely. When I stopped drawing power from myself, the amulet went searching for another source of power. Lucian was standing closest to me, so it latched onto him and stole away some of his power."

Cyrus glanced at the wire in his sister's hand before he raised an eyebrow. "How did Lucian know?"

Biting her bottom lip, Talise turned her eyes downward. "I'm not sure, but I think he could feel it. Once I realized I was drawing power from him, I stopped immediately. I only took a small amount from him. He could still shape fire after I destroyed the wall, but I don't know if it weakened his shaping at all."

Rio continued to tap his chin as he gazed into a corner of the room. His face screwed up. "So, if you only draw a portion of power from someone, it will weaken but not destroy them?"

"I guess." Talise offered the least commitment she could. "But I still don't want to steal power from my enemies."

Even if it would give them a strong tactical advantage, it seemed wrong. It seemed like the kind of thing that would have kept Eben from giving her the amulet in the first place.

For a moment, Wendy's fingers stopped twisting the wire. "We never asked you to draw power from your enemies."

One of Talise's eyebrows tilted upward. "Then why did you want to know about it?"

Everyone stared at Aaden again.

He turned to Talise with a weighted glance. "We want you to draw power from *us*."

Her eyebrows rose so fast it sent a zing through her forehead. They could *not* be serious. Her eyes flitted around the room, landing on each of her friends in turn.

They *were* serious.

She sucked in a breath. "I'm not going to steal your power."

Tempest picked at the end of her braid. "But you wouldn't be *stealing* it. We're offering it willingly."

Hair whipped around Talise's cheeks as she shook her head. "It will weaken you. I have no idea the long-term effects it would have."

Cyrus gave a careless shrug. "Lucian seemed fine when you did it to him."

Curling one hand in her lap, Talise tried to sit up taller. "I might be strong enough to destroy the wall on my own."

"You don't have to do this alone." Fyra's voice came out stronger than Talise had ever heard it. The soldier sat up straighter, continuing with even more determination than before. "Even more importantly, you *can't* destroy that wall alone. Not without hurting yourself."

An admiring smirk adorned Claye's face as he watched Fyra speak. Once she finished, Claye continued right where she left off. "We are fighting toward the same goal as you. Let us give what we can so that we will *all* succeed."

Tears prickled in Talise's eyes when the weight of what they offered finally hit her. She pressed her lips together, trying hard to find words to indicate her gratitude. Instead, she only managed a nod. But her chin quickly tipped upward. "I want to practice first. I want to do a test with a tiny amount of power to make sure it isn't too dangerous."

"Excellent idea." Wendy twisted off a piece of the silver wire in her hand. "Then you'll see it works, and we'll all be fine. With our power, you can easily take down the wall."

It would be anything *but* easy. But just because Talise had to save all of Kamdaria, maybe it didn't mean she had to save everyone by herself.

Wendy handed the twisted piece of wire to Tempest. After her work, the silver almost looked like one of the delicate tines of a tiara.

With the wire in her hands, Tempest reached into her tunic pocket. She pulled out an actual tiara. Except one spot looked empty, as if missing a tine. Using the loose wire at the end of Wendy's piece, Tempest twisted the tine onto the tiara, filling the empty space. Now it was complete.

Delicate silver wires twisted in swirls and peaks. Crystal beads in blue, red, green, and orange were dispersed evenly over the wires. The tiara used simple materials, but they came together in the most exquisite way.

Shrugging, Tempest held the tiara out to Talise. "It was the best we could manage in such a short time."

Wendy chuckled as she nudged Tempest in the side. The sweetest smile filled Wendy's face. "It's perfect, and you know it. You learned a lot from having a jewelry-maker as a father."

A grin turned Tempest's mouth upward. "We thought you needed a proper crown when you faced the emperor, to remind him who you are."

More tears filled Talise's eyes as she set the tiara into her lap. "Thank you." Her eyes swept over the room. "All of you."

Aaden slipped his hand into hers. She squeezed it as she used her shoulder to brush away a tear.

They had a big task ahead of them that day. She swallowed. But maybe together, they had a chance.

Chapter Fifty-Two

Inside the riverboat, minutes passed with excruciating slowness. Talise paced back and forth over a portion of deck that would probably start to wear under her shoes. The amulet buzzed in her hand.

She had practiced drawing tiny amounts of power from each of her friends. To her dismay, it worked. She could take some of their power and use it to shape more than she could on her own. Even Rio and Fyra had intense shaping power to draw from, and they were not skilled shapers.

But that only made things more difficult because now they expected Talise to use their power to take down the wall. As much as she knew it would work, she was still terrified to unintentionally injure her friends in some way.

Anticipation and fear like she had never known sat inside her. It bubbled and boiled with every new second that passed. But then the riverboat came to a stop.

Her insides churned as tingles spread all through her fingers and toes.

They had arrived.

Sucking in a breath, Talise froze in place. Soldiers marched, forming their ranks around her. She feared she would pass out from sheer terror.

Wendy approached, brushing away invisible wrinkles in Talise's colored gown.

The soft velvet trim of the long sleeves tickled her wrists. A full skirt swished over the layers of fabric underneath it. The white chiffon shimmered in the light. Each strand of the embroidered swirls stood out against the white fabric.

Never had Talise worn something so regal. The colors in the embroidery perfectly matched the crystals that adorned her tiara. Blue, red, green, and orange. Four colors for the four elements. Wendy and Tempest had expertly pinned the tiara in place along with the front pieces of Talise's hair. The rest of her black hair hung freely just past her chin.

Wendy used a rag to wipe away any last traces of dirt on Talise's skin. Based on the number of times she wiped, Talise was pretty sure most of the smudges were imaginary. But she let her friend work all the same.

With the fate of Kamdaria on her shoulders, she had never needed so desperately to look like a princess.

At last, Wendy declared her ready.

Aaden came to her side, tucking a warm hand at her lower back. His eyes took in every part of her, but apparently, she had rendered him speechless again.

That feeling alone could sustain her through anything.

When she stepped off the riverboat, her friends stood at her side, and her soldiers stood at her back. But even after stepping onto the ground outside, scores of soldiers surrounded the area. Citizens formed thick crowds. Devotion gleamed in all of their eyes.

They were ready to fight for her.

It took some walking to finally reach the part of the wall where they intended to stand. After traveling a city's length, they finally arrived. Soldiers stood behind her, never wavering. She turned to face them and the citizens.

She would not address them now. The wall separating the Gate and Crown was probably too thick to hear a quiet speech or cheering through, but they didn't want to take the chance.

Instead, Talise brought her fist against her heart. Every person around her did the same. When she raised her fist into the air, they copied the movement with great determination in their eyes.

She held her fist high for several seconds. If there had been enough time, she would have looked into the eyes of every single citizen. She would have nodded to hopefully convey just how much their devotion meant to her.

Since their time was limited, she settled on piercing in the entire crowd with her most grateful stare.

When her fist lowered, a hush fell over the crowd.

Her heart hammered as she approached the wall before her. They had chosen the spot after hours of discussion. The base of a mountain sat on the other side of the wall before her. To her right, the mountain would slope upward with Ridgerock Palace resting at the top of it. To her left, the base of the mountain fed into Kamdaria's capital city.

With no gateway between the wall anywhere near that spot, the people on the other side would certainly not be expecting an attack. Plus, it brought Talise's army as close to Ridgerock Palace as they could hope to get.

Now she just had to destroy the wall.

Her friends gathered around her, ready to let her draw power from them. Behind them, ranks of soldiers stood with their weapons ready.

Swallowing over an enormous lump in her throat, Talise pulled out the amulet. A faint green glow emanated from it. It crackled in her hand, as if it knew what was coming. Squeezing it, she reached her hand out.

As it had done several times now, power sparked at her toes and began filling like a well inside her. Once the power reached her stomach, she cut the amulet off from it. The amulet reached out for a new source of power. It found Aaden first.

His power sparked hot and fierce inside Talise, eager and unwavering. When his power reached her knees, she cut it off and sent the amulet searching yet again.

Wendy's power felt bubbly, but it held a surprising amount of force. Claye's power felt like weights, each part heavy but with a bounce of fun. Tempest's power came next, then Cyrus's, Rio's, and Fyra's.

Each one sizzled and buzzed inside Talise in its own unique way. They filled her, giving her three times the amount of power she had when she destroyed the first portion of wall.

But even as her senses reached for the wall in front of her, she knew it still might not be enough.

The wall was thicker. Sturdier. The materials were stronger than those used in the wall that separated the Gate from the Storm.

With so many people counting on her, Talise had no choice but to do her best.

Her hand formed a fist. Cracks split through the wall in front of her. When her hand gave a twist, the stone began to crumble. Now she pressed her other hand forward. The amulet pulsed inside it. Her second hand twisted, and the wall pulverized to dust before her.

Thick dust floated and filled the air, but her mind was still focused on the wall. Though every part of the wall within her sight had been crushed, she could still sense the parts that hadn't yet been destroyed. Her destruction had broken through half the wall with more crumbling down at every moment.

Punching both hands forward again, she felt more of the wall falling. But her well of power was also falling. She drew from it, clenching her gut against the pain that suddenly zinged through her.

More of the wall crumbled, but one last portion remained. Her hands twisted, but her well of power had gone dry. She took a single breath.

Around her, everyone stood. Waiting.

How could she give up now?

She had done her best. She had taken power from her friends. Could she really give up now when victory was so close?

Of course not.

Her people needed her.

The amulet burned in her hand. Once again, it began drawing power from within her. Instead of starting at her toes, the power sparked in her stomach. Right where she had stopped when she cut it off before. It filled her. She didn't stop it.

It buzzed upward, going higher. Only when it brushed against her heart did she stop. If her life had been less important, she would have just let the power fill her to the top of her head again.

But if she died during this fight, who would lead Kamdaria after they removed her father from the throne?

No, she couldn't be reckless with how much power she used. She had to make sure *some* of her strength would remain. But she also *had* to destroy that wall.

With the last bit of power she drew, she sent a final punch outward. Even as her heart sputtered, she felt the last of the wall crumble to dust. Her knees buckled. She caught herself right away, but Aaden glanced toward her with a fearful look in his eye.

Ignoring him, Talise stood tall. Weakness filled her limbs, her gut. She could feel her legs giving out underneath her. But if she only had a few more moments of being able to stand, she would use it.

The dust settled before her. Finally gone.

Forever.

There was no more Crown. No more Gate. No more Storm.

Now, there was only Kamdaria.

At the base of the mountain, palace soldiers scrambled and dashed forward. Their weapons came out hastily. They fell into haphazard ranks.

Talise stood firm in her position. She straightened her spine. When her mouth opened, even the palace soldiers stopped to hear her.

"I am Princess Talise Ruemon. Go tell the emperor I have a message for him. He must come down to meet with me if he wants to hear it."

At the end of speaking, she fell into a chair someone had placed nearby. Hopefully she moved with the air of regal indifference she'd been going for.

The palace soldiers stared back at her for a moment of stunned silence.

But then one of them moved. He darted up the mountain and toward the palace.

CHAPTER FIFTY-THREE

EVERYWHERE AROUND TALISE, HANDS HELD tight to their weapons. She continued to sit with as much regal grace as she could manage in her chair. Hopefully no one could tell how weak her body was. Luckily, sitting helped give her some of the rest she so desperately needed.

If she got to her feet, her legs would most certainly buckle underneath her. But maybe sitting helped her anyway. Maybe it showed the palace soldiers that she was at ease. And maybe her ease made them even more nervous.

Shivers moved through her at intense speeds, wreaking havoc on her insides. By some miracle, she managed to keep herself from visibly shaking. Blood trailed through her veins. It felt thicker and thinner than it should have at the same time. Her body fought to stay upright.

Despite the weakness crushing her from the inside out, her army gave off swathes of confidence. The palace soldiers trembled, glancing behind them or around them every few seconds. They gripped their swords with too much muscle. It was painfully obvious they had been caught unaware.

And all of them, even the ones standing the farthest away, kept staring at the rubble of what at once been the wall. Soon their gaze would shift straight to her, the princess. She could see their insides working, trying to decide if their loyalty had been correctly placed.

But she didn't want them join her because they feared what else she could do. She wanted them to join her because they believed in the same future she did.

A female soldier came rushing down the mountain. Her hands shook with every step. When she reached the base and stepped toward Talise, the soldier swallowed several times. She ducked her head in a bow but immediately seemed to regret it. She shook her head, as if that could erase the bow.

When she finally looked up, her cheeks had turned pink. She swallowed again. "Emperor Flarius requests your presence in his throne room. He sends his personal guard to accompany you."

Gesturing behind her, the soldier indicated a dozen soldiers in finely pressed uniforms. The silver hems at the bottom of their palace uniforms showed that they were indeed members of the emperor's personal guard.

Talise's eyes flitted over them quickly, but that didn't stop a familiar face from standing out among them. Major Cole. The aging guard had known her since birth. When Aaden had left the palace to spy on Kessoku, the kind major had been eager to offer updates about Aaden. Even when she began to defy her father, Major Cole seemed to believe in her.

An ache stretched through her throat. She knew it would be this way. She knew she would be facing the people who had very recently been on her side. But seeing the major's face twisted her heart into a mess.

Battle would bring death, but every soldier before her was Kamdarian. No matter what side they fought for. Even knowing it was impossible, she wished for an end to war that didn't have to bring death.

But it would bring death. All she could do was minimize it as much as possible.

Sitting up higher in her chair, Talise placed her hands delicately in her lap. "I told the emperor he must come down to me if he wishes to hear my message."

"He will not come." The soldier immediately jerked her head downward as soon as she said the words.

Talise leaned forward. "Then I will wait."

The soldier's eyes widened.

Now Talise sat back with another display of casual grace. "Relay my message to him once more."

When the soldier began climbing up the mountain again, the emperor's personal guard remained. They stood at attention, keeping their eyes on Talise.

The request to have the emperor come down was obviously a show of power. It demonstrated that Talise had just as much right to give orders as he did. But if he complied, it would also give them a strong tactical advantage.

Attempting to defeat the emperor inside the palace would be extremely difficult. It had rooms and passages that made hiding easy. The mountain itself tired anyone who had to climb it to get to the emperor. Not to mention, it gave palace soldiers a strong advantage by having the high ground.

They expected the emperor to comply. After destroying the entire wall around the Crown, they expected him to be so frightened of Talise's power that he would be willing to do whatever she asked.

But perhaps she had underestimated his cowardice. Perhaps he feared her so much that he wouldn't even leave his palace walls.

If he didn't come down, their strategy would suffer. Their plans would have to shift in too short a time. They didn't plan a thorough contingency because they truly expected him to come. If they accepted defeat in this first show of power, it could change everything.

But if the emperor wouldn't meet with her, the battle would never begin.

The female soldier returned. She cleared her throat but immediately hunched her shoulders. "Emperor Flarius will hear your message, but he will hear it at the palace doors. You must come to him."

Glancing to her side, Talise looked at her friends. They had all come to stand around her. None of them seemed weakened like she was after destroying the wall. They could all stand without trouble. Hopefully they truly were as strong as they seemed.

Raising an eyebrow, she looked to her friends. She spoke in a low voice so the palace soldiers across the rubble wouldn't hear. "Do we go to the palace?"

Rio sucked in a breath. "It will give the emperor a strong advantage." As always, Rio spoke the truth no one wanted to hear.

Glancing up the mountain, Wendy gave the softest shrug. "We might not have a choice."

Apparently, that was the end of their council. No one else said a single word, probably because they didn't know any better than Talise did what the best course of action would be.

Waiting any longer would only make her look weak. That probably wasn't the best image to portray right before a final battle.

Holding her head high, Talise turned to face the palace soldier at the base of the mountain. "If my father wants me to meet him at the palace doors, then tell him he must send a palanquin to carry me there."

The woman looked taken aback at the words. Her surprise only lasted a moment before she began climbing up the mountain again. This time, the emperor's personal guard followed behind her.

In a whisper, Tempest asked, "Why the palanquin?"

Claye gave a signature smirk as he let out a chuckle. "It's another show of power, isn't it?"

"No." Aaden's voice came out quiet but so much more urgent than the others. "It's because Talise doesn't have the strength to walk."

So, he *had* noticed after all.

Wendy sucked in a gasp as she reached for her friend's arm. "Why didn't you tell us?"

Guilt lined her actions as Talise shrugged. "When was I supposed to tell you?"

"You had time to tell Aaden," Claye accused.

After a beat of silence, Talise glanced to her side until her eyes met Aaden's. His face held as much awkwardness as hers. How could they explain?

"Oh." Claye's voice fell. "You *didn't* tell him, did you?"

A tiny shake of the head was all the response she offered. "What about the rest of you? Are you weak after I used your power?"

They all insisted they hadn't been weakened at all. After tilting her head to the side with a disbelieving expression, they admitted the truth. They had been weakened slightly but not like she had. It was only the amount they expected after the tests they had done.

Fyra bit into her bottom lip. "But are you sure *you're* okay, Princess?"

Talise waved away the question. "It's fine. I will rest as soon as I finish this first part of the battle."

Aaden tipped an eyebrow up. "You need more than rest. You need a healer."

"Fine." She tried to offer a smile, but it probably looked more like a frown. Where were they supposed to find a healer once the battle began? The emperor had done much too good of job of ensuring the empire's best healers lived inside the palace. And like Aaden had recently said, Kessoku's healers weren't very good.

The likelihood of finding someone who could help her wasn't just low, it was next to impossible.

As they continued to whisper, the palace soldiers began forming tighter ranks. They marched across the street, coming closer to Talise and her army.

Talise cut off the conversation at once. They couldn't afford to have the palace soldiers know what they were talking about. If the emperor had any inkling of the weakened state Talise was in, all the rest of their plans could crumble.

Sitting high in her chair once again, Talise chose to stare right into the eye of anyone who dared glance her way. Most of the time, it made the soldier shrink in place.

Eventually, a palanquin arrived. The emperor's personal guard carried the wooden box. The shimmery paint on the outside gleamed in the sunlight. Silky pillows and drapes filled the inside. As she had suspected, it would only allow one occupant.

Holding onto the long poles that supported the box, the emperor's personal guard slowly lowered the palanquin. Major Cole himself gestured toward the opening. "Your ride awaits, Princess."

Her eyes narrowed at the sight. "Thank you for your willingness, but my own soldiers will carry me to the palace doors."

She shot a look toward Rio that she could only hope he understood. *Don't give them a chance to argue.* He only glanced at Talise for half a moment before he began directing her soldiers toward the palanquin.

Even as Major Cole opened his mouth to protest, Talise's soldiers pushed the emperor's personal guard out of the way. Only once her own people had complete control did she rise from her chair.

Her head went woozy as soon as she stood. With great care, she managed to keep herself standing tall. Each step helped her head feel a little more upright. Though still very weak, she felt ready to stand before the emperor for a short while. Hopefully she could handle it for long enough.

It was time to face her father.

Chapter Fifty-Four

WITH EVERY BUMP AND JOSTLE of the palanquin, Talise's heart stopped. The weight of what she was about to do slammed into her from every angle. Fear didn't exist anymore. Neither did courage. All she had left was a pure, raw emotion she couldn't name.

What she was about to do was far from being good. But it was still the right thing.

At the top of the mountain, her soldiers were puffing for air. She could barely hide that she was too. Not from exertion but from anticipation.

She stepped out of the palanquin, keeping her movements slow and deliberate. She let the sun wash down on her. Spring had nearly arrived, which gave the air a warm thread among its chill. As she stepped, her colored embroidery caught the light.

Her body did not have much strength. Spending every last bit of it, she found a spot to stand in front of the palace doors.

By the time she had turned to glance behind, her soldiers had already moved the palanquin out of her way. Rows of her soldiers formed ranks behind her. They had their weapons at the ready.

But closer to the palace, the emperor's soldiers stood with *their* weapons at the ready.

As devoted as her soldiers were to her, the emperor's soldiers looked just as ready to fight for him.

She only had time for a single breath and then Emperor Flarius emerged from the golden palace doors.

He wore a thick cloak trimmed with fur. The silk of his tunic shimmered in the light, even more than her embroidery did. He wore his usual crown. The golden tines stretched upward. Bright rubies were set in the band underneath each of the tines. It was the same crown she had emulated when she made a crown of ice for him during the Master Shaper competition.

While she studied his crown, his eyes lingered over hers. The slightest flinch passed over his features when he saw the tiara on her head.

His study made her fingers twitch. The moment they did, her friends moved in closer to her sides. Taking a deep breath, she finally opened her mouth.

"Father."

He flinched again. Since the attack on the palace in her childhood, she had never addressed him in such a way. They had both done an extraordinary job of pretending his only relationship to her was as emperor.

But now she acknowledged who he truly was. And he didn't like it at all.

She stood even taller. "I have come to take away your crown."

Ripples moved through the soldiers, especially on the emperor's side. Their heads turned. Their mouths dropped. Many held on even tighter to their weapons.

Emperor Flarius had flinched once more, but his face relaxed a moment later. He stood tall, giving off confidence like she could only dream of. Suddenly, he looked completely unconcerned by her words. "You have no authority to do such a thing. If you attempt to take my crown, I will be forced to throw you in the dungeon until you have learned your lesson."

He leaned forward now, angling his body so that it felt like he was towering over her. "You never have been good at respecting authority."

The patronizing expression on his face once would have made her squirm. At one time, she would have paled at his words, taken them to heart.

But she was a different person now.

She drew power from her friends once again. Not with the amulet, but just by knowing they stood there by her side. She was stronger because of them. She had learned so much. And now she realized, facing her father didn't scare her at all.

Letting one corner of her mouth turn up, she gave a pointed glance straight into her father's eyes. "You are destroying this land and this people. As princess of Kamdaria, it is my right and my duty to protect it. By that law, I *do* have authority to take your crown and your throne. This people will bow to you no more."

Now came the most terrifying part of her plan. She reached into the pocket of her dress and pulled out her ID card. When she opened the card, the silver crescent moon on the front glinted in the light. She raised it high into the air.

"For too long, we have been divided by walls. For too long, the symbols on our ID cards have defined our worth." Her gaze now turned directly at her father. "For too long, we have been led by a man who only has his own interests at heart."

With a flick, her ID card slapped against the stone street. "I am not the only one who stands against you today. Because of your leadership, your people stand against you also." She turned to face the army behind her. "All those who wish to stand in defiance against the emperor, throw your ID card onto this pile."

It was probably a little too brave to claim that anyone else would be willing to be rid of their ID card. But when the moment came, those words felt right. She hadn't spent time considering whether anyone would join her or not. She just said the words.

And now the world fell silent as she waited.

A second slap sounded on the street. When she turned, she saw Aaden's empty hand angled toward the street. His ID card lay directly next to hers. She'd kiss him for that. As long as they both survived.

When another ID card fell to the street, Talise's heart leapt. She only had a split second to see that it came from Wendy because another ID card fell down almost immediately after. Tempest's?

Talise couldn't tell because more ID cards dropped down on top. All her friends had dropped theirs, but the pile had more than just theirs. From behind her, soldiers threw their cards. Those who stood too far away passed theirs ahead until those close enough could drop them onto the pile.

Soon, dozens of ID cards littered the street. Maybe even a hundred. Just when Talise's heart was ready to burst, Rio and Cyrus pulled out a suede bag. Together, they dumped the contents of the bag onto the pile.

More ID cards.

So many more.

They must have been collecting them since Talise first announced she would destroy them.

Emperor Flarius had gone pale.

More weakness spread throughout Talise's body, reminding her she didn't have the strength to stand for much longer.

Standing tall, she faced the emperor's army. Her voice came out powerful and loud. "Today you must choose." She eyed the soldiers in front of her before gesturing toward the emperor. "Do you want my Kamdaria or his?"

With her hand reaching out, a spark lit above her palm.

The emperor sucked in a breath.

Pain sliced through her limbs, but she did her best to ignore it. The spark burst into a flame. Her eyes fell to the pile of ID cards at her side.

"No." The plea left the emperor's lips in a twisted tone. "Don't do it. Don't…"

His words trailed off when he met her eye. He must have seen the determination coursing through her because his jaw went rigid. When he spoke again, it was through clenched teeth. "You will regret this."

Her chin tipped into the air. "I think *you* are the one who will regret your actions."

With that, she threw the fireball at the ID cards. Even that simple action was enough to drain away the last morsels of her energy. She was supposed to shape more flames, but now she could barely stand.

At her side, Aaden threw a large fireball at the pile, growing the fire until it ate into the ID cards. He took her hand. To the crowd, his actions probably just looked like he agreed with her, that he was willing to stand at her side and fight for the same thing.

Luckily, it had the added benefit of helping her stand. While leaning on his strength, she could stay upright just a little longer.

The emperor glared at the burning ID cards until the first speckles of ash began filling the air. He backed up toward the doors of the palace, still eyeing the flames. With one shoulder already inside the doorway, he whispered a single word.

"Attack." He disappeared into the palace immediately after.

All around Talise, weapons were drawn.

Her body shook with the effort to stand. The weakness inside her grew at every second. Standing at the palace doors, the emperor's army had a great advantage.

And somewhere in Kamdaria, Lucian and River and their followers who wanted revenge were still hiding somewhere. Even if Talise removed her father from the throne, she knew those two would be back to fight her for it someday.

Things did not look great. But then again, when did they ever?

Whether they were ready or not, the final battle had begun.

PART FOUR

FIRE STORM

Chapter Fifty-Five

A BARRAGE OF FIRE FILLED the sky.

Talise pulled water from the air, which immediately sent a shaking jolt through her heart. The decision to shape came naturally, but it brought a grim reminder along with it.

Destroying the wall around the Crown had weakened her significantly. Even the one second of shaping water caused a tremor inside. Her veins crackled like lightning. Still, fire poured down from above. From the palace.

With a palm shooting upward, she shaped the water anyway. Her knees shook from the effort, but she couldn't let flames rain down on her army.

As intended, her sheet of water flew over her soldiers like a canopy, just barely protecting them from the attack. In better circumstances, she would have turned the water to ice. Since her heart trembled and skipped inside her at the moment, that wasn't an option.

When the falling flames met her sheet of water, they destroyed each other in a sizzle of steam. Heat from above made it clear that another barrage of fire would come soon. Just as

Talise raised her arms to pull more water from the air, her legs gave out.

Aaden lifted her off the ground before she could fall. His jaw flexed as he turned away from the palace doors. When he turned to retreat down the mountain, her soldiers did the same. Tension split through his clean-shaven jaw as he flicked his eyes toward her. "Do you have enough strength to shape elements right now?"

"No." Her heart twisted in her chest, reminding her just how much strength she *didn't* have.

"Then stop shaping." His voice rustled the hair by her ears. How he managed to carry her and run at such a high speed, she'd never know.

The second rain of fire dropped just as they reached the halfway point down the mountain. Her gut lurched as she glanced over her shoulder. Were her friends okay? Were her soldiers?

Luckily, her previous blast of water provided just enough time for everyone to move into less precarious positions. Her friends ran down the mountain behind Aaden, their faces hardened with focus. Many of her soldiers ran behind that group to keep them safe from attacks. Many had stayed to fight, and even more still stood at the bottom of the mountain, waiting.

With every jarring step, her soldiers moved out of Aaden's way. They stayed close, only moving until the last possible second. With every new step, the way cleared just in time.

The silver and crystal tiara on Talise's head bounced against her head. Wendy and Tempest had carefully pinned it into place, well enough that it stayed attached throughout the bouncing. It jostled and clunked, but it didn't come free.

Even as her heart trudged along with a weakened pulse, it sank lower in her chest. This was why Talise has tried so hard to get the emperor to the bottom of the mountain. If he had followed her request and met her down where she destroyed the wall, her army wouldn't be in this danger now.

After Emperor Flarius refused her multiple requests, she chose to face him at the palace doors. Now his army had a better position than hers. Thundering filled her chest. Would the consequences be worth it?

Her lips pressed together to stop the trembling in her chin. It seemed like a good moment to bury her head in Aaden's shoulder. His grip on her only strengthened as he continued to jog forward.

She allowed herself a moment—just one moment—to pity herself and her army. And then she lifted her head again.

"Put me down."

"You don't have the strength to stand." Aaden's response came sharp and fast. He continued to run down the mountain, nearly reaching its bottom. He didn't ignore her, but he didn't give any room for argument either.

Narrowing her eyes, Talise opened her mouth again.

This time, Wendy interrupted her. She had jogged forward to her side. "What are you going to do in your weakened state?"

While the question rattled inside Talise's mind, they all reached the bottom of the mountain. One of the head soldiers in Talise's army approached. The woman went straight to Rio. "Do we keep fighting?"

Rio gave a stiff nod. "Attempt to enter the palace and capture the emperor like we planned. If the attack gets worse, and you can't get in, fall back. You know what to do from there."

The woman had already turned around to return to her squad. She replied to Rio over her shoulder. "If we have to fall back, we'll revert to our backup plan. We know what to do."

As princess, part of Talise's job was to let other people do *their* jobs. Still, it came as a surprise to see how easily her friends and her soldiers adjusted when the first plan had clearly failed miserably.

"Does anyone know where we can find a healer?" Tightness stretched through every syllable Aaden spoke.

A man stepped forward as he brushed a wrinkle from his Kessoku uniform. "We have a few in our group. They—"

"I meant a good healer." Aaden's words came out even tighter than before. "Do you know anyone who can help with heart problems?"

Silence met his second request. Heaviness carved into the air around them as the silence continued. The man dropped his head to his chest as he walked back to his group again.

After another beat, Tempest screwed her face up into a knot. "Let's just get to my family's house like we planned. Maybe they know someone I don't."

No one spoke as Aaden and the rest of Talise's friends began running once again. Their feet pounded against the stone road leading into the nearby city.

Cyrus offered a charming smile as he ran, probably to encourage Aaden. Since nothing about Cyrus's smile held even an inkling of hope, it did little for the heaviness around them. No one else in their group bothered to try. Desperation took hold of their hurried movements.

The color in Claye's face drained as he gave a small gulp. He reached for Fyra's hand, giving it a quick squeeze.

They had reached the city. The crowded homes and shops stretched out on the stone street before them. Several smaller streets broke off from the main one. Each street carried luxurious shops brimming with glittering clothing, decadent foods, and pristine weapons.

Such finery brought forth a dark reminder that citizens in the Crown had everything the other citizens did not. Most of them had never known want.

"Watch out."

Rio shouted the words, but they came too late.

Boulders as big as heads flew toward them. Swift fireballs followed soon after. Both came from inside a nearby shop. The Crown citizens inside the shop only sneered when Talise made eye contact. With hands punching forward, they demonstrated the excellent shaping skills they had acquired by being raised in the Crown.

Talise and her friends could only run and hope they moved away quickly enough.

They didn't.

Beneath their feet, the stone street split. A wall of earth shot upward from the crack. Rising earth nipped at Aaden's heels fast enough to send him sprawling forward. He held tight to Talise, and quickly curled them both into a side roll. The movement took the brunt of his momentum, so the fall didn't hurt too badly.

They both spent a few seconds on their backs, just heaving. It didn't last long. Aaden glanced to the side, letting his gaze linger on Talise for only a moment. But then a noise crunched around them.

Aaden's shoulders jerked before he yanked her toward the nearest shop. Just as he pulled her away, a combination of hard pebbles and air whips hit the street exactly where she had been.

He lifted her off the ground and into his arms once again. They both glared at the menacing earth wall that still blocked off the street. It separated them from the others. Were they okay?

"Do you know how to get to Tempest's house from here?" He whispered the question as he ducked down one of the smaller streets.

Her mind spun in circles as she tried to make sense of the streets around them. She had been to Tempest's house only once before. And at that time, she had others to help her with the directions. Truthfully, she had no idea how to get there.

While living at the elite academy, she never left the academy grounds. Even after becoming Master Shaper and taking up residence inside the palace, she had only ventured onto the streets of the capital city once. For the Fire Festival parade.

Just as they rounded another corner, a blast of water shot toward them. Aaden angled his palms outward, somehow managing to hold Talise at the same time. Floods of fire burst from his hands, evaporating the water within seconds.

When Talise raised her hands to help, he shot her a glare. After a jerky turn, he ran down a small street just as fireballs flew overhead.

Her body wasn't just weak anymore. Tingles spread all through her, making every pore ignite with sparks. The street ahead of them looked clear, but crashes and booms sounded from every corner. How much longer until the sound of clashing blades joined them?

Of course she never expected the final battle to be easy. But she also never expected to be separated from her friends, too weak to even walk. And right at the beginning. Another twist speared through her heart. It caused a hard shiver to shake her entire body.

Aaden sucked in a breath.

"I'm fine." They both knew she wasn't. Even in his arms, her body curled in on itself with each step. She glanced upward. "Is there a place we can climb up a little bit? Maybe from higher vantage point I'll be able to figure out where we are. Then I can get us to Tempest's house."

The skies grew dark above, which added to the confusion. Hopefully, a higher vantage point would be enough.

With feet slowing, Aaden's eyes moved upward. He scanned the buildings, but concern only contorted his features the more he looked.

He opened his mouth.

A wall of earth crashed into them. They hit the ground before either of them could breathe. Now came the thing Talise had feared only moments earlier.

Daggers sliced through the air toward them. Aaden could glare all he wanted, but that wouldn't stop Talise from reacting. Her hand shot forward. With the amulet clutched in one hand, her shaping could move more air than any other shaper could dream of. The daggers spun away in a funnel of icy wind. Her heart thumped too hard. And then it didn't thump at all.

She forced out a hard cough just as her hand fell.

Heavy rocks rained down on them next. Aaden punched his own rocks toward them. Many of the rocks got blasted away from the force of his rocks. But others still fell.

Talise noted with no small amount of frustration that the rocks that would have hit her were the ones blasted away. The remaining rocks hit hard on Aaden's chest and shoulders. He had clearly known his shaping could only take care of some of the rocks. Of course he took care of her first.

A large rock slammed into Aaden's stomach, knocking him to his back. He opened his mouth as if to cough, but not a single breath came out. His eyes bulged.

Gritting her teeth, Talise shot ripples through the earth beneath her. Their attackers were hiding, but that much movement in the earth would surely drop them to their knees anyway.

By the time she finished, Aaden was breathing again. She let out a breath of relief, which only lasted half a second. Fireballs blasted toward them. When Aaden lifted her off the ground again, it didn't happen effortlessly.

He grunted. Each step landed too heavy, too jerky.

"Maybe I can walk now."

He let out a breathy chuckle at the suggestion. Too breathy. Now he was sucking in a breath that didn't seem to give him the air he needed.

Fear sliced through her veins, cutting without abandon. They were separated from her friends. They had no idea if any of her friends had been injured. They were separated from her army too. And they were running among the very citizens of Kamdaria who hated her most.

Bringing unity would help those in the Gate and Storm. Distributing resources evenly would help them too. But for people in the Crown, those ideals threatened their way of life. They didn't want to let go of the opulence or the decadence. They didn't want to have less.

And because they had been privileged since birth, they had the best tools to fight. The best shaping. The strongest bodies.

Aaden was huffing by the time they moved down another street.

Talise's own breathing had become erratic, but she hardly noticed. She gulped. "Maybe we should try to get closer to the palace again. I know the way to Tempest's house from there."

He shook his head. They both jolted as he nearly lost his balance. When he stepped down another street, his breathing came out heavier than ever. "I have a better idea."

His eyes brightened at what lay ahead of them.

But this street looked the same as all the others. The houses were crowded together. Even in the darkening sky, the paint on the outside of the homes shimmered. They were elegant. Expensive.

Yet relief flooded through Aaden's features with every step they took. She couldn't imagine why until he slipped around the corner of one particularly fine house.

Without a word, he pushed open a door and stepped inside.

CHAPTER FIFTY-SIX

EVERYTHING IN THE HOUSE HAD an air of precision.

It shouldn't have taken Talise as long as it did to realize whose house they were in, but maybe the weakness and the attacks had muddled her mind.

Once inside, Aaden helped her sit down against one wall. Her fingers dug into the plush rug beneath her. "Isn't this dangerous? What if the people who live here come home?"

"They won't." He had already disappeared through a grand doorway, his voice getting quieter with each step.

Her back leaned into the wall behind her, which looked a little too clean. Maybe she had just been in the Gate and the Storm for so long. Every piece of furniture in the room sat at meticulous angles. The room didn't just look refined. It looked perfect. A little too perfect.

Her eyes fell on a large painting of a tree on the wall across from her. The branches stretched out gracefully on the white paper. The leaves had a crispness to them, but they also seemed warm and inviting. Even from her spot on the ground, she could tell it was a family tree.

Many homes in Kamdaria displayed large family trees in prominent places. This one featured exquisite colors and graceful lines. It had been painted by a master.

And then it hit her.

Despite the weakened state of her heart, she forced herself to her feet. It took several grunt-filled steps to hobble across the floor. She clutched her heart with each struggled breath. But she made it. One name sat prominently on the tree trunk.

Sato.

Just above the last name, two more names had been painted.

Blaise. Seraphina.

Beneath those, the name *Lucian* sat with a wide black mark right beside it. Thick and heavy ink obscured the name at Lucian's side.

But those names didn't matter. The most important name of all sat at the bottom of the tree, near the roots. Talise's heart fluttered at the sight of it.

Aaden.

Her finger traced over the calligraphy. She knew he had grown up in the Crown. She had always known. But somehow, she had forgotten. Perhaps it was because Aaden didn't care so much about maintaining his rich way of life, at least not like he used to. Now he cared far more about doing the right thing.

As she scanned the names above Blaise's and Seraphina's, Talise realized this wasn't just his grandparents' home. This was Aaden's home too. This was where he had grown up.

"I found some food." Aaden spoke quietly, as if afraid to break the spell that had come over the room.

But for one moment, Talise couldn't pull her gaze away from the family tree. A realization hit her as she carefully glanced over each of the names once more. She clutched her heart harder as she turned to look at him. Would he know just by looking in her eye that she had realized something?

His eyebrows pinched together once he saw her face. "You really shouldn't be standing right now. You need to rest."

Her heart squeezed in her chest, but it had nothing to do with the weakness inside. Not this time. "Aaden." It came out softer than she intended.

He came to her side, gently guiding her back down to the floor where she could rest. A tray sat near the wall, filled with herb-encrusted rolls, sweet fruits, richly cooked meats, and puffy balls of rice.

"Aaden."

The second time she said it, he glanced at her with a different look. Did he realize now? Jerking his head away, he reached for the tray. "Food will help you get your strength back. And I'm boiling some water to make a draught that should help with the tremors in your heart."

She had her back to wall now. Her shoulders fell as she relaxed the muscles she had used while standing. Aaden knelt almost directly in front of her, reaching for one of the herb-encrusted rolls on the tray.

Just when he tried to hand it to her, she reached out and touched his scar. Her thumb ran over the white line that went over his eye from his forehead to his chin. Aaden abandoned the roll and placed his hand over hers instead. His eyelids fell closed.

"Do you remember when you got this scar?" she asked.

He nodded, still closing his eyes.

"You got it from protecting me."

Now his eyes opened, and a gentle smile filled his face.

She sucked in a breath, just a tiny one. But she needed something to help her force the next words out. "You were so embarrassed about the scar. You were afraid you wouldn't be handsome anymore."

He flinched. Though she had been expecting it, it still squeezed her heart to see it. His eyes narrowed as he once again focused on the tray. "You should try these rolls first. They're delicious."

Her fingers wrapped around the roll he offered, but she placed it in her lap. "You said your name, Aaden, came from your great-grandfather. You said he was known for being handsome, which was why you were embarrassed about the scar. You were afraid you wouldn't be like your great-grandfather anymore."

Aaden swallowed as he met her eyes with an unwavering gaze. "How do you remember that? I told you that months ago."

She reached for his face again, this time letting the tips of her fingers brush over the hair on the side of his head. "But there's only one *Aaden* on that family tree, and it's yours."

He flinched again.

It seemed like a good moment to lean closer. "That means the name *Aaden* came from your mother's side."

His body sat completely still for a few moments. He didn't even breathe. When he finally did, a breath so loud came out, it could have been called a heave. In one swift motion, he dropped to her side and scooped her into his arms.

Though he held her, he had clearly done it to receive comfort for himself. Wrapping her arms around him tight, she gave every measure of comfort she had. He melted into her touch.

"Yes." He sucked in a shuddering breath while pulling her closer. "My name is the only connection I still have to my mother. It's the only proof I have that she was once a part of my life."

Tears followed soon after. Hot, painful, silent tears.

They may have entered the final stages of war earlier that day, but in that moment, they remembered how the war had started all those years ago. Families had been broken. Hope snuffed out.

And the effects of it still hit them now.

As much as it hurt, as much as it stung, being with Aaden helped her cling to the hope of a brighter future.

After the crying, Aaden forced her to eat. The herb-encrusted rolls were as delicious as he promised. The fruit offered sweetness to her taste buds that she hadn't experienced in months. When he urged her to eat the richly cooked meat, she wrinkled her nose and turned away instead.

He raised one eyebrow. "The meat will help sustain you longer than the other foods can."

Her stomach churned at the thought of something so rich while weakness still plagued her body. "Can't I just eat the rice instead?"

His eyes narrowed, and his mouth screwed into a knot. But even as he tried to look serious, she could still see a smile hiding underneath the expression. "You should eat both."

He popped one of the rice balls into his mouth before standing. "I'm going to check on the draught for your heart." He glanced over her once, his eyes landing on the ripped and stained hem of her gown. "And I'll see if I can find something else for you to wear. If we get into another fight, a gown probably isn't the best clothing to have."

She scowled at the meat in front of her, but finally nibbled at one end of it. That was all she needed. Devouring the half Aaden had left her took almost no time at all. By the time he returned, she had eaten the rest of the rice balls too.

A light green liquid filled the steaming hot cup he offered. She took it into her hands but eyed the contents suspiciously. "What kind of draught is this?"

Steaming liquid filled his cup too, but it looked much more inviting. A pleasant cinnamon and nut scent came out of it.

"It's a draught for the heart."

When she responded to his explanation with another suspicious look, he tried again. "My grandmother needs the draught occasionally. She's been using it since before I was born. The recipe came from a skilled healer, and it helps my grandmother. So, it should help you. It's the best alternative we have if we can't get you to a healer."

Talise took a tentative sip of the green liquid. A tangy aroma hit her tongue, filled with fruity spice. After swallowing, a bittersweet aftertaste came. Overall, it was a much better experience than expected. Her second sip was a lot more willing.

A few sips later, her heartbeat had already noticeably strengthened. Her sips turned into gulps. "I think it's working. Are all healers from the Crown this skilled?"

Aaden closed his eyes for a second too long. When he did, a tiny flinch pulsed through his eyebrows. By the time he opened his eyes again, she realized her question had struck a nerve. But what part?

And then it hit her.

His grandmother in the Gate was a healer. She had helped Talise right after Talise destroyed the first portion of the wall. But if his mother's mother was a healer, did that mean…

Gathering the crumbs and dishes, Aaden let out a sigh. "The emperor likes to collect the best healers and keep them all in the Crown. When he finds skilled healers from the Gate, he often encourages them to get to know eligible young men who were born in the Crown."

Talise took one last sip before finishing off her draught. Getting to her feet, she grabbed both cups to bring back to the kitchen. "Is that how your mother met your father?"

"Yes." It didn't seem comfortable for Aaden to have his past dug up like this. But it also seemed like he was dying to finally tell someone the things he had been unable to speak about for so many years.

After setting down the dishes, he directed her toward a room near the back of the house. "You can change out of your gown in there while I clean everything. I need to make sure we leave no trace we were ever here."

"What about the rest of our friends? Do you think they'll come looking for us?"

He considered the words for only a moment before shaking his head. "It's too dangerous to travel at night when the chance of attack is so high. Rio knows that."

Talise bit into her bottom lip. "So, you think they'll go to Tempest's house and wait for us there?"

Aaden nodded. "They should. Either way, we shouldn't leave this house until morning."

Without another word, he gestured toward the same room he had pointed to before. This time, she moved toward it.

The moment she entered the room, she knew it was Aaden's. The spotless walls and precise arrangements matched the rest of the house, but this room smelled more welcoming than the others. Plus, his academy uniforms hung among the rest of the clothes.

She quickly changed out of her gown and into the soft blue tunic and pants he had found. They likely belonged to his grandmother. They didn't fit perfectly, but they fit well enough. And they would be much more comfortable for a fight.

After changing, she found a book of poems on a small table by the bed. Her tiara gave a soft clink as she set it on the table. Then she grabbed the book. She settled onto the floor with her back against the wall as she began flipping through the pages.

Just as she began reading, a loud crash sounded out on the street outside the room. Her heart skittered into a fit, reminding her that the draught had only helped a little with the weakness inside her.

"Talise." Aaden called to her from the other side of the door. His voice came out soft but urgent.

She held the book close to her heart. "You can come in."

When he did, he let out a sigh of relief at the sight of her. Immediately, he moved over to a window. He carefully moved the screen covering the window away just an inch. After a few moments, he moved the screen back in place and let out another sigh. "It was just a neighbor who dropped a pot."

He sat down next to her, putting an arm around her shoulders. His eyes flicked toward the bed. "It's getting late. You should sleep in here, and I'll go to the other room. In the morning, we can try to find the others."

She dropped her head onto his shoulder, nuzzling in close. "I think I'd rather stay here with you for a little longer. Tell me about these poems."

His whole face brightened as he pulled her closer. They read a few poems together, but soon sleep overtook them both. The room darkened as they drifted off, leaning against the wall in each other's arms.

CHAPTER FIFTY-SEVEN

MORNING FLOATED IN SLOWLY. TALISE recognized the scent around her before anything else. The clean, crisp smell had a touch of warmth through it.

After living in the Storm and the Gate for so long, she was used to less than ideal sleeping positions. But when she remembered her pillow was actually Aaden's shoulder, she snuggled in closer to him. He responded immediately by pulling her in even closer still. The wall at her back didn't offer any comfort, and the hard floor beneath her seemed stiffer than ever. But she didn't care.

When her eyes fluttered open, his were still closed. His face looked more peaceful than she had ever seen it before.

He did eventually open his eyes. When he did, it was simply to find hers immediately. The look sparked a fire in her chest, which quickly spread out through all her limbs. But then he gave her a small half smile, which only melted her all over again.

Even sitting against the wall in possibly the most awkward sleeping position ever, she had never been more at ease.

He tilted his head toward her, pressing his fiery lips against hers. It didn't make any sense how every kiss from him could feel better than the last, but it did. Every time.

Just as he leaned in for more, quiet voices sounded in another part of the house. Aaden pulled away with a jerk, his eyes growing wider by the second. He jumped to his feet. By the time he took one step toward the door, he was already turning back around again.

After he offered his hand to help her up, she took it and forced herself to stand.

"How are you feeling?" His whispered words came out too fast.

Skips jumped through her stomach, but those only had to do with the way Aaden looked at her. Her heart on the other hand, that skipped with weakness. She pressed a hand to her chest. "I feel better than yesterday, but I'm still weak."

He nodded. It didn't hide the gulp that trailed down his throat. When he stepped across the floor again, it was to move closer to the window. His feet glided over the floor with the lightest step.

The voices in the house only got louder.

For a moment, both Talise and Aaden stayed rooted to the ground. Listening. Only once the voices stopped did either of them move again. He took her hand, holding it with a gentle but steady grip. He eyed the window.

Before he could take another step, the door to the room opened. A woman stood before them. Her gray hair had been swept up in an elegant bun. Blue swirls ran through the woman's black gown. The dress had a simple design, but the woman held herself with the grace of royalty. Her shoulders were straight. her back perfectly aligned. Everything about her was perfect.

Of course, Talise recognized the woman. She had been a mentor to Talise's mother when the empress first married Emperor Flarius and moved to the palace. Talise had known of the woman since birth.

Seraphina. Aaden's grandmother.

The look on her face so perfectly conveyed disappointment, it was almost enough to crumble whatever resolve Talise had left. When Seraphina let out a disappointed sigh, Talise's gut twisted in on itself. One quick glance told her Aaden felt the same. Or maybe worse.

Seraphina stepped into the room and glanced at someone in the hallway. She raised an eyebrow at the person, as if communicating some unknown thought.

A moment later, another figure appeared. Commander Blaise stood just as straight as his wife. His military uniform was so perfectly pressed, wrinkles probably shrunk at the sight of it. Unlike Seraphina, Blaise's face looked neutral. Not a fraction of emotion peeked through the perfect mask.

He glanced at Talise and Aaden as if nothing but an empty room stood before him. It didn't last. The moment his eyes landed on Aaden's chin—his clean-shaven chin—horror passed over Commander Blaise's face for exactly half a second. The blank mask returned immediately, but it was stiffer now.

His voice came out even stiffer than that. "You shouldn't have come here."

Aaden's shoulders hunched forward. "I'm sorry." To anyone else, the words would have sounded normal. But Talise could hear the crack that went through his voice. Most likely, his grandparents heard it too. Aaden swallowed. He sucked in a breath that was probably meant to calm his trembling words. Now his head lowered. "I'm sorry about my…" The words trailed off as he rubbed a hand across his clean jaw.

All at once, the mask on Commander Blaise's face fell away. Gentleness puddled into his eyes. His expression became soft like Talise had never seen it before. Blaise stepped forward. "I don't care that you shaved."

Aaden glanced upward. The tiniest gleam of hope appeared as he stared at his grandfather. When his gaze moved to his grandmother, she offered a graceful but tender smile.

Commander Blaise stepped forward again. "I'm sure you had a good reason for it, but there's no time to worry about that right now. Emperor Flarius is desperate to find both of you. I held him off as long as I could, but he's sending people out now." His head gave the tiniest shake while a flash of fear went through his eyes. "This is the *first* place he'll look. You never should have come here."

The growing frown on Aaden's face matched his wide eyes a little too well. "I didn't think about that."

With a calm mask painted over his features once again, Commander Blaise gestured toward the window. "If you go out through there, the neighbors won't notice. Make sure you follow the back streets to Fire Square. And don't go directly into Fire Square if you can help it."

Aaden nodded, already moving toward the window with Talise's hand in his.

"Wait." Commander Blaise touched the goatee on his chin. "I'll get you some cloaks that will help disguise you." He turned to walk out of the room but glanced over his shoulder at his grandson. "And you'd better get some extra daggers. Come grab a few from my collection."

Instinctively, Talise reached for the flame-carved dagger hidden in the belt under her tunic. Since Aaden had given her that dagger, it had probably once belonged in Commander Blaise's collection as well. Maybe it had even belonged to Lucian at one time.

Aaden disappeared out the door with his grandmother.

The moment they left, Seraphina gave a pointed glance at the tiara still sitting on the small table near the bed.

Scratching the back of her leg with one foot, Talise gestured toward the tiara. "My friends made that for me." She gulped. "To remind the emperor who I am."

Lifting a dignified eyebrow, Seraphina nodded. "That's smart. Emperor Flarius likes to pretend he's forgotten that, as you well know."

A beat of silence filled the air. Nothing seemed appropriate to fill it. Before it stretched too long, the woman moved across the room with elegant steps. Despite her lofty appearance, something friendly shimmered in her eyes. "I could tell you so many stories about your mother."

Talise stood a little taller at the thought. Were her eyes too eager?

A subtle smirk lifted one corner of Seraphina's mouth. "And Shyna too. Though very different, those two were as close as any siblings I've ever seen." Her eyes fell closed as she reached for the sapphire pendant hanging from her neck. A wince scrunched her face up before she opened her eyes again.

"My aunt Shyna didn't die in the first attack on the palace." Talise blurted the words out without thinking about them for even a moment. Even after speaking, she had no idea why she decided to admit such a thing.

Seraphina's eyebrows rose.

Painful memories roiled through Talise's mind. "My aunt Shyna raised me in the Storm until I was old enough to be tested for a shaping academy. She lived there the whole time I was at the elite academy." Her bottom lip shook as she blinked away the tears gathering in her eyes. "But she died only days before the Master Shaper competition."

Understanding shone on Seraphina's face. With only a few words, the woman seemed to know just how much pain had filled Talise's life. Seraphina swallowed before speaking again. "No one else could have lived as long as Shyna did. That woman could survive on hope alone."

They were just words, but they warmed Talise completely. Since that first attack, she had never been able to talk about her family with someone who had actually known them. The words filled her in a way she had never expected.

Now Seraphina touched a hand to Talise's cheek. "You are the perfect combination of both your mother and your aunt, Shyna. You are loving," her eyes twinkled with mischief, "and fiery."

A quiet chuckle left Talise's mouth. That sounded like a pretty good combination.

When Seraphina's hand dropped to her side once again, she stood even taller than before. "Many people inside the palace are loyal to you. When you finally get inside, they will come to your aid."

The words skipped inside Talise's heart. But the skip immediately turned into a yank that drained her of energy.

Seraphina's eyes grew more intense. "But there are also many who want to crush your rebellion. You must be careful."

Just as she finished speaking, Aaden returned with his grandfather. Commander Blaise handed Talise a rich velvet cloak lined with fur. The soft charcoal fabric was so rich, it almost shimmered. She wrapped it over her shoulders and fastened the polished silver clasp. White fur tickled her neck, but it also began warming her at once. After locating a large hidden pocket on the inside of the cloak, she tucked the tiara inside. Aaden's cloak looked the same as hers but with brown fur instead of white.

When they turned toward the window, Commander Blaise held up one hand. "Just one more thing." His soldierly mask fell away once again, revealing a kind face. "We love you." The words came out tight. As soon as they left his lips, he pulled his grandson into a firm embrace.

"And be careful." Seraphina's words came out as polished as ever, but a few tears streamed down her cheeks. She wrapped her arms around her husband and grandson, who both immediately hugged her back.

Before she knew it, Talise had somehow joined them as well.

The moment ended too soon for all of them. But the morning light in the room grew, reminding them of how little time they had.

With Aaden's grandparents standing by the door, Talise and Aaden moved to the window. They climbed out without too much noise. Once on the street, they pulled the hoods of their cloaks over their heads to hide as much as possible.

Their feet moved quickly over the ground. Aaden whispered to her between steps. "My grandfather says to expect barricades in all the major streets. Fighting has broken out throughout the whole Crown."

Her gut writhed, which only made her heart skitter. "Okay." It wasn't much of a response, but she couldn't think of anything else to say.

His hand reached out for hers, his urgency coming through in the touch alone. "I need you to stay close to me."

She nearly let out a chuckle because she hadn't planned on doing anything else. "And I need you to take care of yourself, not just me."

He glanced toward her now, his eyebrows pinching together. It seemed like her statement hadn't even reached his ears. "Do you think you can find Tempest's house?"

The writhing in her gut only twisted harder. After letting out a hard breath, Talise rolled her shoulders back. "I hope so."

CHAPTER FIFTY-EIGHT

IT TOOK A FEW MORE turns than it should have, but Talise managed to find Tempest's home. Having daylight helped significantly. It also helped that she'd been spent all night thinking about how to get there. Even more importantly, the fancy cloaks disguised her and Aaden enough that they didn't meet a single attack along the way.

Even with the house in view, every step still felt like knives. Fear didn't trickle through her. It roared. It scuffed every nerve and burst through every pore. Sweat prickled on her neck, and it had nothing to do with the warmth of the cloak.

Once at the door, Aaden released her hand for the first time since leaving his grandparents' house. The rapid beating of her heart could not have been good for her condition, but she couldn't do anything about it.

Her knuckles hit the door with a tentative knock.

Barely a moment had passed before the door creaked open a sliver. Through the small opening, Talise saw a man with a white beard and wispy hairs dotting his bald head. At once, she recognized him as Tempest's father. But the man didn't seem to recognize her as easily.

He narrowed his eyes and opened the door a little wider. "Would you like to come in?" The question felt like it had layers of meaning to it.

No hesitation ran through Talise as she nodded and pulled Aaden into the home.

The man closed the door behind them almost as soon as they had entered. The moment they came into view of the front room, a quiet shriek filled it.

"Talise!" Wendy pounded across the floor as tears filled her eyes. Shudders went through her shoulders as she wrapped her arms around her best friend. "We thought you might have died."

The urge to cry hit Talise hard, but she managed to speak first. "I'm sorry. We got lost and—"

Wendy had already pulled away, wiping her tears as she shook her head. "No, you don't need to apologize. It was crazy for all of us when we got separated. I'm just glad to see you. Come sit down."

Talise and Aaden joined Wendy on a rug in the front room. Several others filled the room as well. Rio and Fyra sat on the rug with a few other soldiers.

Rio pressed a fist over his heart as he nodded toward Talise. "It's good to see you, Princess."

Sitting forward on the rug, Fyra blinked much faster than usual as she stared at Talise. "How are you feeling?"

"Um." Since Talise's heart had decided to thump and skitter all at the same time, the answer was probably not good. But she didn't want to admit that.

Before she could answer, Tempest entered the room from a hallway. Her long braid swung as she carried a tray of simple breads and fruits to the rug. Her eyes widened at the sight of

Talise. Immediately, Tempest's gaze turned to Wendy. Once their eyes met, Tempest let out a long sigh of relief.

Tempest set down the tray, and everyone began devouring the food like they hadn't eaten in days.

Talise turned to Rio. "How are things?"

He took in a breath and set his shoulders straight. "There's fighting all over the Crown. It's good that we set up armies in lots of different places. The emperor's army wasn't expecting that, and they're still trying to recover. Right now, we're trying to gather our troops into one location. It's been difficult to send messages because there are barricades and angry Crown citizens everywhere we go."

She nodded long enough to make sure Rio ate something. Once he had food in his mouth, she spoke again. "Where is everyone gathering?"

"Remember how the elite academy was destroyed a few months ago?" Wendy reached for a sugared bun. "Kessoku was trying to capture it to use as a base, so the emperor burned it to the ground."

Talise shook her head at the words. "I forgot about that."

Just then, the door swung open, and Claye entered through it. As soon as he shut the door behind him, he began speaking. "I sent the message to Flint's squad. They know they need to meet us—" He jerked to a stop as his mouth fell open for a moment. "Talise."

She waved a hand through the air. "Yes, I'm alive. We got lost." Her gaze quickly turned back to Rio. "So, we're meeting at the old elite academy grounds? When?"

Whatever the soldier had in his mouth, he swallowed it in one gulp. "We're all gathering there tonight. We're planning to attack the palace as soon as it grows dark."

Talise nodded as she considered the words. "And what about—"

The walls of the home shook as a blast filled the air. Of course their rare moment of peace would be destroyed within minutes. In one blink, half of one wall exploded into nothing. Flames erupted everywhere. In the walls. Across the floor.

Tempest shaped water out of a large barrel at the edge of the room. Her water bounced over flames, putting them out in large clouds of steam.

Her father ran into the room waving both hands in front of his face. "They found us out. Get out of here while you still can."

His hair whipped around his head as he jumped across the floor to shape water over the flames.

Talise lifted her hands to help with the shaping, but the man waved her off. "Just run. We'll take care of anyone who attacks."

Aaden had already pulled Talise to her feet. She wanted to protest. She wanted to help. But every face around her looked ready to vehemently protest the idea. Even Fyra shook her head decidedly.

Rio began moving toward the part of the wall that had just exploded. "Let's go, Princess."

Claye and Fyra moved into position behind her, forcing her toward the exit. Aaden stood by her side as they began moving out of the house. Glancing back, Talise looked hard at her best friend.

Apparently, Wendy had no intention of leaving. She shaped air swirls around the room, which put out the little fires that still remained. "Go." Wendy gave a sharp nod. "You know the plan. We'll meet up with you tonight."

Tempest gave a nod of her own to Talise as she continued shaping water over the destruction of her home.

Talise's gut wrenched with every step. Why did they have to separate? Again? And why did Tempest's home have to be destroyed just because her family had helped Talise? She didn't like it.

But then again, who liked anything that went along with war?

"We still have one last message to deliver." Fyra's voice came out stronger than Talise had ever heard it.

Rio nodded at the words. He gestured Claye and Fyra down a street to their left. "They should be down that way. We'll meet you tonight."

Claye and Fyra moved down the street without another word.

Only one minute passed before another explosion blasted ahead of them. Talise covered her head with her hands while she tried to figure out where the debris would fall.

Crackling embers rained down on them. Aaden put them out in a flash by pulling water from the air.

It was hard to ignore the explosions, but they still had to figure out where to go next. Straight to the elite academy? Somewhere else to rest first?

The moment the questions filled her mind, sharp rocks shot through the air toward them. If her strength had been up, she could have flicked them all away with a little air shaping. Instead, blood drained from her limbs as she tried to duck.

Aaden jumped in front of her. He caught the full brunt of the sharp rocks while she caught none.

They ran.

Rio directed the way down a side street with dust and cobwebs.

A trickle of blood ran down the back of Aaden's hand. After seeing it, Talise glared. "You promised to take care of yourself, not just me."

He stared straight ahead as he marched forward. "I never promised that. And *you* need to stop trying to help. You're draining your energy, which is already low."

His words only caused her to glare harder.

Rio poked his head around a corner before quickly pulling back again. He stared at the two of them for a tense second. "We need to run."

It turned out, running weakened her as much as shaping did. Fireballs and rocks and whips of water shot toward them with every step. They just had to past two streets, but even that was too much.

By the time they moved past the battle zone, her heart beat much too slowly. She stepped forward, but it felt like walking on knives.

A shadow danced across the street in front of them. Her fingers curled while she desperately tried to catch her breath. Would the person bring danger?

But when Rio approached the figure who had found them, he merely let out a sigh of relief.

Cyrus stepped out from around the corner. Sweat drenched his forehead. He heaved in relief at the sight of them, but it didn't stop the shivering that shook through his arms and hands.

"Did you send the message?"

Rio's question came out strong, but Cyrus only tilted his head. After a moment, he shook out his shoulders and squeezed his eyes shut. "Yes." Cyrus touched a hand to his forehead. "They know what to do."

But just those simple words were enough to send him rocking back on his heels. He pressed his head into his hands. "I saw my aunt and uncle with the squad I found."

Narrowing his eyes, Rio urged them all to continue down the street. "Yes, I know. That's why we sent *you* to that squad."

Cyrus's feet stumbled down the road. When he moved his hands away from his face, his eyes were stricken. "My uncle Wade…" Cyrus gulped. "He got hurt badly. *Badly*." His eyes fell to the ground. "He might not survive."

The words sent a knife through Talise's insides. She remembered Wendy's description about that aunt and uncle. They had children. *Young* children. Now Talise wanted to bury her face in her hands.

Cyrus tapped his forehead over and over again, almost like he had forgotten how to speak. "His wife…" Cyrus's feet fell too hard on the street. "My aunt Avery…"

Already, tears had pooled in Talise's eyes. How could the poor woman raise her children if her husband didn't survive? How could she go on?

Hollowness filled Cyrus's voice when he spoke again. "She's dead. My aunt Avery died in an attack."

The street exploded right in front of them, but Talise barely noticed. Her heart was giving out. Her legs. Everything. She knew war would bring death. She *knew* it. But why did it have to be Wendy's aunt?

Under Rio's direction, they ran through several streets. After a few minutes, they found one without any people at all. They crept down the quiet street with their heads down.

The air sizzled with energy. Everyone in their group moved carefully to keep their steps silent. Whenever the slightest noise filled the air, everyone flinched. In a way, the calm was almost as bad as a fight. Their hearts still pounded just as hard while they waited for something to go wrong.

As always, the calm didn't last long.

They started down a new street, and a wave of fireballs rained down on them. Aaden's hands rose into the air just as quickly as Talise's did. He shaped air away from the fireballs, snuffing out most of the ones nearest to him. She shot clods of earth at the fireballs nearest to her, smothering them until there was nothing left.

Her heart jolted as she shaped. By the time they started running again, weakness crowded into every part of her body. They hurried over the stone, turning onto a new street before another wave of fire could fall down on them once again.

Both soldiers and Crown citizens attacked on the streets. Talise and her friends had to move quickly so no one could report their location and coordinate a capture. Rio's quick directions moved them down roads and alleys at random. Hopefully it was enough to keep them safe.

When they entered a new street, even more elements showered down on them from above. Talise's hands raised instinctively. Aaden didn't even glare at her for it, but only because he was too busy fighting off elements.

Rio and Cyrus moved to fight, but fear controlled their actions. They glanced over their shoulders and tripped over their feet. Terror flinched through them with every step.

At the sight of it, a hot rage burned inside Talise's gut.

She and her friends had nearly reached the end of the street. Running didn't seem like the best option anymore. Without a second thought, Talise spun on her heel to face her attackers.

Her feet stomped over the stone street, blasting away any element that flew toward her. Each step brought another slice through her heart. Whatever strength she had came from pure adrenaline.

It wouldn't last.

Soon, the attackers came into view. They wore pristine cloaks and sparkly jewels. Their clothing glinted in the light of the day. When they saw Talise moving toward them, small gasps left their lips.

Though they clearly had no problem attacking others, it looked as though they never expected to *be* attacked. Talise narrowed her eyes at them, raising both hands out in front of her. If they wanted to hurt others, they would get the same in return.

She reached inside her tunic pocket for the amulet, which she had carefully placed there the night before.

After a strong shove, the earth beneath her feet rippled forward. The stone slabs that made up the street shook as they jerked with Talise's shaping. When the ripple of stone reached the attackers, they all fell onto their backs.

Scrambling to their feet, they raised their hands to attack again. But Talise had already marched even closer to them. She knocked away their fireballs and loose stones with simple waves of her hands. Her hands punched forward again.

A second ripple moved through the stone street. The buildings on either side of the attackers began shaking at the movement. Her heart clenched. Stopped. She punched again.

The attackers ran. Their frightened gasps and pleas hung in the air. Talise ignored every one. She sent another ripple through the earth. This one came so strong that a nearby building cracked.

And then it crumbled.

Screams erupted from the attackers' mouths as the building toppled down on top of them. The sight of it probably should have worried Talise. Instead, gratitude filled her. Those who fought for her had already suffered too much. If Crown citizens chose to attack, then Talise would attack them back. Soon, they would know how it felt to have everything taken away.

The straining of her limbs vaguely filled her mind. Her heart was ready to collapse, but she ignored it. When those around her shouted her name, she ignored that too.

The only thought in her mind was to finish the job. Get rid of the attackers for good.

But then she fell.

Her legs buckled. Her heart lurched. Finally, she could feel it. The adrenaline was gone. The shaping was gone. Her body collapsed into a heap. It felt hollow. Dead.

Someone was hyperventilating at her side. Probably Aaden.

After a few moments, a little of the weakness dropped away. She could lift her head at least. Several sets of arms lifted her off the ground and brought her down another quiet street.

Her breaths wouldn't come in fast enough. When she tried to push herself to her feet, her knees shook hard. An arm wrapped around her waist.

"Talise."

Aaden reached out his other arm, ready to lift her off the ground. A harried expression filled his eyes.

She waved him off. "I can walk." But she couldn't.

Weakness cracked through her bones. Even when she spoke, the words came out breathy and stilted.

"You need a healer." Panic laced every one of Aaden's words. His breathing came out too fast as he began pacing over the stone street. "You need one right now."

He turned toward the others. "We can't do this." He shoved a hand through his perfectly combed hair, which sent it into messy chunks. His voice quavered. "She's too weak. How are we supposed to defeat the emperor when she can barely stand? How can she survive?" A shuddering breath shook through him.

All at once, Aaden froze in place. Every bit of color had drained from his face. He turned to Rio with an intense gaze. Both of Aaden's fists clenched before he spoke again. "We have to postpone the attack."

Twinges curled in Talise's veins. Even her voice shook, but she had to speak to keep Aaden sane. "I'm fine."

He spun so fast on his heel that his cloak floated outward. His jaw flexed as he glared. "You are not."

But with him in that position, she noticed something she hadn't before. A little piece of parchment poked out of hidden pocket in his cloak. She pulled it out without thinking.

On the parchment, a name had been written. Talise didn't recognize it. Her face screwed up at the sight of it.

While Aaden also looked confused, he didn't look nearly *as* confused as her. He tapped the name with his finger. "My grandparents know this family. They're good friends."

Rio tilted his head toward the parchment. "Where did you get that?"

A smidgen of hope appeared in Aaden's eyes as he crumpled the paper in his fist. "I think my grandparents want us to go to their house."

Chapter Fifty-Nine

TALISE MOVED FORWARD DOWN THE stone street, but only once Aaden wrapped his arm securely around her waist. She leaned on him more than she cared to admit with each step. Her arms felt like clouds of glass. Erratic beats pounded through her heart. It was impossible to tell what was a heartbeat and what was a pulse of anxiety.

Cyrus walked at their side, but his face had sunken. His eyes dulled. He stepped without purpose or weight. After the unexpected attack, his mind was free to roam again. Based on his body language, his thoughts centered on the death of his aunt.

Pointing toward him with her chin, she whispered to Aaden. "Is he okay?"

Heaviness dropped in Aaden's eyes as he glanced toward his friend. "He'll be fine. Sometimes he needs time to process things like this. It might take a while."

Nodding was the only response she could muster.

"Are you sure this is safe?" Rio marched forward but without the steady steps he usually had. He glanced toward Talise, eyes expectant.

She offered a noncommittal shrug. What else could she say? Of course she didn't know if it was safe. Nothing was sure anymore.

"Who gave you that paper?" This time Rio directed his question toward Aaden.

"My grandparents." At least Aaden sounded less flustered than he had a few minutes ago.

Rio glanced between them as they continued down the street. Twitches went through the muscles in his face a few times before he finally spoke. "Forgive me, but isn't your grandfather Commander Blaise?" Rio gave a pointed glance in Talise's direction. "The emperor's most *trusted* advisor."

"Yes, but his grandfather is on our side." Shakes and tremors rocked through Talise's limbs. Though she had insisted on walking by herself only a few minutes ago, she regretted it now.

After letting out a steady breath, Rio tipped an eyebrow upward. "How do you know that?"

Her stomach crushed in on itself as she tried to move forward. "We already saw him this morning. If he wanted us to get caught, he could have kept us at his house until the emperor's soldiers arrived. He helped us escape instead, so yes, I'm pretty sure he's on our side."

Rio's lips pressed together as he blinked repeatedly. Though the soldier never shied away from saying the things that needed to be said, he certainly looked like he was holding his tongue at the moment. When he finally did speak, disbelief colored his words. "You went to Commander Blaise's house? It didn't occur to you that the emperor might look for you there?"

She had every intention of answering. She wanted to elaborate on how *not* trusting people had caused her a lot more grief in life than trusting them had. She wanted to explain how Commander Blaise and his wife were probably the only people in Aaden's life who ever truly loved him.

But she didn't.

On her next step forward, she buckled over and clutched her stomach tight. Her head barely moved fast enough to keep her vomit from spewing onto her shoes. By the time she finished gagging, Aaden had pulled her hair away from her face. At least her tiara was still in the cloak pocket, otherwise it probably would have fallen off.

She didn't stand up afterward. Aaden lifted her into his arms once again. She could feel a tremor through his arms at the effort of holding her, but of course he held his face still like it was nothing.

Cyrus leaned against the wall, his face still broken. He stared at nothing, not even the vomit on the ground. His body wilted. "Wendy doesn't even know. How am I supposed to tell her our aunt is dead?"

Rio flinched at the words. They all did. Snapping his head toward Aaden, Rio asked, "How far away is this house?"

They all started moving forward again before Aaden answered. He tilted his head toward a nearby street. "It's just a few streets over. And it's on the way to the elite academy, so it won't set us back very far."

With a nod, Rio continued forward with steadier steps. Any hesitancy that lingered inside him had been erased now. His soldierly mannerisms had returned. He scanned each section of the street with an astute eye before leading them onward.

Once they reached the home, Aaden set Talise back on the ground. His arm immediately wrapped tight around her waist while they stood at the door.

They didn't wait long before the door of the house flew open. A young man of about fourteen stood in front of them. His scraggly clothes and rough hands marked as him someone who had definitely not been born in the Crown. By the looks of it, he might have been born in the Storm. Strangest of all, he looked vaguely familiar.

"Are you Aaden?" the young man asked. He didn't look at any of them in particular, instead letting his eyes roam across the three young men before him.

Aaden shot the slightest glance toward Talise before he answered. "Yes."

A wide smile filled the young man's face as he opened the door wider. "Then come in."

The moment they crossed the threshold, the young man closed the door behind them. "Cascade," he called out. "They're here."

The name sent a jerk through Aaden's shoulders. Once again, he glanced toward Talise. But Cascade wasn't such an uncommon name. Surely the young man couldn't have been calling out for Aaden's *sister*, Cascade.

As they moved down a long hallway, footsteps thundered toward them. Moments later, a bright young face greeted them.

Talise blinked once and then stretched out both arms. "Willow."

The girl's face beamed as she darted forward. She wrapped her arms tight around Talise, which didn't help with her weakness. But it did warm Talise's heart. Besides, Aaden still had his arm around her waist to help her stand. What could a hug hurt?

When Willow bounded back down the hallway in front of them, Talise whispered soft enough so only Aaden would hear. "I never asked you before, but is Cascade's home where you brought Willow's family when you brought them to the Gate?"

Aaden nodded in response, but he seemed more intent on staring down the hallway at anyone who might be at the end of it.

Moving closer, Talise lowered her voice another notch. "Didn't you say your mother wanted nothing to do with you when you found her? How did you convince your mother and her husband to take in Willow and her aunt and two cousins?"

"I didn't." Tension split across his shoulders before he spoke again. "My mother made it clear she never wanted to see me again. I've avoided her since then. Luckily, Cascade convinced her parents to take the others in." He let out a soft chuckle. "She can be very persuasive."

The grin on his face vanished as soon as they reached the end of the hallway. His features immediately hardened into a rigid glare. The reason didn't become clear until they stepped into the large room at the end of the hallway. A small crowd filled the room, but Aaden focused on one person in particular. His face twitched at the sight of her.

Aaden's sister jumped to her feet and clapped her hands together. "You made it." Her smile brightened as her gaze turned to Talise.

Rio's eyebrows were now pinched together so tight, a deep crease appeared between them. When he glanced toward Talise, the look demanded an explanation.

Unfortunately for him, Talise only cared about the young woman before her. "Hello, Cascade." Hopefully her smile didn't showcase any of the straining in her heart.

Cascade's eyes filled with awe as she clapped her hands over her mouth. "You know my name?"

Talise nodded.

A scrunch went through Cascade's shoulders as her face filled with the biggest smile. "I can't believe the princess knows me." Her smile grew even wider. She glanced toward Aaden for the briefest moment before she looked back to Talise again. "I've been dying to meet you."

Every word between them only brought more confusion across Rio's face. Cyrus had settled onto the ground, leaning into a wall. He seemed oblivious to the entire interaction.

Aaden folded his arms over his chest, narrowing his eyes into a tight glare. "What are you doing here, Cascade? You *promised* you would stay safe."

"Look at me. I'm safe, aren't I?" A smirk tilted her mouth as she gestured over herself.

Aaden let out a huff. "You shouldn't have followed me here."

"I didn't." A mischievous glint appeared in Cascade's eyes. She glanced toward Talise, almost as if trying to communicate something. Willow clapped a hand over her mouth to stifle a giggle.

Aaden was not amused. His next words came out stiff. "Then who brought you here?"

"I did."

With so much going on, none of them noticed another person had entered the room. The woman standing before them wore a simple tunic trimmed with shimmery gold brocade. A thick gold chain necklace adorned her neck. The beginnings of wrinkles etched her eyes with softness. Wisps of gray strands peppered her black hair. She stared at their group, holding her body much too rigid.

At Talise's side, Aaden had gone completely still. His eyes had widened. His mouth dropped. For a few beats, he didn't even breathe.

Talise knew exactly who the woman was even before Cascade jumped to her side and called her *mother*. Aaden continued to stare without moving. The woman stared back just as intensely.

"I thought you might need a healer." Aaden's mother continued to stare at her son. Her eyes pled for some kind of acceptance. He provided none.

Even Talise couldn't react. She wanted to be angry at the woman for disinheriting her son and refusing to see him when he found her again. But considering she came offering her skills as a healer, this probably wasn't the best time for such things.

"We do need a healer." Rio managed to say the words the rest of them couldn't. He glanced toward Talise expectantly. When she didn't offer any more explanation, Rio gestured toward her. "Princess Talise is badly injured. It's something with her heart. Do you think you could help?"

The woman's face fell at Aaden's continued silence, but she nodded. "Come into this room over here. I have an area set up. Aaden?"

He stiffened but turned toward his mother.

She offered a soft smile. "Could you get me two bowls of water, one warm and one cold?"

He blinked and said nothing.

The woman continued. "Your grandparents said you've been to this house before. The people who live here aren't home, but they said you knew the house well. Do you think you can find bowls for me?"

Aaden sucked in a breath as he gave a hurried nod. He disappeared down another hallway in front of them.

Gesturing toward a small room, Aaden's mother said, "Go lay down in there, Princess. I need to gather a few more things."

Rio followed closely behind Talise as they entered the room. Swathes of white cloth covered the ground. Several stacks of linens sat in one corner. The moment the door closed behind them, Rio jerked his head toward Talise. "Whose house is this? How do we know we can trust these people? And who is that woman?"

"It's Aaden's mother." With her body continuing to weaken by the second, Talise gratefully lowered herself onto the floor.

Rio stood still while a thousand expressions filled his face at once. His eyes scrunched, his mouth dropped, then he looked to the side. Clearly, the explanation didn't actually explain anything at all.

Talise rubbed a hand over her heart. "She disinherited Aaden when he was a child."

Now horror filled Rio's face. But with the horror came the understanding he had been lacking only moments earlier. "And that girl?"

Pulling her knees up to her chest, Talise winced at the pain inside her. "Cascade is Aaden's sister. Well, she's technically *not* his sister. Aaden's mother has a new husband now, and Cascade is their daughter."

Rio kneaded his temples with both hands as realization continued to dawn on him.

"Please don't tell anyone." Talise didn't like secrets anymore, but this secret wasn't hers to reveal. Rio needed to know so he would trust Aaden's mother and sister, but it didn't seem right to let the knowledge spread everywhere unless Aaden himself chose to share it.

With a solemn nod, Rio agreed. "I won't tell anyone. I promise."

By the time he finished speaking, Aaden's mother entered the room. A man with a sun weathered face entered behind her. It must have been her new husband. Moments later, Aaden entered with Cascade. They each carried a bowl.

Aaden's mother knelt down at Talise's side, hovering a hand over her body. It didn't take her long to find whatever it was she was looking for. She looked Talise straight in the eye. "If you stay awake, it will help me know if what I'm doing is working or not." She gulped. "But it's going to hurt. A lot."

Letting the words settle deep in her chest, Talise nodded. "Let's do it."

CHAPTER SIXTY

THE PROCESS OF HEALING BROUGHT even more pain than Talise expected. She had already been through a lot in her life. She had known heartache and sorrow like most people never even dreamed of. But healing the tremors in her heart?

It introduced to her to an entirely new type of pain.

Someone stuffed a ball of fabric into her mouth so her screams wouldn't alert any neighbors, who might then alert the emperor. She squeezed Aaden's hand through the agony, which only brought a small measure of comfort. Tears spilled from his eyes every time he asked his mother if the process was almost over.

Cascade dabbed Talise's head with water, using both cold and warm water depending on her mother's instruction. Willow sat at Cascade's side, helping whenever needed. Rio stood outside the room, guarding just in case someone unexpected appeared.

The process of healing used shaping to manipulate blood and veins and all sorts of other things inside the body. Talise had never studied the healing arts much, but Aaden's mother seemed to have skill equal to any Master Shaper.

Talise couldn't spare any admiration for it because shocks and zings kept slicing through her insides. Just when she'd take in a deep breath, a gasp would steal it away again. Every muscle inside her tensed with aches.

But then it was over. Aaden's mother closed her eyes as she held her hand over Talise's heart. She gave a quick nod and turned to her son. "It's done. She should be able to shape again without any injury or weakness."

Scooping Talise into his arms, Aaden nodded at the words. He buried his face in her hair. Hot breath rustled around it, which had a calming effect.

It took several long breaths before Talise could finally speak again. By then, the others had filed out of the room. They must have known she and Aaden wanted privacy.

"Can you feel it?" Strains leaked into Aaden's voice. "Does it feel better?"

Resting a hand over her chest, Talise nodded. The pain lingered, but at least it didn't sting or slice. "It does feel better." For her own benefit, she reached a hand out and shaped a small fire above her palm. When the action didn't cause any twisting or wrenching inside her heart, she shaped the flames higher.

Aaden's eyes widened at the sight, fear dancing across his features. "Does that hurt?"

With a small smile, Talise shook her head. "It's even better than after I got healed the first time. It must have helped significantly to have me awake during the process. I feel normal again."

The disbelief in his eyes shone like a beacon toward her.

She gave a short shrug. "Well, I'm still tired, but at least I don't feel weak."

He accepted that answer without a single eye raise. When he helped her to her feet, she moved without any of the internal creaks or groans that had filled her the last two days. Now she could stand without even feeling lightheaded.

Just when she glanced up at his face, his lips more specifically, everyone else entered the room once again. Cascade and Willow skipped across the floor to retrieve all the bowls and bandages still strewn about. Intermittent giggles interrupted their quiet chatter. Soon, they disappeared through the door with their arms full.

A few more items still littered the floor. For a moment, Aaden bent as if to pick them up. But then his mother entered the room. When she looked his way, his spine immediately straightened.

"I'm going to go check on Cyrus." He gave Talise's hand a gentle squeeze before rushing out of the room.

Talise found herself face-to-face with Aaden's mother. It turned out, Talise had practically nothing to say to the woman. After a very short nod, Talise said, "Thank you." Then she plucked a few items off the floor just to keep her hands busy. At the last second, she plucked her cloak off the ground, which she had removed for the healing process.

By the time she entered the hallway, no one else lingered nearby. It took a few minutes to find the kitchen. She quickly dropped off the bowls in her hands and then turned back to the hallway to find Aaden.

He stood at the very end of the other hallway. Willow and Cascade stood just to the side of him with their heads bent toward each other. They kept peeking into the large room that came off the hallway. After every peek into the room, giggles would erupt between them.

Talise was already smiling by the time she reached the three of them. Glancing at the girls, she tipped an eyebrow upward. "What are you two giggling about?"

Aaden looked toward her with his own eyebrow raised. "A boy named Terreth. He's *so* handsome, apparently."

Hearing such a statement from Aaden, of all people, was enough to spread a grin across Talise's face. When she stepped closer to him, he slipped an arm around her waist.

Willow and Cascade looked back into the room and let out identical sighs. Cascade shook her head wistfully. "He's the handsomest young man I've ever seen."

A light chuckle escaped Talise's lips before she could stop it. "Well, where is he? Now I have to see what he looks like."

With eyes bright, Willow grinned. "You saw him already. He answered the door when you got here."

"Oh, I remember him." Talise took the moment to rest her head on Aaden's shoulder.

Cascade's eyes went wide. "Terreth grew up in the Storm, not in Willow's city though. He lived by the River Gate. You have to hear his story though. He always knew Storm citizens would be able to shape again someday."

The story certainly sounded intriguing, but Aaden's inquisitive expression stole all of Talise's attention. "Do you still have the amulet?" he whispered.

She quickly checked that it still sat in her tunic pocket. After feeling it, she gave a nod.

"Good." Now Aaden glanced above her. "You should put your tiara back on. We are close to the academy grounds. Everyone will want to know when their princess arrives."

Nodding again, Talise reached into the hidden pocket of her cloak. Aaden helped her pin the silver and crystal tiara back into place. When he finished, they both stepped into the large room where a small crowd had gathered.

Terreth stood at the front of the crowd, looking like he was about to tell a story. Once again, the sight of the boy caused a sense of familiarity to strike Talise.

Cyrus sidled up to them before Talise could dwell on it too long. Wendy's brother looked different than earlier. His eyes were bright again, his smile back. "You got here just in time. You'll never believe this boy's story."

Luckily, they didn't have to wait long. Terreth stood tall as he began to speak. "When I was four, I met a girl from the Storm who could shape the elements."

That alone caused small gasps to ripple through the crowd.

Terreth grinned. "She wasn't new to the Storm either. My mama said the girl's clothes were worn, so she had to have been there for at least a year, probably more. By then, *everyone* loses their shaping. But this girl didn't."

The words prickled at the back of Talise's mind. Something inside her sparked after hearing them.

The boy continued his tale. "My mama and I were on a riverboat, and I cried and cried because I hadn't eaten in days."

Just like that, the spark bloomed into a memory.

Raising his hands up, Terreth continued. "The girl was only a few years older than me, but she shaped a ball out of earth and bounced it into the air." He leaned forward with a grin. "And then she made an earth snake and slithered it around. As you can imagine, I was so entranced, I stopped crying immediately."

At some point, Talise's mouth had dropped. Her fingers pressed against her lips while a flood of memories filled her mind.

Dropping his hands, Terreth gave a significant look into the crowd. "My mama always said she knew Kamdaria would change someday. And now it finally will."

Whispering, Aaden leaned closer to her. "That sounds impossible. Do you really think—" But he didn't finish because he had finally turned enough to see her face. Now his own mouth dropped. "It was *you*, wasn't it? You were the girl." He no longer whispered. The words dropped from his mouth, full of astonishment.

Unable to speak, she merely nodded. His eyes brightened at the sight of it.

"Princess Talise?" Terreth spoke from his spot in front of the crowd.

Turning her eyes forward, she realized everyone in the room was staring at her now. She gulped. They expected an answer, but she could only manage one word. "Yes."

A half smile broke across Terreth's face. It must have been too charming because Cascade and Willow both sighed at the sight of it. The young man grinned even more. "You were helping people from the Storm even before we knew it. Kamdaria is lucky to have a princess like you."

At the sound of those words, everyone in the room dropped into a deep bow. Even Aaden.

Good thing her heart had been healed because otherwise, it would have completely burst at the sight before her. Forcing herself to take steady breaths, she kept most of the brimming tears inside her eyes. "Thank you." She gave a short bow back to them as she said it.

Silence filled the room for another second before someone asked for another person to tell their story. Everyone's attention turned back to the front of the room once again. Except now someone else had come to Talise's side.

Aaden's mother was back. The man who had been with her before stood at her side. He didn't introduce himself, but Talise was certain he was Cascade's father.

"Excuse me." Aaden's mother spoke barely above a whisper. She looked between Talise and Aaden, apparently choosing to ignore how Aaden avoided her eye contact. "I wanted to have a word with both of you."

With Aaden so close, Talise could feel how his shoulders stiffened.

Aaden's mother took in a breath. "I need to ask about your heart."

Though the stiffness in Aaden's shoulders didn't disappear, he still nodded. As he and Talise followed his mother down the hallway, he squeezed Talise's hand with clear tension.

Soon, they entered the healing room. Aaden's mother and Cascade's father stood side by side. So did Talise and Aaden, but obvious discomfort filled them both. Cascade tentatively entered the room with Willow on her heels.

Aaden's mother scratched at her nails on one hand before glancing Talise's way. "How is your heart? Can you feel it beating as strong as it should be?"

Though Talise nodded, it probably looked rigid. "Yes. I think the healing was effective. I'm still tired but not weak."

The ghost of a smile appeared on the woman's lips. "Good." When she opened her mouth, no words came out. Now she glanced up at her husband.

They shared a look for only a moment before he started speaking. "We also wanted to say something to you, Aaden."

Tension cut into the air. Aaden's fists twitched at his sides, but his expression remained blank.

Unhindered, the man continued. "You know how things are in Kamdaria. To leave her marriage, your mother also had to disinherit you."

It seemed like a good moment to reach for a dagger. She didn't, but that didn't stop Talise from *wanting* to reach for it. Her jaw clenched tighter with every second. If she was this angry, she could only imagine how Aaden felt.

The man wrapped an arm tight around his wife's shoulders. "We are glad to have our family. I am especially grateful to have my wife and daughter." He took in a breath. "And we know what the law says about you…" He trailed off for a moment while sharing another look with his wife. Nodding, he turned back to Aaden. "We know what we said before, but we don't care anymore. You're our family too, Aaden, no matter what the law says."

Despite the rising anger, the tiniest spark of warmth burst inside Talise's chest. She glanced to her side.

Aaden looked as stiff as ever. Stiffer even. He swallowed and blinked without uttering a word. He stared at the man and woman before him with no amount of affection. He swallowed again. Harder. When he did speak, his voice came out thick. "I don't know if I'm ready to forgive you."

His mother let out a whimper as she put a hand over her mouth.

Clenching her jaw tighter than ever, Talise squeezed tight onto Aaden's hand. "Then you don't have to forgive them." Dropping his hand, she stepped in front of him and shot a glare toward his mother. "He doesn't have to."

Willow and Cascade had stayed silent throughout the entire conversation. Now they shared a look with each other, which clearly said they weren't surprised by the turn of events.

But Aaden's mother was. Tears pooled in her eyes as she looked to her husband once again.

He gave her shoulders a gentle squeeze, while still maintaining eye contact with Aaden. "You *don't* have to forgive us yet. But if you ever are ready, we'll be here for you."

The room probably would have exploded with tension, except Rio entered at that exact moment. His eyes locked onto Talise's, as if unaware of the tension. She knew him well enough to know he probably did recognize it but chose to ignore it anyway. She'd have to thank him for that later.

"It's time for us to go." Rio jabbed a thumb backward over his shoulder. "Cyrus and I have spoken to several people here who want to join our ranks when we attack the palace tonight. But it's getting late. We can't stay any longer."

"Right." Nodding, Talise took a step toward the door.

Aaden glanced at his sister. "Promise that you'll stay here." His head titled as he seemed to reconsider the words he had just said. Narrowing his eyes, he continued. "In this house, I mean. And promise that you'll be safe."

Talise put both hands on her hips as she looked at Willow. "*Both* of you."

The girls shared a far-from-reassuring giggle before Cascade nodded. "I promise."

Willow gave Talise a quick hug.

But the moment ended far too soon. With night approaching, they had to move. It wouldn't be long now.

It was time to attack the palace.

Chapter Sixty-One

Talise held her head high as she marched toward the old academy grounds. Aaden, Rio, and Cyrus marched with her but so did many others. The attacks from Crown citizens continued once they reached the streets. Luckily, the farther they got from the city, the fewer attacks they encountered.

From all directions, soldiers marched toward the ruins that had once been the elite academy. Some wore Kessoku uniforms with neat black tunics and three interlocking circles adorning the chest. Others wore burlap or linen tunics with dirt smudging their faces.

The weapons they carried didn't have the fine workmanship of those in the Crown. Some only had large sticks or heavy rocks. But the fire in their eyes was unmatched by any of the Crown citizens Talise had seen.

Her heart jumped as she remembered once again why this battle was so important. The people had been oppressed for too long. They were willing to fight to the death to gain their freedom again.

As they neared the old academy grounds, a few familiar faces appeared in the crowds. Wendy and Tempest moved through a line of soldiers, offering food and pouches of water. Talise let out a long sigh at the sight of them.

No emotion could explain the relief she felt at seeing them alive and safe. She allowed herself a moment to feel it and then she turned toward Cyrus. Aaden had turned toward him at the same time.

Cyrus met their eyes, but then dropped his chin to his chest. It had taken a while for him to regain some semblance of normalcy after they had found him on that street. Now, creases appeared around his eyes. A shudder shook through his shoulders.

Talise glanced toward Aaden, but he only shrugged.

Rolling her shoulders back, she looked at Cyrus once again. "Aren't you going to tell Wendy what happened to your aunt and uncle?"

His entire body flinched at her words. "Of course I will." He ran a hand through his hair, but any feigned bravado was lost before he finished. "Just not right now. We have to attack the palace. She doesn't need any distractions right now."

Talise tipped an eyebrow upward.

It only caused Cyrus to stand taller. "I'll tell her about it after we defeat the emperor."

With another glance toward Aaden, Talise finally shrugged. If Cyrus didn't want to tell his sister that their aunt had died, she wouldn't force it. At least not yet.

They reached the rubble of the old academy grounds. Scorch marks covered the gravel pathways. Burnt wood chunks were strewn across the ground. Soldier after soldier filled the area. They sharpened weapons, donned uniforms, and spoke in hushed tones.

Talise joined the soldiers, ready to help with anything she could. Those nearest to her looked straight at the top of her head. When their eyes found the tiara sitting there, they all began dropping to one knee. They bowed deep. When one line of people would bow, it opened the way for the people behind them to see her standing there. And then those people would bow too.

It wasn't just the people at the academy grounds either. Everyone stopped in the tracks, even those still marching forward. While they knelt before her, the weight of her responsibility cracked in her chest.

She pressed a fist to her heart and then held it into the air. The people mirrored her action and then they stood and went right back to work. They didn't expect a speech or any kind of miracle from her. They had simply wanted to express their devotion to her.

Her eyes filled with tears at the thought.

"Princess." Fyra stumbled forward from the back of the crowd. Her eyes were alight as she grabbed onto Talise's hand. "Look who it is."

Talise's feet began moving before she even processed what had just happened. Soon, Fyra gestured toward an older woman standing alone.

The woman stepped forward tentatively. Her sharp features could silence a classroom in an instant, but Talise knew from experience the woman was softer than she looked.

"Mrs. Dew." Talise rushed forward to embrace her old academy teacher. Maybe Mrs. Dew wouldn't think it proper or something, but Talise didn't care. She had been through too much to care about that sort of thing.

After a short hug, Mrs. Dew smiled at Talise. "It is good to see you again."

Talise bit into her bottom lip. "What happened to all the other instructors? Do any of you have jobs? Are you okay? What happened after the elite academy got destroyed?"

Mrs. Dew shook her head as a chuckle left her lips. "This is hardly the time to worry about any of that."

Despite her experiences in the past year, Talise almost felt like a student once again. She wanted to ask more questions, but now her mouth clamped shut. Waiting for instruction.

In a flash, Mrs. Dew's eyebrows knitted together. "I have something important to tell you. I wasn't sure who else I could trust with the knowledge."

Tightness spread through Talise's limbs as the weight of this supposed knowledge hit her. Just like that, she became the princess yet again. "What is it?"

Mrs. Dew pursed her lips like she always did before saying something unpleasant. "The emperor has a secret weapon."

Nothing could have prepared Talise for the way her stomach twisted into a knot. This was not the kind of news she needed just before their attack on the palace. Gulping, Talise nodded. "What is it?"

A twinge went through Mrs. Dew's forehead. She shook her head. "I don't know for sure. I think the emperor knew I was loyal to you, so he tried to prevent me from getting the information I sought."

The woman's features pinched as she stared at the ground. "I know it involves fire, but I don't know much else."

Nodding, Talise's thoughts turned back to the day before. "They threw fire on us when we got to the palace yesterday."

Mrs. Dew shook her head. "No, it's more than that. Bigger. I know he hasn't used the weapon on your army yet." She took in a breath, but it didn't appear to give her the fortitude she expected. "You need to be careful. The emperor is certain he can defeat your army."

She stood and placed a hand on Talise's shoulder. "You have fire inside you. If anyone can defeat the emperor, it's you. But even if you can, it won't be easy."

After a short bow, Mrs. Dew disappeared into the crowd.

The words dug deep into Talise's heart. They pulsed with jagged beats. Though scores of people surrounded her on all sides, Talise's senses closed in on a single person.

Aaden. Did he know what she was thinking? Based on his expression, he clearly had at least some idea.

Without a word, he led her through the crowd and found a quiet spot just far enough away to have a somewhat private conversation. "You're thinking of your father?"

Her fingers found the hem of her tunic. "Yes."

He let out a heavy breath. Pain flitted through his eyes, which perfectly mirrored the pain in her heart. He leaned in closer and lowered his words to a whisper. "We aren't planning to kill your father. You instructed us to capture and imprison him."

Tears prickled at the back of her throat as she nodded. Saying the next part would be easier because she knew Aaden had already guessed that too. Still, her voice cracked over the words. "But what if capturing him isn't enough? What if it takes more than that to defeat him?" Her voice lowered again. "What if killing him is the only way?"

"I'll do it." Aaden whispered quiet enough that no one else would hear. He spoke with such surety it was clear he had been rehearsing the words in his head for some time. "If you ask me to, I'll do it for you." A hard swallow passed through his throat. "I can't imagine having to kill my own father. You shouldn't have to kill yours."

She buried her head into his chest instead of answering. Truthfully, neither of them knew what would happen once they entered the palace. But she did know, if the emperor had to die, she definitely didn't want to do it herself.

Having Aaden offer was more than she ever could have hoped. But hope was only one of many emotions swimming inside her.

Time had caught up to them. She'd visit one last place and that was it. The attack on the palace would begin.

Chapter Sixty-Two

The palace graveyard sat between the old academy grounds and the palace. Talise stood in front of a short wooden fence that still separated the two. She could look over the fence just far enough to see the graves of her mother and brothers and sisters who had died in the first attack all those years ago.

What would they think of what she was about to do?

While alive, her mother had been the only person who could help her father see when he had gone too far. After she died, the emperor had done nothing *but* go too far.

Would her mother agree that he needed to be removed from the throne? Would she be disappointed?

No matter how long Talise stood staring, she couldn't decide on an answer. Her body felt cold and empty, without any emotion at all. But considering what they were about to do, she should have felt *something*. But maybe it was just the calm before the storm. Maybe her heart knew she needed to save up those emotions for after the battle.

Because the chances were high that more people she loved would die.

A pair of footsteps moved carefully over the gravel to stand at Talise's side. They were quiet and unassuming but ever so steady. Just like her best friend had always been.

Wendy glanced into the graveyard, probably just now noticing the graves that were visible from this spot. And now, she was probably realizing why Talise had come here to think so often during their academy years.

After a gentle touch to the forearm, Wendy set her face. "Everyone is ready. They're just waiting for you to give word."

The first drop of emotion burned in Talise's chest. Fear? Rage? Anticipation? She didn't know what to call it. The feeling sent razors through her insides, scraping and gnawing away at whatever semblance of calm dared to exist inside her.

It was time.

Words didn't follow Talise on her way to the head of the army. Only somber looks met her eye just before each person bowed. Speeches had been given. Orders had been given. All that remained was action.

At the head of the army, an empty spot stood waiting for her to fill it. Aaden stood next to that spot with a gaze as intense as ever. Tempest and Rio stood directly behind him with another empty spot for Wendy. Behind them, Cyrus, Claye, and Fyra stood. And behind them, her army.

Once Talise reached her spot, she raised one fist into the air. At the top of the mountain, the palace army had seen them gathering all day. She didn't have time to give a long speech or talk about their plans. But she wasn't going to send her army into battle with nothing.

She stood tall, feeling the full weight of the tiara pressing down on her. "For a future where every citizen has enough. For a future where we are not separated by the marks on our ID cards." Her fist raised into the air. "For Kamdaria."

Everyone shouted the last two words back at her, but something more entered the air at the same time. Strength. Resolve? That energy didn't have a word either, but it struck through the army hard enough that everyone could feel it. Their faces grew more focused. Their fingers twitched with readiness.

They were ready. She was too.

With that last moment, the charge began. When Talise began marching, those behind her marched in perfect time.

Maybe the emperor had a secret weapon like Mrs. Dew said, but they had a secret weapon too. The emperor knew they had Kamdar's amulet, but he didn't know how well Talise could use it. He didn't know how much she had grown since she left the palace.

Whatever weapon or element he threw their way, surely the amulet would be able to fight against it.

Marching forward brought back painful memories. Less than a year ago, she and Aaden had been on the palace grounds in another battle. They used shaping to fight off the Kessoku coming to attack the palace. Her heart hammered as she remembered standing near a chrysanthemum bush waiting to fight her enemy.

Now she stood on the other side, waiting to fight an enemy who had once been her ally. Once they passed the palace graveyard, a steep climb awaited them.

Squeezing the amulet tight in her hand, Talise reached out. Every part of the mountain sparked and buzzed with energy, as if answering a call from the amulet. With almost no effort at all, she shaped wide steps into the mountainside. Her soldiers would still have to climb, but it would take far less effort with stairs to step on.

Her heart pattered in her chest. Fear coursed through her veins. After being on the emperor's side during that fight all those months ago, she had some idea of what to expect.

Strong shapers would meet them on the palace grounds, ready to pick off as many soldiers as possible. Once the army marched too close, those shapers would retreat.

Talise would face those shapers personally. She and Aaden were the only Master Shapers left in the entire empire, *and* she had the amulet to help her.

That first challenge would be their easiest victory.

After that, archers would be hidden inside the palace. They would shoot their arrows out through thin windows that would be difficult to penetrate.

Kessoku had brought their earth cannons to help with that part.

By then, Talise would be focused on the doors. The thick wooden doors were reinforced with gold and other metals. Even with the amulet, burning through the thick wood might take too long. Behind the doors, barricades would be set up. It wouldn't be easy, but they'd get through. They had to.

Nearly at the top of the mountain, Talise spared a glance toward Aaden.

He returned the look, hardening his features with resolve. His fingers gripped around the hilt of his sword. "You can do this." Had he known she needed a little encouragement at that exact moment? He nodded, the resolve on his face growing even more. "And I will be by your side every step of the way."

Her heart soared. They were just words. Simple phrases. But like he had from the moment he met her, Aaden found a way to touch every sense inside her. His words ignited with a power that would sustain her throughout the fight.

She nodded back at him.

And then she stepped onto the palace grounds.

Wind crashed into her with the speed of a tornado. Pulling from the air behind her, she used the amulet to blow the wall of wind back toward the palace.

While her attackers were still busy being shocked at their wind blowing backward, she used her other hand to shape icy whips of water toward them. As the whips cracked, the ice inside them crushed into sharp fragments. By the time her whips slapped against her attackers, the ice punctured their clothing and skin.

Gasps filled the air.

From another side of the palace grounds, a second group of attackers appeared. They sent heavy rocks shooting toward her soldiers. Even with her face turned toward the ice whips, the amulet sensed the rocks.

It only took a sharp twist and clench of her fist to raise a wall of earth from the ground to stop the rocks.

More elements flew.

By now, there were enough elements that she couldn't keep track of them all. But she wasn't alone.

Aaden used two hands to block and beat the obstacles. His skills as a true Master Shaper had never been so evident.

Wendy and Cyrus formed tunnels and whips and walls of wind that blasted into attackers. Their moves were practiced and more powerful than anyone expected from air shapers.

Tempest pulled water from the streams and ponds inside the palace gardens. The liquid hit hard against the palace soldiers. Claye used earth shaping to catch and hold the feet of palace soldiers as well.

When even more attacks hit, the soldiers in Talise's ranks fought back with ease.

They were winning.

It was far too early to claim victory. They hadn't even reached the part of the grounds where the arrows from inside the palace would be able to reach them. But in that moment, they were winning.

Talise stomped forward. Her hands whipped around in every direction as she blocked attacks. Her training with the amulet helped her react instinctively. Now that she wasn't drawing on a well of power, she could use the amulet without weakening her body.

With each step forward, the palace grew larger. More oppressive. That only caused her to move faster. Stomp harder.

When the arrows began to fall, she shot precise fireballs at each one. Their wooden shafts burned to ash long before they reached their targets. More arrows rained down. With her earth shaping senses, she could feel the stone arrowheads at the tips. It only took mild concentration to find each arrow in the air and demolish it.

The palace shapers retreated. They fell back in the palace gardens, far from the chaos of battle. It was a small victory. Talise took it all the same.

Gilded wood doors towered above. She stepped toward them. Her eyes narrowed. The arrows continued to fall, and she continued to burn them up. But if she was going to get through that door, she'd have to stop worrying about the arrows.

Luckily, Kessoku's earth cannons soon began firing into the small openings that the arrows came out of. The first wave of earth slowed the attack, but it soon became apparent that the earth cannons weren't enough. Arrows continued to fall.

Talise punched fireballs at the arrows as she turned to the side. Aaden shot a blast of water so hard that the shower of rocks flying toward him changed direction mid-fall. She lifted her eyes upward. His eyes followed.

He glanced at the arrows and then he glanced at the doors. Even while his face pulsed with deep thought, he continued to shape threats away. "What if we build a tunnel over ourselves? Can you shape earth up from our sides and over our heads?"

The idea was sound. It came at a crucial moment, proving once again that Aaden was more than just the one she loved. He could offer council and strength when she needed it. And he believed in her power too.

But sometimes, those things weren't enough. Sometimes even the greatest preparation couldn't prepare someone for what lay ahead.

She should have known. Mrs. Dew had warned them. Even then, it came as a shock.

With the amulet in one hand, Talise stretched her arms out. Ready to shape a tunnel of earth over their heads to protect them from the arrows.

That's when the fire storm began.

Flames erupted all around them. Holes appeared at random intervals all around the palace grounds, and fire shot upward from them. The fire burned hot and high. In minutes, the heat caused sweat to break out over everyone's foreheads.

Regular fire would have been easy to put out. Talise's shaping senses combined with the amulet could have shaped away the fire in less than a breath. But these fires didn't come from fuel or regular flames. People were shaping these fires.

There must have been some network of tunnels underneath the palace grounds that allowed soldiers to shape flames up the holes. In fact, the fires burned so large, there must have been several people contributing to each fire.

And if someone else controlled an element with their shaping, no one could wrest that control away.

The fires grew.

From beneath the earth, the shapers fed the flames. The orange light licked the ground, moving outward in slow and steady intervals.

Earth beat down on the fires. Water splashed down against it. The efforts helped, but they didn't extinguish the fires completely.

And then more fire came from above.

Flames poured from every opening inside the palace. The tiny windows that had arrows falling from them only minutes earlier, now had hot fireballs coming out.

Explosions burst out from the earth cannons. Just like with the flames coming from the ground, the earth from the earth cannons failed to put out the fires. It continued to rain. To burn.

Gripping the amulet, Talise formed a canopy of water over her army. Before she could turn it to ice, more fireballs blasted through the liquid. Her heart shook as she pulled more water from the air. The water kept her soldiers safe, but it heated up more every second.

Her jaw clenched as she made another attempt at turning the water to ice. She failed.

It wasn't like when she and Aaden used fire and ice on the poison factory in the Storm. It wasn't like when they used fire and ice to form trees that would impress the emperor.

This fire worked against her. It showered down, falling harder and faster before she could get control of her water. Her feet pressed down into the soil as she tried to measure her heart beat and her internal temperature. Just when she'd know how much cold she needed to shape to create ice, more fire would rain down.

The canopy of water warmed. It boiled. It sizzled into steam. Then she couldn't worry about ice because she had to pull more water from the air to maintain the canopy.

Flames continued to fall. To shower. The fire above was bad enough, but the fire around them continued to grow as well. Even with the ability to shape ice, Talise's body still pooled with heat.

A crack in her canopy appeared. Her arms waved and pulled and shaped, but she couldn't keep up. The first fireball burst through. A scream promptly followed. It came from someone in her army.

Her arms moved faster.

Another crack appeared.

She swallowed as the fire continued beating down. Her friends moved frantically around her. They fought the fire with all sorts of creative shaping, but they couldn't keep up. The fire storm would engulf them soon. It would consume them completely with no regard for their life.

Talise glanced at the doors once again. If they could just get inside the palace, they could escape the fires.

More screams erupted throughout the army. Screams that squeezed her heart in a knot.

Her hand balled into a fist as she formed another canopy of water overhead. The water was thin, but it would hold for a few moments.

Even as her heart dropped down to her toes, she knew what she had to do. It still hurt. She had to swallow over a large lump in her throat just to keep her voice from cracking.

Holding her fists high, she turned to face her army. And then she shouted the word she'd been dreading since the beginning.

"Retreat!"

CHAPTER SIXTY-THREE

SHADOWS CREPT IN AS NIGHT descended upon them. Tents cropped up around the old academy grounds. Talise roamed among her ranks, desperately trying to convince herself that she could speak to every single soldier.

Many had burns. Others had bruises. At least none were dead. Not yet. Those who had the worst injuries were sent back into the capital city where Aaden's mother could heal them.

Trembling worked through her jaw, but she couldn't stop reassuring the soldiers. Every soldier.

Her feet stumbled over the smallest pebbles. At least no one noticed. Or perhaps they only pretended not to notice. When Claye and Fyra came toward her, she tried to hold her head high. Did they need encouragement? Advice?

"We have an idea." Claye paired the words with his signature smirk.

No sweeter words could have been spoken. Not daring to let out a breath of relief yet, Talise merely gestured that he should continue.

Fyra spoke next. She bit into her lip. "We just need a few more shapers."

The reluctance to let out a sigh of relief now brought a pit into Talise's stomach instead. "How many?"

Claye's smirk faded into a fake smile. "At least a dozen."

Tension joined the pit in Talise's stomach. Her face must have conveyed enough because the pair of them frowned at the same moment.

"We don't have any extra shapers?" Fyra asked.

Aches stung in Talise's throat as she shook her head.

Claye waved the words away as he and Fyra moved back toward the soldiers. "Don't worry about it. We'll figure something out."

They wouldn't. How could they? As soon as they disappeared into the crowd, Talise spoke to her soldiers with even more vigor than ever. If she kept busy, she wouldn't have to face the impossible task before her. The epic failure that awaited them all.

How could she defeat an army with the resources and training the palace provided? She had already retreated twice against the emperor's army. Maybe tomorrow would be different since they knew what to expect, but maybe it wouldn't. And they didn't have any extra shapers. They just had Talise, who had no idea what to do.

Even if she used an earth tunnel to protect her soldiers from the arrows and the fire storm from above, that still wouldn't take care of the fire that came up from the ground.

"Talise." Aaden had found her again. She kept sending him off on pointless errands because she knew what he would say once he got a minute alone with her.

Rest. Stop trying to fix everything all at once. You need to sleep.

But she couldn't bear to hear any of those things. She had to keep talking to the soldiers. She had to keep moving through the crowds with some sort of purpose. If she stopped, she'd be alone with her thoughts. And her thoughts would tell her hope was lost.

Though she'd been saying it over and over again to her soldiers, they couldn't simply try again the next morning. If they did, they'd just fail like they had that evening. Maybe she could tear down the palace walls using the power of the amulet but doing so would only weaken her heart again. If the process killed her, Kamdaria would be left hopeless anyway.

The truth was hard enough to brush away and ignore. How could she ever face it head on?

When Aaden reached for her hand, she felt heat coming off him like it always did. The touch brought comfort but not enough. Pulling her hand away, she tried to stand taller. "I have to talk to another group. I need you to…" Excuses weren't as easy to come up with when he stood so close.

"Talise." He tilted his head to catch her eye. When that didn't work, he angled his body toward her.

She turned on her heel, deliberately avoiding eye contact. Her fingers kneaded over a sore spot in her arm just so she'd have something to do with her hands. "It will be better tomorrow. We'll try again in the morning when the air is still chilled, but the light is bright."

Her feet began moving but not toward the group she supposedly had to talk to. Instead, she found herself drawn to same spot of comfort she had visited many times throughout the years. To the fence between the academy grounds and the palace graveyard.

"Talise."

The third time did her in. His voice came out softer. Gentler. He knew what she was avoiding. It was clear in his tone alone.

When he reached for her this time, she didn't pull away. Instead, she buried herself in his arms. Her body shook as the first tears left her eyes. She couldn't cry too loudly or the soldiers would hear. But her heart was too spent to stop the tears completely.

From her position near the palace graveyard, none of the other soldiers could see her very well anyway. The shadows helped even more.

Aaden held her just long enough to calm the beating of her heart. When she pulled away, she still felt defeat down to her toes. What good had it done to survive Kessoku's dungeons, and River's attacks in the Storm if she was just going to fail at this final hour?

Taking a deep breath, she leaned closer to Aaden. It didn't solve anything, but at least she didn't feel as though she was being crushed from the inside out. Now she looked into his eyes.

She expected him to wear an expression of understanding. Or comfort even. Instead, expectancy filled his eyes. He had let her cry because that's what she needed in that moment. But it suddenly became clear that he hadn't approached her for that reason alone.

His head tilted ever so slightly toward the head of their makeshift camp. "There's someone here that you need to see."

Wiping away the residue of her tears, Talise straightened her back. She combed through the knotted strands in her hair. She had no idea who the mysterious visitor was, but for a wild moment she thought maybe it was the emperor. Had he seen her army's power and been afraid?

She brushed dirt from her soft blue tunic and then touched a hand to the tiara on her head. "How do I look? Do I look—"

"Frazzled?"

Her mouth bent in a frown. The fact that he had correctly guessed her question without any hesitation did not bode well.

"No." He said it without a hint of deception.

She lifted one eyebrow up on her forehead. She could only hope it conveyed the skepticism she felt.

He shrugged. "If you do, everybody does, so there's no need to worry. I'm pretty sure she won't care. She might not even notice."

She? So, it wasn't the emperor then. That was probably a stupid thought anyway, but that didn't get Talise any closer to guessing who it was. Cascade? No, the young woman had promised she would stay at that home in the Crown. Aaden's mother then?

It wasn't.

When Talise reached the area Aaden indicated, fear sparked inside her. Wild eyes stared back from a frighteningly familiar face. The woman's indifferent posture had a way of setting Talise on edge. Talise had been expecting to see this woman again, but she always imagined it would be at the end of a sword.

River sat on a log glowering at the ground the way she always did. When she noticed Talise coming near, she let out a huff. "Finally."

Sucking in a breath, Talise reached for the amulet and the dagger hidden under her tunic at the same time.

Rolling her eyes back, River let out a scoff. "If I wanted to hurt you, do you think Aaden himself would have led you over here?"

It did seem unlikely once it was pointed out like that. Talise lowered her arms to her sides.

With a subtle squeeze around his sword hilt, Aaden leaned toward the older woman. "I'll still kill you if you try anything."

River flinched at the words, which she immediately tried to hide through another eye roll. "I know. You've said that at least a dozen times. And you killed my two best soldiers before your little escape to the Storm, so I'm well aware what you're capable of."

Even without moving a muscle, the intensity in Aaden's eyes grew. "You sent them to kill *me*. It's your own fault they're dead. And since they were both even more bloodthirsty than you, the world is better off without them."

The second flinch that went through River's face shook less than the first. Still, her shoulders jerked along with it, as if trying to shake away his words. It did seem strange that someone more than a decade older than Aaden could fear him so much, but considering he had killed her two best soldiers, the fear made sense.

With her defenses lowering by the second, Talise raised one eyebrow. "If you're not here to hurt me, then why *are* you here?"

A sigh went through River, forceful enough to rustle the hairs on her forehead. "I'm here to offer help. My entire team of soldiers wants to help as well. I know you hate me, and let's be honest, I don't like you that much. But I'm a good fighter. The other soldiers on my team are good fighters too. With our help, you have a much better chance of getting inside the palace."

"Um." Talise blinked as the words sank in. Was there a diplomatic way to respond to such shocking words? Apparently not. She screwed up her face into a knot. "You know we aren't planning to kill my father, right? We're just going to imprison him and remove him from the throne."

Though River winced at the words, she followed it up with a nod. "I know."

Muscles all through Talise's face continued to contort with utter confusion. "I thought you only wanted revenge. What about your family members who were sent to the Storm?"

Though her spine had been straight and stiff the entire time, River hunched forward. "My aunt's children? Their families?" She let out a hateful scoff. "They're dead. They're *all* dead. After we made that hole in the wall, it took me a few years to find out where they had been sent in the Storm. Three of her children got sent to one city and two of them got sent to another. By the time I figured out where they had been sent, my aunt's children and families were all dead. One of them did have a child before she died, but I couldn't find the child when I was searching for her a week ago. She's missing, which probably means she's dead too." Despite her hardened stare, true sorrow shimmered in River's eyes. "Nobody ever lives long in the Storm."

The words shouldn't have affected Talise considering everything River had put her through. But the way she spoke about the missing child, it filled the air with thick energy. Talise found herself reaching for the hem of her tunic. "I'm sorry."

River stared at the ground without acknowledging the words. "I thought if I could bring the child to the Gate then everything would be okay. She wouldn't come when I asked a few years ago, but I thought things would be different with the wall destroyed. But now even she's gone too." Her head shook side to side as she curled one hand in a fist. "I finally realized; it doesn't matter what happens to the emperor. My family members are still dead. Nothing can bring them back. All I can do now is try and stop the same thing from happening to other people."

Pain spread across the woman's face as she forced the words out. Each one brought a deeper strain through her voice.

Talise glanced at Aaden. He stared at the woman the same way Talise had only moments earlier. It came as a shock that

River could exhibit normal expressions such as sadness and regret. Especially since she had only ever showed interest in one thing previously. Revenge.

Clearing her throat, Talise attempted to stand taller. Aaden's elegant grandmother came to mind as she positioned her face. "So, now you actually want to help us?"

All at once, River's face turned blank. Cold but with an insane amount of focus. She dropped to one knee and bowed her head deep. "I swear loyalty to you, Princess. My hands and my weapons are yours to command."

War certainly had a way of bringing out the most unexpected actions from people. Whatever calm existed on Talise's face before contorted into shock. She had to repeat the words in her head three times before they sank in.

After a swallow, Talise gestured her hand upward. "Thank you, River. We accept your help."

The woman followed the direction completely and then stood in front of Talise, as if awaiting another command.

Biting her bottom lip, Talise threw a quick glance toward Aaden. He stood staring at River with shock still painting his features. Turning back, Talise decided to ask her question as quickly as possible or else she might lose courage. "What about Lucian? Is he with you?"

River sucked in a long breath. Twitches appeared all over her face from her eyebrow to her nose to the corners of her lips. Only after clenching her jaw and shaking her head did she finally speak. "I know he still wants you dead. He thinks that if he kills you and the emperor, it will leave him as the next logical leader of Kamdaria. He thinks the members of Kessoku will support him in his attempt to take the throne. But he's determined to kill you and the emperor first."

A hard puff escaped Aaden's nose as he took a step closer to Talise. He gripped his sword tight as his shoulder bumped against hers. "Where is he?"

Shrugging in response, River said, "I don't know. I tried to follow him, but he got away. He's somewhere close, but I doubt you'll know where until he wants you to know."

Of course. Just when unexpected help arrived, of course another wrench had to enter their plans.

"Excuse me, Talise?" Claye stepped toward her from behind. "Rio and I think we might be able to use some of the shapers that marched at the back of…" His eyes had been focused on a piece of paper in his hand. When he glanced up and saw River, he stopped speaking entirely. His nose immediately wrinkled as he took a step back. "Uh, should I be worried?"

Giving a noncommittal shrug, Talise answered. "River is on our side, I guess. Her team of soldiers is too."

His expression of shock only lasted a moment before it morphed into something just short a smirk. He glanced at the parchment in his hand and then he looked back up again. "How many of your soldiers know how to shape earth?"

Pulling her eyebrows together, River lifted one shoulder. "I don't know, twenty maybe. How good do they need to be? You've seen my earth shaping skills. Are they good enough?"

Claye nodded eagerly. "Yes, that's perfect. Twenty will make an enormous difference." He turned toward Talise and again held out the paper in front of him. "Fyra, Rio, and I snuck up to the edge of the palace grounds earlier with a few other soldiers. I used my earth shaping senses to find all the holes where the fire came out during that attack. This is a map of all the holes."

Talise's eyes drifted down to the paper in front of her. It was filled with a basic sketch of the palace grounds. Colored circles dotted the design.

Fyra stepped forward eagerly, pointing to the paper. "Now that we have a map of the holes, we can shape earth over them to prevent fire from coming out. The soldiers in the tunnels might be able to shape more earth to break through, especially if those of us shaping aren't very good shapers. But it doesn't matter. If that happens, we can just shape more earth over top and the fire *still* won't be able to get through."

From behind Fyra, Rio came forward. "Aaden told us how you were going to create an earth tunnel to block the arrows from above. Now that we have more shapers, Claye can gather a team to do earth shaping to block the fire from below. As long as you can create that tunnel before the palace soldiers send fire down on us, we should be able to get inside the palace with no trouble at all."

The tiniest spark of hope burst inside Talise. She kept staring at the parchment for a loophole, a mistake. She found none. While she had been worrying and comforting the soldiers, her friends had come up with a plan. A good plan.

Things really *would* be different tomorrow. And with the help of River's team, they stood a chance.

CHAPTER SIXTY-FOUR

A CLEAR DAWN MET THE horizon the next morning. Bright sunrays cut through the chilly air of a winter trying to linger for too long. With the clear sky came hope. Talise never expected it to be easy, but standing before her soldiers again, entering the palace truly seemed possible.

She stood as tall as she could on a log to address her army. With the palace at the top of the mountain next to them, she merely spoke in a slightly louder voice than normal. Those near the front of the crowd, relayed her message to those behind, which continued until those at the very back had heard the words.

"When we fight today, we don't do it for power. We do not fight for money or privilege or position. Instead, we fight for a better future. We fight to reunite families. We fight for equal opportunity." She put a fist to her heart. "We fight for a better Kamdaria!"

When her fist raised into the air, every fist in the army mirrored it. Her heart thundered in her chest as she turned, but she held her head high.

The second march up the mountain felt different. Her soldiers were well rested. Her own heart and mind were well rested. Everyone in the crowd stomped forward with the knowledge that they had a way past the emperor's fire storm. The only true difficulty would be getting past the palace doors.

Once they reached the top of the mountain, palace shapers slammed wind and rocks toward Talise and her friends. Just like they had the night before, Talise and her friends slapped the elements away with almost no effort at all.

In the morning light, they could better see how frightened their opponents looked. Even better, their opponents could see how confident Talise and her friends looked. They only fought for a few tense minutes before the palace shapers fell back.

The arrows rained down next, but everyone was ready for them. Blasts of air and shots of fire removed the arrows while Talise reached for the amulet inside her tunic pocket.

Her fingers squeezed the cool metal. Everything buzzed around her as the amulet sensed the elements. Holding both arms out to her sides, she slowly raised them up until her two fists met high above her head.

While her hands moved, two long walls of earth popped out of the ground. They stretched upward, eventually curving toward each other until they formed a long tunnel. She couldn't hold the shaping in place once she got to the palace doors, but she held onto it for several moments. Hopefully then, the palace soldiers would stop trying to control the earth because they could tell her shaping had control of it already.

Shouts sounded all around them. Many came from below. Many came from above.

Puffs of heat burst above the ground's surface, sizzling in the cold air. But so far, no fire burned around them. Claye's plan was working. The earth tunnel was working.

When she stepped up to the palace doors, she finally released control of the earth tunnel. Her gaze turned to those standing nearest to her.

Wendy wore a sweet expression as she raised her hands out in front of her. Tempest and Rio drew their swords while their fingers gripped them tight. Cyrus tipped an eyebrow up in his sister's direction as he raised his hands. Claye and Fyra shaped earth over the nearest fire holes but took a moment to nod toward Talise. River and her shapers worked under Claye's direction.

Finally, Talise looked at Aaden. He had drawn his sword as well. His left hand was up as well, ready to shape any element if needed. When he glanced her way, her stomach flipped. "We're ready when you are."

The stomach flipping continued as she squeezed the amulet again. Having friends who believed in her power was great but having the power to actually change things was even greater.

She sucked in a short breath. And then the shaping began.

Fire.

Flames burst from Talise's palm engulfing the palace doors completely. Holding tight to the amulet, she carefully considered the balance inside her mind. Emotion flowed through her. Anger at how her people had been treated and determination to change it. But with the emotion flowed an equal amount of logic. Changing Kamdaria would take time. This was only the first of many steps.

Once she found a perfect balance, she then drew on the amulet's power even more. Her flames shifted from orange to white. After another burst, the flames turned blue. They ate through the palace doors like a child crunched on candy.

Chunks of burnt wood fell away while the rest turned to ash. Even some of the metal reinforcing the door burned hot enough to melt. It slid down to form boiling puddles of silver and gold.

Soon, the door had crumbled away. Talise's blue flames vanished as she closed her fists.

The smoke cleared away. She carefully tucked the amulet back into her tunic pocket. The faces that greeted her from inside looked like they had never truly known fear until that moment.

The palace soldiers held their weapons so tight, their entire hands had turned white, not just their knuckles. Chins trembled. Shoulders trembled. Knees trembled. Though the palace soldiers stood in defensive positions, they all seemed to have forgotten how to fight.

Sounds of chaos erupted behind Talise as part of her earth tunnel caved in. Apparently, someone on the emperor's side must have realized they could now take control of the earth she had once controlled. The earth tunnel was quickly being dismantled.

After once last glance toward her friends, Talise raised her hand and charged into the palace.

Swords clashed. Grunts erupted from mouths on both sides. As Talise's feet hit the palace floor, her heart pounded with each step.

An arrow flew toward her. She burned it to ash before it could strike. Clods of earth shot at her. Pulling water from the air, she froze ice around the clods. The action made them heavy enough that they dropped to the ground just before slamming into her.

She continued forward.

Even as she sliced and smashed and plummeted her way down the hall, her mind focused in on her destination. The emperor's living quarters. After hours of discussion, she and her friends had finally decided the emperor was most likely to hide there. In case he wasn't there, her friends would all check other parts of the palace at the same time.

Her feet stomped with every bit of determination she could muster. The elements she sent outward changed from air whips and dirt clods to fireballs and deadly icicles. As much as she didn't want to hurt anyone, the necessity of it became clearer by the minute.

A swarm of palace soldiers entered the hallway before them. Just as Talise raised a hand to fight, a familiar face stopped her.

Ember. Talise remembered the palace soldier. Ember had helped Talise escape the palace during the summer. As the young woman bounded forward, another memory flitted through Talise's mind.

She remembered how Rio had sent a message for Ember when Aaden traveled to the palace while they were living in the Storm. Rio had feelings for the young woman, though Talise didn't know how strong they were.

In the midst of the fight, Ember bounded forward, straight into Rio's arms. Joy split across his face as he lifted her off the ground and spun her around in a circle. When he set her back down again, they shared a kiss that could have stopped time.

But it didn't. The war continued all around. After only a moment, the two of them raised their weapons and continued to fight like nothing had happened. When another swarm of soldiers rounded a corner to enter the hallway, they shot weapons forward without abandon.

More weapons clashed. More blood splattered.

It took effort just to move forward toward the end of the hall.

At the end of the hallway, Talise and her friends turned a corner into a new corridor. Her feet faltered at the sight of the emptiness before her. Was the new hallway too empty? With a quick glance over her shoulder, she realized the palace soldiers had gathered far away from her. Or were they gathering far away from that particular hallway? The empty one?

Before any type of conclusion could settle in her mind, an explosion erupted from one side of the empty hallway. Clumps of the palace wall burst into the air while flames licked everything in sight.

Only then did Talise realize her body was flying through the air. Her back slammed into the opposite wall in the next second. Whatever breath she had quickly got knocked out from her chest.

Her eyes widened as she tried to cough. Slapping a hand against her chest didn't help either. She leaned forward, attempting another cough. Finally, a small bit of air entered her body. It took several gasps before she could breathe again.

The shock of the explosion had dulled her senses enough that she hardly noticed anything going on around her. But once she had air, she frantically glanced up and down the hallway. Aaden rubbed the back of his neck while winces wrinkled across his face.

Claye and Fyra sat coughing like Talise had been only moments earlier.

Tempest shook out her muscles while her face twisted in pain. As she moved, her eyes roamed the hallway just like Talise's did. They both found the same body at the same moment.

With a face drained of color, Cyrus knelt at his sister's side.

Wendy.

Talise gulped.

Wendy's legs bent at strange angles, making it clear she hadn't been conscious when she landed on the ground. A small trickle of blood slid down her forehead.

Whatever air Talise had gotten into her body before had vanished now. The entire world stopped as Talise stared at her best friend. If she stared long enough, she'd see Wendy breathe. Or twitch. Or *something*.

Cyrus gave a heavy gulp before he touched his sister on the shoulder. With the touch, Wendy stirred. Her eyelashes fluttered until they snapped open.

Talise shared a look with Tempest as they both let out deep sighs of relief. In a moment, Tempest was at Wendy's side, helping her sit up and wiping the blood from her forehead.

Relief filled every vein in Talise's body as she glanced down the hallway at the rest of the soldiers. Many of them had been injured, though none as seriously as Wendy. Luckily, Wendy was already pulling herself to stand.

But even as that thought struck Talise, a part of her felt she had missed something. Or maybe someone.

"Talise." Aaden stood at her side, close enough that his shoulder brushed against hers. But the heat that always accompanied him didn't burn as hot as it usually did. One glance into his face showed a stark, raw fear.

Her stomach sank before she even knew why. That nagging feeling of missing someone hit her even stronger. Except now she remembered. She knew whose face she hadn't seen.

The relief she had felt only moments earlier burned into ash.

Before she even finished turning in the direction Aaden indicated, she had already grabbed on tight to his arm.

Blood splattered the walls at the end of the hallway. Too. Much. Blood.

A piece of the wall had been smashed to pieces. The splintered wood pierced straight through two chests.

Ember. And Rio.

The two who had only been reunited moments earlier now lay lifeless in thick pools of blood.

But war didn't care for how the heart broke. It didn't care for the lives it took. It only wanted more. More blood. More death.

Another wave of palace soldiers entered the hallway from another direction, forcing Talise and her army to run.

Chapter Sixty-Five

NO AMOUNT OF SWALLOWING COULD loosen the lump in Talise's throat. It nestled deep, aching more with each breath. For a wild moment, she thought the lump might take over her throat completely. Maybe it would close off her air supply, and she'd die. But at least then she wouldn't have to face the nightmare of reality.

Rio was dead. Ember too.

A part of her clung to the silly hope that they could have survived. But she'd seen too much death now. She knew they were gone.

The aching inside her pulsed. It felt more real than the pounding of her heart or the slapping of her feet against the floor.

Her arms waved on instinct. She shot elements forward, taking down anyone who dared stand in her path. They moved down another hallway. As she fought off palace soldiers, she instinctively led her group to an alcove that was hidden by a tapestry.

Her army continued to fight as they had planned, but the rest of them—her friends—they joined her inside the alcove with eyes drawn to the ground.

The only sound louder than their heavy breaths were the constant gulps.

Cyrus held his hands against his temples, shaking his head side to side with slow, deliberate shakes. "First Aunt Avery and now Rio?"

Wendy's face cracked with horror as she grabbed onto her brother's shoulder. "Aunt Avery? What happened to Aunt Avery?"

Cyrus couldn't respond. His face was too twisted.

Fyra started crying. Claye offered her a pat on the back, but it lacked comfort because tears slid down his own cheeks.

Tempest slammed her fist into the wall. She kicked it next.

At the edge of the alcove, Aaden stared at the rest of them. He took deep breaths in and out, but it didn't stop his face from contorting every few seconds. His hand gripped tight on his sword, which he still had drawn. Every small noise caused his arms to twitch, as if ready to fight again.

Apparently Talise had started crying too. She hadn't even noticed. The heavy weight pressing down on her chest was much more apparent. Her limbs felt too heavy to lift. Her lungs felt too tired to breathe.

Nothing felt real.

"We have to find the emperor." Though pain laced Wendy's words, she still managed to speak with conviction.

Aaden nodded before she even finished. "We'll have time to mourn, but not now. We have to go on or we'll lose."

The words didn't stop any of the crying, but they did help everyone stand a little taller. Talise's voice cracked when she tried to speak. After clearing her voice, she tried again. "Wendy and

Tempest, you go to the treasury as planned. If the emperor is there, don't fight him. Just find the rest of us, and we'll fight him together."

Even though she had been the first to snap them out of it, Wendy only gave a half nod. Pain had replaced all the sweetness in her expression. Tempest scowled at the ground as she nodded.

Swallowing for the twentieth time, Talise continued. "Claye and Fyra, you head to the library. Aaden and I will go to the emperor's living quarters like we planned."

Cyrus's chin still quivered as he stepped forward, but he was clearly making a strong effort to pull himself together. "What about the throne room?"

Silence reigned again. Cyrus was supposed to go to the throne room to look for the emperor, but he wasn't supposed to go alone. They planned for Rio to accompany him.

It hurt to gesture toward the hallway on the other side of the tapestry. Talise's heart twisted as she tried to settle her face into an expression of determination. "We have plenty of soldiers within our ranks. Find one of them to go with you."

When they stepped into the hallway again, not a single tear adorned any of their cheeks. But just because they had stopped the tears didn't mean they had stopped the pain.

War would continue to steal from them as long as it lasted.

And they stepped back into it anyway.

Chapter Sixty-Six

CHAOS FILLED EVERY PART OF the palace. When Talise and her friends split up, they agreed to meet near the ballroom after their searches to share what they found. The rest of Talise's army fought against palace soldiers with the strength of those fighting for their families.

Her heart still ached with each step. Her feet still lingered back even as she urged them forward. She fought off elements and weapons, but she didn't feel it. Darkness crept inside her, chilling every vein and limb.

She fought on pure instinct alone. The only time her mind could actually focus was when she caught sight of Aaden's face. Nothing about it held neutrality. He glared with the anger of a raging fire. For someone so passionate, he usually masked his emotions a little too well. But now they sat open on his face. Pure rage backed every slice of his sword. Hatred filled every fireball he shot.

The look didn't suit him. She missed the softness in his eyes that was so subtle, she had to look deeply to see it. At least the emperor's living quarters were getting closer. When they reached the final hallway, her heart pounded at the sight before her.

Too many memories filled this area of the palace. Memories of her childhood. Memories of fighting with Aaden for their places as Master Shaper. Memories of going to the living quarters after the masquerade ball. Memories of waiting for Aaden to return from Kessoku only to be disappointed when he never did.

While she had memories of every area in the palace, this particular hallway boasted the strongest and darkest of them all. It felt natural to be there when the aching inside her twisted and tangled as it did.

A dozen soldiers marched into the hallway from behind another hidden alcove. It probably should have taken her by surprise, but maybe nothing could surprise her anymore. The ambush just felt like every other thing she'd experienced that day.

Her fingers twitched at her side while she tried to decide whether or not she should reach for the amulet. Twelve soldiers against two weren't the best odds. But then again, she and Aaden were Maser Shapers. If she didn't need the amulet to defeat them, why use it?

The palace soldiers each sent a barrage of fireballs toward the two of them. With his jaw clenching tighter every second, Aaden shaped oxygen out of the air, extinguishing the fires instantly. He sent his own fireballs in return, twelve in quick succession.

Yelps escaped the palace soldiers as they tried to dodge the hot flames. A smile very nearly turned Talise's mouth upward. Perhaps she *didn't* need the amulet, but only because Aaden could defeat all twelve soldiers on his own.

Forgoing more fireballs, the palace soldiers charged forward. As they did, more charging footsteps sounded from behind.

Talise glanced over her shoulder. Another dozen soldiers charged toward them from the other side of the hallway. Now they had two dozen soldiers to defeat. Reaching into her pocket, she turned toward Aaden.

He seemed to have the same idea as her. Without a word, they stood back to back and prepared to fight off the soldiers charging toward them.

It only took one touch on the amulet before power surged through Talise's veins. In a split second, she pulled water out of the air to form a tall wall between herself and the palace soldiers on her side of the hallway. In almost the same moment, the wall froze to a solid block of ice.

Two arrows shot through the air, but they got caught in the wall just as it froze. When she turned around, Aaden had used a wall of wind to knock half the soldiers before him off their feet.

More arrows sliced the air, all of them aiming toward Aaden. A single wave of Talise's hand blew the arrows off course. They struck the wooden wall instead.

By then, the palace soldiers behind her had melted her ice wall. Their sharpened swords aimed for her as they continued to charge. From Aaden's side, more arrows flew. Two swords clashed against his as he swung his own to protect himself.

Despite fighting against twenty-four soldiers, the two of them still held their own for a surprising amount of time. Every time the soldiers gained an advantage, Talise would use the amulet to throw up an element they couldn't possibly defend against.

But with every minute, they closed in. With her back against Aaden's, she shot a tornado forward. It bounced against soldiers as they fought to regain their balance. The moment of respite lasted only a few seconds before the soldiers closed in again.

A sword swung at her, but she was too busy pulling water out of the air to block it. The blade left a nick in her arm before she could jump away. Aaden glared at her attacker, but he was too busy fighting off three swords at once to come to her aid.

The blade swung toward her again. This time, she pulled enough water from the air to create staff of ice to block it. Her staff held for only a moment before the force of the sword sliced through it.

Ice shattered to the ground. When the blade met her skin a second time, it left a shallow gash just under her collar bone. Though he stood behind her, Talise could feel the tension seeping from Aaden as the blade continued to fly.

Elements worked better from a slightly farther distance. Up close, she needed a weapon. Her fingers found the flame-carved dagger under her tunic. When the sword swung at her again, she met it with her polished blade. Using all the strength in her arms, she pushed the sword away.

The palace soldier stumbled backward, not expecting her to have a real defense against his weapon. But as soon as he moved back, another soldier took his place.

They were all so dedicated. So soldierly. She gulped. They reminded her of Rio.

Her jaw clenched as her fingers wrapped tight around the amulet. Though she and Aaden had fought valiantly against a crowd that should have defeated them, it had gone on long enough.

She still had to find the emperor.

Punching her hands out, flames erupted from the ground upward. Tall pillars of fire encircled every soldier who fought against her. In a flash, her attackers were immobilized. With one clench of her fist, they'd be dead.

Heat scorched the air, causing sweat to bead across her forehead. The soldiers must have been scared, but they didn't make any noise. They didn't call to each other or try to break free of their prisons. The only sound that did puncture the air around them came from the panting breaths erupting from Aaden's mouth.

They both turned toward each other while Talise held the life of every palace soldier in her twitching hands. Aaden's jaw flexed at the sight of the blood dripping down her arm and pooling under her collar bone.

White stretched across his knuckles as he gripped his sword tighter. The rage that had painted his features earlier only deepened. Darkened.

He wanted blood. She could see it in his eyes. Since her own stomach still writhed at the thought of Rio's mangled body, she wasn't far off from wanting it too.

Would he try to stop her if she clenched her fist? Would he be disappointed if she burned every one of those soldiers to death?

The heat in the air burned hot enough to cause crackles and pops. Though the soldiers continued to stand in complete silence, the amulet felt their energy fading. They were scared. Stricken.

Their lives belonged to her.

Her fingers itched to close. To tighten. Strangely, the words inside her head that stopped her came from someone who probably hated her more than anyone.

It doesn't matter what happens to the emperor, my family members are still dead. Nothing can bring them back.

Since the moment Talise met her, River had only cared about one thing. Revenge. But at the final hour, even River had turned away from it. She realized revenge wasn't productive, it was selfish.

While the flames continued to sizzle, Talise's mind went back to the garden where she had first trapped soldiers in pillars of flames. The guardian of the amulet had taught her balance. He had taught her restraint. No matter how she tried to justify it in her mind, she couldn't kill these soldiers.

Letting out a slow breath, she lowered the flames. They continued to burn in pillars, but the pillars only burned as high as each soldier's chest. One more deep breath.

Now for the thing she should have done from the beginning. Time to speak.

"Kamdaria is broken. Some citizens have barely enough to survive. Other citizens have been poisoned." Her head turned as she looked over the soldiers before her. Many tried to glance away, but others allowed direct eye contact. When they did, she offered her most imploring expression. "The emperor does not care that Kamdaria is broken. He continues to break it with every decision he makes."

Perhaps her expression had done it, or perhaps the soldiers couldn't help but see truth in her words. But soon, more eyes looked up at her. More anger melted away.

Talise stood taller. "I know it seems wrong to turn against the one who controls the empire." She took a deep breath. "But as princess, it is my right to protect this empire, even if that means protecting it from my own father."

Now the faces before her began glancing between themselves. They looked at each other with questions in their eyes.

The soldier directly in front of her had a blank expression. But after another moment, it hardened. He glanced down at the fire before him. Though she could only see his face, his intent was still clear. He wanted a way out.

Her jaw tightened as she raised her fire pillars once again. Now the flames licked just under the chins of each soldier. Her eyes narrowed. "I could kill all of you now."

Enough fear stared back at her to confirm she had made her point.

She lowered the flames down to their chests again. "But I'd rather have you on my side."

The quiet sound of crackles filled the air before a voice finally broke over them. "I will fight for you, Princess."

A soldier in the back had spoken. Her voice came out barely above a whisper. The soldier beside her raised his eyebrows high on his forehead at the sound of her voice. His mouth began to drop, but before it did, another voice came out.

"I side with you, Princess."

She had seen it before, but her chest still squeezed with warmth as heads in the crowd before her began to bow. The fact that she held their lives in her hands probably made it easier to side with her, but they still did it.

Not all of them. A few hardened faces in the crowd only twisted even greater at her proposition. They glared at every soldier who joined her side. But in the end, enough people joined her that those who didn't were quickly outnumbered.

When she lowered her flames, those on her side tied up the soldiers who refused to join her. She glanced at Aaden while they worked. A bit of anger still lingered in his eyes, but something in them had softened too.

The soldiers who joined her began leading those against her toward the antechamber that led to the dungeon. She stopped the last one just before he could step away.

"Where is the emperor?" Hopefully her eyes conveyed her desperation.

Sorrow split across the soldier's face. "I don't know. Nobody knows. After you came to the palace doors yesterday, he disappeared. There are rumors that his personal guard knows where he is, but I don't know if I believe it." The soldier's head hung. "I don't even know if he's still in the palace. I think maybe he ran away."

The words bit into Talise with surprising sharpness, but she reached for even the smallest measure of gratitude. "Thank you."

He offered a small nod before following after his fellow soldiers.

As they disappeared down the hall, Aaden shoved his sword into his sheath. He kicked the wall while his jaw clenched tight enough to make his veins bulge. "He ran away?" Aaden spit the words out in a burst of air. "You've been leading your army from the front line, and the emperor ran away while his soldiers die for him?"

"I don't think he actually ran away."

Aaden let out a scoff. "Why not? What has he ever done that was remotely honorable? He sent you to the Storm when you were only five. He made you live in those harsh conditions without any extra money or food to help you survive. Instead of doing anything to improve the empire like Kessoku asked, he just hid you away so he wouldn't have to be reminded of the mistakes he made."

By the end of Aaden's words, anger filled his eyes once again. His face was red, his fists clenched.

But for once, Talise's mind sparked with clarity. "He wouldn't stay here because of honor. He'd stay because this palace is the only thing he has left. Even his most trusted advisor is on our side, and I'm pretty sure he knows it."

Glancing down the hallway, her eyes focused on the door that led to the emperor's quarters. "He's here. We just have to find out where."

Chapter Sixty-Seven

A HIDDEN LATCH KEPT THE emperor's quarters locked. Talise had learned how to open the door before she even learned to bow properly. She wasn't supposed to learn about the lock until she was older, but she had had six older siblings. And they didn't keep secrets very well.

She pushed the door open slowly, but her heart was already sinking in her chest. The emperor knew she could unlock the door. He knew she had done it before.

And if she could unlock it so easily, why would he ever hide from her in such a place?

She already knew the rooms would be empty even before she saw them. Despite that, she and Aaden still dutifully checked every possible spot. The living quarters began with a basic office and sitting area. Those led to a bedroom, a washing room, a room dedicated to playing Forces, and several other offices.

All of them were empty.

They both went through the rooms a second time to check under furniture and behind tapestries. The second search still revealed nothing.

Back in the entrance room, Talise backed into the desk in the middle of the room. Her heart couldn't sink lower because it had already slid down to her toes. Hair brushed across her cheeks as her chin dropped to her chest.

Just when an ache twisted through her, something new brushed across her cheek. Aaden touched her with the warmth he always carried in his fingers. Tilting her chin up gently, he gave her a look that cured some of the heaviness in her chest.

Seeing emotion of any kind on his face was always nice. But seeing desire? And seeing that desire directed at her? Nothing would ever top that feeling, she was sure of it.

His mouth tilted upward in the slightest smile. He held her captive with the intensity of his gaze. And based on his expression, he knew exactly the effect he had on her.

But being in that room brought back too many memories. It had been less than a year earlier when they stood before the emperor with their fire and ice trees that were meant to impress him. Her eyebrows pinched together as she turned away from him. "I never trusted you then." The words came out in a whisper. "When I found out who your father was, I assumed you would be like him." Her arms folded over her chest, creating a barrier between her and Aaden. "But you never did anything dishonorable toward me. I never trusted you, and I should have."

Trying to move closer, Aaden shrugged. "I don't care."

"Really?" It only took one eyebrow raise to change his mind.

He let out a sigh as his gaze turned upward. "Fine, yes. It hurt me. But," he shrugged again, "I just needed to you know it hurt me. Now you know, and I don't care anymore."

Her eyes narrowed as she shot him with a hardened stare. "You should care. I judged you for your father's actions instead of paying attention to your own." She had to turn away as her gut twisted. "Besides…" Her eyes drifted over to the space in front of the desk. Months ago, they stood before the emperor with their ice and fire trees. And of course, the emperor chose that moment to teach them a lesson. He said one of them could become Master Shaper, but the other would have to be imprisoned in the dungeon. They had to choose who would receive which consequence.

Talise's heart thumped as the memory flooded her mind. She shot another glance Aaden's way, hoping he could see how her face twisted in regret. She gulped. "You only fell for me because of a lie. When we did the ice and fire trees, the emperor threatened to throw you into the dungeon. I told him to punish me instead. You thought I was sacrificing myself for you." Her head hung. "But I wasn't. I knew my father would never throw me into the dungeon right after I had finally returned to the palace. I didn't sacrifice myself for you. I was simply asking my father to not hurt you."

Aaden let out a scoff loud enough that she looked up at him. His eyes rolled back. "Yes, because that one moment is the only reason I fell for you. I definitely wasn't enamored by you from the moment you introduced yourself to me. I *definitely* didn't fall hard when you helped me befriend the palace soldiers despite my painfully awkward attempts. Oh, and I've *certainly* never been entranced by your beauty or your determination or anything."

Talise felt her lips twitch with a smile. He reached for her again.

Brushing his thumb across her cheek, he leaned in. "That was smart what you did with those soldiers and the fire in the hallway. I probably would have killed them, but you found allies instead."

Biting down on her bottom lip, she grabbed onto Aaden's tunic just so she could tug him closer. Leaning into his chest, she looked up at him through her eyelashes. "You liked that?"

Whatever words had been on his lips vanished in an instant. Now he only had one thing on his mind.

He kissed her so fiercely that fire sizzled inside. His arms wrapped around her tight. One around her shoulders and one at her lower back, falling lower by the second. His touch had a remarkable way of healing the pain inside her. It also had a remarkable way of curling her toes in delight.

They probably would have stayed there all day if a noise in the hallway hadn't stolen away their attention. Aaden glared at the door when he pulled away. By the time he glanced at her again, fiery desire danced in his eyes.

She looked down at the desk just behind her while warmth floated in her chest. "You've kissed me in this same spot before."

His fingers slipped through her hair as he leaned in close again. "I know. Since you got kidnapped in the middle of our first kiss, I thought it was fitting that we should get it right a second time."

She smiled at the words, but the sounds in the hallway continued to grow. They both swallowed at the same moment, stepping away from each other.

Aaden reached for his sword. "I'm going to go check all the rooms one more time. If there are hidden alcoves and secret locks in this palace, there's a distinct possibility that there are secret passageways too. I'll do what I can to find any."

Nodding, Talise walked around the desk only to sit down behind it. "I'll go through the papers in here. There might be clue to my father's whereabouts."

After a stiff nod, Aaden disappeared into another room.

The first stack of papers from inside the desk consisted of numerical reports that didn't make any sense. There were percentages and dates, but without context, they meant nothing. One pattern became obvious. The percentages increased over time. Though the dates began years earlier, the percentages in the latest months were exponentially higher than any of the previous years.

At the bottom of the final paper, a short note had been scribbled.

Increase sharply so they can't develop immunity. Deaths irrelevant.

Nausea yanked through her, but she refused to acknowledge it. Her heart had already been through too much. Besides, she just wanted to find clues to her father's whereabouts. She didn't need any horrifying revelations at the moment.

Pulling out a second stack of papers, she decided to start at the bottom of the pile. It only took a few moments of reading to send another yank of nausea through her.

The words were familiar. Not just familiar, they were hers. Though written in different handwriting, Talise immediately recognized her own words and phrases. Words she had written to Marmie. Letter after letter after letter.

She couldn't even enjoy reliving the memories because the implication hit her like a stone. Someone had copied, word for word, every letter she had ever written to Marmie. And then those letters had been given to her father.

It wasn't that the letters were filled with any great secrets. It wasn't that she ever said anything that might have given away her identity. It was simply the invasion of privacy that cut down to her core. Both her father and some unknown scribe had been reading her letters without her knowledge. All those years when she'd been writing to someone she trusted more than anyone, her words had been exposed to others without her knowledge.

Every line she scanned brought another twist through her insides. By the time she reached the top of the pile, her stomach was ready to spew its contents. But familiar words stared back at her. Words that burned and ached inside.

He did fire sculptures like I've never seen before. Somehow, he managed to get little cherry blossoms to burst out of the fire branches. I'll admit it, Marmie. I'm scared. I've tried so hard to win, but I think he's better than me. At least I'm not a child anymore. If I have to go back to the Storm, I'd probably survive now. And then I'd get to be with you again. That doesn't sound so bad.

She'd been writing about Aaden. At the very bottom of the letter, more words had been written. Even in the scribe's handwriting they looked hastily scrawled. *Please don't worry, I'm still going to try.*

When her gut churned inside her again, it wasn't with nausea but with rage. More words had been scribbled at the bottom of this page too. But this handwriting she did recognize. The same as the note at the edge of the other paper, this handwriting belonged to her father. The words felt like ice inside her.

She cannot escape her destiny. Action must be taken. Her reason for returning to the Storm must be eliminated. Forty-eight percent is a lethal dose, but it will not raise suspicion. Put in food so no one suspects poison. It will look like malnourishment.

Breathing no longer seemed important. She wanted to rage, but too much ice had filled her heart. The evidence sat before her with no chance of rebuttal. She fought to find fault with it anyway. She failed.

"Aaden." Her voice cracked hard when she forced herself to speak.

He appeared in the room in only a few seconds. She couldn't see her face to know what it told him, but she could see how his own expression paled. His shoulders stiffened. "What happened?"

A lump burned in her throat when she tried to swallow. Her voice came out thin. "Remember when you said you'd kill the emperor if I asked you to?"

Aaden's eyes jumped down to the papers on the desk before he looked back at her again. Questions burned in his eyes, but he didn't utter any of them. He just stood silently. Waiting.

She gestured toward the paper, unable to touch it herself another time.

When he picked it up, he held the hilt of his sword while scanning the words. Confusion worked across his features. "This is a letter you wrote? To Marmie?"

Talise sat completely still. Her muscles couldn't move even if she wanted them to.

Both of his eyebrows rose. "It's about me." Almost as soon as the words left his lips, his entire face fell. The parchment crinkled as his hand closed into a fist. Every muscle in his face tightened. "The emperor poisoned Marmie." Aaden's eyes raised to meet Talise's. "He's the reason she's dead."

Hearing it sounded even worse than realizing it, which didn't seem possible. Her stomach churned.

But war reared its ugly head once again. It didn't even allow her the luxury of vomiting when the truth hurt too much.

Palace soldiers spilled into the room, waving their weapons wildly. One glance into their eyes told Talise they couldn't be persuaded to fight for her no matter what she said to them.

These soldiers were firmly on the emperor's side.

<h1 style="text-align:center">Chapter Sixty-Eight</h1>

TALISE SENT A WALL OF wind toward the palace soldiers, but they were prepared. They raised thin metal shields and walked into the wind. By the time the wind finished blowing, the soldiers had moved closer than before.

Their shields blocked a wave of fireballs next. The shields themselves absorbed the heat and turned bright orange. But there must have been something attached to the other side of the shields that the soldiers could hold because they continued to march forward without any hesitation.

None of the soldiers gave much notice to Talise. Their eyes only turned toward her when she blasted them with attacks that had to be deflected.

But they did have a clear focus. Even while they fought every attack, they moved forward. Toward Aaden.

She reached for the amulet now, ready to end this for good. It pulsed in her hand. More soldiers spilled into the room, filling every corner. A breath later, even more soldiers entered.

At one point, the power of the amulet allowed her to shape ice over every shoe and ankle belonging to the palace soldiers. It would have helped more except soldiers continued to file into the room. Just like with the fire storm, there were too many of them. Too many moving parts. Even with the amulet, she couldn't keep track of everything.

So many soldiers had entered the room now that they stood shoulder to shoulder. She couldn't even see Aaden. Her heart leapt into her throat as she pushed a group of attackers against one wall. That afforded her a small glimpse of Aaden.

They had him.

The palace soldiers had lifted him off the ground and were carrying him toward the door leading out to the hallway. Her fingertips sizzled, ready to throw fire in every direction. But she couldn't. Wild flames would injure the palace soldiers, but they might injure Aaden too. Without knowing his exact location, she feared throwing out any attack.

In her hand, the amulet pulsed with energy. It wanted to blast down a wall or send in a flood. Instead, she pushed herself through the crowd. Once she knew Aaden's exact location, then she could make a plan.

By the time that thought passed through her mind, he was gone. The soldiers had carried him out the door and into the hallway. The soldiers left in the room paid no attention to Talise. They just filed out of the room, getting in her way while she tried to do the same.

Her fists clenched tight as she shoved through the crowd. Fire burned inside her. The urge to destroy something came stronger than ever.

When she finally reached the hallway, her eyes turned straight to Aaden. He squirmed in the arms of his captors. They held him tight. Thick gloves had been shoved onto Aaden's hands, gloves that also curled his hands into fists. For most people, the gloves prevented shaping.

But Aaden was a Master Shaper. He knew how to shape through such defenses. The terror in his eyes explained his hesitation. Like Talise, he had probably been unwilling to release too big of an attack when he didn't know if it might hurt her.

For now, he could only react. That wasn't enough to free himself from his captors.

But it didn't matter. Talise could see him now, and the amulet buzzed with anticipation. Just before she raised her arms to use it, the slightest movement at the edge of the hallway caught her eye.

The emperor.

He hid behind a statue, his fur cloak clasped tight around his shoulders. The golden crown embedded with rubies sat neatly on his black, glossy hair. The world seemed to stop when his eyes met Talise's.

His shoulders twitched with indecision. For a moment, he shrank back, as if anxious to hide behind the statue again. Another moment later, he leaned forward, perhaps realizing his position had been revealed and hiding would do nothing.

Jerking her head up and down the hallway, Talise searched for someone on her side. Anyone.

But the only other person nearby who was loyal to her was Aaden. The emperor's soldiers still held him tight, carrying him down the hallway toward the dungeon.

All at once, the problem became clear.

The emperor would make her choose. Just like he had all those months ago.

Marmie or the competition. Aaden or the emperor.

Duty or love.

With her eyes on her father, Talise's feet were rooted to the ground. Frozen.

It didn't matter that the choice wasn't fair. It didn't matter if making her choose was a cruel, unnecessary trick. She couldn't refuse the choice.

Her nose wrinkled as she jerked her body around. Aaden. Of course she had to choose Aaden. She had chosen duty when faced with Marmie's funeral or attending the Master Shaper competition. Maybe that had been the right choice, but it never felt like it.

This time, she'd choose love.

Just as her feet began moving toward the palace soldiers carrying Aaden, the tiara on her head bounced. The weight of it pressed down on her. The weight of Kamdaria.

What would happen to the empire if she let the emperor get away? What would happen to her? The rest of her friends? The citizens of the Storm?

Sensations blazed inside her while the impossible choice only seemed more impossible by the second.

Turning on her heel, she faced the emperor once again. Was that a smirk hiding under his glare?

He knew exactly what he was doing. He always knew. Once again, he presented her with two choices, but they weren't really choices at all. Both options benefitted him and hurt her.

If she went after Aaden, the emperor had a chance to regain control. If she went after the emperor, her mind would be too focused on Aaden to do anything of consequence. Either way, her father would have the advantage.

A shot of fire burst through the air. Talise turned.

Aaden had freed himself from his captors. He fought fearlessly, shooting any and every element against them. They had taken his sword, but he hardly seemed to notice. For one single moment, their eyes met.

The truth hit her with clarity she hadn't known in a long time.

This choice wasn't about love versus duty. The emperor did everything in his power to frame it as such, but that didn't mean Talise had to fall for his tricks again.

It was about trust. Something the emperor knew absolutely nothing about.

Talise nodded at Aaden at the same moment that he nodded back at her. She had to trust that he would be okay. His skills were great. His determination even greater.

The palace was filled with soldiers loyal to her.

The ambush had taken them both by surprise, but hadn't Aaden always trusted her? Hadn't he always believed in her shaping abilities, her skills as a leader? Surely, she could trust him in this moment.

She could believe that he would be okay. And if she could believe that, she was free to do what needed to be done. Thrusting her palm forward, she froze the feet of every palace soldier to the ground. Even if she didn't stay to fight, that would at least help Aaden escape.

Now, her body whirled around for the last time. When she began marching down the hallway, the emperor's eyes widened. He gulped as he backed away.

A flaming wall of fire shot from his palms before he broke out into a run.

Shaping a thin layer of ice over her skin, Talise walked straight through the wall of fire without a second thought. Steam sizzled off her when she reached the other side. The tiara on her head warmed against her head.

No more running. No more pawning the job off to someone else.

It was time to face her father.

CHAPTER SIXTY-NINE

THE DOORS TO THE BALLROOM swung wide before Emperor Flarius disappeared through them. Talise's footsteps only stomped harder down the hallway. The palace soldiers behind her shouted as they fought against Aaden.

Her resolve only deepened with each step. Aaden would be safe. She believed it just as much as she believed it was time to face her father.

Swinging the ballroom doors again, she marched into the room.

The moment she stepped inside, a large boulder toppled down from a precariously built tower. She had to launch herself forward to avoid being hit. The boulder crashed onto the floor, letting out a resounding crunch through the entire ballroom.

Only once she confirmed that no part of her tunic or pants had been stuck under the boulder could she pay attention to anything else. Glancing backward, thumps filled her chest.

The boulder completely blocked the ballroom doors. She could use the amulet to crush it, but that would take time and concentration. As long as she was busy fighting, neither she nor her father would be able to leave the room.

More important, no one else would be able to enter. Sucking in a deep breath, her limbs shivered with a hum. Was it a good thing none of the palace soldiers would be able to come in and fight against her? Or was it a bad thing that none of her own soldiers could come in and help her fight against the emperor? And what about Aaden?

Shaking out the thrumming in her arms, she turned back to the strange tower at her side. The emperor stood atop it with some sort of lever still in his hands.

He gulped at the sight of her. His eyes flicked toward the boulder, clearly upset that she had gotten into the room before the boulder closed it off completely. The surprise only lasted a few moments. By the time she blinked, a fearsome expression filled his face.

Streams of fire blasted from each of his palms. They burned hotter than most fireballs she encountered. Though he was the emperor and usually spent his days in the throne room or in offices, she knew how much effort he had put into his shaping skill. Too much. Unfortunately, his sword skill was equally dangerous.

Fire shot toward her while her father scrambled down from the tower. It only took a flick of the wrist to swallow his flames up with water pulled from the air.

At the bottom of the tower, he shed his fur cloak and pulled a sword from his sheath. His blade turned orange as he shaped fire into it.

Perhaps it was petty, but Talise couldn't help showing off a bit. Pulling more water from the air, she froze a solid layer of ice around his blazing sword. Even as he increased the heat inside it, she merely added more ice to the sword.

His nose wrinkled as he dropped the sword from his hand. Pain twisted through his features while he stretched out his fingers. Had her ice frozen his skin?

When he glanced around the ballroom, she noticed small bowls lining the floor. During her training as Master Shaper, she had used the same bowls many times. Each bowl held earth or water.

Drawing earth from the nearest bowl, the emperor shot hard clods of dirt toward her chest. She pushed bursts of air against them with gentle flicks of her wrist. Each clod of dirt fell to the floor in a puff of dust.

Her feet slapped the floor, moving forward once again. The emperor glanced at the bowls surrounding him, but he blinked too fast to focus on them. Her Master Shaper training had come from the emperor himself, so he probably never expected her to have the skills to defeat him.

But she had been through a great deal since leaving the palace. Now she had Eben's training. Now she had Kamdar's journals. Now she had the amulet.

While the emperor scrambled for another element to shoot, her fingers squeezed around the cool metal in her hand. At one time, she would have hesitated to attack her own father.

That was before she found those letters in the emperor's quarters.

Before she found out who he had killed.

Raising her arms high, she stopped deflecting his attacks and began attacking him instead. She sent a wall of earth made from the bowls lining the ground toward the emperor until it knocked him off his feet.

When he threw a pair of daggers at her, she used water to grip them by the hilts and pull them to the ground. Fireballs rained down on her father, which he only barely managed to put out before getting burned.

She continued marching forward.

More elements flew, but each one became less minor and more lethal. Their slices and swipes aimed for the kill.

Even with the amulet in her possession, her father was still a worthy opponent. His attacks didn't come nearly as close to hurting her as hers came to hurting him. Still, he continued to escape her attacks no matter how many she sent his way. And maybe there was still a tiny part of herself that held back.

It didn't stop her from marching forward. When she had him pinned into a corner of the room, he didn't even notice until his back hit the wall behind him. Sucking in a breath, his eyes went wide. He glanced at the wall. A wild frenzy filled his eyes for a single moment. By the time he turned back to face her, everything about him had turned calm.

With a twist, she formed a long icicle that came to a deadly point. The cold burned in her hand as she pulled it back to strike.

The calm on her father's face never wavered. "You're going to stab me with ice?" He let out a patronizing scoff. "Can your ice shaping even withstand the heat inside a body?"

Her nose twitched at the words. Even now he was goading her. Correcting her.

Tightening her grip on the icicle, she took a step toward him. "I saw you make every one of my siblings cry. For most of them, you did it weekly."

He scowled. "They deserved it. Just like you do. No child has the right to turn against a parent."

A chuckle so light left her lips that it barely made a sound. "Don't you remember what Mother always told you? You expect too much. You push too hard. Did you really think you'd never have to suffer consequences for it?"

His face turned bright red as he blasted hot fireballs at Talise. When she extinguished them with earth, he growled. "Do not speak of the late empress to me."

Talise took another step forward. "Why not? Does it fill you with too much guilt to remember how you could have prevented her death? If you had listened to your people in need, Kessoku might not have attacked the palace. She would still be here."

Fireballs flew toward her so fast, she nearly didn't have enough time to stop them. Flames singed the ends of her hair while a fireball blasted across her cheek. Another fireball burned through the fabric covering her knee. She managed to shape water around both of them before they could do anymore damage.

But more attacks followed.

Now the emperor was the one stepping forward. His eyes blazed with wild rage. No longer did he cower in fear of what his shaping might to do himself. He only seemed to care that his attacks hurt Talise. It didn't matter if he hurt himself in the process too.

A stone slammed into her chest hard enough to make her cough. Her feet stumbled backward while she tried to refill her chest with air.

On the ground, a light layer of earth was sprinkled. The emperor sent water at it, turning it into slippery mud. Her feet danced over it while she tried to regain her balance. As she teetered, the emperor sent a blast of wind. It knocked her onto her back.

Though her body slammed against the floor, her mind focused on the cool metal in her hand. Losing her balance had nearly made her lose her grip on the amulet. She closed her fist around it once again, but the moment cost her.

Cold mud slithered up her feet and ankles. Soon, it wrapped around her legs to just below the knees. The mud trapped her against the ground. Her grip on the amulet tightened. Pressing both hands to the ground, she attempted to lift herself to a standing position.

The moment her fingers brushed against the ballroom floor, mud crawled around her hands and wrists. Now both her hands and feet were pinned down. Stuck.

Her body writhed against the pressure. She tried to use the amulet to send blasts of air to free herself, but she couldn't find a position strong enough to counter the emperor's earth shaping. She tried to wash away the mud with waves of water, but the emperor just shaped even more mud around her.

She was stuck. She couldn't melt or freeze the mud. Even if she did, it wouldn't help. Fire wouldn't help either. Air and water clearly did nothing. Her legs shook as she tried to shake herself free.

A smile curled onto the emperor's face as he watched her struggle. He did nothing to stop her. He didn't attack either. He just watched, enjoying it a little too much.

The pounding in her chest thundered until it ached. Inside her hand, the amulet buzzed. Blazed. It burned. It was like the amulet could sense her danger.

But it could do nothing to free her.

The emperor was shaping the earth around her feet and hands. And once an element was controlled by one shaper, another shaper could never steal that control away.

That was a law every student learned in their first year of shaping. Even those who never attended a shaping academy knew elements could only be shaped by one person at a time. Kamdar's journals confirmed the same thing. During her few months inside Kessoku's base by the Ember Gate, she trained daily with the amulet. Though she attempted many impossible things in those trainings, she had never come close to stealing control of an element from someone else.

But her life hadn't been in danger back then.

Now it was.

She couldn't explain how she knew it, but the amulet could tell. It knew how she fought and struggled against her bonds. It knew what she needed to do to escape.

A warm glow filled her chest. It spread through her arms and down to her legs. The warmth sparked and crackled, filling her veins with an energy she had never felt before.

Clarity blossomed in her mind. She could sense every element in the room. She could sense every bit of it. When she focused in on the mud around her feet and hands, it sizzled. It acknowledged her.

Squeezing tighter on the amulet, even more sensations filled the room. Suddenly, she could sense tiny threads that connected her father's hands to the mud pinning her down. The threads showed the connection between her father and his shaping.

The warmth inside her continued to grow. The smallest smile played on her lips. If she could sense the threads, surely, she could do something *to* them as well.

Using nothing but her mind, she snapped the threads. They whipped through the air while her own threads reached out. Her threads were stronger. Thicker. And now *they* controlled the mud around her.

With a single swipe, the mud fell away from her around the palace floor. She pushed herself off the ground and stood taller than she ever had.

The emperor's mouth dropped. His arms fell. He took slow steps backward until he ran into the wall once again.

She had all the control. Nothing could stop her now.

CHAPTER SEVENTY

ICE CRYSTALLIZED OVER TOP OF the mud on the palace floor. Talise stomped over it. Unyielding.

The emperor kept opening his eyes wider. He'd stare at the mud, then turn his gaze toward her. Did he know how she stole control away from him? When he glanced at her a second time, something sparked in his eyes. His eyes drifted downward until he stared at her fist that held the amulet. When he looked back into her eyes again, that spark only grew.

Something different took hold of his expression then. She had seen it too many times to count. In too many people.

Greed.

Ignoring it, she pulled water from the air and formed another lethal icicle. She pulled her arm back, ready to plunge her weapon deep.

Her father's face twisted. "How dare you attack me."

"Marmie died right before the competition." Talise's voice came out even colder than the ice in her hand.

With a twitching nose, the emperor clenched his jaw. "That woman was never your mother."

"She loved me like one." Though Talise's words spoke of warmth, they came out even colder than before.

Sneering, the veins in the emperor's forehead pulsed and bulged. "She was your mother's *sister.*"

Talise leaned forward. "That means she was *your* sister too. And yet, you killed her."

His eyes flashed with the thinnest thread of surprise. It only lasted a moment before he shrugged. "You wanted to return to her. I had to take away that option to ensure you came home."

Talise squeezed her icicle so tight that cracks spread through it. "You could have brought her to the palace. You could have hidden her." Hot, angry tears prickled in Talise's eyes. "You didn't have to kill her."

Shaking her head, Talise melted and refroze the water inside her icicle, ensuring that none of the cracks remained. She looked her father in the eye again. "But that's your favorite solution to every problem. When the citizens of the Storm started complaining, what did you do? You poisoned them until they were too defeated to care."

Another flash of surprise swept across the emperor's features. His shoulders hunched forward.

Clenching her jaw tight, Talise continued. "When Kessoku attacked the palace last spring, what was your plan? You chose to kill every enemy except one soldier just so you could make a point."

The emperor's expression hardened as heat flushed in his neck.

She shook her head. "Have you ever faced any of your problems? Any at all? Or do you just kill people until the problem stops bothering you?"

Taking a steady breath, the emperor began plucking bits of earth from his wool tunic. "You forget that we share blood. Can *you* face your problems? Are you going to *kill* me? Your own father?"

Whatever hesitation still lingered inside her got blasted away at the sound of those words. Releasing her grip, she dropped the icicle to the ground. Both she and the emperor glanced down at the shattered ice at their feet.

Ice would never do against the emperor. He deserved a more symbolic death.

"I don't want to kill you, but it is my duty to protect the empire." She sucked in a breath. "Even if I have to protect it from you."

When they both looked up again, Talise held her hand out with the palm facing forward.

The emperor released a cruel laugh at the sight. "You do not even bring a proper weapon against me?"

It took no effort now to ignore his hateful words. At one time, his words would have had more weight than those of any other person. But she had changed since then. She had learned to care about more than her father's opinion.

Narrowing her eyes, she squeezed the amulet tight. Power sparked in her toes. She felt it fill inside her like a well. Her own power coursed with the same glowing warmth it always did. It only reached her knees before she cut it off again.

Now, the amulet reached out. It found another source of power. Dense energy began filling her, starting at the toes. It churned with strength, but it almost felt empty. Dead.

The moment the dense power began filling her, the emperor threw a hand to his heart. He clutched it. His eyes widened as he stared at Talise's shaping hand. A cough erupted from his throat while his gaze intensified.

He knew. The way he clutched his chest and stared at her. He knew she was stealing his power away from him. When he backed into the wall at his back, savage fear filled his eyes. He glanced toward her fist again, the one holding the amulet.

"Stop this." Even with his life in her hands, his voice still came out like a command. "Kamdaria is my responsibility, not yours."

The dense power continued to fill inside her. She kept most of her focus on it while she spoke. "Whether I like it or not, Kamdaria *is* my responsibility. If you want me to stop, you'll have to get rid of me for good."

Once his power filled her up to her stomach, she cut it off. With a snap of her fingers, a fire sparked.

The fire didn't originate near her hand or anywhere around them. Instead, the fire sparked inside a heart. The emperor's heart.

Frantic breaths escaped him as he clutched his chest tighter. Still, he stared down at her with a sneer. "Do you want me to kill you?"

The threat didn't have much weight. It would only take one little squeeze from Talise to make the fire grow. One little flex and her father would be burned from the inside out. What could he do against her now? Raising an eyebrow, she kept the fire inside him at a low simmer. "You could always disinherit me instead."

He let out an icy laugh. "Don't be ridiculous. This is Kamdaria. Family lasts forever."

The words stretched around her like frosty tendrils. They froze her in place as the reality of what she was about to do hit her too hard. Could she really do it? Could she kill her own father?

It only took a split second for the thoughts to pass through her mind, but that split second was too long. The moment of hesitation cost her.

Lunging forward, the emperor's shoulder slammed into her gut. Air escaped her as she fell onto her back. He wrenched off her tiara with one hand, pulling out hairs along with it. Tears pooled in her eyes. When he slammed a knee into her gut, more air escaped her.

Too much pain and shock filled her to pay any attention to her father. When he pried open her fist, she hardly took notice. It wasn't until the cool metal left her palm that she realized his intention.

The amulet.

Punching both hands forward, she sat up with a start. Her fingers reached, trying to take the amulet back again. The emperor moved too quickly. Her hands brushed against his fingers, just missing.

Inside her, the buzzing well of power drained away. As long as she held the amulet, her well of power stayed intact. But the moment it was stolen from her, the power sizzled and popped until it vanished.

The emperor must have had his power returned to him. He grinned as he stared back at Talise. She still sat on the ground. Her limbs ached as she tried to push herself to her feet.

He held the amulet between two fingers, smugly showing it off. "I have everything now."

Gulping probably made her look weak, but she couldn't help it. Claye had told her the amulet was bonded to her. He said it wouldn't work for him or River the way it worked for her. But would it work for someone who shared her same blood? Would it work for her father?

Even now that she had gotten to her feet, he towered over her. His posture made it clear that not a single part of him believed he could be beaten. He had taken her crown, her amulet, but those were only his most recent conquests. He had taken

Aaden from her too at a time when she needed him desperately. And Marmie.

From Kamdaria, he had taken even more.

Her desires didn't matter anymore. She didn't *want* to kill him, but he had to die. The only thing that mattered now was doing it without hesitation. No more holding back. It didn't even matter that he held the amulet. Once her resolve solidified, she realized she didn't even need the amulet.

He squeezed the amulet and lifted a large portion of water from the bowls scattered all around. It didn't seem like more water than he could shape without the amulet, so maybe it wouldn't work for him after all.

While he moved, she shaped earth from the remaining bowls. With the amulet, she could have lifted more. But she was still a Master Shaper. Her fingers curled into fists as she packed the earth tightly together. It had to be dense enough to cause damage.

By the time her father sent a wave of water her way, she was ready. She punched the densely packed earth forward. The moment it flew, she used air shaping to push it forward even faster. Her stomach churned with nausea because she knew how much force that earth had. It would crack ribs. Crush insides.

Her father would never survive.

Only then did she realize the emperor's wave of water included a few deadly daggers. She continued to shape more air behind her earth even as she ducked to avoid her father's wave of water. He ducked too. Not fast enough.

The dense earth slammed into his shoulder, sending a loud crack through the air. Breath left his mouth in a hard gasp.

But something else hit him too.

Tingles spread over her body as she noticed two more elements slam forward. Water in the shape of a point blasted him on the opposite side. He fell onto his back and a whip of fire burned around his neck and chest.

His arms jerked. He let out a weak cough. Blood splattered around his mouth when he forced the cough out. Whatever life he had left wouldn't last long.

But Talise could only stare at the water and fire. Where had they come from? Was it the amulet? Had it bonded to her so greatly that even without touching it, its power came to her aid?

No.

The answer wasn't mystical or unearthly in any way. Clearly, the other elements had come from other shapers.

"Finally."

The woman's voice sent a zing through Talise's spine. Fear so potent filled her body that turning around felt like wading through mud. But she had to. She had to see it, though part of her already knew who she'd see.

Two shapers stood just behind her. They only ignited more fear.

Lucian and River. The woman's eyes were as wild as ever.

Lucian stroked his goatee while a terrifying smirk adorned his face. "Now we just have to get rid of the girl."

※

CHAPTER SEVENTY-ONE

TALISE REACHED FOR HER HEART. She stumbled backward still trying to comprehend the sight before her. Her eyes flicked toward the ballroom doors. The large boulder still blocked them completely.

So, how did Lucian and River get inside?

Gulping, Talise continued to stumble backward. She glanced at River while her insides writhed. "You said you wanted to help us. You said you didn't care about revenge."

The woman scoffed. "And you believed me?" She chuckled and curled her hands into fists. "That is why you're going to lose. You're too stupid."

Without thinking, Talise reached inside her tunic pocket. But the amulet wasn't inside. Her father still clutched the amulet in his palm, even as he lay on the ground. A shiver jerked through her shoulders. "But you helped us. We couldn't have gotten past the fire storm without your team."

Lucian and River shared a look that send another zing through Talise's spine. Lucian's mouth curled upward. "And *we* couldn't have gotten inside the palace without helping you."

As they stepped forward, River sneered. She flashed her teeth at the ground, as if remembering something. "Unfortunately, the rest of my team *did* want to join you. They thought you had a better chance of winning than we did." She shrugged. "So, Lucian and I devised a plan. We decided to pretend to join you. Then when you and the emperor *accidentally* killed each other in a fight, Lucian would have the perfect opportunity to take the crown."

It probably should have shocked Talise more, but it didn't. She should have known. The two people before her hated her even more than her father who had just tried to kill her. Despite the betrayal, Talise didn't regret trusting the woman and her team of shapers. The help came at a time when they desperately needed it. She could deal with a little fall out.

At the moment, Talise was more interested in finding out how they entered the ballroom with the doors blocked off.

That question got answered when she noticed a tapestry rolled up and tied off. An open door sat behind it, which led to a dark tunnel.

Aaden had been right. Apparently, the palace did have secret passageways Talise knew nothing about. And since Lucian had been a high-ranking soldier before he traded secrets with Kessoku, it made sense that he knew of the passageway. If the emperor had treated Talise as a true Master Shaper like he should have, she probably would have known about the passageways too.

Fear should have gripped her more, but the passageway only brought one thought to Talise's mind.

Now she had an escape.

Lunging forward, Talise moved toward the passage.

Boiling hot balls of water pelted her from above. Her throat locked as she shot spears of ice over her shoulder. At least the ice would cool the boiling water before it hit her.

When the boiling water had no effect, other elements rained down on her. Whips of fire cracked against her from every side. A wave of water blasted into Talise, temporarily whisking her off her feet.

They expected her to fight back, but she didn't. She only cared about escaping. Her father had been taken care of. If he wasn't dead yet, he would be very soon. It was pointless to fight River and Lucian on her own when she could just as easily escape the room and find help.

As Talise ran for the passageway, rolling mounds of earth slid across the floor right in her way. The earth shaping didn't take much skill, but it didn't matter because it still tripped Talise up at a crucial moment. Even though she jumped over and past many earth mounds, doing so still slowed her down.

Her focus never wavered. She deflected the attacks raining down on her but continued to run for the passageway. Just when she moved closer, she noticed a figure standing inside the passageway.

Had someone come to her aid already? Aaden?

But the figure was short. Young.

By the time the girl emerged from the shadows of the passageway, Talise's heart thumped hard. She froze in place while a pair of eager, young eyes stared back at her.

Clenching both hands into fists, the girl shouted into the room. "Stop trying to hurt the princess!"

"Willow." Talise's voice came out breathless. "You shouldn't be here. It's too dangerous. You could…" But she couldn't finish the sentence because the horrors of what could happen were too great to speak.

From behind, Lucian let out a throaty laugh. "A child has come to save you, huh? How fortunate." He chuckled again. "For us."

Sucking in a breath, Talise jerked her head toward Lucian and River to assess the situation. How could she most effectively protect the girl?

But a strange sight met her eyes. Lucian continued to lumber forward, ready to destroy anything that got in his way. On the other hand, River had frozen in place. The woman's mouth had dropped as she stared ahead. She didn't even blink.

"Willow?" River said the name with an almost reverence. "Your name is Willow? And your hands are cracked and weathered like someone from the Storm."

Talise shared a glance with Willow, but the girl's face only twisted in confusion. This didn't seem like the most logical time for such observations.

River's eyes widened even more. "What is your mother's name?"

When the girl just stared back with her face screwed into a knot, River finally stepped forward. For a moment, Lucian had paused, staring between the two of them.

A spark filled River's eyes. She leaned forward and repeated the question. "What is your mother's name?"

At only thirteen, Willow probably couldn't think of a way her dead mother's name could be used against her. She shrugged, and said, "Violet Okada."

River clapped a hand over her mouth. "You're…" Her shoulders shook as she sucked in a breath. "You're the one who went missing." For the first time ever, River's eyes turned bright. The wildness melted away. "I'm your aunt. Well, sort of your aunt. Your mother was my cousin. You're the only one left from that line."

For a moment, stillness hung in the room. Nobody moved or spoke or anything. Willow glanced toward Talise, as if asking what she should do. But Talise was still too shocked to even think.

With a shrug, Willow reached out one hand. A flick of her wrist caused a large rock to rise up from the ground. She bounced the rock through the air a few times, perhaps showing off her ability to shape. Finally, the girl faced the woman before her. "Well then, Aunt River," she raised the rock higher. "You should be ashamed of yourself."

Her hand sliced through the air, which sent the rock down fast. It hit River's neck at such a perfect angle, the woman collapsed into an unconscious heap.

Talise had no time to admire the remarkable shaping skills Willow had just demonstrated because Lucian shaped a fire over his palm. Maybe River had let the girl distract her, but Lucian wouldn't make the same mistake. Even worse, he probably wanted to harm the girl.

"Willow." Talise filled her voice with urgency. She tilted her head toward the secret passageway behind her. "Go get help."

The girl nodded and darted toward the passageway without question.

As she disappeared into the shadows, Talise called after her. "And be careful!"

Talise couldn't leave the ballroom now. She had to take care of Lucian before he made any attempt to injure the girl. At least River was still unconscious.

Lucian's fireball blasted toward Talise, sizzling as it flew. She knocked it away with a burst of air. He snarled. "You stole my son away from me."

Shots of air burst from Talise's palm as she blasted away more fireballs. "I *stole* him? You might recall that *you* are the one who *left* him. Your only son. He had already lost his mother, no doubt because of how you treated her, and then you left him too."

The fireballs turned into a long fire whip. As it flicked toward her, Talise pulled water from the air to smother it.

Fire burned even hotter in Lucian's eyes as he stepped forward. "I did what had to be done for Kamdaria. He'll understand someday."

Talise's fists clenched as she glared at the man. "No. You did what you wanted to do. You expect Aaden to love you unconditionally, but when have you ever done the same for him? Have you ever been there for him when he needed you? Or have you only ever been there when it was convenient for you?"

Letting out a growl, Lucian leapt toward her. Fire engulfed his hands as he reached for her neck.

Pulling the dagger out from under her tunic, she sliced a gash into his palm.

His hands jerked back the moment her blade touched his skin. Blood trickled over his palm, but he didn't seem to notice. The dagger held his attention completely.

When he clenched his jaw, the goatee on his chin bristled. "That is my dagger." Fire engulfed his hands once again. "You *dare* use my own weapon against me?"

Taunting her attacker probably wasn't the best idea, but she couldn't help it. Her lips curled upward as she tightened her grip on the flame-carved dagger. "It's mine now."

He hissed as he lunged toward her again. The flames engulfing his hands left scorch marks on her tunic. She stabbed the dagger at him without hesitation. It only sliced through some of the skin on his shoulder, but at least he could tell how serious she was.

When he took a step back from her, his chest heaved. He panted like an animal ready to kill. She adjusted her grip on the dagger, wishing she still had the amulet.

His hands whirled around as he formed another fire whip. The flames immediately pinned her against one wall. She would have pulled water from the air to put the fire out, except he shaped flames over her hands too. Fire flickered in between each of her fingers. If she moved even a fraction, she'd burn.

While she tried to think of a way out of her predicament, Lucian drew a sword. He eyed her neck with too much delight. At first, she had just been eager to free herself from the bonds. But now?

Now she realized how close she was to death.

If she had the amulet, she could have stolen control of his fire just like she stole her father's control of the mud. But the only thing she had now was fear. Crackling, burning fear that sent sparks all through her veins.

He pulled the sword back, eyeing her neck again.

Just when she almost closed her eyes, another blade appeared. A sword stabbed straight through Lucian's chest from behind. His eyes bulged as blood seeped into the clothing over his heart. He dropped to his knees.

Behind him, the emperor stood with absolutely no color left in his face. He glared as he lifted his blood-soaked sword again. "You already killed the rest of my family. I won't let you kill my daughter too."

The emperor shot his blade forward, stabbing Lucian a second time. The last breath left Lucian even before his back hit the floor.

Talise stood rooted to the ground. The fires around her vanished the moment Lucian died, but still she couldn't move. She just blinked. Stared.

Her father dropped to his knees, letting out a cough that splattered blood all over the ballroom floor.

Sucking in a breath, Talise finally stepped forward. "You were going to kill me yourself."

Since her father had just saved her life, it probably wasn't the best moment for an accusation. She didn't care.

Her father nodded as he lowered himself onto his back. "I was." More blood splattered from his lips. "I was going to kill you." The words caused his face to twist with pain. He laid on the ground now, his breaths too shallow. "I wanted to break Kamdaria the way it had broken me. I didn't want you to stop me." He turned toward her then. "But…" Reaching up, he brushed a hand across her cheek. The smallest smile covered his face.

He stared at her for only a moment. His lips parted to say more, but he didn't.

Instead, his hand fell. His shallow breaths vanished.

He was dead.

528

Chapter Sventy-Two

THE COLD TOUCH OF HER father still lingered on Talise's cheek. She stared down at him with no idea how to feel. *Could* she feel anymore? Could she be grateful to the man who had both ruined her life and saved it?

Feeling nothing, she pulled open the fist he made at his side. The amulet still sat in his palm. It buzzed when she touched it. At least she could feel that.

Slipping the amulet back into her pocket, she looked back to the face of her dead father once again. Maybe the feelings would come later. Maybe she just needed more time to process everything.

As she sat there, more pressing thoughts moved forward. The passageway gave her an escape. Willow had only recently darted down it, which meant her life could be in danger.

The biggest threat—the emperor—had been eliminated. But that didn't mean the war was over.

Getting to her feet, Talise took the golden crown from off her father's head. Blood splattered and dripped off it. If anyone need proof of his death, that crown would provide plenty.

Her heart continued to beat as she moved toward the passageway. Still, she felt almost nothing. Her feet trailed slowly down the shadowy tunnel before her. She had no idea where the tunnel would lead.

Should that have frightened her? It didn't.

Time passed as she moved forward, but she couldn't tell how much. Everything inside her still felt dead. Soon, a light appeared at the end of the tunnel. Voices shouted through it. She could hear footsteps thundering past. Nearing the end of the tunnel, she realized a tapestry covered this entrance too. Light poured in from a small hole in the tapestry.

Though many voices shouted beyond the tunnel, it came as no surprise that her brain processed the words of one particular voice first.

"Where?" Aaden had never sounded so scared.

Willow's eager voice answered him. "It's just behind that tapestry there."

Talise lifted the tapestry away, stepping into a hallway of the palace near the throne room.

At the sight of her, Aaden sucked in a breath. Tears immediately formed in his eyes as he bounded forward. No sooner had she drawn a breath than he had her in his arms. He squeezed her tight, but she didn't mind.

"You're alive." He whispered the word into her ear then immediately started kissing her. His lips left fiery heat everywhere they touched. Her ear, her cheek, her lips. They all tasted the passion he made no attempt to hide. When he pressed her up against the wall, she could feel how his limbs shook. Hers did too.

He kissed her again, even harder than before. Then his hand slipped into her hair. "I love you."

He whispered the words, but it didn't matter because she felt it. She felt it all the way down to her toes. The emptiness inside her came to a screeching halt as his words filled her like nothing else could.

She leaned into him, finally feeling alive once again.

"Um, Aaden." Cyrus's voice sounded far away, but Talise knew he actually stood close to them.

Gripping her tighter, Aaden turned toward the voice. "She's alive."

Wendy appeared at her brother's side, which brought another burst of emotion through Talise's chest. "And the emperor?" Wendy asked.

Aaden stiffened as he turned toward Talise. Even without a word, he knew to glance down at the bloody crown in her hands. "He's dead?"

Tension rippled through her as she nodded. Now she had to swallow over the thick lump that had formed in her throat. "Your father is dead too."

For a moment, he didn't move. When he did, it was only to nod. But then he swallowed and pulled her even closer still. "I'm sorry I wasn't there. I tried to get into the ballroom, but the doors were stuck."

With each word, more emotion trickled into Talise. The reality of everything came in slowly though. It moved just fast enough to give her time to process. "There's a boulder blocking the doorway. I'll have to use the amulet to remove it, but I didn't have time to do it. What about the soldiers who were fighting you? What about everyone else?"

Instead of answering, Aaden turned to Cyrus and Wendy.

Wendy's face beamed as she gestured down the hallway. "We'll show you."

Aaden gripped Talise's hand as they started walking forward. At the end of the hallway, they turned down another hallway that led to the throne room. No weapons clashed through these hallways. No elements flew.

When they reached the throne room, rows of soldiers greeted them. Claye, Fyra, and Tempest all directed groups of soldiers. At the sight of Talise, everyone in the room stopped.

Aaden squeezed her hand tighter. "We have control of the palace. After you followed the emperor, I managed to get to the throne room. Cyrus had a squad of soldiers who helped get me free. Another squad from our army joined not long after. We took control of the throne room while other squads did the same thing throughout the entire palace."

Talise's lip trembled as the truth finally settled inside her. "So…"

With a smile as bright as ever Wendy answered. "We won. Kamdaria is yours to rule."

CHAPTER SEVENTY-THREE

A LIGHT SPRING AIR RUSTLED all around. Talise looked out her window at the palace garden. The chrysanthemum seed she had planted the night before sat just beneath her window. It would take several years before the seed would grow into a full bush, but she didn't mind waiting.

Chrysanthemums had always been her mother's favorite flower.

Normally, she would have waited until the day of Earth Festival to plant the seed. Every family planted a new seed in their garden for the holiday since it was all about new life. Usually, it was the first thing they did on Earth Festival morning.

But Earth Festival would be different this year. The coronation would take up the entire morning.

Just as that thought entered her mind, a knock sounded at Talise's door. Soon, several people entered her rooms to help her prepare for the day. They helped her into her gown and tied off the sash.

The rich green silk wrapped around her, almost like a tunic. The high collar was trimmed with shimmery white and gold brocade. A forest green belt wrapped around her waist. Her short hair got curled and pinned so it would stay out of her face. Finally, she stepped into soft velvet shoes. The others declared her perfect.

When she stepped into the hallway, soldiers and servants filled it. Their eyes brightened at the sight of her. As much as she enjoyed their smiles, the face she most wanted to see waited for her at the end of the hall.

Aaden also wore green silk, but his was a deep sage. The frog closures down the front of his jacket were made with fine, silver cords. His hair had been combed with precision. The scar over his eye was lighter than ever.

He offered his arm to Talise, which she took eagerly.

"Are you nervous?" He whispered so the others around them couldn't hear.

She bit her bottom lip and held onto him tighter. "Yes." She let out a sigh. "But your grandfather insists it won't take long. We still have Earth Festival to celebrate after all."

Each step moved too quickly. She tried to appreciate every noise and sight before her, but they still made it to the throne room in almost no time at all. Rows of citizens filled the large room. Their clothing indicated that people from all over the empire had come to celebrate. Some wore luxurious velvet, but others wore threadbare cotton. All were welcome.

Every head bowed as she moved down a long aisle. At the head of the room, a large throne sat waiting for her. Rich black upholstery adorned the chair with silver-painted wood trimming it.

Near the front of the room, the crowd ended. Aaden stood with them while Talise had to walk alone up the throne. Commander Blaise stood next to it, waiting for her.

She gulped when she reached him, but he offered the tiniest hint of a smile. At once, he began the ceremony. He started by talking about her heritage and the emperors and empresses who had come before her. Then he talked about her deeds and how much she had done for Kamdaria. Everything sounded a lot better coming from him than it had felt in real life.

At the end of the speech, a soldier stepped forward with a silver crown in his hands.

The crown featured ornate twists and opulent crystals. It looked similar to the tiara Tempest and Wendy had made, but this one used richer materials. And it was bigger. A *lot* bigger.

Commander Blaise listed the promises Talise would make by accepting rule of Kamdaria. When she uttered her acceptance, he placed the crown on her head. He continued on with more words, but she was too distracted to pay attention.

Aaden grinned at her from the front row. She didn't want to wait another minute before she could stand with him once again. Luckily, she didn't have to wait long.

With a grand flourish, Commander Blaise bowed to her. Everyone in the room followed his example. As she stepped down the aisle again, she did it as empress.

Empress of Kamdaria.

Thinking of it filled her with all sorts of doubts, so she focused on Aaden instead. He offered his arm again, and together, they walked to the ballroom.

With the coronation out of the way, everyone could enjoy Earth Festival. Long tables were filled with trays of food especially made for the holiday. Green salads with delicious dressings dotted each table. There were also bowls filled with a variety of green fruits: honeydew, kiwi, pears, and grapes.

On other trays, green wraps covered portions of rice and smoked meat. One of Talise's favorite dishes had always been the asparagus drizzled with a tangy lime sauce.

But of course, Earth Festival desserts sat among the food as well. Cakes were decorated with the cherry blossoms that had just begun to grow on the trees outside the palace. Chocolate candies shaped like tree branches were dotted with red fruits to look like blossoms and green frosting to look like leaves. Everything about the desserts spoke of new life.

"Have you finished your wishes?" Aaden pulled her closer when he asked.

She loved it when he did that. Reaching into her dress pocket, she pulled out a folded piece of parchment. "I have mine ready. What about yours?"

He patted the pocket of his tunic. "I finished mine a few days ago."

As part of Earth Festival, every citizen wrote about or drew pictures of the wishes they hoped would come true in the next year. But the wishes were always secret. No one ever shared what their pages with others. Despite that, Talise couldn't help wondering what Aaden had wished for.

Before she could dwell on it too long, Wendy joined them wearing as innocent a face as ever. She took both of Talise's hands and let out a sigh as she looked at the crown on her head. "I'm so glad this day has come."

Talise squeezed back before they both dropped their hands. The last few weeks had been so crazy, she'd barely had a moment to speak to her friend. "How are you and Cyrus doing?"

Wendy smirked. "Cyrus loves being back in the palace. He missed the finery."

With a nod, Talise asked, "How do you like working for General Gale again?"

Once the emperor was gone, very few of the palace soldiers remained loyal to him. Most everyone was eager to support Talise's rule. General Gale had once trained the army for Emperor Flarius. Now he did it for Talise.

The smile on Wendy's face faltered as she glanced into the ballroom. "It's fine."

Tilting her head to the side, Talise raised an eyebrow. "But?"

Wendy shrugged. "Now that conditions are improving throughout Kamdaria, it's not as important for me to live in the palace."

The words hit Talise hard, but deep down, she had known this was coming. And ultimately, she understood. "Would you move to be closer to your family?"

Wendy's eyes sparkled at the question. She must have feared Talise's response. But since Talise didn't scold or complain, Wendy's mouth turned up to a grin. "That's what I'm thinking, but it wouldn't be soon. Maybe in a year or two. Tempest's family has been doing well with jewelry sales. Her father wants to open another shop in a new city. He thinks Tempest could run it herself."

"That sounds nice." Aaden nodded toward Wendy, but he gave Talise's hand an extra squeeze when he did.

As much as Talise wanted her friend to be happy, it would still be sad to have her leave the palace. That thought brought forth another. With a swallow, Talise turned her eyes downward. "Have you seen Rio's grave yet?"

Wendy touched her heart as she gave a slow nod. "Yes, I saw it yesterday. I like that you buried him the palace graveyard. He deserves that honor."

Talise's throat prickled with an ache as she nodded. "His family just moved nearby, so I thought it would be fitting. Now they can visit whenever they like."

Tears pooled in Wendy's eyes. "That's nice."

Aaden cleared his throat, probably trying to dislodge an aching lump from it. They all stood in silence for a moment. Remembering. The war had taken a lot from them, but Rio's loss would hurt more than the others.

As they stood, Claye approached with a signature smirk. "How does it feel to be empress?"

The jovial question sent a chuckle to Talise's mouth. "I don't know if I can answer that since I haven't even been empress for an entire day yet."

Claye shrugged as he ran a hand through his hair.

"How do *you* feel about teaching?" she asked him.

The smirk on his face quickly turned to a smile. A new elite academy was still being built, but for now, academy classes were being held inside the palace. Claye was one of the newest teachers.

He stuffed his hands into his pockets. "It's just nice that I don't have to hide my skills anymore, you know?"

The words twisted inside Talise. She did know. And even though she was glad Claye was happy now, it still hurt to remember how he had lied to her about so many things. At least in their new roles, they wouldn't see each other much.

Aaden scratched his chin. "Do you like the children?"

Claye answered with an eager nod. "I love them. They think I'm very cool, which is always fun. And they never get bored when I talk about Forces."

Talise chuckled at that. Claye always did have an obsession with Kamdaria's favorite game. "And how's Fyra doing?"

A splotch of pink filled Claye's cheeks. "She's doing well. I don't know if you remember, but her parents work here in the palace too. They're doing even better now that they're paid reasonable wages. Hey," Claye's smile widened even more, "Here come my favorite students."

Willow, Cascade, and Terreth came toward them wearing tentative expressions. The apprehension fell away once Talise beckoned them forward.

Talise herself insisted they all have a place at the elite academy. Apparently, it was going well.

Claye gestured toward each of them. "Cascade already has exceptional healing skills, which isn't too much of a surprise since her mother and grandmother are both healers already. Terreth is great with fire, which makes me laugh. I always love it when someone's primary doesn't match their name. And Willow." Claye shook his head with a grin. "This girl succeeds at every task with tenacity alone. They really are the best students."

Willow's feet shuffled over the ballroom floor as she glanced up at Talise. "Thank you for letting us train at the elite academy. It's such an honor."

Warmth spread in Talise's chest as she nodded. "Of course. Everyone should have the chance if they want it, not just those born to privilege."

"Cascade." Aaden's mother called to her daughter from across the room. When she realized the girl stood with Aaden, her mouth clamped shut.

So far, Aaden had only spoken to his mother once since the final battle. He did extend forgiveness to her. But they both quickly realized that forgiveness was just one step forward. It would take several more steps before they felt like a true family again.

Talise leaned closer to Aaden as he gave an awkward wave to his mother. Maybe it would be difficult, but Talise fully believed they'd get there someday.

After more mingling and lots of eating, the time finally came for the wishes. Talise moved to her spot at the head of a table. The room hushed all around her as she pulled her parchment from her pocket once again.

She took a deep breath as she stared over everyone in the room. "Earth Festival is different this year. Though the holiday always marks a new year, this time, it also marks a new Kamdaria. As we release our wishes, I hope that everyone feels as I do, the wish for something better."

With that, she sparked a fire in her palm and burned the parchment to ash. They believed the fire would separate the wish from the paper and release it into the air. Most of her wishes that year had to do with improving Kamdaria. One specifically was about traveling back to the poison factory in the Storm. Now that she had the amulet, she could create fire hot enough to destroy that poison. She also wanted to build more glass houses and rebuild so many things. But amongst the wishes for Kamdaria, there was one that was different.

While others used fire shaping or candle fire to burn their papers, she turned and glanced at Aaden. One of her wishes, maybe the most important one, was all about him.

EPILOGUE

THREE YEARS LATER

TALISE stood relaxed on the deck of a riverboat. A misty breeze drifted all around her, rustling the skirt of her dress. The smell of wet earth filled the air. When the riverboat jostled, Talise grabbed onto a railing and grinned.

Nothing could sour her mood today, not when she was going to visit Wendy.

Even better, Aaden appeared from behind a pillar of the riverboat. His lips twitched into a smile at the sight of her. Just like hers did at the sight of him. He wore his silver crown today. The thin band wrapped around his head of perfectly combed hair. It was much smaller than the silver crown on her own head.

Though everyone called him emperor, they made sure his crown and throne made it clear that he had less ruling power than Talise. Not that he cared. He still spent every morning telling Talise how lucky he was to have found her.

She stepped right up to him and wrapped her arms around his waist before planting a kiss on his ever-fiery lips. Since others roamed the riverboat with him, she held herself back from doing more. But she could see in his eyes that he desired more just as much as she did. Her lips curled upward into a smile. They'd just have to wait until they returned home to the palace.

Considering all the fights between her own parents that she witnessed as a child, she never expected marriage to be so wonderful.

"Look." Aaden pointed toward the land just past the river. A small crowd had gathered to watch their imperial riverboat pass.

Talise lifted both hands into the air. She never missed an opportunity to indulge the citizens. With quick swipes and jabs, she pulled water from the air in the shape of stars. With a twist of her wrist, the water turned to ice. She punched her hand forward and the ice shattered outward into a showing burst.

The citizens cheered loud at the sight of it. Her heart warmed as she raised her hands to do it again.

Soon enough, they passed the city. The riverboat slowed as they reached their destination. Horses waited for them on the shore. After an hour of riding, they reached a little home that stood quiet at the end of a street.

Wendy beckoned Talise and Aaden inside with cheeks plump and eyes shining brightly. Wendy's entire family greeted them with warm embraces. Tempest was there too. They shared a delicious meal, but soon, Talise pulled her friend away.

Aaden knew the real reason for the visit, but Talise hadn't told anyone else. It didn't seem like the kind of thing that could be sent in a letter or with a messenger. By the time Wendy settled into a chair across from Talise, she blinked expectantly.

Talise had spent weeks practicing this conversation with Aaden, but still, she had no idea what to say. Maybe blurting the words out would be best. "I want you to be the new guardian of the amulet."

No expression filled Wendy's face as she stared back. "What?"

Letting out a sigh, Talise leaned back into her chair. "I needed the amulet to take down the walls and to take back the empire, but I don't think I need it anymore. Its power is great. I don't want to be tempted by it. I want the amulet to be hidden away again, just like it was when I found it."

"Wow." Wendy reached for a section of hair, which she began twirling around one finger. "That makes sense, but wow." With a gasp, she brought a hand to her lips. "Wait. You want *me* to guard it?"

A crooked smile fell over Talise's mouth. "Yes. You've always been there for me, Wendy. Always. I'm confident no one could do the job better than you."

With blushing cheeks, Wendy put a hand over her heart. "I'm honored. I'm more than honored." She reached for a section of hair again, but then her expression fell. "But..." She glanced upward only to stare at her lap. "I can't have children, not if I stay with Tempest. I'll have no one to pass the amulet on to when I die."

Talise gave a shrug. "In Kamdaria, we believe that family is the most important thing." She leaned forward. "But maybe it doesn't have to be the only thing. Sometimes family members aren't the only ones who are there for you. Sometimes the bond of friendship is just as strong."

Wendy placed a hand over her heart as she nodded. Her head tilted as she twirled the hair around her finger. "But if I don't pass the amulet on to my child after I die, who else can I pass it on to?"

Pulling the amulet from her pocket, Talise dropped it into her friend's lap. "I trust you to guard the amulet during your lifetime." She turned her mouth up in a smile. "I also trust you to find someone *you* trust to guard it afterward."

Wendy's face turned solemn as she touched the metal.

"Since the amulet is bonded to me, I don't think it will work for anyone else during my lifetime anyway. But that will probably change once I die." Talise gestured toward the entrance of the house. "I brought the journals as well. I figured they should stay with the amulet. They're outside with the horses."

The solemnity on Wendy's face only grew. "I promise I will take good care of them. And the amulet."

It was nice to have the reassurance, but Talise didn't need it. She knew Wendy would do well. That was why she asked her to be guardian in the first place.

After tucking the amulet carefully into her pocket, Wendy's eyes brightened again. "How is Claye doing at the academy?"

Talise let out a chuckle. "Apparently, the children get into all sorts of trouble. Willow, Cascade, and Terreth are the worst. But they get away with it because their hearts are always in the right place."

Now Wendy chuckled at the thought.

Visiting longer would have been nice, but as empress, Talise had to get back to the palace. Before evening fell, she and Aaden were back on the riverboat again.

Heaviness lingered inside Talise's heart as she stared out at the passing empire. New buildings were being built, but leftover rubble still offered a stark reminder of what the empire had been only three short years ago.

When a cool breeze fluttered around her, Talise tried to rub heat back into her arms. "Am I doing the right thing?"

Rubbing his own hands over her arms, Aaden glanced out at the land before them. "By hiding away the amulet? I thought you said it was time."

She bounced her head up and down. "I know, I know. If I don't need it, there's no reason for me to have it." She bit into her bottom lip. "But we still haven't cleared away all the debris left over from the walls. The soil is still poisoned in some areas. Only uninhabited areas, but still. And things are still being rebuilt."

As he ran his hands up and down her arms again, he nodded. "It's true. You haven't fixed everything in Kamdaria."

Her heart dropped at the sound of those words.

"That would be impossible," he said with a smirk.

She looked into his eyes for a moment before letting out a soft chuckle.

Circling behind, he wrapped his arms around her stomach and pulled her close. "But there is one thing I know for certain."

She nuzzled into him. "And what's that?"

"You've changed Kamdaria for the better."

ACKNOWLEDGMENTS

Thank you so much for reading! This series took me on a journey that brought both joy and tears. Finishing this last book brought so many mixed emotions. It's great to have everything wrapped up for these characters, but it's hard to say goodbye too. Thank you for sticking with me until the end. It means the world!

Next, I must thank my incredible editor, Deborah Spencer. Thank you for all your notes to make sure my geography and descriptions stayed on point.

To my awesome cover designer, Angel Leya, thank you for creating book covers that capture the heart of this series.

Everyone on my ARC team deserves heaps of thanks. You were all so dedicated to get those reviews up on time. Thank you!

My bookstagram ARC team is also extremely dedicated and artistic. Thank you so much for your awesome pictures! If you're on Instagram, you should definitely follow these amazing people.

@ashleys.reading.cafe @booksandtheblacktea @jcaesara
@bookslesstravelled @books_over_everything
@ninis_bookshelves @sarahsbookadventures
@the.fictional.brunette @erins_adventures_in_the_pages

Queens of the Quill, you ladies are the best! You have believed in me and cheered me on along the way. Thank you. Thank you Abby J. Reed, Alison Ingleby, Charlie N. Holmberg, Clarissa Gosling, Hanna Sandvig, Joanna Reeder, Kristin J. Dawson, Rose Garcia, Stacey Trombley, Tessonja Odette, and Valia Lind.

And thank you to my most wonderful husband. It doesn't matter how many times I say it, you are the best. I couldn't have done any of this without you.

Visit **kaylmoody.com/kamdaria** to download *Winds of Flame*, a prequel short story that takes place at the elite academy.

KAY L. MOODY is proud to be a young adult fantasy author. Her books feature exciting plots with a few magical elements. They have lots of adventure, compelling characters, and sweet romantic sub-plots. Most of her books have a dystopian flair. They include a variety of technology levels and lots of diversity. Kay lives in the western United States with her husband and four sons. She enjoys summertime, learning new things, and doing her nails with fancy nail art.

THE FAE OF BITTER THORN
BOOK 1 IS AVAILABLE NOW!

CHAPTER ONE

SWORDS CAME FIRST.

Love could come later—maybe never—but Elora would die before she went a day without lifting her sword. Her father usually sparred with her, but now that he was too busy arranging her marriage to a rich, old merchant, she'd just have to find a new partner herself.

Her blade sliced through the brittle red leaves that clung to a bush by her home. Each gave a soft crunch before drifting to the cracked dirt below. The chilly air cooled her brow as she swung the sword again.

The leaves would have fallen on their own in another week or two. That made it less satisfying to chop them away, but it was also less destructive.

When only bare branches remained on the bush, she took her sword to the trunk of a nearby tree. The sharp metal of her sword cut into the rough wood. Chips of bark flew as she ripped her sword away to do it again. It didn't take long for the trunk to be covered in gashes. Her mother would have sighed at the sight of it. Her father would have chuckled.

None of it made Elora feel any better. She let out a huff as she sliced the tops off a lovely clump of wildflowers.

Was it normal to be so angry while waiting to meet one's betrothed?

The mere thought caused her simmering emotions to bubble up. Though her bottom lip trembled, she refused to acknowledge anything but the sword in her hand. It cut through the air, this time slicing another bush that had red leaves trying to hold on for dear life.

Even after the leaves had been eradicated, her sword continued to spin and slice. The muscles in her arms ached, but that wouldn't stop her from swinging the blade like her life depended on it.

Anything to keep the tears at bay.

When her sword glanced against a tree instead of against its intended target of a bush, a shudder ripped through her shoulders. Pain stung through her throat when she tried to swallow. Her arms slumped to her sides, feeling heavier than usual. Hard pants puffed from her mouth while drops of sweat trickled down her neck.

Gripping her sword hilt tight, she pressed her forehead against the nearest tree trunk. Its familiar scent of rich bark and sticky sap wafted into her nose. Would her new home have trees that smelled the same?

Her lip was trembling. Again.

With a sniff, she shoved herself away from the tree and slid her silver blade inside its sheath. The belt that was wrapped around the bottom of her leather corset held the weight of the sheath and sword, distributing it evenly across her hips.

Even in the brisk air, her skin felt too warm. She wrinkled her nose at the limp fabric covering her arms. The long-sleeved underslip might have been lightweight, but it always got in the way when she used her sword. Her woolen skirt she didn't mind. She'd learned to fight in a skirt years ago. The leather corset actually helped her sword skill since it acted as a torso support and as a kind of armor. But the linen underslip?

She would have sliced the long sleeves right off if she hadn't been certain her mother would faint at the sight. And perhaps Elora *should* have been more concerned about her appearance, considering she was about to meet her future husband and all.

At least the rich purple dye in her skirt had lasted longer than her family's wealth. And at least it still fit her. Her light brown hair hung freely down her back in gentle waves. It wasn't a common hairstyle: no braids, combs, or even a ribbon. But she had only been able to make so many concessions when getting ready that morning. Hopefully her betrothed liked long hair.

A lump pricked her throat, which would have been easier to ignore if tears hadn't puddled in her eyes at the same moment. She blinked them away before they could fall. It didn't change how her corset seemed too tight and her heart seemed too heavy.

Ignoring those things, she traced a finger over the leather wrapped hilt of her sword. There was no reason to be emotional anyway. This was a marriage, not a death sentence. With her eighteenth birthday a month away, she had been hoping for a *little* more time at home. A little more time to be free.

But her father's forge was close to ruin, and her marriage was the only thing that could save it—and her family.

Mother always said Elora was lucky for being so beautiful. Now her beauty would buy a husband who could save her parents and two younger sisters from financial ruin. All she had to give in return was her entire self to a complete stranger.

Lucky indeed.

The veins in her hand pulsed as she gripped her sword hilt tighter. She forced deep breaths in and out of her nose, urging her heart to stop racing. It refused. Why could her heart do whatever it wanted but her head still had to accept marriage?

Before her thoughts could spin too far out of control, she reached under her corset for a reminder of her one last goal. She wanted to win her very own sword fighting tournament. Of course, women were not allowed to participate, but she had been preparing for this goal for weeks. To hide in plain sight at the tournament grounds, she just needed the right clothes.

With a gentle tug, she pulled a piece of parchment out from under her corset. Handling the parchment gently, she smoothed out the creases as she traced a finger over the drawing. Thin pencil lines and colored paint combined to portray a knight in full armor. Her father had recently acquired a full book of drawings that depicted life in a nearby castle. The images and descriptions of the gardens and clothing were captivating, but this drawing of the knight was her favorite.

Letting her finger linger over the knight's sword, she carefully studied his stance. Years of sword training with her father taught her plenty about correct stance. Still, the man in the drawing somehow seemed nobler and more gallant than her.

Straightening her back, she unsheathed her sword and attempted to stand in the same position. As it had been doing a lot lately, the air hung stagnant all around with no hint of breeze. She made her own wind by swiping the sword diagonally in front of her body.

In her mind, the leather corset and woolen skirt were gone. Instead, she imagined herself wearing a heavy suit of chainmail with a belted white tunic on top. Matching clothes sat in a dusty trunk in her father's forge. His old tournament clothes *might* be recognized by others in their village, but they were the only men's clothes she had access to. They would have to do.

Her eyes remained closed as she struck her sword forward in lethal jabs. After a moment, she peeked through one eyelid at the drawing of the knight. She adjusted her feet to match the stance and closed her eyes to move again.

When she slashed her sword through the air again, she didn't just imagine herself in the clothes. Now she imagined herself standing across from Theobald, the greatest sword fighter and sword maker the land had ever seen. His prowess was well known due to all the tournaments he'd won.

Theobald was also her father, though she imagined a slightly younger version of him to fight against.

Age had caught up to him now, but her father had once boasted incredible sword skill. During her childhood, he spent as many days forging new swords as competing in dangerous sword fighting tournaments. She remembered sitting on her mother's knee in a crowded arena while her father effortlessly beat any opponent who crossed him.

When Elora's skirt rippled around her legs, her arms dropped to her sides again. The illusion vanished in a heartbeat.

Even with the right clothes, she still might not get away with sneaking into a tournament. And too many people would be angry if they found out. That gloomy truth always crept around the corners of her mind, but she did her best to ignore it. No matter what everyone else thought about a woman wielding a sword, she *had* to participate in a tournament. At least once.

For a single moment, the air sizzled around her. Hairs prickled at the back of her neck while the sensation of being watched flooded through her. Before she could glance into the woods, a strong gust of wind blew the drawing of the knight out of her hand. Her eyes flew open as she jumped to snatch the parchment from the air.

Instead, another gust carried it past the clearing where she had been practicing. In only a moment, it drifted toward the front of her family's cottage. Despite the dirt and leaves she had to trudge through, Elora raced toward her drawing without question.

As a tangible reminder of the tournament she hoped to win, nothing could stop her from protecting that parchment.

Her feet tripped over crunchy leaves and dry twigs. The page finally stopped flying when it wrapped itself around the front leg of a chestnut brown horse. Her husband-to-be had arrived on that same horse not long ago. He and her parents were still discussing the particulars of the upcoming marriage. The horse probably wouldn't appreciate a stranger grabbing at its leg, but she *needed* that paper.

Heavy thumps pounded in her chest as she reached out. Her fingers pinched over the page just as the horse snorted with a distressed neigh. Its teeth chomped down, nearly taking a chunk of out her arm. She had stepped back just in time.

Despite the pounding pulse that strummed through her, a smile tugged at her lips. She held the drawing against her heart for a beat before folding it and tucking it neatly underneath her corset.

The horse continued to neigh, but her relief seemed to calm it slightly. She took a step back and lowered her head. Reaching out a flat palm, she let the creature sniff her until its muscles relaxed.

"Elora." Her mother appeared through the front door of their cottage wearing her finest blue shawl. She gave a pointed grimace at Elora's dust-covered hem before turning back toward the inside of the cottage. "I discovered the cause of the horse's fright. Elora must have been eager to meet it."

While the sound of footsteps neared, Elora shook her skirt to loosen most of the dirt. Her back had only just straightened when a man appeared in the doorway beside her mother.

The beam on her mother's face could have brightened a moonless night. "Elora, meet Dietrich Mercer, your betrothed."

A curtsy came automatically. Elora could only hope it hid the scowl taking over her features. By the time she rose from the curtsy, her father had joined the others. He closed the door of the cottage behind him as the three of them stepped toward her.

Mr. Mercer was shorter than her father and had less defined features. His round belly poked out above his belt. He did have a fine head of curly blonde hair, which paired nicely with his bright blue eyes. But it looked as though the most intense sport he had ever performed was writing a letter. At least he wasn't as old as her father. The man was much closer to her father's age than to hers, but he still had a *bit* of youth in him.

Heat flushed into her cheeks when he nodded his head in return. Somehow, she managed to stop herself from reaching for her sword hilt. Instead, her sweaty palm stroked over the horse's chestnut mane. "I apologize if I acted out of turn, but your horse caught my eye. Such a beautiful creature."

Mother always said flattery could smooth over anything.

Mr. Mercer must have agreed because the slightest smile twitched at his lips. "You have a good eye." He glanced up and down her body as he spoke, but at least he had the decency to pretend he was eyeing his horse. "This mare has strong legs that have carried me through many villages. It can carry a cart full of wares all by itself."

"How impressive." Her mother touched a hand to her necklace as her jaw dropped.

That caused a bigger grin on Mr. Mercer's face before he turned to look at Elora again. "But I usually take two horses, so I don't put so much strain on this one."

"What a humane thing to do." Somehow, Elora had adopted her mother's dulcet tone. Getting married to a stranger was the last thing she wanted, but she didn't want to upset her betrothed during their first meeting either.

Mr. Mercer stepped forward to rub between the horse's eyes. He gave her the briefest glance before staring back at his horse. "Once we marry, perhaps we could go horseback riding together. I have a lovely meadow where the flowers bloom beautifully."

His blue eyes flicked toward her again, this time looking brighter than before. She allowed one corner of her mouth to tilt up in a smile. "I'd like that." The most surprising thing about her statement was that it actually held truth.

The words seemed to give him courage. He reached into the leather pouch hanging from his horse's saddle. "I brought you a book from my library."

A tiny gasp escaped her when he dropped a thick leather-bound book into her hands. "You have a library?"

His chest puffed out as he nodded. "Yes, your father said you'd like that."

She glanced back at her father whose thinning brown hair looked wispy over his head. He gave a short nod that said more than words could have. He had promised to find her a good husband, and so far, things weren't as bad as they could have been.

Her father cleared his throat and gave a pointed look toward her betrothed. "And you said you had a bit of woods where she can practice her sword fighting every day, correct?"

Red burned through Mr. Mercer's neck and face. He ducked his head and looked studiously at his horse's mane. "Uh, yes. I can provide for your," he glanced at Elora through the side of his eye, "eccentricities."

She tightened a fist but did it beneath the folds of her skirt. Her father had promised to find her someone who would let her continue to practice her sword skill. She should have known her betrothed would only barely be able to tolerate it.

Still, *eccentric* was one of the better words used to describe her skill. Most people considered it downright unseemly for a woman to know how to wield a sword.

Mr. Mercer cleared his throat and looked deeper into his horse's mane. "As long as the sport doesn't interfere with her childbearing."

Her muscles stiffened at once. It was lucky her betrothed continued to stare at his horse. He wouldn't have liked the scowl that screwed up her face. It wasn't that she found marriage or children inherently disgusting. But this conversation made her feel less like a person and more like an object in some business arrangement.

When her mother invited everyone back inside to discuss the details, only Elora's body accompanied them. Her mind was off imagining a tournament. In it, she wore chainmail and boots, and no one criticized her for carrying a sword. Then again, in her father's old clothes, no one knew she was a woman either. The thoughts brought a smile to her lips.

They could make her get married, but they *couldn't* take away her dream. Before her wedding, she'd sneak into a tournament. No matter what the cost.

That same strange sensation of being watched prickled over her skin again. Rather than fearing it, she found herself longing for it. Maybe someone new in her life was just what she needed. She'd welcome any number of new people… as long as she could fight them with her sword.